DESPISED
AND *Desired*

THE MARQUESS' PASSIONATE WIFE

Also By Bree

Historical Romance:

Suspenseful Contemporary Romance:

Middle Grade Adventure:

Paranormal Fantasy:

DESPISED
AND *Desired*

THE MARQUESS' PASSIONATE WIFE
(#3 LOVE'S SECOND CHANCE SERIES)

BY

BREE WOLF

Despised & Desired
The Marquess' Passionate Wife
By
Bree Wolf

This is a work of fiction. Names, characters, businesses, places, brands, media, events and incidents are either the products of the author's imagination or used in a fictitious manner.

Any resemblance to actual persons, living or dead, or actual events is purely coincidental.

Cover Art by Victoria Cooper

Copyright © 2016 Sabrina Wolf

www.breewolf.com

ISBN-13: 978-3964820051

To My Son, My Little Man
My Knight in Shining Armor
A Mother's Love is Unconditional and Forever
Never Doubt That

ACKNOWLEDGEMENTS

As always, my biggest thanks goes to my family, without whose loving support I would have neither the time nor the patience necessary to sit down and write.

Again, I am very grateful to Michelle Chenoweth. For her keen eyes and careful instructions have been a wonderful help to my own error-prone eyes. You are a wonderful teacher!

A great big thank-you goes to Monique Taken and Zan-Mari Kiousi for beta-reading my first draft and providing honest and insightful critique, which is absolutely priceless.

DESPISED
AND *Desired*

PROLOGUE

England 1794 (or a variation thereof)

eads of sweat formed on Ellie's brow and ran down her temples. Trying to shield her face from the scorching sun, she pulled her bonnet deeper into her face. Ellie knew she ought not to be here, and yet, she could not help herself.

The rising heat of this year's unusually hot summer had her escape the earl's garden party in search of a little refreshment.

Excitement had seized her when she had heard other children whisper about the small brook that snaked its way through the forest to the south of the manor. However, uncertain whether or not to dare go against her mother's rather stern instructions of proper conduct, Ellie had waited until the very last moment before she was sure she would melt away. Only then had she dared sneak away.

Now, following in its general direction, Ellie soon heard the soft babbling of the small brook as it fought the sun for its continued existence.

Stepping over large boulders and wading through a sea of long-stemmed grass, Ellie glimpsed the brook's shiny surface, glistening in the sun like an oasis in a desert. Hurrying her step, she hastened toward it at the very moment it seemed to beckon her closer.

A smile spread over her face as she beheld the cool water before her feet. Kneeling down, Ellie reached out a hand, and a soft moan escaped her lips when the fresh water touched her heated skin. For a moment, she closed her eyes, feeling a slight chill run from her submerged hand up her arm. It felt wonderful!

Opening her eyes, Ellie scanned her surroundings and found a cluster of trees a little farther down the stream providing ample shade. Reluctantly withdrawing her hand from the cooling brook, she strode through the grass and then sank down under the trees' large canopy. She removed her bonnet and leaned forward, hand searching for the refreshing wet. Collecting a little water in her cupped hand, she brushed it across her arms, enjoying the tingle that ran through her. And yet, it wasn't enough.

Not nearly enough.

Eyeing her shoes and stockinged feet with a hint of disgust, Ellie took a deep breath. She really ought not to. Even at twelve years old, Elsbeth Munsford was very much aware that a lady ought not to remove her clothing in public.

Glancing around, Ellie frowned. *What public?*

A mischievous smile spread over her face as her nimble fingers worked to loosen her shoes. When they came off, her stockings quickly followed, and Ellie delighted at the feeling of soft grass under her bare feet. Then she glanced at the water and wiggled her toes.

Taking a deep breath, she pushed all thoughts of her mother away and rose to her feet. After making sure that she was, indeed, alone, Ellie slowly pulled up the hem of her dress, revealing her ankles. Grinning from ear to ear, she bit her lower lip in excitement and then stepped toward the brook.

As the cooling water rushed over her skin, Ellie sighed with delight, wiggling her toes and digging them into the muddy stream bed. For a moment, she closed her eyes, savouring the moment until she realised it still wasn't enough.

The coolness barely spread to her knees, let alone chase away the beads of sweat still popping up on her forehead.

Lifting up her skirts to just above her knees, Ellie revealed a small birthmark that resembled a bird taking flight. Although her mother had always considered it an oddity, relieved it was in a place covered by clothes, Ellie had always felt special because of it, wishing that she, too, could simply spread her wings and fly.

Sighing, Ellie waded deeper into the stream. When the water swirled around her calves, she finally felt its cooling effect spread into every part of her body. Welcoming the slight chill chasing away the hot air resting on her skin, Ellie once more closed her eyes.

Lost in a moment of pure pleasure, Ellie did not hear them coming.

Only when they broke through the underbrush, their boots snapping dry twigs as they went, did Ellie's eyes snap open.

Instantly, shock froze her limbs, and she stared at the three young men standing but a few feet from the water's edge.

In that moment, Ellie was too stunned to observe anything else but the cold that slowly spread through her body, bringing with it an old fear. *What would her mother say?*

Then, she swallowed, and her eyes travelled from the tall, dark-haired youth, who—as her mother had informed her—went by the name of Frederick Lancaster, second son to the Marquess of Elmridge, to the two others standing to his left and right, Oliver Cornell and Kenneth Moreton. While Frederick bore an expression that did not betray his thoughts, his friends looked rather surprised to find her in the stream, the corners of their mouths slowly drawing up into a smile, clearly showing their amusement.

Tears began to form in Ellie's eyes as she slowly backed away toward the other side of the brook.

As though in trance, their eyes followed her until Frederick turned to his friends. "Go back," he ordered them. "Speak of this to no one."

For a second, Oliver seemed ready to argue, but Kenneth grabbed his arm and pulled him back through the underbrush.

Frederick, however, remained behind.

Crossing the stream in a shallower spot, he came toward her, his eyes never leaving hers. When he reached her side, he held out a hand, offering to help her out of the stream.

Uncertain what to do, Ellie looked from his hand to his face.

"Do not be afraid," he spoke. "I mean you no harm."

His dark blue eyes shone as clear as the water still swirling around her legs, and her heart beat slowed. Swallowing, Ellie took his hand, surprised at how hot his skin felt compared to her own, which at this point was rather chilled. A shiver went through her, and he pulled her out of the water.

He smiled at her. "You should put your shoes back on."

Ellie blushed and then hurried back to the shady spot where she had left them. Sitting down, she noted that he stood with his back to her, giving her privacy, and she quickly pulled her stockings over her legs and slipped on her shoes.

Then she stood up, not knowing what to say.

"Are you properly attired?" he asked.

"Yes," Ellie breathed, wondering if he judged her as she knew her mother would as soon as she learnt of this.

He turned around then, a friendly smile on his face. "Allow me to escort you back."

Ellie took a deep breath before closing her eyes for a brief moment. When she opened them again, he stood before her, and she shrank back.

Seeing the fear on her face, he instantly retreated a step. "I apologise. I didn't mean to startle you, but you seemed troubled. Are you injured?"

Ellie shook her head. "Please leave," she whispered, her voice pleading.

He frowned at her. "I cannot leave you alone. Who knows who else might be in these woods?"

Never having contemplated the possibility that a threat might be looming near, Ellie glanced at the tree line in his back. Was he right? Was there danger out there?

"If you are worried about being seen with me," he said, trying to catch her eyes, "I assure you I have no intention of compromising you in any way. I merely suggest that I escort you as far as the gardens. From there, you can make your way back on your own. I will stay back and assure that no harm comes to you." His deep blue eyes looked into hers, and he spoke with a sincerity beyond his years. "No one will know."

"What about your friends?" she asked, twirling her bonnet in her hands.

He shook his head. "They will not say a word," he assured her.

Ellie took a relieved breath, and a shy smile came to her lips. "Thank you."

"You're welcome," he said, returning her smile. Then he stepped back, gesturing at the path ahead. "Shall we?"

Ellie nodded and fell into step beside him. Brushing her blond curls back, she fastened her bonnet, keeping the sun out of her eyes.

He glanced down at her. "May I ask your name?"

"Ellie," she whispered and met his eyes, feeling a warmth spread to her cheeks that she could not blame on the sun.

He smiled. "I'm Rick."

For a long time, they walked in silence, a silence that felt comfortable as though they had known each other for a long time.

When the hedges of the estate's garden finally came in sight, Ellie whispered, "Will you tell my mother?"

He shook his head, and relief flooded her body. "I would not dare bring any harm upon you," he said looking down at her.

Again, Ellie felt herself blush. "Thank you."

"She is highly critical of you, is she not?"

Ellie nodded. "She counts my faults on a daily basis."

Rick smiled. "That shouldn't take her long." As they stopped by the long hedge, running along the gardens, his eyes shifted to hers. "I cannot find a single one."

Again, Ellie felt herself blush and quickly averted her eyes.

"You should go," he said, "before anyone sees us together."

Nodding, Ellie smiled at him, then turned and headed back toward the noise of the garden party. Although she was tempted, she did not dare turn around to see if he was still there. Even if she could not see him, she still felt his eyes on her, watching over her safe return.

Frederick Lancaster, she mused. He would be a wonderful man one day. Ellie was sure of it. After all, he had saved her

1

A BLESSING IN DISGUISE

Twelve Years Later

"ave you heard?" Madeline Jeffries exclaimed, almost choking on her tea as the
words flew out of her mouth. Coughing,
she tried to regain her composure, her dark curls bouncing up and
down with each fit.

"Heard what?" Ellie asked, setting down her teacup. She flexed
her right hand to loosen her tight muscles and then absentmindedly
massaged the scarred tissue between thumb and index finger. Would
she ever regain the flexibility she used to have?

Two years ago, a candle left unattended had burned down half
the house, almost claiming the life of Ellie's little brother Stephen. Although Ellie had been able to save him, she had paid a dear price.
While the house had since been restored to its former glory, Ellie's skin
still spoke of the day that had changed her life.

"Frederick Lancaster is returning from the war."

At his name, Ellie's eyes snapped open, her tense muscles forgotten. "He is?" she gasped before trying to lend her enquiries a nonchalant air. "Was he injured?"

Madeline shrugged, taking another careful sip now that she had shared her news. "I do not know. If he was, I believe it was nothing too severe. Otherwise, I am certain I would have heard of it."

Closing her eyes, Ellie took a deep breath. Although they had not spoken in years, Ellie had never been able to forget the honourable youth who had saved her reputation that hot afternoon long ago. Her mother had never found out, and neither Frederick or rather Rick—as she secretly thought of him—nor his friends had ever let anything slip of her daring adventure that day.

"I am glad that he is well," Ellie couldn't help but say. Her friend, however, didn't seem to think it an odd statement as she continued sipping her tea. "I worried that something might happen to him especially now that his father has passed. I am sure he will be of great comfort to his mother."

"I suppose so," Madeline said. "Unfortunately for him, he is not returning to claim a title. He is still the same man he was before his father passed, and as a second son, he will always be."

Ellie frowned. "Even if he had inherited the title, he would still be the same man. He would only have different responsibilities."

Madeline laughed. "These responsibilities—as you call them—are what make and break a man. If he had inherited his father's title, he would now command his family's assets and could choose any woman he wanted for his bride. Her dowry in turn would allow him to further his family's standing, which he then could pass on to his heir." Madeline shook her head. "A title is the fine line between significant…and worthless."

"He is not worthless!" Ellie snapped. "How can you speak so?"

"I'm sorry, Dear Elsbeth. I did not mean to offend your delicacies, nor did I mean to offend him. I am certain Frederick Lancaster is a marvellous man. I was merely pointing out that as a second son, his possibilities are severely limited."

"Then maybe it is a blessing in disguise," Ellie said smiling.

"How do you mean?"

"Since he does not need to choose a wife based on obligation, he is free to marry for love."

Shaking her head, Madeline chuckled. "You are a dreamer, my dear Elsbeth. Love is nothing tangible, nothing to rely on, nothing to set your sights on. People only speak of love when they have nothing else to show for themselves." Patting Ellie's hand, Madeline sighed. "Love is fleeting. You cannot trust it." She took a deep breath before meeting Ellie's eyes. "And I thought you of all people should know, having learnt that lesson in such a harsh manner."

Ellie couldn't help but cringe as her friend's words re-opened the wounds that had only just begun to heal.

Although two years had passed since a servant's oversight had almost cost Ellie her life, even today, she remembered the heat searing her skin as she had fought the flames with her bare hands to save her brother's life.

Only six years old at the time, Stephen had knocked over a candle, which had quickly set the room ablaze. Alerted by his screams, Ellie had come to his aid. Her attention completely focused on him, she had barely felt the flames until Stephen had been safe. Then all of a sudden, excruciating pain had brought her to her knees as the flames had burned away her skin.

Yet, somehow she had survived and fought her way back into life. Today, she could smile and laugh again, and whenever her eyes fell on her little brother, she knew it had been worth it.

Glancing out the window into the gardens, she caught a glimpse of her brother playing with his dog, Rupert. Smiling, Stephen scratched the hound's belly as the dog licked his master's face.

Yes, everything was as it should be. Her brother was alive and well.

Swallowing, Ellie shifted her eyes from the peaceful scene outside the window to the ugly scars that would remain a part of her forever.

The doctor had given her a special balm to massage into her damaged skin. For although new skin had formed, it was still tender and whenever she would stretch her limbs, the skin would feel as though it might be pulled apart any second. Her hands were the worst. The fire had consumed them both. Never again would Ellie be able to sit down to embroider a cushion or draw her friend's image. Her fingers refused to handle such a delicate task. Even holding a teacup now presented a small challenge.

However, none of this had been able to take away her zest for life. In Ellie's eyes, the world still held wonders that needed to be explored and happiness that begged to be found. She had been happy again even if only for a short time.

What had finally crushed her spirit had been the loss of the man she loved. Albert Cartwright, Viscount Haston.

During her recovery, her dream of a shared future had given her strength. Albert had always been so attentive and caring, always considerate of her opinion. Whenever she had set foot in a ballroom, his eyes had immediately found hers, lighting up with the love he had for her.

However, after scars tainted her beauty, travelling from her right cheek, down her throat, over her shoulder and down both arms to her hands, the light had dimmed, and now lay dead at her feet. All hope was lost.

"Maybe the dream I had ended badly," Ellie whispered, forcing back the tears she could feel clinging to her eyelashes, "but that does not mean it is always futile as you say." She lifted her eyes and met her friend's pitying gaze. "I know that you only mean to caution me, and I thank you for that, but what is life without hope for a future? Maybe I will never again have the love that I thought I once had. But that does not mean that others can't find it." She took a deep breath, feeling the tension in her heart spread into her limbs. "Frederick is a good man, and he deserves more than obligation. With or without a title, he is not worthless, and I am hoping with all my heart that one day he will find a woman who will make him feel…treasured."

Madeline swallowed, then opened her mouth and closed it again, not knowing what to say.

"You don't have to explain yourself." Shaking her head, Ellie smiled at her. "I know we look at life differently, and there is nothing wrong with that. I do not want to live without someone who loves me by my side: be it a husband, a sister or a friend. I know that now." She squeezed Madeline's hand. "You have to find your own way."

Her friend took a deep breath. "I'm sorry. I didn't mean to bring tears to your eyes."

Hearing Madeline's words, Ellie only then noticed the small drop rolling down her cheek until it reached the corner of her mouth. Brushing it away, she dabbed a handkerchief to her eyes. "I know," she said, trying to smile. "I am grateful for your friendship and for your honesty. Most people only see the scars I bear and not the person underneath. They tiptoe around me as though a harsh word could do me harm. And yet, they are surprised when I smile since they are certain that nothing in the world could ever bring me joy. Many believe I should have died two years ago." Madeline opened her mouth to object, but Ellie shook her head. "Yes, it is true. If I have no claim to happiness in my current state, what purpose does my life have?" She shrugged her shoulders. "On some days, I wonder about that myself. Even though I have a large dowry and my family is highly respected, I have no delusions about ever being a married woman." A sad smile lifted the corners of her mouth. "I am on the shelf as they say, but does that mean my life is over?"

For a moment, Madeline simply looked at her before a mischievous gleam came to her eyes. "It most certainly is not," she announced, reaching for Ellie's hands. "Life has a lot to offer, and husbands are just one small part of it."

Ellie laughed, treasuring the friend who had stood by her through all of this.

"Let us speak of more important matters than husbands," Madeline continued, her usual eagerness once more taking over. "The Midnight Ball is in a fortnight. What are we going to wear?"

2

A HERO'S RETURN

rey clouds hung over Elmridge as Frederick Lancaster returned home. How long had it been since he had last been here? He wondered. Long enough for him to feel like a stranger, someone who did not belong. And yet, this was his home.

For a long time, Frederick sat on his gelding a good distance from the manor and stared at the house that he knew so well. He saw the window that he and his brother had climbed out of more than once in yet another search for adventure, the rose garden that his mother tended with the same care and devotion she bestowed on those she loved as well as the small family cemetery that now housed his father's remains. The property looked like it always had, and yet, nothing was the same.

Never again would he hear his father's gentle voice as he spoke to him about the many wonders life held. Never again would he see his mother's smile as she looked at them, love shining in her eyes. Never again would he feel safe, almost invincible, as he had all those years he had spent on his family's estate.

The harsh truth had finally found him, sinking its cruel talons into his flesh, refusing to ever release its hold on him. No, nothing was the same anymore.

Urging his horse on, Frederick felt a looming dread settle in his bones the closer he came to the manor. As he pulled up the reins, a stable boy came running to take the horse. "Welcome back, Lord Frederick."

Nodding at the youngster, he turned and climbed the stairs, his feet heavy as lead. Two footmen opened the large double-doors, and Frederick entered the grand hall of Elmridge, his footsteps echoing through the vaulted room like thunder rolling off the mountains.

He should never have returned.

"Frederick!" his mother exclaimed behind him, and he turned toward her with a heavy heart.

Forcing a smile on his face, he slightly bowed his head to her as her dainty feet carried her across the marble hall and she all but threw herself into his arms. Her fragile arms closed around him, embracing him with a strength he never thought possible.

"Welcome home," she whispered in his ear before she stepped back, her watchful eyes searching his face. Although clouded with grief, they still held a mother's undying love for her son, and an unexpected warmth washed over his cold heart.

As her gaze slid over his face, taking in the small scar on his left temple, her hands gently brushed over his shoulders and down his arms as though asking about the wounds that lay hidden from her sight. She swallowed then and closed her eyes for a brief moment. When she looked at him again, a delicate smile played on her lips. "I am glad you have returned. I only wish your father were here to see you."

Bowing his head, Frederick swallowed. "As do I, Mother."

"Come," she said, linking her arm through his. "You must be exhausted. I will have a bath drawn and food brought up to your room."

As they walked up the large staircase, Frederick glanced left and right, waiting for the rest of his family to appear. All remained quiet though.

"I asked them to give you some time," his mother said, once again knowing exactly where his thoughts had strayed. "Do not believe that they did not wish to see you," she assured him, a tender smile curling up her lips. "However, I thought you might want some time to

yourself first." Her hand gently squeezed his arm. "I can call them if you wish."

Frederick shook his head. "Not yet."

She nodded and escorted him to the room that had been his for as long as he could remember. There she stopped, took his large hands in her small ones, looked deep into his eyes and then gave him a tender kiss on the forehead. "I'm so glad you are home," she whispered, her voice choked with tears.

"As am I, Mother," he said, hoping she could not read the lie in his eyes.

A smile came to her face, and she once more squeezed his hands before turning to go. "I'll have water brought up," she repeated as though reluctant to leave him.

"Thank you, Mother," he said and entered his room, desperate to be alone with his thoughts.

Soaking in the tub, Frederick closed his eyes, enjoying the soothing warmth that engulfed his tense limbs. The water felt wonderful like a thick blanket wrapping him in its safety, and yet, it could not wash away the pain that lived in his heart.

With a deep sigh, he grabbed the soap and rubbed it along his tired limbs. The dust from the road washed away quickly, the scars, however, remained. Staring at the stab wound in his left shoulder, Frederick remembered the day he had received it.

The bayonet had come out of nowhere. He hadn't even seen his opponent until it had been too late, and the cold steel had already dug its way into his body. A searing pain had brought him to his knees, and black spots had begun to dance before his eyes.

Slumping onto the blood-soaked earth, he had been certain his end was near.

The terror of the battlefield echoed in his ears as cries and shouts mixed with the heavy firing of canons and the lighter and faster firing of muskets. The stench of dying men, their hopelessness and fear mingling with the sweet smell of rain and the copper aroma of blood, still clung to his nostrils. No matter what he did or where he was, Frederick was forever doomed to relive these memories. They sought him out again and again as though his torment sustained them.

Like the bayonet, Kenneth, his childhood friend, had appeared as though rising from the earth itself.

Before the French soldier could finish Frederick, Kenneth bolted forward, his face twisted in an angry snarl as he came to his friend's aid. Not hesitating for a moment, he had flung himself at the enemy soldier. They had exchanged a few blows; however, Kenneth had disarmed the man swiftly, who had then stared up at him, a dumbfounded expression on his face as Kenneth sunk his bayonet into his chest.

Relief had flooded Frederick's heart upon seeing his friend succeed, knowing he would never have been able to live with himself if any harm had come to Kenneth because of him.

Still, he had returned to England alone.

With a deep sigh, he rose from the depth of the water, feeling the chill in the air on his wet skin. He dressed slowly, dreading the inevitable.

As he stood before the mirror, his eyes travelled over his appearance. How often had he looked into this mirror? A million times and more? Now, however, what he saw scared him. Somehow the dark in his heart had spread into every fibre of his being. He was not the man he once had been.

Now, his black hair seemed even darker as did his eyes, which were like looking into an abyss. They held nothing soft or tender but pierced their opposite with an icy stare. His strong chest and muscled arms ended in large hands that could rip a man to pieces. Hands that had taken more lives than he could remember. Hands that had not been able to save the one life he had cherished. Even above his own.

Looking at himself in the mirror, all Frederick saw was a monster.

Swallowing hard, he took a deep breath and left his room. Would the others notice? He wondered. How could they not?

As he approached the drawing room, happy chatter reached his ears, and his muscles tensed. Involuntarily, he reached for his pistol, shaking his head as he realised the insanity of that action.

Clearing his throat, he walked into the room.

Instantly, it fell silent.

All eyes turned to him, and Frederick's hands balled into fists as he forced himself to remain rooted to the spot. His legs quivered with the effort it took him not to bolt from the room.

Coward! His mind screamed.

Seated on the settee, his mother smiled at him, her eyes warm and full of affection. The sight almost turned Frederick's stomach upside down.

Then his gaze shifted to his big brother as he stood by the mantle, his head turned to the door, one hand gently cupping his wife's cheek. A big grin broke out on his face as he beheld Frederick, and dropping his hand, he strode forward. "Little brother, home at last!"

"Leopold," Frederick said, slightly bowing his head.

His brother frowned. "Don't be so formal," he laughed before he drew Frederick into his arms, affectionately slapping him on the back. "It is good to see you."

Feeling rather awkward, Frederick returned his brother's embrace half-heartedly. In a far corner of his mind, he seemed to remember that such a sign of affection had come to him easily once. Now, however, it felt unnatural, and his muscles were unable to relax, tense almost to the point of breaking.

Standing back, Leopold smiled at him, his soft brown eyes searching his brother's face. "You must tell me everything."

Frederick cringed inwardly. "Later," he mumbled, evading his brother's eyes.

"Certainly." Shaking his head as though suddenly remembering the other family members in the room, Leopold stepped back, grinning from ear to ear. He held out his hand, and his wife stepped forward, a smile on her beautiful features as she slipped her hand into his.

"Welcome home, Frederick," Maryann said, a gentle smile curling up her lips as she placed a soft hand on his hard arm, planting a tender kiss on his cheek. "We are so relieved to have you back with us."

"Thank you," Frederick mumbled, not sure what else to say. He drew in a deep breath as Leopold as well as Maryann remained by his side, their closeness unnerving him more than the feeling of detachedness that he couldn't seem to shake. He grew increasingly uncomfortable and wished for nothing more but the safe retreat to his room.

"Supper will be served shortly," his mother announced as she rose from the settee, her eyes on him. "Would you care for a walk?"

The ghost of a smile crossed Frederick's features. "I would like that. Thank you, Mother."

"Sounds like a marvellous idea," Leopold agreed, offering his arm to his wife. As he led her out the door, Frederick's heart sank. What he wouldn't do for a little peace and quiet?

His mother softly slipped her arm through his and drew him forward. "You must be patient with them," she whispered. "They have been very worried about you especially since…"

"Father's death?"

His mother nodded before looking up at him, and he could see the hint of tears clinging to her eyelashes. "They wish to be happy again, and you coming home is the greatest gift we could have hoped for especially in such a dark hour."

Frederick swallowed, his gaze fixed on the setting sun as they walked down the small gravel path to the garden labyrinth that bordered the manor to the west.

Leopold and Maryann walked a few feet ahead of them, her arm through his, his hand gently cupping hers. Now and then, his brother would lean over and whisper something in her ear, and her eyes would turn to him, gazing up into his with a deep love shining in them.

At his side, his mother remained silent, and Frederick took a deep breath, enjoying the late afternoon air as it filled his lungs. Delicate fragrances danced on the slight breeze, and he felt the beginnings of a headache subside. As his muscles began to relax, he closed his eyes for the briefest of moments, cherishing the quiet stillness that engulfed him and soothed his aching heart.

However, with supper, he found himself in hell once again.

Seated around the large dining room table, the family engaged in friendly conversation. Besides his mother, Leopold and Maryann, their six-year-old daughter Mathilda sat at the table, eyeing him with open curiosity.

Frederick wanted to squirm.

Occasionally, they addressed him as though feeling the need to include him in their conversation. Frederick, however, would have preferred to be left alone, and so he answered with mind-numbing indifference. Most of the time, he had no idea what they were talking about, and yet, he could not bring himself to care.

As the evening progressed, the conversation shifted from societal events and the estate's business to the war, and Frederick felt the blood pulse in his veins. As time passed and no one sought his opinion of the matter, Frederick began to relax until Leopold turned to him, inconspicuous interest in his eyes, and asked, "We have heard that Napoleon uses a new, lighter kind of canon. Do they truly work more efficiently?"

For a long minute, Frederick stared at his brother. More efficiently? He thought. In what way? Tearing men's bodies apart?

He glanced at his little niece, munching on her roast beef. What was he to say? Ought he to explain how a cannon ball tore apart a human body, scattering its parts over a great distance, soaking the earth with litres of blood?

Shaking his head, Frederick swallowed, and looking at his brother, he knew as clear as day that nothing in this world could ever paint a true picture of the horrors of war. Leopold did not know. For all the intelligence he possessed, he could not comprehend the savagery and gruesomeness that could be found on a battlefield. Like animals, civilised men tore each other apart, their eyes burning with hatred for an enemy they did not know. An enemy who thought of them the same way. As time passed, that hatred would vanish replaced by numbing stillness until one could not even glimpse remnants of the soul anymore. Even if one survived, one would be dead. A hollow vessel, for the spark of life had been extinguished.

For good.

Clearing his throat, Frederick nodded, his eyes focused on his plate. "Indeed, they are."

Sensing his brother's reluctance to speak about his experience, Leopold steered the conversation back to a more neutral topic. "Lord Branston reminded me of the invitation to his annual Midnight Ball. I already reminded *him* that you will not be attending since you are still in mourning," he said to his mother, who nodded, her fingers reaching for the small silver bracelet her husband had given her for their first anniversary almost thirty years ago. "However," he continued, turning to Frederick, "he is very eager for you to make an appearance."

The blood froze in Frederick's veins.

Leopold laughed. "I suppose as a war hero you would be quite the attraction at any event. The ladies will be all over you."

"Leopold!" Maryann chided, slapping him good-naturedly on the arm. However, she was instantly comforted by his charming smile and apologetic words.

"I told him you would be happy to come," his brother continued when his wife turned her attention back to the food on her plate.

"I hope that was all right? I figured you would enjoy an occasion to reconnect with your friends and acquaintances."

Swallowing a rebuke, Frederick nodded, forcing the hint of a smile on his face. "Certainly."

His brother's brows narrowed. "You do not wish to attend?"

Frederick sighed and met his brother's eyes. "No, Leopold," he spoke, his voice harsh with suppressed anger and open frustration. "To tell you the truth, I have no desire to be surrounded by old tattletales, scheming mothers and envious, disgruntled gentlemen, who are merely interested in elevating themselves by association. All they care about is tales of heroic deeds as though such a thing truly existed. They know nothing of war, and what is worse, they don't want to know. Not the cold, hard truth, at least."

Silence hung over the dining room, and Frederick felt a pang of guilt as his family looked at him with sorrowful eyes.

He took a deep breath. "I apologise. I didn't mean to spoil everyone's appetite." Rising from his chair, he bowed to his mother. "I believe it best I retire early tonight. My travels have worn me out. I trust a good night's sleep will do me some good."

His mother nodded, and yet, her eyes said that she didn't believe him. "Good night, Frederick. It is wonderful to have you back home."

Smiling at her, Frederick turned and left the dining room without looking back. His feet carried him up the stairs and into his room. He closed the door and locked it behind himself. Leaning against the smooth, wooden surface, Frederick closed his eyes.

He should never have returned.

Despite the sliver of hope that had carried him through the day, Frederick knew beyond the shadow of a doubt that there was no way back to his old life. The man he had once been didn't exist anymore, and the man he had become did not fit into the life he had left behind.

What was he to do now?

Dropping down onto the bed, Frederick didn't bother to undress. However, as he closed his eyes, images resurfaced that he had hoped to have left behind.

It had been a futile wish.

An anguished moan escaped his mouth, and he rubbed his hands over his face. The one person who would have understood what it felt like to be thrust back into this life was dead. His remains buried somewhere on the continent. Lost and forgotten.

No one who had not walked to the edge of the world and almost fallen off would understand the despair that lived in his heart, poisoning him a little more each day until one day there would be nothing left of him.

Then he would be truly dead.

Frederick hoped that day would come sooner rather than later.

THE LOSS OF A FRIEND

 rapped in a drawing room with his mother and his sister-in-law as well as a handful of female visitors, Frederick was ready to shoot himself. Standing to the side of the armchair Maryann currently occupied, he did his best to blend into the background as the ladies, most of whom had not called on Maryann or his mother in a long time, chatted on eagerly. Again and again, he found adoring eyes sweep over him in a scrutinising manner as though trying to unearth his secrets.

And yet, worse than the stares were the rather uneducated and insensitive questions they asked.

"How many enemies did you kill?" *I didn't stop to count.*

"Were you wounded?" *It was war. What do you think, my lady?*

A chubby matron elbowed the woman who had asked the question. "My dear Lady Bertram, do you not see the dashing scar on his temple?" She winked at him. "I say it makes you look like a pirate."

Frederick took a deep breath.

"Do you still carry a pistol?" *I wish I was.*

"Do the French truly look like evil men?" *They are no more evil than you and me.*

All these questions hailed down on him in a matter of minutes that Frederick didn't even know where to begin, much less how to answer without causing affront. However, to his great relief, he soon realised that an occasional nod or shake of his head sufficed, and the ladies flew into yet another rant about what a marvellous experience war had to have been for him.

Slipping out of the room after half an hour, Frederick breathed a sigh of relief, his feet directing him toward the stairs and the safety of his room without conscious thought.

"Brother!"

Frederick froze, and for a moment, he closed his eyes, willing Leopold to simply walk away.

Unfortunately, it didn't work.

"Would you care to join us?"

Reluctantly, Frederick turned around and found his brother standing by the foot of the stairs, a group of men crowding around him.

Not unlike the ladies, the gentlemen eyed him with a mixture of admiration and curiosity; and yet, some faces held a hint of envy etched in their eyes.

Forcing a somewhat pleasant expression on his face, Frederick joined them in the study for a glass of brandy and a cigar. Talk soon circled around to the war, and Frederick once again did his best to retreat into the shadows, hoping to be overlooked.

Unfortunately, it didn't work.

Although the men's questions were of a more technical nature, they were no less insensitive. Gritting his teeth, Frederick tried to stay calm as he felt the blood pulsing in his veins. If he could only show these fools that war was neither a game nor a business endeavour!

Before he could explode, his brother placed a hand on his shoulder, steering the conversation back to the Midnight Ball that was to take place in three days. Especially the younger, unmarried gentlemen were eager to discuss the attending ladies, and soon Frederick was able to escape the room in much the same fashion as before.

Shaking his head, he wondered how much more of this he could take before losing his mind.

In the hall, he came upon his mother. As unease seized his heart, he quickly scanned his surroundings for a potential flock of chattering ladies following close on her heel.

A gentle smile came to his mother's face. "I am alone," she said, brushing a hand down his arm. Lately, he had noticed that she sought a physical contact as though needing to reassure herself that he was really there.

He sighed. "I cannot understand what these people are doing here," he moaned, doing his best to keep the desperation he felt out of his voice so as not to alert his mother. "Are there not enough war stories circling around that they have to beg for more?"

His mother cupped a hand to his cheek, gentle eyes looking into his. "Just humour them. Tell them what they want to hear," she advised, "and before long, they will leave you alone."

Frederick nodded. "I suppose you are right, Mother. However, I do not know how much more of this I can bear."

"Why don't you go for a ride?" his mother suggested. "Get some air and clear your head. You'll feel better."

Again, Frederick nodded, and after thanking his mother, he headed straight for the stables.

As the wind whipped in his face and he saw the horizon shine in the distance, Frederick felt some of the strain of the last few days fall from his weary muscles.

The ache in his bones, however, remained.

"You have a visitor, Lord Frederick," Wilton, Elmridge's butler, announced as they sat down for dinner.

"Who is it?" Frederick moaned. *Would this never end?*

"The Earl of Cullingwood."

Almost jumping to his feet, Frederick turned to his mother, who nodded her head, a pleased smile on her face. "Do not worry about us. Go see your friend."

"Thank you, Mother," Frederick replied and hurried out of the room. Long strides carried him down the corridor and toward the front drawing room. For a moment, he stopped outside the door and took a deep breath. It had been a long time since they had last seen each other; not since he and Kenneth had gone off to war, and Oliver had remained behind.

Entering the room, Frederick found his friend staring out the window, a glass of brandy in his hand. Although a hint of melancholy hung about him, he looked like he always had. His auburn hair gave his rather pale complexion a bit of a glow as he stood tall, shoulders squared, and sipped his drink. His pale blue eyes were distant, and frown lines darkened the face that used to shine with laughter more than any other Frederick had ever seen.

When he closed the door behind himself, Oliver turned from the window, and their eyes met. "It is good to see you, old friend," Frederick greeted him, unsure whether they could simply continue their friendship as it had been before.

"It is, indeed," Oliver agreed, and the corners of his mouth curled up into a smile. "I hope you don't mind," he lifted the glass in his hand, "but I helped myself."

Involuntarily, Frederick felt the corners of his mouth tug up in reply. "I can't say I am surprised." Stepping forward, he gestured for his friend to sit and then took a seat himself. "What brings you here?"

"Do you truly have to ask?" Oliver set down his glass and leaned back, his eyes even more piercing than Frederick remembered. "I thought you would come to see me or, at least, send word." A hint of disappointment showed on his face. "Or do you still hold a grudge?"

Frederick frowned. "A grudge? What about?"

Shaking his head, Oliver smiled. "You truly do not hold it against me, do you?"

"I have no idea what you speak of." Leaning forward, Frederick rested his arms on his knees, his eyes searching his friend's face. "I'd be much obliged if you would explain yourself."

"I should have gone with you," Oliver said without preamble, and Frederick felt a shiver run down his back. "I knew I should have. I knew it even then." He shook his head. "I never should have listened to my father."

Closing his eyes, Frederick drew in a deep breath before once more meeting his friend's eyes. "Your father's counsel was wise. We should all have heeded his words. Neither one of us should have gone." He looked at Oliver imploringly. "He saved your life. Do not hold it against him."

"You make him sound more caring than he truly is," Oliver objected with a snort. "The only reason he was concerned for my life was

because I am his only heir." He rolled his eyes. "And he did not counsel me. He ordered me to stay behind." Frederick could see the guilt on
his friend's face as clear as day. He, himself, only knew too well how it
felt to have regrets that tormented him with every breath he took.
"And still, I could have gone. I could have stood up to him, at least
once, and made my own way. But I didn't. If I had, maybe…"

"What?" Frederick asked. "Kenneth would still be alive?"

Oliver shrugged, not meeting his eyes.

"You couldn't have saved him," Frederick said as the images of
their friend's death played before his eyes. "I was there, and I
couldn't." He took a deep breath. "Do not torment yourself for it
would be in vain."

"Don't you?" Oliver asked. "I can see it plainly on your face, so
do not deny it."

Once again feeling the desperate need to escape the room, Frederick gritted his teeth as his hands balled into fists. Every muscle in
his body tensed, and a drumming pain settled behind his forehead. "I
am not denying anything!" he forced out through clenched teeth. "I am
the very reason he…" His words trailed off, and he forced more air
down his lungs.

Oliver nodded. "How did it happen?"

Frederick closed his eyes. He had feared that this moment
would come. A moment that would force him to relive the most horrible seconds of his life. And yet, he could not deny Oliver's request. He
had a right to know what had happened.

"Do not ask me which battle it was for they all blurred together
a long time ago," he began, his voice sounding hoarse to his own ears
like that of an old man. "I only remember sweeping hills and a sunrise
so beautiful that I thought for sure all this had to be a bad dream. How
could the world be so breath-taking when good men lost their lives
upon its soil day after day?" As Frederick closed his eyes, he heard his
friend draw a strained breath. "When the battle began, we charged
ahead. The icy wind whipped our faces as our horses carried us closer
to the enemy. We could see their weapons, polished to perfection,
gleaming in the early morning sun."

Frederick swallowed, and as he met his friend's eyes, he saw in
them the same reluctance to hear what had happened that he felt to
recount it. Still, neither one of them had a choice. They owed it to
Kenneth. "We spotted the cannons from far away," he continued, remembering the day like no other, "as we had many times before. But

we did not see it coming. Even if we had, I doubt that there would have been anything we could have done."

For a long time, Frederick remained silent, trapped in a memory he could not escape, watching his friend's face twisted in the agony of death.

"What happened then?" Oliver asked, his voice merely a whisper as though he was afraid to disturb Frederick's thoughts.

"They fired," was all he said, and once again silence hung between them. A silence that stretched into a heavy burden settling onto their shoulders. A burden they would carry with them for the rest of their days.

"One second, he was right next to me," Frederick finally continued, "and the next, the cannon ball cut down his horse's legs. As it slumped to the ground, Kenneth was flung out of the saddle. Only a moment later, he landed on the ground with a sickening crunch."

Wringing his hands, Oliver looked paler than he ever had.

"And that was it," Frederick said, meeting his friend's eyes. "He was gone. From one second to the next, Kenneth was gone. He broke his neck upon hitting the ground." Rising to his feet, Frederick started to pace. "I keep thinking that it shouldn't have happened like that. Soldiers, who die in a war, are shot or stabbed. It should have been the cannon ball or a sabre or…" Trailing off, he shook his head. "And then I think it does not matter how it happened. Dead is dead." He turned to look at his friend. "But shouldn't he have had a hero's death? He fell off a horse!" Frederick shook his head, feeling an all too familiar madness engulf him. "I still can't believe it. And I don't know what to think or how to look at his death. I don't know anything anymore." Coming to stand by the window, Frederick stared past the neatly trimmed hedges and the orderly gravel path leading up to the front steps. His eyes focused on the horizon where earth met sky, a line that looked the same no matter where he went.

"It was not your fault," Oliver spoke from behind him. As they stood side by side, he placed a hand on Frederick's shoulder. "You could not have saved him. I know that if anyone could have, it would have been you."

For a brief moment, Frederick closed his eyes. "I know. Somehow I know that, and yet, there is a part of me that knows nothing of reason, of rational thought or of cause and consequence. It is that part that I feel rising to the surface lately. Everything I thought I knew is just…It's gone, replaced by a black abyss, and it's drawing me in."

"I don't know what to say," Oliver admitted, worry clinging to his words. "If I had gone with you, I might not have been able to save Kenneth, but maybe we could have saved each other. Now, you're alone."

Looking at his friend, Frederick nodded. "Thank you for listening to my rambles. I appreciate it."

Oliver shook his head. "Do not speak as though you're standing on the brink of a cliff with no intention of turning back." Oliver grabbed him by the shoulders and gave him a hard shake. "I lost Kenneth, but I will be damned if I lose you, too."

Frederick stared into his friend's eyes, and for the first time, he thought that maybe all hope was not lost.

4

THE MIDNIGHT BALL

*T*he stars sparkled in the night sky like diamonds as Ellie and Madeline ascended the stairs to Lord Branston's residence for his annual Midnight Ball. Even early in September, the late hour brought with it a slight chill in the air, and Ellie drew the delicate shawl closer around her shoulders. Although she had chosen a dress that covered most of her scars, her neck and lower face were naturally still exposed, and so she had insisted on the shawl in order to further cover herself—as far as that was possible.

Of course, everyone in the county knew about the accident and had heard or even seen how badly she had been injured, and yet, Ellie couldn't shake the feeling that most people preferred not be to reminded of it. As though looking at her would spoil their fun, she sensed their reluctance to receive her in their midst.

Taking a deep breath, Ellie smiled at Madeline as they walked through the grand foyer side by side. Not hindered by unseemly scars, her friend had chosen a more revealing dress, its shades of dark violet enhancing the glow of her raven-black hair. Next to her, Ellie felt devoid of colour. Her own pale blond curls sat atop a simple, white dress, a light blue sash tied around her slender waist.

As they entered the ballroom and the music reached her ears, Ellie smiled. Oh, how she loved the lively atmosphere of such an event! The laughing and dancing filled her heart with such a vibrant energy that she hardly knew how to contain herself. As though of their own accord, her feet started tapping to the rhythm, and she longed to dance.

Her gaze followed the smiling couples as they spun across the dance floor, and a wistful glow came to her eyes. If only she could dance again. At least one last time.

Ever since her accident, men generally treated her like an old matron, someone who watched the proceedings but did not participate. They treated her with respect, offered to fetch refreshments and enquired if she required anything, but they didn't see the young woman she was: the young woman who longed to dance, who wanted nothing more but to forget the past for a few hours and enjoy herself.

As expected, eligible and not so eligible gentlemen crowded around Madeline as soon as they entered the ballroom. All smiles, they sought her attention and asked for the next dance. With a dazzling smile of her own, Madeline drew their interest, and yet, avoided promises she did not care to make. Ellie admired the ease with which her friend manoeuvred through the sea of admirers that met her at every event.

"Do you never tire of all the attention?" Ellie asked as they headed for the table of refreshments set under a looming arch by the French doors leading out onto the terrace.

Madeline chuckled. "Certainly, I do. Even I do not care for the regard of a man I have no interest in. I merely seek to draw out the one man who deserves my undivided attention."

"Is that so?" Ellie smiled, pouring herself a glass of punch. "And have you made any progress?"

A hint of disappointment in her eyes, Madeline scanned the crowd. "I'm afraid not, which I find rather frustrating. It is not like my expectations are so unreasonable. However, so far it seems like there is no man in the whole of England whom I would even consider."

"That is disheartening," Ellie mumbled suppressing a laugh. As much as she adored her friend, Madeline had a tendency for dramatics; and as far as her expectations were concerned, they were, indeed, rather unreasonable. Not that Ellie would ever tell her that.

Her eyes still sweeping the crowd, Madeline suddenly froze. Then she spun around, grabbed Ellie by the arm and pulled her to the side.

"What is the matter?" Ellie gasped, wondering what had brought on such a strange behaviour. "Are you all right?"

"Yes, certainly," Madeline stammered, her eyes straying to the crowd beyond Ellie's shoulder. "I just thought…I saw…a mouse."

Ellie's eyes narrowed. "A mouse?"

A sheepish grin came to Madeline's face, and she reluctantly met her friend's eyes. "Maybe it was just my imagination."

"Madeline, what is going on? What did you see?" Ellie tried to turn around, but Madeline once more grabbed her arm and pulled her back. Staring at her friend, Ellie's eyes narrowed. "What could you possibly have seen that would explain this rather extreme behaviour of yours?"

Feigning surprise, Madeline released her arm. "Me? Nothing. How about we take a turn about the room?" she asked, steering Ellie farther away from the dancing couples. "This way."

"All right." Pretending to follow her friend, Ellie only took two steps before turning back. Before Madeline could stop her, she spun around, her eyes scanning the crowd.

As she spotted them, the blood froze in her veins.

"I'm sorry," Madeline whispered beside her.

Ellie swallowed, unable to tear her eyes from the man she had wanted to marry as he danced with another woman. As he looked down at her, a deep smile came to his face. A smile that Ellie recognised. A long time ago, that smile had been meant for her.

A heavy lump settled in her stomach.

"Who is she?" Ellie asked, not sure if she wanted to know the answer.

"Abigail Turnton, Lord Smithen's daughter."

Ellie nodded as her eyes filled with tears. Blinking them away, she took a deep breath. "This is not a mere dance, is it?" Ellie asked. "What do you know?"

Madeline sighed before reluctantly answering Ellie's question. "They are betrothed. He asked for her hand a fortnight ago."

Closing her eyes, Ellie once more drew in a deep breath. As the world began to spin, Madeline's hand closed around hers, squeezing it gently. "Come," her friend whispered. "You don't have to look at them."

"Yes, I do," Ellie stammered, knowing that there was no way for her to avoid seeing them while at the same time enjoy herself out in society. If she did so, she might as well return home and never set another foot outside again. "I have to make my peace with it. There is no other way."

As her eyes followed the happy couple as they spun around the dance floor, Madeline's hand remained on hers, a lifeline that would keep her sane when her mind threatened to spin out of control and her heart ached so fiercely that Ellie thought it would burst into a million pieces.

Until a familiar face drew her attention, and the breath caught in her throat.

"What?" Madeline asked, looking at her with worried eyes.

"He's here," Ellie gasped as her gaze swept over his tall stature as if a magnetic pull held them trapped. He stood to the side, his elder brother, the marquess, and his wife as well as his friend Oliver Cornell at his flanks. Although he looked every bit the gentleman, with his hair neatly brushed back and his attire meticulously groomed, he still seemed somehow out of place considering the exuberant gaiety of the evening. His eyes were hard, troubled even, and his lips were pressed into a thin line. Whenever someone would walk up to him, he bowed his head in greeting. However, the hint of a smile that came to his features seemed forced, and it disappeared as quickly as it had come.

Despite the joy that had flooded her heart upon seeing him, Ellie was not blind to the pain so apparent in his eyes. What had happened to him? She wondered, glimpsing the thin scar running down his left temple. What nightmares had he witnessed?

"Who's here?" Madeline asked, interrupting her thoughts.

Ellie swallowed and then nodded her head in his direction. "Lord Frederick Lancaster."

Following her friend's gaze, Madeline smiled. "He is a handsome man, is he not?" she mused. "Easily distracts from the more important men at his side."

Ellie's eyes snapped to her friend's face and found a teasing smile curl up her lips. "Why do you tease me?"

"Because I can see that you care for him," Madeline said, squeezing her hand. "Is that not the reason why you defended him so passionately the other day?"

Feeling a blush warm her cheeks, Ellie averted her eyes. "I do like him, yes. Or rather I did." Seeing the curiosity in her friend's eyes,

Ellie added, "Years ago, he did me a service, and it endeared him to me." She smiled shyly. "But that was years ago. I have no way of knowing what kind of man he is today."

Madeline shrugged, a conspiratorial smile on her face. "In my experience, people rarely change. At our very core, we are who we are. If you liked him then, he must be a good man."

For a moment, Ellie stared at her friend in surprise. Never would she have thought Madeline to be capable of such deep musings. And yet, her friend was one of only a handful of people who was able to see past her scars. "Yes, I believe he is."

"Do you wish to be reacquainted with him?"

Ellie shook her head. "No," she whispered, eyes straying to his tall form once again. "I could not compete." A small stab pierced her heart as she watched other young ladies vie for his attention, their smiles and glowing eyes untainted by ugly scars.

"If you believe in love as you say you do, then there is no competition," Madeline objected. "Either he is your match or he is not. The scars you bear, either one of you, do not matter. Maybe because of them, you're all the more suited for each other."

Looking up at her friend's glowing eyes, Ellie smiled. "You have a hidden depth, Madeline, that very few people ever get to see."

Eyes opening in feigned shock, Madeline gasped, "I would certainly hope so! After all, I have a reputation to protect." Laughing, she took her leave and joined the other couples on the dance floor, now and then glancing back at Ellie, letting her know that she was not forgotten.

While Madeline danced and flirted for the rest of the evening, her cheeks flushed from exertion and excitement, Ellie remained hidden in the shadows of the large room, her eyes involuntarily straying to the one man she felt certain could heal her broken heart. And yet, she did not dare speak to him. Would he even remember her?

Hushed whispers floated to her ears when the music stopped, and although Ellie did her utmost not to listen, her heart could not shut out the words she heard.

"Look at her. Even after all this time, you can still see where the fire touched her skin."

"I know, poor thing. What do you suppose she is doing here?"

"Maybe her mother urged her out of the house for some entertainment. It cannot be beneficial to be alone all the time."

"Are you certain? The baroness is not even here. I heard she is ailing."

"The poor girl does not look happy, does she?"

"How could she?"

Ellie sighed and for a moment closed her eyes. When the musicians began to play a lively country tune, drowning out the next pitying remark, she felt herself relax. Watching the couples take their positions, she once more glanced across the room.

This time, a number of gentlemen crowded around Frederick, their faces eager and laughing as they chatted, occasionally turning to the returned war hero in hopes of new stories to repeat for years to come. Ellie had seen it before. Men who returned from the war were often hounded by those who had remained behind as they eagerly sought sensational anecdotes to enrich their otherwise uneventful lives. They were like blood hounds, which had caught the scent of their prey.

Ellie shivered, thinking about the insensitivity people often displayed. Could they not imagine the pain that their thoughtless remarks caused? Had nothing painful ever happened to them?

As her eyes returned to Frederick, she found the marquess by his side. Seeing the strained expression on his brother's face, Leopold stepped forward, arm sweeping to the side, holding back the men that sought his brother's attention, and ushered Frederick through the crowd. Oliver spoke up then, and the heads turned back to him as he drew their interest with an entertaining story. Soon, the men were laughing, allowing Frederick to escape.

Ellie smiled, relieved to find that he was not alone in his pain. Maybe one day, he would be able to smile again, the same heart-felt smile she remembered from so long ago.

5

LOSS

*S*tanding on the terrace, Frederick drew the chilled night air into his lungs. He felt smothered by the crowd of people who refused to leave him alone, completely blind to the agony their thoughtless remarks dragged to the surface.

For a moment, he closed his eyes and wished himself far away.

"Better?" Leopold asked, placing a hand on his shoulder.

Frederick shook his head. "Why won't they leave me alone?" He spun around, eyes fixed on his brother. "You might as well inform them that I have no intention of ever revealing any details with regard to any battles I have found myself in. It is not for them to know, and I swear, next time someone asks, I will not be so lenient!" Feeling steam come out of his ears, he gulped down another breath, savouring the slight tingling in his chest as the cold air touched his lungs.

"I know how you feel—"

Frederick's brows rose into arches.

"Fine," Leopold relented. "I don't know how you feel. However, I am telling you that it is most unwise to snub the people you will find yourself dealing with for the rest of your life. These are your friends and neighbours, and despite their eager thoughtlessness, they do not mean any harm by asking you these questions." Again, Leopold placed both his hands on his brother's shoulders, his eyes intent on Frederick's. "Please, be patient, and wait it out. They will stop. It will not be like this forever."

Frederick snorted. "I do not know how much longer I can bear this."

"I know. But that is what I am here for," his brother said, an affectionate smile curling up his lips. "I will keep them away from you as best as I can."

Frederick nodded. "Thank you, Brother."

"Think nothing of it," Leopold said before giving his brother an encouraging pat on the back. "I'll go back inside." His eyes found Frederick's once more. "Do not stay out here for too long." Turning back to the festivities, Leopold reached for the handle when the door swung open. He stepped back, and a smile spread over his face. "Oliver," he said, sounding pleased. "Good! He could use some company."

Frederick sighed when his friend came to stand beside him, taking his brother's place. "Do you have more encouraging words to say? For I am not sure I want to hear them, much less if they would do any good. I am not really in a receptive mood right now."

"Unfortunately, I am not the bearer of good news," Oliver said, tension lending a slight quiver to his voice.

"What is it?" Frederick asked, feeling a wave of apprehension wash over him at the sight of his friend's slumped shoulders and distraught face.

For a moment, Oliver hesitated, his eyes fixed on Frederick's face as though trying to determine whether or not to share with him what he had learnt. Then he swallowed and drew in a deep breath. "Charlotte is here."

The blood froze in his veins as Frederick stared at his friend, unable to believe his ears. "Here?" he croaked. "She is here? Right now?"

Oliver nodded. "She wants to talk to you."

Closing his eyes, Frederick took a deep breath as the world began to spin.

"You cannot avoid her forever," Oliver pointed out. "She has a right to know."

"I know," Frederick mumbled. Then he opened his eyes and looked at his friend. "How am I to face her after what I've done to her?"

Oliver shook his head. "She will not blame you. After all, it was not your fault, and I believe she knows that."

"All right," Frederick nodded. "I'll talk to her." From the moment, Kenneth had died, Frederick had known that one day he would have to face her.

"I'll fetch her," Oliver said, and Frederick watched him return inside and cross the ballroom until he was lost from sight.

Thinking about Charlotte, Frederick's hands balled into fists, and he gritted his teeth. What was he to tell her? What would she ask of him? He shook his head, trying to clear it. Then he spun around and began pacing the length of the terrace, raking his hands through his hair.

"Frederick?" Oliver's voice stopped him in his tracks.

Swallowing, Frederick slowly turned around.

In the light of the moon, she looked paler than he had ever seen her. A handkerchief clutched in her small hands, she lifted her chin, and her hazel eyes looked into his. A shiver went through her, but Frederick doubted it was from the cool night air.

"Charlotte," he whispered and stepped forward.

Oliver cleared his throat. "We'll be over there."

Momentarily shifting his gaze to his friend, Frederick found him retreating to the other end of the terrace, Charlotte's mother at his side.

"It is good to see you," Charlotte said, her voice echoing of emotions held in check. Unshed tears clung to the corners of her eyes, and the hint of a smile she forced on her lips almost broke his heart.

"It is," Frederick agreed, not knowing what else to say. He ought to be able to help her, ease the pain, and yet, his own held him trapped.

Stepping around him, she walked over to the banister and looked out into the night. "After it happened, I thought you would write to me," she said, not looking at him.

Nevertheless, Frederick felt the full weight of the accusation she laid at his door.

"At first, I thought that you had been injured, too, but then..." She turned her head, her hazel eyes looking into his. "Why?" A tear rolled down her cheek, and she quickly brushed it away. "With no word from you, it didn't seem real." A sad smile crossed her face. "Do you know what I mean? A part of me felt certain that he would return, that one day he would come walking through the door."

Frederick nodded. "A part of me still believes that."

"I don't anymore." Her eyes held him captive as he witnessed the harsh truth spread over her face. "When you returned without him, I knew." She swallowed, dabbing the handkerchief to her eyes. "Now, all hope is lost." Eyes fixed on his, she stepped forward. "Why didn't you come to me? When I learnt that you had returned, I felt certain you would finally call on me." A frown drawing down her brows, she shook her head. "But you didn't. Why didn't you?"

Taking a deep breath, Frederick still didn't know what to say. After all, there was no explanation, no rational excuse to make her understand. Guilt had been holding him back as well as the insane notion to hope that maybe what he knew to be true was not, after all. Delivering the news of his friend's death to his fiancée would have confirmed the truth. And despite everything that had happened, a part of Frederick hadn't been ready to accept the fact that his friend was truly gone.

Now, seeing the truth on her face, loss once more hit him with the full force of its tragedy.

His hands balled into fists as he tried to maintain his composure. "I needed time," he pressed out through clenched teeth, desperately trying to force the pain back into the abyss he had banished it to the day Kenneth had died.

"Time?" Charlotte echoed, her eyes void of emotion. "I only came here tonight because I needed to see you. I needed to know. I could not go to Elmridge, a place where we had all been together before." Her voice broke, and she shook her head vehemently as though expecting him to contradict her. "I couldn't have come. I would have expected to see him there. I…"

Frederick took a deep breath. "I'm sorry, Charlotte. I didn't mean to hurt you, but I wasn't ready to face you yet."

Fixing him with a defiant stare, she challenged him, "Are you now?"

Frederick met her eyes and then nodded. "I don't believe I have a choice," he said. "You have a right to know."

She closed her eyes then and turned back to the gardens shrouded in darkness at their feet. Resting her arms on the banister, she bowed her head. "Tell me then. How did it happen?"

Once more, Frederick unlocked the memories that pained him daily and braced himself to relive his friend's final moments. Forcing himself to remain calm, he spoke with an even voice, explaining the situation they had found themselves in on the battlefield and the unexpectedness of Kenneth's death.

Tears rolled freely down Charlotte's cheeks, and she didn't bother to brush them away. However, no sob escaped her lips, and Frederick marvelled at the strength that resided within her. She bore the loss of the man she loved with dignity and grace, and he felt selfishly grateful for not having to witness her breakdown as his words confirmed what her mind already knew: Kenneth would never return.

"Did he suffer?" she asked, her voice barely loud enough to reach his ears.

Frederick shook his head. "I do not believe so. It was…sudden." He swallowed. "I don't believe he realised what was happening." He drew a deep breath, determined to set her heart and mind as much at ease as he possibly could. "I saw him…later …when…His face held no signs of pain or agony. He seemed at peace."

Charlotte nodded before she raised her eyes to his. "Thank you for telling me. I am glad you were by his side when it happened."

And yet, I couldn't save him, Frederick thought.

Ignoring his own demons, he stepped forward and took her hands. "He cared for you deeply. He told me so every day," he whispered, watching new tears spill over and run down her cheeks. "More than anything, he wanted to return to you. Nothing but death could have ever kept him from your side."

At his words, Charlotte closed her eyes, and when she opened them again, a hint of determination shone in their hazel depth. She took a deep breath and withdrew her hands, once again wringing the handkerchief that had already caught too many of her tears. "Thank you for telling me this," she said, her eyes shifting past his shoulder. "I need to go."

Frederick nodded. "Be well, Charlotte. Should you ever need anything, do not hesitate to call on me."

"I will," she said, then swallowed and walked back to the terrace doors where her mother met her and escorted her back inside.

"Are you all right?" Oliver asked, coming up to stand beside him. "You look like hell."

A snort escaped his lips, and Frederick shook his head. "You have no idea. I've been in hell ever since it happened. Coming home, I thought maybe I could somehow leave it all behind, but…" Again, he shook his head. "Somehow it is worse. I'm thinking about going back."

"Going back?" Oliver gasped. Grabbing his friend by the shoulders, he looked deep into his eyes. "Talk to me, Rick. What is going on?"

Shrugging off the hands that held him, Frederick stepped back. "This world is not mine anymore. I don't know how to…be here anymore." Raking his hands though his hair, he closed his eyes. "I feel like I am going insane."

"You cannot go back," Oliver proclaimed, the tone in his voice not allowing for an argument. "I know you. With all this pain haunting you, you'd recklessly throw yourself into danger." Determined, he shook his head. "No, you'd never come home."

Frederick sighed. "Maybe that would be for the better."

Oliver stared at him with wide eyes. "You cannot mean this."

"I can, and I do." Turning around, Frederick headed back inside. However, before the door closed behind him, he heard Oliver saying, "I will talk to your brother about this. Together, we will find a way to help you. I'm not giving up on you, Rick."

Sighing, Frederick closed the door, knowing that there was nothing they could do.

6

THE WEIGHT OF PAIN

*T*he exuberant joy that hung about the ballroom radiated by the many couples dancing and laughing, enjoying the music, the drinks and the late hour, felt like a slap in the face to Frederick.

After speaking to Charlotte and watching her heart break into a million pieces, he looked at the world around him, and the madness began to rise once more. As the blood in his veins started to boil and pulse, Frederick gritted his teeth, willing himself to remain calm. How could such opposites exist in the same world? The misery and terror of the battlefield as well as the joy and ease of a night of dancing? How was this possible?

Hurrying over to the refreshment table, Frederick reached for something stronger than a glass of punch. He knew he was trapped in this place; however, he would do whatever necessary to ease the pain that rested in his bones, in his soul, in the very core of his being. And to hell with everyone who disapproved!

Standing in a corner of the large room, half-hidden behind stately artefacts, Ellie watched him gulp down one drink after another. Something had happened out on the terrace; she was sure of it. Something awful. Something that had crushed his spirit.

When his brother had ushered him outside, he had looked relieved to be escaping the throng of people vying for his attention. However, the moment he had reappeared, she had been able to tell that a heavy burden had come to rest on his shoulders, a burden as torturous as any she could imagine.

Could it have something to do with the young woman who had gone to see him?

From what Ellie had been able to observe, they had spoken to each other privately. Her face, too, had seemed flushed when she had re-entered the ballroom at her mother's side. However, the look in her eyes had not held the same agony she now glimpsed in Frederick's.

Wringing her hands, Ellie knew that it was none of her business. And yet, she desperately wished to know what had transpired between them. Were they in love? Had it been a lovers' quarrel?

Ellie bit her lip as the thought brought on a small sting in her heart. She was surprised at how deeply she cared for him even though it had been years since they had last spoken to each other. How could she care for someone she didn't even know? Or had Madeline been right? Did people not change at their core? Could he possibly be the same man she had met all those years ago?

Slowly, the music faded away as did the laughing couples. The lights dimmed, and Frederick felt himself relax his hold on the glass in his hand. How many had he had? He couldn't remember. Enough to be given a reprieve from the agony twisting his heart.

He sighed and poured himself another drink.

"Are you out of your mind?" a voice snapped next to his shoulder, and Frederick winced as its loud pitch pierced the fog numbing his pain.

Slowly, he turned his head and found his brother glaring at him. "Come again?" Frederick queried, wishing with all his might that Leopold would just walk away and leave him alone.

Of course, he didn't.

"I spoke to Oliver," Leopold growled. Then his eyes swept over Frederick, and a disgusted frown came to his face. "Drinking your pain away?" he asked in a softer tone.

"Unfortunately, that's not possible," Frederick mumbled, once more downing the contents of his glass. "However, I am willing to give it my utmost."

Ripping the empty glass from his brother's hands, Leopold slammed it onto the table. "Frederick, you need to come to your senses. This is not you. I had hoped that speaking to Charlotte would allow you to put all this behind you."

Frederick's eyes snapped open. "You told her I would be here? Is that why you insisted I attend?"

"I apologise for the deception," Leopold said, his eyes dark with sadness. "However, I did not know what else to do. I can see how much losing Kenneth tortures you, but you have to find a way to move on. I know that this is easy for me to say because I cannot even begin to understand what you went through," he stepped forward and placed his hands on Frederick's shoulders, "but it is the only way."

Frederick closed his eyes, then took a step back and shook his head. "It is not the only way."

"You cannot be serious!" Leopold snapped, and his eyes narrowed. "Going back will only get you killed. How does that help Kenneth?"

"It doesn't," Frederick stated, knowing that no matter what he said his brother could not understand how he felt. Yes, he missed Kenneth, and he felt guilty about his death. But that was not all of it. The world looked different now, and Frederick couldn't bear to look at it. "However, it will end this pain."

As Leopold continued to stare at him, disbelief showing in his eyes, a footman stopped beside Frederick, a tray balanced on his hand. "For you, my lord."

Without looking, Frederick took the offered drink, and the footman walked away. "I'm sorry, Leopold," he said. "I know you mean well. But there is nothing you can do or say that will change my mind." Giving his brother a sad smile, he lifted the glass to his lips.

"No!" Leopold snarled, determination shining in his eyes. "I don't care what you say. You are my brother, and I will help you whether you like it or not." Snatching the drink from Frederick's grasp, he looked at him through narrowed eyes. "Go get some fresh air. We will talk about this later when your mind is not clouded by this poison."

Frederick sighed. He had half a mind to argue his point but then decided against it. His brother meant well, and he deserved to be treated better than this.

Nodding his head, Frederick once more headed for the terrace.

Her heart beating in her chest, Ellie felt a low current run through her body as she watched the brothers' heated exchange. She was glad to see how determined Leopold was to make his brother see reason. However, from the untouched mask on Frederick's face, she could tell that he was fighting a losing battle.

When Frederick turned around and headed for the terrace, Leopold remained behind, defeated eyes following his brother's retreating figure. And yet, she saw the tension in his jaw as his hand gripped the glass he had taken from him more tightly. His sinews stood out white, and for a moment, he closed his eyes and took a deep breath.

Large strides carried Oliver to Leopold's side then, and the two men spoke to each other in low voices. Occasionally, they would glance at Frederick's silhouette standing on the terrace, not leaving any doubt in Ellie's mind who they were talking about.

If only she could help! Ellie thought, knowing that such a wish was futile. After all, she didn't even know the reason for Frederick's pain. Nevertheless, she was relieved that he had family and friends who cared for him deeply and who would do everything within their power to help him.

Trying to glimpse Frederick's face through the throng of people barring her view, Ellie's head snapped sideways when a loud clatter reached her ears.

As her eyes once more searched the area around the refreshment table, the breath caught in her throat as she found Leopold lying on the floor, his face twisted in agony.

Oliver knelt by his side, his face white as a sheet. Then he looked up with frantic eyes. "Someone call a doctor!"

Everything happened as though time had slowed down, and yet, Ellie's nerve endings felt like they were on fire, unable to keep up with the events before her eyes.

A scream tore from a woman's throat, and the crowd instantly parted to allow her through. Eyes wide with terror, she sank to her knees beside Oliver, her hands gently touching Leopold's ash-white face.

Ellie recognised her as the marquess' wife.

Tears welled up in the woman's eyes and rolled down her cheeks as she pleaded with her husband to look at her.

Leopold's gaze, however, went past her, staring into the distance as his body contorted painfully. Now and then, his eyes would narrow as though he was determined to fight the spasms shaking his body, only to relax a moment later, staring at his wife, yet unseeing.

Ellie was frozen to the spot as were most of the attendees that night, trapped in a tragedy so forlorn that it broke her heart. Only when footsteps echoed from the terrace did Ellie's head snap up, and her eyes fell on Frederick's terror-stricken face as he beheld his brother lying on the floor.

Hurrying to his side, he dropped to his knees beside Oliver. "What happened?" Although Frederick did not yell, his voice carried to the far corners of the ballroom as it lay in shocked silence.

Oliver shook his head. "I don't know. We just stood here, talking about...and then he suddenly dropped his glass and clutched his hands to his chest."

"Leopold?" Frederick called. A hand on his brother's shoulder, he gave it a gentle shake. "Can you hear me?" Tears welled up in his eyes when his brother didn't respond, and Ellie felt the full weight of his pain as if it were her own.

Surrounded by the people who loved him, Leopold heaved a few more laboured breaths before his body became still and his features relaxed as the pain left his body.

"No!" his wife cried, throwing her arms around him. "Please!"

Sitting on the floor, Frederick stared at his brother's lifeless body and the woman clinging to the man she loved.

More than anything, Ellie wanted to avert her eyes, pretend that none of this had happened; however, the calm, unfeeling expression on Frederick's face kept her gaze fixed upon him. What had just happened?

Only a moment before, she had seen terror on his face, fear and pain, but now, there was nothing there. It was as though he had somehow rid himself of the emotions that plagued him. His eyes became cold, heartless even, and when he rose from the floor, he moved like a man untouched by life's influence.

The sight froze her heart, and she realised that Frederick's pain went deeper than she had ever thought possible.

Although she knew how selfish her thoughts were considering a man had just lost his life, Ellie couldn't help but wonder what would happen now.

Now, that his brother was dead, who would protect Frederick from himself?

7

A MOTHER'S RIGHT

n keeping with the rhythmic drumming behind his temples, the rain pelted the windows to his father's study. Although now, it was his. Frederick thought. It had been his for over six months. And yet, he felt as though he didn't belong there as though he had taken it by unlawful means.

Wherever he looked, he would find himself reminded of the past, of his brother and father. Not sufficient time had passed for the wounds their loss had inflicted to heal so that the memories that rose to the surface were not of a pleasant nature. Frederick felt their loss acutely because he was now forced to shoulder the burden of the estate and the title that came with it.

Sighing, he leaned back in the large leather armchair and closed his eyes. Six months had passed since his brother's passing, and Frederick couldn't help but think that they would not recover from that loss.

While still mourning her husband, his mother had broken down at the news of her eldest son's death. She had not been the same since then, walking the halls of Elmridge like a ghost. Physically present, her heart and mind seemed to have vanished, leaving her an empty shell. Although lately Frederick thought to have felt her eyes on him every now and then as though she was watching him. A shiver went over him whenever it happened, and he couldn't help but wonder what she saw when she looked at him.

Like his mother, Maryann was a mere shadow of herself. Witnessing her husband's painful death, she still woke up screaming in the middle of the night, waking the whole house. His mother would comfort her then, for a moment leaving behind the detached stillness that hung over her soul, and ease the heart-breaking sobs that rose from Maryann's throat.

For all intents and purposes, Elmridge had turned into a tomb, housing those unfit for life. Their hearts and souls haunted by loss and pain, they walked the halls alone, spending their days locked in their own misery. Frederick counted himself among them, knowing that his own eyes held the same weariness of life theirs did.

The only ray of sunshine that reached within the old stone walls was Mathilda. Although her heart felt the heavy weight of her father's loss as well as her mother's grief, her childish innocence saved her from losing herself to the same pain. Stealing outside whenever she could, she found playmates in the few servants' children living on the estate. While her governess tended to her education, Mathilda's wild spirit rebelled against anything that would force her to spend time indoors.

Before long, Frederick hardly caught a glimpse of her during the day, and he felt relief flood his heart. If she kept away from them, if she found a place where she could be happy, then maybe she would survive the curse that had so crippled their family.

A knock on the door startled Frederick, and he cleared his throat before calling, "Enter."

The door swung open and revealed his mother standing in its frame. The ghost of a smile showed on her face as she looked at him.

Surprised to see her, Frederick rose to his feet and hastened toward her. Gesturing for her to sit, he asked, "Would you care for a refreshment?"

Taking a seat, she eyed the assortment of liquor on the side table apprehensively before shaking her head. "Thank you, but, no. I prefer to keep a clear mind."

Frederick nodded, sitting down in the armchair next to her. A clear mind? He wondered, remembering the distant look in his mother's eyes whenever he'd seen her. "Is there anything I can do for you?"

Folding her hands in her lap, she took a deep breath. "I came to speak with you about something rather important." Her eyes met his. "And I ask you to keep an open mind and hear me out. Will you promise?"

A frown drew down his brows as Frederick felt a sense of dread settle in his stomach. Nonetheless, he nodded. "You have my word."

"Thank you," she said, and he could see a slight tremble in her hands as she collected her thoughts.

More than anything, Frederick wanted to bolt from the room but forced himself to remain where he was and met his mother's eyes.

"I believe the time has come," she paused, and he felt her eyes look all the way into his soul, "for you to choose a wife."

Frederick blinked, for a moment unsure if he had heard her correctly. Then his eyes flew open, and his jaw dropped. "What?" Of all the things he feared she might say, this had been nowhere near consideration.

An indulgent smile appeared on her face as she reached for his hand. Her eyes, however, remained as unflinching as he had ever seen them. "I apologise for speaking so bluntly. I did not mean to cause you distress; however, I believe that this issue cannot be postponed any longer."

Staring at his mother, Frederick shook his head. "Any longer?" he echoed. "We are still in mourning. Leopold has been dead a mere six months."

Tears pooling in the corners of her eyes, his mother nodded, reaching for a handkerchief. "Your words are true," she admitted. "Believe me, I have considered all social ramifications, and yet, the conclusion I have come to remains the same." She dabbed the handkerchief to her eyes.

"Social ramifications? You think my objections are based on social ramifications?"

Meeting his eyes, his mother shook his head. "I do not. I merely thought to mention that I had already considered every aspect."

Loosening his cravat, Frederick sat back. "And what aspect is it that has you convinced it is time for me to choose a wife?"

Squeezing his hand, she smiled at him with sad eyes. "Two years ago, I was…happy," she said, a wistful gleam lighting up her eyes.

"I had a husband I loved and two wonderful sons." Again, she squeezed his hand, and he felt a lump form in his throat. "Today, however, most of that happiness is gone, and I fear that more can be lost."

A frown settled on Frederick's face.

His mother cleared her throat. "Of course, there is the aspect of succession. You are now the Marquess of Elmridge, and as much as I detest reminding you of it, it is your duty to provide an heir, who upon your own...death will carry on the title." She took a deep breath, and for the first time, Frederick thought to detect a hint of fear in her eyes. Was she worried to lose him, too?

For a moment, she closed her eyes as though steeling herself for what she was about to say. Then she met his gaze, and her own held such a pleading expression that Frederick felt his muscles tense. "We need help," she all but whispered, and the resolve that had held her upright seemed to fall from her shoulders. Frail and exhausted, she sat before him, and once again, Frederick wondered where she found the strength to continue on. "This family is dying," she continued. "I barely have the strength to rise in the morning," he averted his eyes as she echoed his thoughts, "and the same holds true for Maryann. Abandoned by her family, Mathilda is running wild, still able to ignore the pain. Eventually, it will find her though, and then she will be in need of guidance and support." His mother shook her head. "How are we to help her if we cannot even help ourselves?"

Closing his eyes, Frederick exhaled.

"And you," his mother began, and his eyes snapped open, "you need someone, too. Do not deny it."

"But not a wife!" Frederick exclaimed, shooting to his feet. "I need...I need...To tell you the truth, I need to get away!"

"No!" Coming toward him, she took his hands in hers, her eyes determined. "You will not leave. Do you hear me?" Frederick wanted to look away, but he couldn't. "I don't know what it is that blackened your soul or what it will take to bring you back, but I know that you cannot find it on a battlefield."

Frederick's eyes narrowed.

"I know you've been thinking about returning," she admitted, and his eyes opened wide. "Do not look so surprised. I am your mother. Even if I cannot understand it, I am not blind to your pain." She took a deep breath, her small hands squeezing his as though she hoped she could bind him to his home by sheer willpower. "You need to stay and face your demons or they will eat you alive."

Flexing his tense muscles, Frederick tried to extract his hands from hers, but she wouldn't yield.

"If you do not want to do it for yourself," his mother continued, "then do it for this family. We can only remain here at Elmridge if you continue on the lineage. You need an heir, who will inherit the title and this estate. An heir, who will provide for this family." Her eyes implored him. "Do it for us. After all, it is your duty."

Staring at his mother, he shook his head and took a step back, pulling his hands free. "Guilt," he snarled, a hint of disgust in his voice. "You would use guilt to bend me to your will? To keep me here?"

Her small hands balled into fists, and she drew herself up straight. As she glared at him, Frederick could tell that his words pained her, and yet, he could see uncompromising determination in her eyes. "To keep you alive? Yes!" She nodded her head vigorously. "I am your mother. I will do whatever I must to keep you safe. Even if it means protecting you from yourself."

Knowing when a battle was lost, Frederick sighed. "I am not fit to choose a wife. In my current state of mind, I cannot court a woman. It would be hopeless."

A hint of relief came to his mother's eyes, and her shoulders relaxed. "If you do not want to make a choice yourself, then with your permission, I will do it for you."

Frederick nodded, unable to believe that he was truly agreeing to his mother's plan.

"Good. Give me a fortnight," his mother said. "I have a young lady in mind. I will speak to her parents, and should they approve the match, I will inform you thusly."

Again, Frederick nodded as his eyes stared into the distance, and he came to realise that his life was no longer his own. And yet, he did not feel a great sense of loss. After all, the life he was living had little value to him. Why would he not give it up in order to protect his family? He couldn't think of a reason.

"Do not worry yourself," his mother said, wrapping him in her small arms. "All will be well."

Frederick doubted that very much.

8

AN UNEXPECTED PROPOSAL

An icy chill once again clung to the air as April came along. Few flowers were brave enough to bloom, yet, afraid new frost would steal their crown. Huddled inside next to a roaring fire, Ellie poured tea. "Would you like a cup?"

Holding out her hand, Madeline nodded. "Yes, please. Even from the short walk inside, my fingers feel as though frozen stiff." She shook her head, a frown of disapproval on her face. "After the temperatures rose last week, I had hoped to leave winter behind for good." She glanced out the window. "This does not look promising."

Wrapping her own scarred hands around the warm teacup, Ellie sighed. "A little warmth would be wonderful indeed." After breathing in the scented steam, she took a sip, enjoying the hot liquid as it warmed her from the inside.

"Will you join me at the theatre tomorrow?" Madeline asked. "I hear the play is rumoured to be quite entertaining."

"Entertaining?" Ellie asked, observing the gleam in her friend's eyes. "Pray tell. Is it the play that holds your interest or rather someone in the audience?"

A deep smile spread over Madeline's face.

"Who is it?"

"The Earl of Townsend," she replied. "He is rather fetching, wouldn't you say? His family just bought a new townhouse as well as an estate down south. And after all, he is an earl."

Smiling, Ellie shook her head, all too familiar with her friend's peculiarities by now. "Is that important to you?"

Eyes snapping open, Madeline stared at her. "But, of course, it is. I am an earl's daughter; therefore, I should not place my regard any lower than that." Musing, she put a finger to her lips. "However, a marquess or a duke would still be preferable. Unfortunately, the new Marquess of Elmridge is not in Town this season."

The breath caught in Ellie's throat at the mention of his name. Not since that fateful night over six months ago had she laid eyes on him. However, her dreams sometimes took her back to that evening, and she once again found herself observing his every move. Disinterested, he had moved among his peers, his eyes detached, and yet, a veil of misery had hung upon him as though the world held only pain and only ever would.

"The family is still in mourning," Ellie said, forcing her thoughts back to the present. "It has only been half a year since the late marquess' death."

Madeline nodded, her expression serious. "I do remember, yes. That was an awful night. Did they ever find out what happened to him?"

Ellie shrugged. "I do not believe so. I heard it rumoured that it might have been poison; however, there had been no way to prove it, much less find the one responsible."

"Yes, I heard that, too."

Ellie was not surprised, certain that if anyone in London knew anything noteworthy at all, it was Madeline Jeffries. Despite her age, she was usually far ahead of the game even counting the old tattletales.

"At least now, he can make a favourable match," Madeline mused as her cheerful nature chased away any lingering thoughts of the family's misfortune.

"I doubt that a favourable match is on his mind right now," Ellie objected. "First, he lost his father and then his brother." She shook her head, remembering the day she had almost lost her own little brother. "I believe it will take a long time for him to recover."

Madeline shrugged. "Fortunately for him, men have the luxury of marrying late in life without fearing to be considered on the shelf too long. However, I do not believe that dwelling on one's misfortunes is beneficial to one's health or state of mind. He ought to find himself a wife as soon as possible and continue his line."

Narrowing her eyes, Ellie looked at her. "Are you saying you wouldn't mind if he asked for your hand?"

"Of course, not," Madeline confirmed, and Ellie felt a slight stab in her heart. "However, I will not actively pursue him." Her eyes met Ellie's, and a deep smile came to her face.

Feeling a tug on the corners of her mouth, Ellie asked, "Why not?"

Madeline squeezed her hand. "Whether you like to admit it or not, I know you care for him. And I have no wish of seeing you in pain or risking our friendship merely to obtain a husband." A gleam in her eyes, she chuckled. "After all, there are so many potential candidates that one hardly knows whom to choose."

Ellie laughed. "I admit I feel for the man who will one day make you his wife."

A devilish gleam in her eyes, Madeline leaned forward conspiratorially. "My dear, Elsbeth, do not for a second believe that I would allow a man, any man, to choose me for his bride. Quite on the contrary, it will be I who chooses." Sitting back, she chuckled. "Isn't this a marvellous game? If it wouldn't inconvenience me, I'd probably stay unmarried for the rest of my life and simply collect offers."

Smiling at her friend, Ellie shook her head. "Madeline, you are truly impossible!"

"I am who I am, my dear friend. I will not apologise for that," she vowed solemnly before the corners of her mouth curled up into a smile. "But at least, I made you laugh."

A knock on the door made them turn their heads before a moment later Carlson, the butler, entered the drawing room. "I beg your pardon, Miss Munford, but your parents wish to see you in your father's study."

"Thank you, Carlson. I will be there shortly."

A frown appeared on Madeline's face, and after the door had closed, she leaned forward. "Do you know what this is about?"

"I haven't the faintest idea," Ellie admitted, quite puzzled herself. But whatever it was, it seemed urgent; otherwise, her parents would not have interrupted their tea.

Rising from the settee, Madeline shrugged, "Whatever it is, you can tell me tomorrow."

"I surely will."

After seeing her friend to the door, Ellie hastened to her father's study. She gave a quick knock and was immediately ushered inside. Looking from her mother to her father, she found both of their faces flushed with excitement, their eyes sparkling like she had never seen them.

Smiling at them, she observed, "I suppose you have good news to share."

Her mother nodded eagerly, and her father beamed, "Good news indeed!" He glanced at his wife, who instantly stepped forward, taking her daughter's hands. With a delighted smile on her face, she said, "We have received an offer of marriage for you, which, of course, we instantly accepted especially considering the circumstances."

Ellie's smile froze on her face as she felt her mother's disapproving eyes glide over her scars. Although, naturally, her mother had been relieved that Ellie had saved her little brother's life, deep down, she had never been able to forgive her for tainting her beauty and ruining her prospects.

"What?" Ellie gasped, feeling the blood pulsing in her veins. "A proposal? But...?"

"Isn't it wonderful?" her father chimed in as her mother took her hand and led her to the two armchairs under the bay windows. "We expected you to be relieved. After all, no woman in her right mind would want to live the life of a pitiable spinster."

Although Ellie had resigned herself to her fate long ago, she had never quite thought of it in that way. Staring at her parents, she came to realise that in their eyes, at least, she was worthless as long as she remained unmarried.

"You've accepted the proposal?" she asked, feeling her hands begin to tremble. Although she had never sought a love match, Ellie had fancied herself in luck when Lord Haston had openly displayed his feelings for her. However, that dream had ended in a nightmare, and after losing the man she had come to love, Ellie wasn't sure if she could settle for less. Especially now that all people ever saw when they looked at her were the scars that, according to them, defined her. Could she bear to live with a husband who looked at her the same way?

"Certainly," her father said, his brows raised at her in surprise. "We were quite hopeful during Lord Haston's courtship. However, after it quite understandably ended, we feared there never would be another." He clasped his hands together, eyes beaming at his wife, who nodded in agreement, her own eyes shining with pride as well.

Ellie shook her head, trying to focus her thoughts instead of allowing panic to overtake her. "Another?" she asked, feeling confused. "But there has not been another courtship. For the life of me, I don't even know who you're speaking of."

Once more taking her hands, her mother smiled at her. "It is the Marquess of Elmridge."

Again, Ellie's blood froze in her veins, and she stared open-mouthed at her mother. After a small eternity, she swallowed, feeling her heart slowly resume its rhythm. "The Marquess of Elmridge," she mumbled, certain she had strayed into a dream. "Are you certain?"

Her mother nodded. "I know it might be considered a little improper of him to ask for your hand so soon after his brother's passing, but," again, a delighted smile drew up the corners of her mouth, "he is a marquess. How could we refuse? His family has even more prestige than Lord Haston's. However did you manage to draw his attention?"

"I didn't," Ellie croaked, feeling overwhelmed. "I haven't even spoken to him since..." Not since that hot summer day more than twelve years ago. "Why would he ask for my hand?"

Her father laughed. "While some people believe a curse was put on their family, I cannot help but think that we are among the few fortunate ones. After the Duke of Kensington so unexpectedly and for no good reason asked for Rosabel's hand, now it is the Marquess of Elmridge, who desires to make you his wife."

"And for no good reason," Ellie echoed.

"Exactly," her father beamed, caught up in the excitement. "Everything is falling into place. Fortune smiles on us."

Ellie swallowed. "Does he...does he not mind my scars?" Slowly, lifting her eyes off her lap, she looked at her parents, afraid of the answer she might receive.

Her mother shrugged. "Since he asked for your hand, I suppose he does not."

Remembering the night of the Midnight Ball, Ellie shook her head. There had been a moment, only a split second, when he had looked in her direction, but Ellie was certain that their eyes had met. And yet, she had not seen even the faintest glimmer of recognition in them. He did not remember her. "Did he not give a reason when he spoke to you, Father?" she asked, wishing to understand.

Her father shook his head. "I only ever spoke to his mother. After his brother's passing, business detained him at Elmridge, and so she delivered his proposal."

"I see," Ellie mumbled, finally understanding the reason behind all of it. Rick had never asked for her hand. His mother had chosen her—for whatever reason—and he had merely agreed. It was a match-making scheme between their parents, and the tiny hope that her heart had harboured since learning of the proposal withered away. He did not want her. He probably didn't even know what she looked like. Would he be appalled when he saw her?

Ellie shivered at the thought. Why had his mother chosen her? What did she have to offer that no other woman could?

"I thought you would be delighted," her mother stated, a frown drawing down her brows. "Didn't you always wish for an advantageous match?"

"I did," Ellie mumbled as her thoughts strayed to the man she was supposed to marry. Would it be a wise choice though? Her mind had doubts, and yet, her heart rejoiced at the thought of marrying Rick. All those years, she had never been able to forget him. Something about him had touched her heart. Even at so young an age, he had been most honourable, and the way he had looked at her and listened to her, she felt like he had really seen her, seen who she was.

But would he see her now? Would he still smile at her despite the scars that covered the lower left side of her face, her neck, her arms and hands? Ellie closed her eyes. Lord Haston had not been able to look past them. What were the chances Rick could?

Ellie knew it would be wise to listen to her mind's counsel. However, when she remembered Rick's laughing eyes, her heart jumped and a smile spread over her face. In that moment, Ellie knew she was lost.

Yes, she would marry him.

If anyone could see past her scars, Ellie was certain it would be Rick.

9

THE MAN SHE REMEMBERED

*T*ying her bonnet, Ellie walked across the front hall toward the door. However, when she approached, it swung open, revealing a chilled looking Madeline in its frame. When her eyes beheld Ellie, she smiled and hurried inside. "It certainly does not feel like spring out there."

Ellie did her best to still her trembling hands. "I am sorry, Madeline, but I am actually on my way out."

Looking surprised, her friend asked, "May I accompany you then?"

Ellie hesitated, not sure what to say. She didn't want to hurt Madeline's feelings, but her heart was in such an uproar that even the slightest delay felt like torture.

Madeline's eyes narrowed. "What is the matter? Is something wrong? You look pale." She took a step closer, her gaze searching Ellie's face. "What happened yesterday? What did your parents have to tell you?"

Ellie swallowed, and Madeline's eyes narrowed further.

"I…Well, they…," Ellie stammered, not knowing where to begin. There was so much to say, and yet, everything was so entangled that Ellie felt her mind spin.

Taking her friend by the arm, Madeline steered her toward the drawing room. She pushed her down onto the settee before closing the doors, and then she sat down beside her. "You look like they delivered a death sentence," Madeline jested, her voice, however, sounded strained. "What did they have to tell you?"

Ellie licked her lips and then swallowed. She lifted her eyes off her trembling hands and looked at Madeline. "An offer of marriage was made for me."

Madeline's eyes opened wide, and for a moment, her mouth gaped slightly open. Then she swallowed, and a smile spread over her face. "But that's wonderful!" she beamed, giving Ellie an enthusiastic hug. "Why do you look so sad? Do you not like him?" Again, her eyes widened. "Who offered for you?"

Closing her eyes, Ellie shook her head, knowing the words would feel like a lie on her tongue. "The Marquess of Elmridge."

"What?" Once more, Madeline's mouth stood open. "He did? I didn't know you knew each other. From what you said, I thought—"

"We don't," Ellie interrupted. "That is just it. From what my parents told me, I am not his choice, but his mother's." She hung her head, her hands playing with the hem of her sleeve. "I believe he doesn't even know who I am."

Madeline took a deep breath before she reached over and gently pulled Ellie's hands into hers. With tender eyes, she looked at her, and a smile played on her lips. "Do you care for him?"

For a second averting her eyes, Ellie nodded.

"Then don't be sad," Madeline said. "Even if he doesn't know who you are now, he will. He liked you once, he will like you again."

Looking into her friend's eyes, Ellie wished she would feel the same conviction in her heart that rang in Madeline's voice. "I don't even know if he liked me then. He was kind to me, but that doesn't mean he cared for me."

Squeezing her hand, Madeline smiled. "How could he not? My dear Elsbeth, you are the most wonderful creature I've ever beheld." Embarrassed, Ellie averted her eyes, a slight blush creeping up her cheeks. "Don't look so bashful!" Madeline laughed. "If I were a man, I would have asked for your hand a long time ago."

Ellie chuckled, feeling the tension in her muscles subside.

"I am serious," Madeline insisted. "You're kind and caring and absolutely sweet-tempered. It is a delight to be around you. And yet, you are brave and courageous. You do what needs to be done. You care for others more than for yourself, and despite everything, you look at life with a smile on your face." Again, Madeline squeezed her hand, and Ellie looked up at her. "Very few people can suffer what you did and still enjoy life. You are a rare woman, Elsbeth Munford, and Frederick Lancaster can call himself lucky that you agreed to marry him."

Looking at her friend's caring eyes, Ellie felt a soothing warmth spread through her. "Thank you," she whispered. "What would I do without you?"

"Suffer endlessly, I'm certain." Madeline smiled at her before her eyes went wide. "You did agree to marry him, didn't you?"

Laughing, Ellie nodded. "I couldn't help myself. Even if I have doubts, I...," she bit her lower lip, feeling a flush warm her cheeks, "I want him."

Stepping from the carriage, Ellie looked up at the imposing townhouse. Despite Madeline's encouraging words, Ellie had felt the need for an open talk between married—or in her case, soon-to-be married—women. And so she had ushered her friend out the door without being too obvious and had instantly set off.

The butler directed her across the large foyer to the drawing room. Stepping through the door, he announced, "Miss Elsbeth Munford."

Following on his heels, Ellie walked into the elegantly furnished room, and her eyes immediately went to the smiling woman rising from the settee. As the doors closed behind her, she hastened toward her friend. "Rosabel, it is so good to see you."

Wrapping her in a tight embrace, her cousin agreed, "Indeed, it is. How long has it been?" Stepping back, Rosabel looked at her, her eyes gliding over Ellie's scars. "Do they still hurt?" she asked, compassion ringing in her voice, not pity.

"Occasionally," Ellie admitted, knowing that Rosabel would instantly detect a lie. "Especially when the skin gets dry, it feels tight." Ellie shrugged. "I have a special balm I use daily to keep it smooth or, at least, as smooth as possible." She smiled at her cousin, feeling the need to change the topic. Glancing at her cousin's midsection, Ellie asked, "How much longer until the baby comes?"

Rosabel smiled, brushing a gentle hand down her flat belly. "At least, six months," she said, gesturing for Ellie to take a seat, "if everything goes well."

"It will," Ellie said. "Do you wish for a boy or a girl?"

Pouring the tea, Rosabel shrugged. "I already have a wonderful little girl as well as a wonderful little boy, so…it doesn't matter. I only hope for a healthy baby and a safe delivery."

A smile on her face, Ellie took the offered cup. "Have you thought of names yet?" she asked, sipping her tea and welcoming its warmth.

"No, not yet," Rosabel laughed. "It is a bit early for that." Eyeing her friend over the rim of her cup, Rosabel asked, "What brings you here, Ellie? Your note didn't say. However, the look in your eyes has me a little worried."

Ellie swallowed, setting down her teacup. She took a deep breath and met Rosabel's eyes. "I am getting married."

Remaining silent, Rosabel's eyes did not waver from her face. Instead, they narrowed as though looking at her cousin more closely. "You do not sound happy," she finally observed.

Ellie shrugged. "I'm torn. I…"

"Who asked for your hand? I wasn't aware that someone was courting you."

Ellie drew a deep breath and in a few words related what had happened as well as her concerns regarding her betrothed. "I'm not sure if I did the right thing," she admitted, shaking her head in confusion. "What if he does not want me? What if he comes to hate me because he cannot stand to look at me?" Despite Madeline's assurance that all would be well, Ellie couldn't help but look into the future with fearful eyes.

"You do care for him, though, do you not?" Rosabel asked. "I still remember how you told me about the service he had done you all those years ago." A soft smile played on her lips. "Your eyes glowed when you spoke of him, and they still do."

Once again, heat flooded Ellie's cheeks.

"Why do you blush?" Rosabel asked. "Did you not think that I knew?"

Sighing, Ellie shook her head. "I'm not sure. It is just that…ever since the accident, ever since my face was openly disfigured,

I feel as though that is all people see, and they make me feel as though the life I once had has come to an end. As though I have no right to dream of love," she swallowed, "because who could love someone like me? Therefore, it would be safer for me not to love at all so that I am not disappointed when my love is not returned."

"Do you truly believe that you don't deserve to be loved?" Rosabel asked, sadness clinging to her voice. "That no one can possibly love you?"

Ellie shrugged, feeling uncomfortable at baring her soul, and yet, she knew that if she wanted her cousin's advice, she needed to be open about how she truly felt. "Of course, the accident was traumatic and painful...and," she closed her eyes for a moment, "and it changed everything. But deep down, I always felt like I was still the same person. Yes, I will never look at fire the same way as before, but...," she shrugged, "I was me. Does that make sense?"

Squeezing her hand, Rosabel nodded.

Relieved, Ellie continued, "I did not wake up one morning thinking that I had nothing to live for anymore, realising that no one could possibly look upon me and consider me beautiful. I mean, I knew I looked different, but..." She sighed. "It was them, not me."

"Them?"

Ellie shook her head. "All those people who looked at me with pitying eyes, who whispered behind me back, who assumed that all of a sudden I didn't want to dance anymore." Feeling tears sting her eyes, Ellie swallowed. "At first, I was determined to make them see me as I saw me. But after a while, I suppose their words changed how I saw myself after all. Right now, I am not sure what I think much less what to do." She looked at her cousin with pleading eyes, and a single tear spilled over and ran down her cheek. "Please, help me, Rosabel. I feel so lost, and I don't want to make a mistake and ruin his life along with my own."

Leaning forward, Rosabel drew Ellie into her arms, holding her tight as she rocked from side to side.

Slowly, Ellie felt herself relax. The sense of dread that had settled on her heart upon beginning her story turned into a sense of hopeful expectation. If anyone could help her find her way, it was Rosabel. "You truly have a mother's touch," Ellie whispered, brushing the tear from her cheek.

Smiling, Rosabel sat back. "Georgiana taught me," she said, love shining in her eyes, "in a moment when I myself had no hope for a happy future."

"But you are happy now."

"I am," Rosabel said, "and you will be, too."

More than anything, Ellie wanted to believe her. "But how?"

Clearing her throat, Rosabel took a deep breath. "I will not lie to you, Ellie. From what you told me, the road ahead does not seem to be easy to travel." When Ellie's heart sank, Rosabel took her hand. "However, if anyone can turn this into a happy ending, it is you."

Ellie smiled. "But what should I do?"

"Be yourself," Rosabel said. "We can only ever be who we are. He will like you for who you are."

"I'm not sure he will," Ellie admitted, suddenly feeling defeated again. "What if he cannot see past my scars? Most people cannot."

"When you first met him all those years ago," Rosabel began, "do you think he liked you then?"

Biting her lip, Ellie frowned. "How am I to know? He certainly didn't say anything."

"That would have surprised me," Rosabel chuckled before her eyes grew serious again. "Forget how you feel today. Forget other people's remarks as well as your own fears for the future. Close your eyes and remember. Remember how he looked at you, how he spoke to you. Do you think he liked you then?"

Closing her eyes, Ellie once more felt the burning sun upon her smooth, untainted skin. The heat had the sweat running from her pores, and yet, she had felt light and carefree. She remembered the shock at being discovered in the brook, her skirts pulled up over her knees. She remembered Rick's clear, blue eyes as he had looked upon her, neither judgement nor disapproval showing in them. He had sent his friends away, swearing them to secrecy, and helped her out of the water. Tactfully, he had averted his eyes, and yet, a delighted smile had played on his lips. Ellie remembered the tingle that had coursed through her as their hands had touched.

A smile came to her lips, and she opened her eyes. "Yes," she whispered, "he did like me."

"Good," Rosabel said, squeezing her hand. "My dearest cousin, let me tell you what my own experiences have taught me." Ellie nodded eagerly. "Marriage is not easy even under the best of circumstances. We cannot look into another's heart and mind and know them like we know ourselves, our own wishes and fears, our own hopes and dreams." Rosabel shook her head, remembering. "Heaven, sometimes we don't even know who we are ourselves."

Ellie smiled, knowing only too well how true her words were.

"If you care for him," Rosabel continued, her eyes imploring, "then look at him with open eyes and an open heart. Remember the man you knew, but never forget that life shapes who we are. Years have passed since you last spoke. Years that changed you as well as him. At his core, he might be who he has always been, but who knows what happened to him? What might have changed his dreams and wishes, his fears and dreams? He might not even recognise himself after what he has been through."

Ellie nodded. "You mean the war?"

"Yes," Rosabel said, shaking herself as though a shiver had run over her. "I cannot even begin to imagine what it must be like to find yourself in a soldier's position, to take lives and watch people you care for lose theirs." She drew a deep breath and once again squeezed Ellie's hand. "However, it is probably not only the war that has had its effects on who he is. He lost his father while he was still away, and from what Graham told me, they had a close relationship. Then his brother dies under highly suspicious circumstances, and he suddenly finds himself the marquess. Upon his shoulders now rest all the responsibilities that come with such a title. I can only think of it as a burden, especially since he wasn't prepared for it since birth."

Again, Ellie nodded. Much of what Rosabel had said had already occurred to her, and yet, hearing Frederick's life put into simple words helped her understand what he had gone through in the years since their encounter.

"Get to know the man he is now," Rosabel said, a knowing smile on her face, "even if he does not want you to see him. If you allow him to push you away, you will both suffer for it. Take my word for it even if you feel despair crushing the life from you, never give up. The day will come when all your efforts will be rewarded."

Ellie took a deep breath, knowing the difficult path that lay ahead, and yet, looking into Rosabel's encouraging eyes, she knew it could be done. After all, Rosabel and Graham were among the happiest couples she had ever seen. The love and devotion that shone in their eyes every time they looked upon each other spoke volumes and gave her heart the inspiration it needed to even attempt to win Rick's heart for herself.

"Who knows why his mother chose you?" Rosabel said, interrupting Ellie's train of thought. "Maybe she saw the strength that resides within you. The strength that allowed you to overcome great tragedy and reclaim your right to be happy." She squeezed her hand. "Maybe she is hoping that you will be the one to help her son leave the shadows behind and find his smile again."

Feeling a heavy burden lifted off her shoulders, Ellie sighed.

10

AN AGREEMENT

After years of making life-and-death decisions in the field on a daily basis, Frederick raked his hands through his hair at the insignificant problems that plagued him now. Petty disputes between tenants with regard to borderlines and such drove him mad. Why could they not see the bigger picture? He cursed, momentarily mad at his brother for abandoning him and leaving him alone to deal with these issues.

Resting his back against the soft leather armchair in his study, he closed his eyes and took a deep breath, trying his best to release the stress that was starting to pound behind his temples.

After returning home from the continent, Frederick had already fancied himself in hell. Now, however, things had actually gotten worse. Every morning, he woke up with the single desire of being left alone. He did not want to face the world, nor see or speak to anyone. Not even his family.

Only because it was his duty did he go about his business or the estate's business for Frederick had yet to come to terms with the fact that he now was the marquess. He didn't feel like a marquess, and he sure as hell wasn't worthy to be one.

Why did Leopold have to die? He cursed yet again, feeling an instant pang of guilt when he remembered his mother's and Maryann's solemn faces.

Frowning, Frederick sat back. Did he not grieve his brother's passing? He wondered. He did not know. All he knew was that his eyes did not brim with tears every time his brother was mentioned. He did not long to have him back. He did not curse the night that had taken him from them. Or rather he did; however, his reason was usually that he was annoyed with having to handle the estate.

These days, Frederick didn't experience a variety of emotions. The only one he repeatedly felt was annoyance. Everything else had receded into the background, barely there, almost forgotten.

And on top of everything, he was to be married soon. Frederick shook his head. He could only hope that his mother would take her time choosing his bride for the mere thought of having a wife brought a sense of dread to his stomach, like a block of ice settling in and spreading its cold into every fibre of his being.

After all, marriage was the centrepiece of deep emotions; emotions such as love, affection, trust and hope. Remembering the way Leopold and Maryann had always looked at each other, Frederick shook his head. He was not capable of these feelings. He didn't even know if he ever had been. Before the war was a time that he barely recalled. After all, it had no significance for his life now.

Everything had changed. The innocence of those days could never be regained.

His head snapped up when a knock sounded on the door.

"Enter," he called, shuffling the papers on his desk from one side to another. He would deal with those tomorrow.

"Frederick, I have good news," his mother announced, flying into the room. Although she still seemed as fragile as a porcelain figurine, her eyes shone with a new-found purpose. Frederick even thought to detect a glimmer of hope in her gaze.

Clearing his throat, he rose to his feet, gesturing for his mother to sit. However, she merely shook her head, grasping his hands. A smile on her face, she looked up at him.

"You said you have good news, Mother," he reminded her, wondering what had put that twinkle in her eyes. Whatever her news was, he thought it would be a most welcome exception to the norm.

Lately, all news had rather been of the unpleasant kind, the kind he could do without.

Her smile deepened. "I've found the perfect woman for you."

Frederick's stomach twisted as though he had just received a punch in the gut. "What?" he gasped, unable to believe his ears. This was definitely not good news!

"Her parents agreed to a short engagement," his mother continued, pulling him forward toward the seats under the window front, "so that the wedding will take place a month from today."

"A month," Frederick echoed, sinking into the armchair next to his mother's. All strength left him as his mother chatted on happily.

"They were a bit surprised," she admitted, "however, her father instantly agreed." Her eyes settled on his face, and she raised an eyebrow at him. "Don't you want to know who the woman is?"

Frederick shrugged. "What does it matter?"

His mother frowned at him before patting his knee. "I know that this is not what you had in mind, but believe me, a wife is exactly what you need right now. Your brother," she swallowed, and a hint of sadness returned to her eyes, "was a bit lost, too, when he came of age. However, as soon as Maryann had stepped into his life, he was focused and steady in his plans; and most of all, he was happy." A deep smile drew up the corners of her mouth, and yet, sadness still clung to her eyes. "I want you to be happy, Frederick. You are my son, and I cannot bear to see you so lost day in and out."

"I'm not lost," Frederick protested.

His mother cocked her head, her eyebrows rising into arches.

Frederick shook his head. "Fine. I admit I am far from happy at the moment; however, that is not reason enough for me to get married."

"But you agreed," his mother countered, a hint of apprehension on her face. "You agreed, and now, you are betrothed. You cannot go back on your word. Everything has been arranged." She took a deep breath. "I did not wish to bother you with the details of this arrangement for I know how busy the estate keeps you. My intention was not to keep you out but to lighten the burden you carry."

Squeezing his mother's hand, Frederick nodded. "I meant no disrespect," he conceded. "I was merely surprised."

"I know all of this is rather abrupt," she said, once again patting his knee, "but I ask you to put your faith in me. I only have your best interests at heart."

Again, Frederick nodded. Maybe his mother was right. After all, he had no idea what he needed at the moment.

All of a sudden, his life was tied to Elmridge, and the only things on his mind were the duties and responsibilities that came with it. He had forgotten what he wanted a long time ago. After all, it did not matter. So, why shouldn't he marry? He needed an heir in order to protect his family.

However, once he had fulfilled his duty, there would be little reason for him to stay. A steward could handle the day-to-day business of the state until his son would be of age. Yes, once he had an heir, he would be free to return to the continent.

"All right," his mother said as the frown lines left her face. "Shall I tell you about her?"

Frederick shrugged. Did it matter who she was? After all, she would be a stranger; someone who did not have the slightest idea of who he was, either. Then again, how could she? He didn't even know himself anymore.

"Would you at least care to know her name?" his mother asked, shaking her head. "Frederick, you really ought to take an interest. After all, this is your future wife we are talking about."

"Fine." He sat up straight and met her eyes. "What is her name?"

"Miss Elsbeth Munford. She is Baron Harlowe's eldest daughter."

Frederick shrugged. "I don't believe I've ever met her. Her name does not sound familiar."

"You have been gone for a long time," his mother reminded him. "Most of the young ladies out now were still too young then."

Frederick froze. Swallowing, he addressed his mother, "She is not...I mean, this is not her first season, is it?"

"No, it is not."

Relief spread over him at his mother's words. He could not imagine marrying an eighteen-year-old debutante. He would probably frighten her to death. Poor girl!

"She has been out in society for a few years. However, a while back, she had an accident, which got in the way of her prospects. Most consider her on the shelf, as they say; however, when I saw her, I knew she was the one."

Frederick nodded. "Good," he mumbled, hoping that a few extra years had hardened her to the way of the world. Strangely enough, he pitied her for having to marry him. After all, her new home resembled a tomb while its inhabitants moved about like lifeless puppets, and her husband was a mere shadow of himself. Yes, she would need all the strength she could find in order to survive under such gloomy circumstances.

"Then we are in agreement?" his mother asked, expectant eyes searching his face.

"We are," Frederick confirmed. The sooner he fathered an heir, the sooner he would be able to take his leave.

11

A NEW LIFE AWAITS

Her heart pounding in her chest, Ellie looked out the carriage window at the vast pastures stretching to the horizon. Early May had come on swift wings of a summerly breeze, giving colour to the green land as it came to life under a warming sun. Far in the distance, she spotted Elmridge Manor as the land sloped down and ran toward a massive forest, which surrounded the estate like a protective wall.

"Now, at all times, do remember your manners," her mother counselled for the hundredth time since they had set off from London. "After tomorrow, you will be a marchioness, and it is paramount that people see you as such. I want you to hold your head high, but do be polite."

His head resting against the carriage wall, her father slept soundly, the occasional snore disrupting her mother's monologue. Watching him, Ellie wondered if she ought to feign sleep herself. Would her mother even notice?

"By the way, I made sure that Lord Haston received an invitation—"

"What?" Ellie gasped as her head snapped around, and her eyes stared at her mother. "Why?"

Shaking her head, her mother looked at her with disapproving eyes. "It is rude to interrupt, Elsbeth. After we secured such a favourable match for you, the least you could do is honour us by behaving your best."

"Yes, Mother," Ellie mumbled. "Why did you invite him?"

Her mother frowned at her as though the answer should be fairly obvious. "After he ended his courtship, I am certain he felt you would be on the shelf for good." *Didn't you as well, Mother?* Ellie thought. "However, now, you are marrying a man who is his social superior." Her mother chuckled. "That ought to teach him to snub us."

Ellie sighed, relieved that after today she would not have to deal with her mother's matchmaking schemes any longer.

Settling back into her seat, she stared out the window as they drew nearer to the manor, ignoring her mother's prattling as best as she could. Her heart beat in her chest, and the breath caught in her throat when she finally realised what changes tomorrow would bring. This would be her new home, and his family would be hers.

Closing her eyes, Ellie took a deep breath. Then she opened them again, and a smile spread over her face. Whatever tomorrow would bring, she was ready. A new life awaited her, and she wanted it more than she had ever dared admit to herself.

Ellie's eyes swept the large hall as the butler escorted them to the southern drawing room. Following after her mother and father, she kept a careful eye on her younger siblings, trailing behind them, and yet, her attention was repeatedly drawn to her surroundings. This was her new home! Would she come to *feel* at home here? Ellie wondered.

When the butler left to announce their arrival to his lordship, Ellie's mother turned to her husband, a disapproving frown on her face. "Should they not have been out to welcome us at the carriage? After all, we are not mere visitors. Our daughter is the future marchioness."

Her father, however, merely humphed as his eyes surveyed the splendour around them, and before long, her parents' attention settled on more important matters as they voiced the delight they felt at having their daughter marry into such an upstanding family.

"The grounds are larger than I expected," her father observed, looking out the window. "And everything is in top condition." A big smile on his face, he turned to his wife. "Quite obviously, they are not in need of the sizable dowry I am able to bestow on my daughter."

His wife chuckled, her eyes aglow with excitement. "Certainly not." She gazed about the room. "These furnishings are exquisite." Shaking her head as though lost in a dream, her mother turned to Ellie. "My dear child, I cannot tell you how glad I am that Lord Haston lost interest. Undoubtedly, it is his loss and our gain."

Feeling the heat burn in her cheeks at her parents' open appraisal of her fiancé's assets, Ellie breathed a sigh of relief when the door opened and the dowager marchioness walked in. A frail woman of medium height, she walked with grace and dignity, her large eyes glowing with kindness.

Ellie liked her instantly.

"Welcome," she greeted them, a deep smile on her face. "Welcome to Elmridge." After giving her father and mother a quick nod of the head, she turned to Ellie, her soft eyes gliding over her.

For a moment, Ellie felt uncomfortable under the woman's searching gaze. However, when their eyes met, Ellie read no pity or disappointment in them, and her muscles relaxed.

The dowager marchioness took both of Ellie's hands in her own wrinkled ones, and with a deep smile on her face, she looked into her eyes. "My dear child, thank you for coming here. I cannot express how happy I am to see you within these walls."

Feeling tears threaten, Ellie blinked, savouring the warm welcome she had not expected. "Thank you, my lady. You are most kind." Looking at the short woman, Ellie felt the strength that rested in her old hands, and she thought to see a flicker of recognition. She had seen this woman before; however, she could not recall where. Maybe Rosabel had been right. Maybe the dowager marchioness had chosen her for a specific reason. Ellie only hoped she would not disappoint her.

"Call me Theresa," the dowager marchioness whispered and gently squeezed Ellie's hands. "We are a close−knit family and do not stand on ceremony."

Too touched to say anything, Ellie nodded.

"Wonderful," Theresa beamed before an apologetic smile came to her face. "I do hope you can forgive us for not greeting you properly. However, my granddaughter had gotten herself into a rather precarious situation, which required our immediate attention. " Turning to Ellie's parents, she added, "I hope you've had a safe journey here. Would you care for some refreshments?"

The next half-hour, they spent in the drawing room, exchanging pleasantries and chatting about inconsequential matters while enjoying the Cook's exquisite lemon cakes. Although Ellie enjoyed herself immensely, she could not help but wonder where her future husband was. Why did he not welcome them? Despite Rosabel's warning as well as her own knowledge of the situation, she could not help but feel a sting of disappointment.

Patience, she counselled herself. *You will have the rest of your life to get to know him.*

The rest of the day passed in a pleasant manner. After being shown to their chambers and changing out of their travelling attire, they followed the dowager marchioness into the gardens. Tall-growing hedges formed a labyrinth, hiding shady spots within their midst. Flowers of all shapes and colours bloomed around them, their sweet scent dancing on the soft breeze caressing Ellie's cheeks. Feeling the warm sun on her skin, Ellie stopped and closed her eyes for a moment, enjoying the sense of peace that washed over her.

When she opened them again, she saw the rest of her family turn around a corner before they were lost from sight.

"What are you doing?" asked a small, inquisitive voice.

Clasping a hand to her chest, Ellie spun around and found herself looking at a young girl, her hair dishevelled and dirt stains decorating her face. "You scared me," she gasped, exhaling audibly.

"What were you doing?" the girl repeated, eyeing her with a critical gaze.

Once she had regained her composure, Ellie smiled at her. "I was merely enjoying the sun. It feels wonderful, does it not?" The girl shrugged. "What is your name?"

"Mathilda," the girl said. "What's yours?"

Ellie was a tad surprised at the girl's lack of manners. "My name is Elsbeth, but my friends call me Ellie."

Mathilda's eyes narrowed. "Can *I* be your friend?"

"Certainly," Ellie said. "I'd be delighted to have a friend like you. Tell me, Mathilda, do you know the way back to the manor? I fear I am lost."

"It is right over there," Mathilda said, pointing over her shoulder. Then she took Ellie's hand. "Let me show you."

Following the young girl, Ellie remembered what the dowager marchioness had told them, which led her to believe that the girl was the former marquess' daughter. "Your Grandmother said you...eh...had a rather eventful morning."

Mathilda looked at her appraisingly. "She did?"

Ellie nodded, hoping she had not just betrayed Theresa's trust.

After a while, Mathilda shrugged. "I climbed up a tree."

"You did?" Ellie asked in surprise. "I suppose you are not allowed to."

Mathilda shrugged. "Usually, they don't know."

"And today?"

Stopping, Mathilda met her eyes, a hint of embarrassment in them. "I couldn't get down."

"I seee," Ellie mumbled, slightly awed by the adventurous girl by her side. "What about your dress? Did that happen climbing the tree?" she asked, eyeing a tear in the hem.

The girl eyed her critically. "Will you promise not to tell?"

Hesitating at first, Ellie smiled. "I swear. On my honour as your friend, I will not breathe a word to anyone."

"Good." Satisfied, Mathilda nodded. "It got caught on the ladder."

"The ladder?"

"Yes, the ladder to the hayloft in the stables," Mathilda elaborated as she led Ellie past the last tall-growing hedge.

Ellie nodded. That would explain the golden straws sticking out of the girl's chestnut locks, her hair braided down the back. Ellie shook her head. If this morning represented the norm of Mathilda's activities, then the future would be quite *eventful* indeed.

"There. See?"

Looking across the courtyard, Ellie spotted the stables in the far back. "What were you doing in the hayloft?"

"Visiting the kittens," Mathilda said, a mischievous twinkle in her eyes. "Mother says I am not to go there. It is not lady-like, but Pearl needed me."

"Pearl?"

"The mama kitty," Mathilda explained as they climbed the steps to the terrace. "She is taking care of her kittens all day, and no one takes care of her." She looked up at Ellie, a bright smile on her face. "I bring her milk."

"That is very sweet of you," Ellie said, returning the girl's delighted smile. "I am certain she appreciates your help."

"She lets me hold her babies," Mathilda said as they walked up to the terrace door. "I'm the only one who is allowed. Everyone else who comes near gets a nasty scratch."

Slipping inside, Ellie closed the door behind them and found herself in a beautifully decorated room. A pianoforte stood in the corner, and a large fireplace donned the west wall.

"Are you going to be Uncle Frederick's wife?" the girl asked, turning around to look at her.

Taken aback, Ellie swallowed. "Well,…yes, I am."

"Good," Mathilda nodded, then turned around and led Ellie out of the room and down the corridor. "He needs a wife."

"He does?" Ellie asked, surprised and yet intrigued. "Why?"

"He is always so sad."

"Sad?"

Mathilda nodded. "And not sad like Mummy or Grandma," she explained, guiding Ellie back to the foyer. "He is angry sad. Grandma says he is haunted." She looked up at Ellie. "Do you believe in ghosts?"

"Well, no, I suppose I don't," Ellie answered, not sure what to say. Clearly, with the whole family grieving, the little girl was left to her own devices most of the time, and yet, she had the uncanny ability children often have to absorb the tension around them. Mathilda didn't know the details, but she knew what was going on.

"I don't like ghosts," the girl admitted, nervously glancing about.

Kneeling down, Ellie took Mathilda's hands into hers and met her eyes. "I don't think your grandma meant to say that there were ghosts here." A bit of the tension fell from the girl's face. "I think she meant that your uncle is haunted by memories, bad things he remembers from his time as a soldier. Do you understand?"

Mathilda nodded, and a smile came to her face.

"There you are," Theresa's voice echoed across the large hall. "I feared we had lost you." Followed by her parents, who bore a rather displeased expression on their faces, she walked toward them, casting a loving glance at her granddaughter. "I see you have met Mathilda."

"Yes," Ellie said, rising to her feet. "She saved me. I got lost, and she showed me the way back."

Beaming with pride, Mathilda looked at her grandmother. "I did. Truly."

"I am very proud of you," Theresa smiled, brushing a hand over the girl's unruly hair. "Now, hurry on upstairs. Supper will be served shortly, and you look like you could use a bath first."

As the girl rushed up the stairs, Theresa turned to Ellie. "Her father's death has unhinged her world quite a bit." She met Ellie's eyes. "I think she could use a friend, a friend who is not stricken with grief."

"Oh, we are friends already," Ellie smiled. "She even told me a secret, which I am afraid I cannot share with you since I am bound to secrecy."

Theresa chuckled, but her eyes shone so brilliantly that Ellie's heart flowed over with happiness. "I'm so glad you're here," Theresa said for the second time that day. "I knew you belonged with us."

"Thank you," Ellie said, feeling her hopes rise into the sky. Never would she have expected to feel at home on her very first day at Elmridge. Now, all she needed to find out was whether or not her future husband could feel about her the same way.

Ellie fervently hoped that he could.

12

MAN & WIFE

escending the large staircase down to the front hall, Ellie's stomach was in knots. On trembling legs, she followed her parents toward the dining room, eager to glimpse her future husband. Surely, he would be present at supper, wouldn't he?

Upon entering the dining room, Theresa greeted them with the by now familiar warmth that Ellie had come to rely upon within the few short hours she had spent at Elmridge. Her parents returned the greeting, and yet, Ellie thought their demeanour could not rival Theresa's with regard to sincerity.

"Allow me to introduce you to my son," Theresa said, stepping aside. "Lord Frederick Lancaster, Marquess of Elmridge."

Ellie's breath caught in her throat as Frederick stepped forward and slightly bowed his head to them. Although her eyes travelled over him, she did not see the elegant clothes he wore or the impeccable manners with which he greeted her family. All she saw was the smile on his face that seemed out of place as his eyes spoke of a hidden pain.

Her heart ached for him, and yet, his mere presence made her hands tremble with excitement. When he bowed to her and took her hand in his, she was certain her heart would give out. Although his eyes barely met hers, she held her breath as he bent forward and kissed the back of her hand. His lips were so soft, and they chased a delicious tingle up and down her body.

A shiver came over her, and she quickly averted her eyes.

Ellie breathed a sigh of relief when they were finally seated around the enormous table. Her knees felt more than just a trifle wobbly, and she feared they would abandon their post altogether at any moment. However, once that worry was removed from her mind, Ellie felt herself relax, enjoying the company of her old as well as her new family.

While she had a rather estranged relationship to her parents, her younger siblings meant the world to her. Seeing them now cast curious glances at Mathilda, who in turn eyed them through narrowed eyes full of suspicion, put a deep smile on her face.

Looking at the dowager duchess, Ellie noticed the way her eyes swept those in her company. With a smile and a kind word, she assured that all felt comfortable and no one was left out. In Ellie's mind, Theresa clearly was the heart of the family. Although a veil of grief hung about her, Ellie could see the strength and kindness that rested underneath and immediately knew her to be a survivor. Life had dealt her harshly, taken away her husband as well as her eldest son; yet, here she was, determined to save what remained of her family.

Although Maryann's eyes spoke of kindness as well, the former marquess' widow lacked the strength her mother-in-law possessed. Ellie could see the effort it took for her to hold her head high and keep her shoulders back. She seemed like a feather, delicate and vulnerable, and at the mercy of every breeze to blow her way. A storm would surely finish her.

And then there was Frederick. Ellie remembered well the young man who had assured her he would keep her secret that fateful summer, and yet, the man before her seemed to have forgotten those times long ago. It did not surprise Ellie that he did not remember her; however, he also seemed to have forgotten who *he* once had been, who he still was deep down at the very core of his being hidden under layers of pain and guilt.

Frederick barely contributed to the conversation, which was mostly carried by Theresa as well as Ellie's parents. Although he asked the occasional question and answered any query directed at him in a cordial fashion, his eyes remained distant as though he was not really there, as though he did not see the people before him. Unlike Maryann, whose gaze was focused on her food, her fork absentmindedly pushing a carrot across her plate, Frederick appeared…unconcerned, unaffected by grief or pain or loss. His eyes were open, his gaze enquiring, and a charming smile played on his lips.

A mask, Ellie thought. Was he even aware he wore it?

Throughout the evening, she tried to catch his eye. However, when he did look at her, she was certain he did not see her as though determined to ignore her presence. Had he only agreed to the marriage at his mother's urgings? Ellie wondered, fighting to keep discouragement from flooding her heart. Or was he merely disappointed by his mother's choice?

Glancing at her hands, Ellie couldn't help but wonder about the wisdom of the choice his mother had made. After all, could anyone ever truly see past the ugly scars that decorated her skin?

"I trust that your journey here was pleasant?" Frederick asked, and Ellie's head snapped up.

Meeting his eyes, she felt her heart hammer in her chest, and her mouth became dry. She swallowed, desperately trying to remember what he had said. "Yes," she croaked and cleared her throat. "It is indeed a most wonderful spring. Everything is in bloom."

Feeling the heat rush to her cheeks, Ellie couldn't help but gaze into his eyes. They were so blue, so unbelievably blue, and they reminded her so much of that dazzling smile that had lit up his face all those years ago. More than anything, she wished she could see it one more time.

However, the same eyes that looked into hers held no mischief, no sparkle, no happiness. In a strange way, they seemed to lack all emotion as though what they saw could not reach his soul. He had erected a wall around his heart, around his soul, around the very part that made him who he was so that no one and nothing could ever touch him again. It was a safe way to live, and yet, it was a lonely one, too.

As tears came to Ellie's eyes, she smiled at him, silently vowing to stand by his side and never close her eyes to the pain that so clearly shone in his.

When the sun finally lurked into his room, its rays sneaking in through the small gaps between the curtains, Frederick moaned. How could it be morning already? Had he even closed his eyes at all?

For a long moment, he just lay on his back and stared up at the ceiling.

Today was his wedding day.

A groan rose from his throat as he realised what he had agreed to. How could he have been so foolish? Yes, he was the marquess now, and it was his duty to continue his line, and yet, how could he ever have thought that he was capable of doing so?

While Elsbeth had clearly experienced the harshness of life, her eyes had glowed with untainted innocence. What would become of her once the darkness in his own heart also found its way into hers? Could he share her bed and still keep his distance? Could they both remain untouched by the experience? Could he protect her as well as himself from the poison that would undoubtedly arise should he be unable to shield her from the misery that held his heart in its clutches?

As though in a daze, Frederick got dressed and went downstairs. He noticed the festively set ballroom as well as the floral arrangements. He saw servants rush from here to there tending to last-minute matters, and he heard his mother's determined voice, welcoming guests and directing servants. And yet, none of it mattered, none of it touched him. As long as he kept his distance, he would be safe.

And so he kept to his study until his mother finally opened the door. Her gentle eyes looked into his. However, none of the care and concern he read there mattered, either. "It is time, Dear," she said, and he rose from his chair, brushed down his overcoat and left the study.

On his arm, she led him through the house, out the terrace doors and toward the small chapel that he had last visited upon his brother's funeral. How strange some places were? He mused. Sad occasions. Happy occasions. All the same.

Then, he hadn't shed a tear.

Now, he barely smiled. What was the use?

Walking down the aisle, Frederick glanced at the many friends and acquaintances that had answered his mother's invitation. He offered a nod here and a smile there until they stopped at the altar. His mother turned to him then, her nimble fingers setting straight his cravat. "Do try to smile, Dear," she counselled as a gentle smile curled up her lips and her eyes looked at him almost pleadingly. "This is a happy occasion."

Was it? Frederick wondered. He couldn't remember why.

The daze returned then, and Frederick barely remembered standing before the priest. His thoughts strayed to moments past; some moments held joy, however, most of them were moments of pain and loss. Absorbed in his own memories, Frederick barely saw Elsbeth as she came to stand next to him. The priest's words droned in his ears, and yet, he couldn't have repeated a single one.

However, he felt his mouth open and his lips form the words 'I will.'

A kiss was expected. He remembered that much. Could he kiss her and not feel anything?

As Frederick turned to his wife, her blue eyes gazed into his own, and he saw a shy smile curl up her lips. A slight blush coloured her cheeks, and her eyes remained fixed on his as though she was trying to look into his core.

Had he gazed into these eyes before? He wondered. She looked at him as though she knew him.

Frederick swallowed. Then he took the step separating them and leaned down. She closed her eyes then, and so did he.

When their lips touched, relief flooded Frederick's body. He didn't feel anything. This wasn't so bad. He could kiss her, and still keep himself at a distance.

When he opened his eyes, he found her looking at him once more, her lips curled up in a shy smile. Had she felt anything?

The crowd cheered, and well-wishers drew them apart. Frederick shook hands here and there, accepted congratulations and offered his thanks in return. Then he led his new bride back to the manor where the musicians began to play a quiet tune. They sat down for their wedding breakfast, and cheerful conversations reached his ears. He saw delighted smiles on many faces as they drank and ate, and yet, nothing he saw touched his heart.

Inwardly, Frederick congratulated himself. In the few short weeks since his mother had first spoken to him about choosing a bride, he had successfully steeled his heart. If he could not experience emotions, then they could not hurt him or others. If he kept his heart locked up, then none of the pain and misery he knew was still there could travel from him to another.

And yet, as he glanced at his bride, he couldn't help but wonder what it would feel like to kiss her. To really kiss her.

It had been a long time since someone had touched him without inflicting pain.

Someone who was not his mother.

13

A WEDDING DAY

s he led her onto the dance floor, Ellie marvelled at the softness of his touch. Although he barely glanced at her, his touch spoke of a generous and kind man.

His eyes, however, seemed more distant than the night before. He smiled and conversed animatedly with his guests, and still there was a coldness in his gaze that spoke of a tortured soul, a soul that had retreated to keep itself from further harm.

Ellie watched him carefully, and her mind slowly added up her observations and came to a simple conclusion.

Frederick did not want her.

Instantly, Ellie chastised herself for having dared to hope. She hadn't even been aware of it at the time. However, looking at him now, it pained her to have him disregard her so completely. Especially since it stood in such stark contrast to his mother's warm welcome.

Ellie took a deep breath, reminding herself that today was merely her first day as his wife. There would be many more to come. Many more for her to find out what pain resided within his heart. Many more for him to understand that she was determined to bring him back.

Seeing equal determination to separate himself from everyone else around him in his eyes, Ellie only hoped that she would have the strength to stand her ground.

As the steps carried them to one another again, she looked at him with searching eyes, a smile on her face despite the words that left her lips. "You did not wish to marry me, did you, my lord?"

Instantly, the veil that constantly clouded his eyes vanished, and he stared at her...if only for a moment. Before Ellie could congratulate herself on her small victory, his eyes glossed over once more, and a polite, yet distant smile came to his face. "If I have offended you in any way, my lady, I do apologise. Whatever it was, it was not my intention to cause you distress."

Ellie bowed her head, acknowledging his apology, and yet, her eyes would not move from his face. Remembering the one short moment she had glimpsed the man underneath, Ellie felt more determined than ever. If she had to shock him into dropping his guard, then by God, she would.

Out of nowhere, a hand landed on his shoulder, and Frederick spun around, eyes wide, as though he had been shot.

Upon seeing his expression, the smile slid off Oliver's face, and his brows drew down into a confused frown. "Are you all right?" he asked, eyeing him carefully.

Frederick swallowed before shaking off the sense of dread that so often lingered in his bones these days. "Certainly." He forced a smile on his face. "I hope you are enjoying yourself."

"I am," Oliver said. "Or rather I was." Again his friend's eyes swept over him. "However, now I am rather worried." He took a step closer, and his voice dropped to a whisper. "What is going on? You look like you've seen a ghost."

Clearing his throat, Frederick scoffed. "Do not be absurd."

Oliver's eyes narrowed.

"And would you quit staring at me?!" he snapped, momentarily forgetting the rest of their guests surrounding them like a swarm of bees. Fortunately, their continued buzzing drowned out his own rather loud remark. "Nothing is wrong. I was just...thinking."

"About what?"

"Nothing that concerns you," Frederick hissed under his breath. "Now, go and dance. After all, this is a wedding."

"It certainly is," Oliver replied. "Which begs the question why you are looking so glum." Taking him by the arm, Oliver led him to a less crowded corner of the room. "Talk to me, Rick. Why do you look like you're about to face the gallows? This is your wedding day. You should be happy."

Frederick sighed, feeling the desperate need to get away boil in his veins. He shook his head and then raised his eyes to meet his friend's worried gaze. "I am not the man you all expect me to be. I am not my brother, and—"

"We never—"

"Yes, you do!" Frederick snapped as his hands curled into fists, his fingernails digging into his palms. "You all do!" He took a deep breath. "I am doing what is my duty, but you cannot expect more of me. I was never meant for this life. However, now that it is mine, I am doing the best I can. I cannot give you more than that."

"I am not asking for more," Oliver objected. "This is not about the marquessate. I am not talking about the duties that are yours now." He lowered his head, his eyes as scrutinising as Frederick had ever seen them. "I am talking about your wife. Do you not care for her?"

Frederick shrugged, glancing at his new bride. "How could I? I don't even know her."

Oliver frowned. "Then how—?"

"My mother," Frederick interrupted. "She insisted I marry to continue the line."

"I see," Oliver mumbled. "When I heard about your wedding, I believed that such a short betrothal spoke to a love match." He shrugged. "I suppose I wanted to believe that you had fallen head over heels for a wonderful woman and would be happy now."

Shaking his head, Frederick laughed. "I doubt that I am even capable of such feelings."

Oliver's mouth opened and then closed. His eyes, however, betrayed the sorrow that lived in his heart whenever he looked at his friend. "Rick, please!"

Frederick could see it as clear as day, and yet, he knew that Oliver would have to learn to live with it.

Happiness was not in store for him. Maybe not even content-edness. All that was left was to do his duty, to do right by the people that he loved.

Did he? Frederick wondered. He knew he had loved them once. But now, he couldn't be sure. What did it feel like? He couldn't even recall the feeling.

Maybe it was for the best.

Ellie sighed as her feet began to ache.

Wherever she went, stares and whispers would follow her. To-day was her wedding day, and yet, all people saw were her scars. Like at any other event, they gossiped behind her back, their prying eyes following her every step.

Oh, how she wished Madeline were not indisposed! If she only hadn't caught a cold, she would have been a shoulder to lean on.

Standing in line to receive well-wishes and congratulations from their guests, Ellie glanced at her husband. He, too, seemed rather un-comfortable in this sea of spectators, and she thought to see the des-perate need to get away in his veiled eyes. However, just like herself, he nodded and smiled, spoke politely and bore the intrusion into his life with a patience she could not help but admire.

Following his example, Ellie did her best to ignore their guests' inquisitive stares as they glanced back and forth between them, un-doubtedly wondering what had persuaded him to marry her. And yet, Ellie felt a stab in her heart every time she saw it, her own already wounded pride suffering again and again.

"I offer you my congratulations," a familiar voice spoke, and Ellie's head snapped up.

Her heart hammered in her chest as she found herself staring at the man she had thought to marry so long ago. Why did her mother have to invite him? She cursed, forcing her lips into a tortured smile.

Undoubtedly, Lord Haston knew that he looked as strikingly as ever, his light hair offsetting his dark eyes. The same dark eyes that now swept over her and took in every deficiency in her own appear-ance.

Ellie felt herself cringe under his gaze, knowing that he, too, wondered why the marquess had married her. After all, what did she have to offer?

"I wish you well, my lady," he added, his eyes distant all of a sudden as though they had never been more than mere acquaintances.

"I thank you, my lord," Ellie forced out, hearing her own voice tremble as she spoke. Anger surged through her then, and she had to control herself not to slap him across the face. How dare he belittle her in such a way?

"You are a beautiful bride."

As her cousin's caring voice reached her ears, Ellie's anger vanished immediately, and she turned to look at Rosabel with a heartfelt smile on her face. "I am so glad you could come," she said, embracing her cousin. "It wouldn't have been the same without you."

"We are happy to be here," Rosabel's husband agreed, his dark eyes shining with a happiness that Ellie knew had only found him due to his wife's persistence. Their road had been one of many obstacles as well, and their story gave Ellie the hope she needed to face her own future.

As Rosabel hugged her yet another time, Graham turned to Frederick. From her cousin, Ellie knew that although they were not the closest of friends, they had known each other all their lives. "Congratulations," she heard him say. "You have chosen wisely. Elsbeth is a rare treasure."

Ellie's heart warmed at his kind words, and she hoped that one day her husband would feel the same way. Was it possible? Would she ever be able to win his heart?

"Do not let anyone spoil this day for you," Rosabel whispered, glancing to her left at Lord Haston's receding back. "He is not the man you thought him to be. And although they've brought you pain," she added, her gentle gaze travelling over Ellie's scars, "maybe they are a blessing in disguise. Without their interference, you would have married Lord Haston. However, even with your beauty intact, he would never have been able to love you the way you deserve." A warm smile lit up her face as she glanced at Frederick. "Maybe everything happened for a reason. Maybe you were always meant for him."

An indescribable feeling flooded Ellie's heart then, and she sighed with delight. A deep smile tugged up the corners of her mouth in a way they had not in a long time, and her eyes shone as tears gathered and clung to her lashes. "Thank you," she whispered, embracing her cousin once more. "What would I do without you?"

"Remember to be patient," Rosabel implored. "His eyes hold deep pain, but I am certain that behind it, he is hiding a kind heart."

Ellie nodded. "I will." She brushed away the tears, reluctantly let go of her cousin's hand, and with an honest smile on her face, she turned to the next well-wisher.

Night had fallen, and still Frederick sat in his chamber, yet another glass of brandy in his hand. The house was silent, slumbering peacefully, while Frederick's heart beat in his chest, not allowing him a moment of peace.

Again, he downed the contents of his glass, and again, he refilled it.

After yet another hour he had spent sitting in the dark, a sense of detachedness finally spread over him. It began as a slight tingling sensation in his hands and feet, like pins and needles delicately pricking his skin, and then spread into every region of his body. To his relief, his mind did not remain unaffected, and he closed his eyes as a sense of indistinct languor flooded his being. His heart beat relaxed, and he took a deep breath.

Opening his eyes, the moonlight shining in through the window appeared to have lost its brightness as though it had been shrouded in a dark veil. The glass under his fingertips felt no longer cool to the touch, and the cold parquet floor under his bare feet did not freeze his limbs. However, neither did he feel warm. In fact, he felt almost nothing at all.

Taking another deep breath, he finally set down his glass and rose to his feet. On his way to the door connecting his own chamber to that of his new bride, Frederick glanced up and beheld his own reflection in the mirror.

Instantly, he froze in his steps and gaped at the hollow face staring back at him. Dark eyes that he did not recognise as his own fixed him with a penetrating glare.

As he stared, the sense of detachedness slowly began to fade and darkness spread through his heart once more.

Frederick quickly closed his eyes, willing the darkness back into its cell.

For a long moment, he stood on the cold floor, uncertain what to do. He contemplated simply going to sleep but knew that his duty required a different path from him. He shook his head then, knowing that there was no use in prolonging the inevitable.

After all, she was his wife now and had entered the marriage with certain expectations. The least he could do was give her a child. Women wanted to be mothers above all else, did they not? And once he had fathered an heir, he would be free to leave.

Deep down, Frederick knew that his mother thought a wife and children would forever bind him to Elmridge, and a part of him felt guilty for allowing her to believe as she did. However, he knew that should he make his honest intentions known, they would never allow him to leave.

Forcing his eyes to ignore the apparition in the mirror, Frederick approached the door that would ultimately lead him to his freedom.

Forcing her trembling limbs to still, Ellie lay in bed waiting. As the candle slowly burned down, shadows danced across the wall, and every now and then, a shiver ran over her. Would he not come to her? She wondered.

Curious about the ways between husband and wife, but nervous nonetheless, Ellie began to gnaw on her lower lip when the door suddenly slid open.

Instantly, her trembling limbs stilled, and she stared at her husband.

Wearing a nightshirt, he stood in the doorway. Darkness engulfed him, and she could scarcely make out his features. His eyes barely saw her before they travelled to the remaining candle, casting a dim glow about her bedchamber.

In two steps, he reached it and extinguished the flame.

Blackness filled the room, and Ellie froze as her heart hammered in her chest.

Robbed of her sight, she strained her ears, listening to the dull thud of his footsteps as he approached the bed. Then the mattress shifted as he lowered his weight upon it, and Ellie's hands curled around the bed cloth.

Why did he not say anything? She wondered, staring into the darkness. Deep down, she knew him to be a kind and caring man, a man she had always felt attracted to and a man with whom she was more than eager to share the intimacies of the marriage bed. However, in that moment, he was all but a stranger. A stranger who wouldn't even look at her. A stranger who refused to let her see him.

If she could not see his eyes, how would she know how he felt? Had he approved of his mother's choice? Or was he disappointed? Did her scars repulse him? Was that why he had extinguished what little light had remained? So that he wouldn't have to look at her?

"My lord?" she whispered into the dark, but no reply came.

Then she felt a tug on the bedding as he slid beneath the blanket, and the warmth radiating from his body rose goose bumps on her chilled skin.

"Frederick?" she tried once more, but he remained silent.

He slid closer, though, and his body touched hers.

Ellie gasped.

Then he rolled over, and she felt him hovering above her as he carried his weight on his knees and lower arms. His warm breath brushed over her cheek, and a tingle ran down her spine.

Inexperienced as she was, Ellie could tell from the way he moved that he tried to touch her as little as possible, and she couldn't help but wonder whether he did so because he wanted to be considerate of her feelings or his own.

Would he kiss her? She wondered, lying in the dark waiting.

He didn't, and Ellie soon learnt that the mystery of the marriage bed held rather disappointment than pleasure for her. Regret filled her heart at the distance he forced between them; not merely the physical distance but more acutely the emotional one.

He would not touch her beyond what was necessary, neither with his body nor with his soul. After consummating their marriage, he simply slid from the bed and vanished without saying a single word.

Still staring into the darkness, Ellie curled up into a ball and cried. Despite knowing better, she had allowed herself to hope, and now, her foolish hopes had been dashed. He did not care for her—she knew that now—and yet, he was her husband.

Patience. Rosabel's voice echoed in her head, and despite her own misery, Ellie realised that she had expected too much of him that night. Frederick was a broken man. Even if he wanted to, he could not take the first step. It would be up to her to find a way to him.

If only she knew how.

14

SHARED TEARS

taring at her reflection in the vanity mirror, Ellie took a deep breath. This was it. She was a marchioness now and the mistress of this household; more importantly, she was Frederick's wife. How her life had changed in one night!

As her maid pinned up her hair, humming a cheerful melody as she worked, Ellie swallowed, and her eyes slid over the red scars that had brought her here to this house to this life. In her heart, Ellie wanted to believe that Rosabel was right, that she was meant to be Frederick's wife. And yet, doubt sneaked into her heart as well, and she desperately wished to know how her husband felt about her appearance.

In the beginning, Ellie had mourned her beauty just like her mother. However, at some point, she had realised that a life of regret wasn't a life worth living; and Ellie wanted to live. Even if her initial dreams and hopes for the future had been dashed, she still wanted to enjoy her days on this earth.

Still, her scars reminded her daily that life had changed, that now people saw her differently and met her with pity or even disgust, most of the time only thinly veiled by forced politeness.

"Done, my lady," Betty trilled, stepping back. "Is there anything else you require?"

Ellie rose from her chair and turned to the young maid. "No, that is all. Thank you so much, Betty. This truly looks wonderful." Turning before the mirror, Ellie examined her maid's handiwork. While the back of her hair had been piled on top of her head, strands in the front had been forced into corkscrew curls that danced down from her temples on both sides; on the left rather effectively hiding most of her scars.

"You're welcome, my lady," Betty beamed, a deep smile lifting the corners of her mouth.

Leaving her bedchamber, Ellie smiled when another cheerful melody reached her ears. Yes! She thought. We should all be happier!

As new determination grew in her heart, Ellie descended the staircase and headed toward the breakfast parlour. Unfortunately, upon entering, her own good mood received a serious dampener when she was met by rather solemn faces.

Although her parents looked rather delighted with the situation in general, her new family appeared rather out of sorts. While Mathilda was absent, both Theresa and Maryann had dark circles under their eyes, their faces haggard and exhausted as though they had not slept at all the night before. Frederick, too, looked far from cheerful; however, the detached expression Ellie found on his face rather spoke of annoyance than exhaustion.

When they all sat down to breakfast, Ellie carefully glanced around the parlour, her eyes flitting from one to another. Her parents seemed oblivious to the general melancholy that hung about the room and cheerfully complimented their hosts on their exquisite taste with regard to anything that caught their attention. Occasionally, Theresa would smile and comment; however, she seemed rather monosyllabic this morning. Ellie wondered what was wrong.

Taking another bite from her muffin, Ellie shifted her gaze to her husband. From under her eyelashes, she looked at him, wondering how they would meet after the previous night. Although their encounter had been brief, Ellie now felt a deeper connection to him and hoped that they would have a chance to get to know each other in the days to come.

When she reached for her teacup, Frederick looked up, and she felt his eyes on her. Although feeling slightly unsettled, Ellie raised her gaze to his.

"I trust you slept well, my lady," he said, and although he did not avert his eyes, neither did he look at her in a way that led her to believe she truly had his attention.

"Yes, quite well, my lord." Returning her cup to its saucer, Ellie kept her gaze on him. "And you as well, my lord?"

"Indeed," he said, and yet, for a brief moment, his eyes flickered to his plate before returning to hers, and Ellie thought to detect a slight tremble in his rather tensed jaw. However, then he cleared his throat and seemed back in control. "Business will keep me occupied today. However, I trust that my mother and sister-in-law will keep you good company."

Ellie's heart sank. "Will you not be joining us, my lord?"

"I'm afraid I cannot," he said before he returned his attention to the footman, gesturing for him to remove his plate. Apparently, he considered their conversation to have come to an end.

After breakfast, Ellie bade her parents and siblings goodbye and wished them a safe journey home. A part of her was sad to see them go while another rejoiced at the opportunity to settle into her new life without her mother's reproachful eyes on her.

As she watched their carriage disappear from view, Ellie sighed, a smile curling up her lips. Then she turned around and found Theresa standing behind her.

Slightly startled, she clutched a hand to her chest. "I'm sorry, I did not see you there."

A smile on her face, Theresa waved her concerns away. "I should have made my presence known. I apologise. I had no intention of intruding on your farewell." She took Ellie by the arm and led her to the front drawing room. "It is never easy for parents to part with their children." Leaning closer, she whispered, "I have to confess I was always glad I only had boys, hoping that they would stay closer to home." She chuckled, but sadness clung to her eyes. "I suppose, once they had outgrown their childhood years, I was not prepared to lose them. I did not see it coming."

Ellie squeezed Theresa's hand. "How could you? What happened was a tragedy!"

"It was," Theresa nodded, then closed her eyes for a brief moment and took a deep breath. "Well, what was was. It is no use crying over spilled milk." She turned to Ellie and gestured for her to sit. "May I ask a favour of you? I know I am terribly rude considering this is your first day here at Elmridge, but I am at my wits' end."

"No, not at all," Ellie said, gently placing a hand on Theresa's as they lay folded in her lap. "I am happy to help. If there is anything I can do, please do not hesitate to ask."

Some of the tension left Theresa's shoulders, and she took a deep breath. "These days, I feel life is only filled with worry." She shook her head. "I worry about my son, my granddaughter and my daughter-in-law. Some days, the sadness that rests on this house is unbearable."

"What can I do?" Ellie whispered. She knew she was a stranger, and yet, these people were her family now.

"It is Maryann," Theresa whispered. "My son's passing broke her heart. Almost every night, she has nightmares, and sometimes she even wakes up screaming and kicking, then curls up into a ball and weeps." For a moment, Theresa closed her eyes, and a shiver shook her small frame at the memory. "Last night was one of those nights that particularly torment her. I go to her, and I hold her, but I don't know what else to do. Right now, I don't have the strength."

On impulse, Ellie wrapped her arms around her mother-in-law, and she rested her head against Ellie's shoulder as though they had known each other for years. "I will go to her," Ellie whispered against the woman's greying hair. "Do not worry. Go upstairs and get some rest. I will take care of her."

"Thank you," Theresa breathed, and for a moment, Ellie thought she had already fallen asleep.

After seeing her mother-in-law to her chambers, Ellie went in search of Maryann. As she entered the back parlour, she found the woman standing by the tall windows, staring into the distance. Her posture spoke of a crushed soul as though she barely had the strength to keep herself upright.

Approaching her, Ellie spoke softly, careful not to startle her. "Maryann? Shall we take a turn about the garden? It is such a beautiful day."

Slowly, her sister-in-law moved her gaze from the horizon and looked at her with eyes that seemed as distant as Frederick's. Seeing her desire to be left alone, Ellie took Maryann by the arm and led her outside before she could turn down her offer.

The sun shone brightly, warming the earth, and birds chirped in the trees bordering the gardens to the west. A small fountain trickled in the centre, encircled by tall-standing hedges casting a welcoming shade over intricately carved benches.

Stepping down from the terrace, Ellie held Maryann's arm tightly in her own, softly squeezing the woman's hand. "I haven't really had a chance to speak with you, yet," Ellie began. "I wanted to thank you for your warm welcome. I already feel quite at home here."

A shy smile came to Maryann's features as she glanced over to Ellie. "I am sorry. I suppose my welcome was lacking quite a bit."

Ellie shook her head. "Do not worry yourself. I understand it must have been hard for you to see a wedding at Elmridge so soon after your husband's passing." From her own experience, Ellie knew that loss only got worse when it was left to fester. In order to find her smile again, Maryann needed to face the pain and speak about her husband and what losing him had done to her.

As expected a heart-breaking sigh rose from Maryann's throat. "It brought back so many memories."

"Did you get married here, too?"

Maryann nodded, and a slight gleam came to her eyes. As they walked the labyrinth, Ellie listened as her new sister-in-law spoke of her husband, of their wedding, Mathilda's birth, their life together and the one day it had all come to an end. Again and again, tears came to Maryann's eyes. Sometimes they would spill over and quietly run down her cheeks, and sometimes she would break down in heaving sobs and Ellie would hold her as she wept.

"I never truly met him," Ellie admitted as they sat side by side on a bench by the fountain. "But from the few times I saw him, I thought he had kind eyes, compassionate eyes. He was a family man, was he not?"

Maryann nodded, dabbing a wet handkerchief at her swollen eyes. "He loved Mathilda. I know, many men do not know what to do with their daughters, but Leopold would sit and play with her for hours." A deep smile came to her face as fresh tears ran down her cheeks. "During the summer, we often went outside with a big picnic basket and spent the whole day by the lake."

"The lake?"

"Yes, there is a lake about a half-an-hour's ride from here. We would usually take the carriage and play games along the way." Maryann closed her eyes, then opened them again and shook her head. "It makes me so sad that Mathilda will never have that again." She glanced at Ellie. "I haven't been a good mother to her lately. She only just lost her father, and now, I'm…I just can't…"

Ellie took Maryann's hands, squeezing them gently. "You're not a bad mother. Don't ever think that. Mathilda loves you."

"But she is in pain, too, and I can't help her. All I do is cry…all day." She swallowed. "I try to keep my distance so that she won't see, but I think she knows."

Ellie nodded. "She does." Maryann's eyes went wide, and she buried them in her hands. "No, don't," Ellie interrupted, pulling Maryann's hands off her face. "Don't hide your tears. Although I have not seen Mathilda cry, I am sure she does. She tries to be strong because she believes you need her to be, but deep down, she mourns her father just as much as you do."

"I always knew that," Maryann confessed. "But I don't know what to do."

"Share your pain," Ellie said, her own heart heavy at the sight of such loss. "You cry alone, and she cries alone. Maybe you should stop pretending that either one of you is fine. Share your pain, and share your tears."

A hint of hope shone in Maryann's eyes as she looked up at Ellie through a curtain of tears. "Do you not think it would hurt her more?"

Ellie shook her head. "I think it would help her." She squeezed Maryann's hand, and the woman smiled at her. "You know, it is truly beautiful out here. Maybe you should not break with tradition and still go see the lake this year." Ellie knew their wounds would only heal over time if they were tended to, and if they did not start now, precious time would be lost.

Maryann's eyes went wide before a flicker of understanding came to them.

"I think it would be a good place to remember her father."

A deep smile on her face, Maryann hugged her.

15

SHARED PAIN

 itting at his desk, Frederick stared at the papers before him. As much as he tried to concentrate, his thoughts would constantly stray to the previous night.

Everything had worked out as he had hoped. He had consummated his marriage, and yet, he had kept his distance. He remembered how she had called his name, and a hint of guilt surfaced at having ignored her so completely.

At the same time, he knew that if he had acknowledged her presence, he would not have been able to keep himself separate from the emotions that he could still feel lurking beneath the surface.

With a clenched jaw, Frederick nodded his head, determined to continue as planned. He would share his wife's bed, but he did not want to know who she was or communicate beyond normal pleasantries. What was the point? After all, he had no intention of staying longer than was necessary for her to conceive an heir.

Glancing down at yet another social function he had received an invitation to, Frederick sighed. He did not remember being in such high demand before going off to war or before becoming the marquess. However, it didn't matter which aspect had sported this newest invitation, neither one shed a favourable light on him as a person. Aside from his family, did anyone truly know him? Did anyone care to?

Oliver did. Frederick knew that. And yet, neither he nor his family could possibly understand how his life had changed, and he didn't know how to make them understand. And so he avoided them, separated himself from them and pretended everything was fine.

So far everything had worked well. Soon, he would be free to leave.

Rising from his chair, Frederick walked around the room, feeling the need to move in his trembling legs. Never before had he spent this much time sitting in a chair, tied to a desk. His shoulders felt tense, and a dull pain settled in his lower back.

Stretching his limbs, Frederick walked over to the window. The weather was perfect. The sun was shining, not a cloud in sight, and yet, the temperatures had not yet climbed so high that any form of exercise would be ill-advised.

Yes! He needed to get out, out of this house and away from all these people, who looked at him with sad, yet hopeful eyes.

A hard ride across the fields would do him good. It would chase away the nagging guilt that encroached on his heart every time his mind was unoccupied. It would give his limbs something to do, something to feel instead of the numbing ache of past injuries. And it would allow his mind to pretend that life was simple, simple enough for him to climb on a horse and leave. For good.

If only.

As his eyes returned from the distant horizon, they found two figures sitting on one of the benches by the fountain. Squinting his eyes, Frederick recognised his sister-in-law and to his surprise his wife.

Their heads bowed toward each other as they sat close together; Maryann's left hand wrapped in both of Elsbeth's. Their lips moved, and Frederick couldn't help but wonder what they were talking about. As he looked closer, a jolt went through him when Maryann suddenly buried her face in her hands, weeping openly.

Never had he seen his brother's widow display such emotion. A dark cloud had always hung about her since that one fateful day. However, she had rarely shown her grief openly in such a loud manner. At least not since the day her husband had died.

In the next moment, Frederick was even more stumped when his wife pulled Maryann into her arms, gently rocking her as though soothing a young child.

Frederick swallowed. Maybe his mother had been right. Unlike himself, Elsbeth seemed to know exactly what his family needed. A marchioness not even a day, and she was already healing his family's wounds. His mother had indeed chosen well.

From the corner of his eye, Frederick caught a movement.

Hiding behind a large bush, Mathilda cowered, her dress once more ripped beyond repair. As she stood bent forward, peering at her mother and new aunt from her hiding place, her little hands came up, and she wiped her eyes. Tears sparkled on her cheeks, and Frederick wondered what else the child had witnessed without anyone noticing.

Within the next few days, a routine developed that allowed Ellie to find her place within the family. While her husband was otherwise occupied, she mostly spent her mornings with Maryann strolling the gardens. At first, their only topic was Maryann's grief over her husband's death, but occasionally Ellie noticed that it helped her new friend to learn of her worries as well and give advice herself.

"He hardly looks at me," Ellie said, once more feeling defeated. Her days were marked by ups and downs, moments of confidence and those of doubt. "Sometimes I feel like he looks right through me."

Maryann nodded. "He looks at all of us this way," she reminded Ellie. "Do not feel bad. He needs time. Two nights after he returned, Leopold…," she took a deep breath, "…he told me that Frederick was a mere shadow of himself. It scared him to see his brother so miserable, and he didn't know how to help him."

Stopping in her tracks, Ellie turned to her friend. "Neither do I. But how can I even try if he refuses to spend any time in my company?"

A careful smile played on Maryann's lips as her eyes swept Ellie's face. "You truly like him, do you not?" Ellie blushed. "I only ask because from what Theresa said, I thought it was not a love match."

"No, it wasn't," Ellie admitted, unsure what to say. At the moment, she was rather uncertain about her own feelings. "All I know is that I do like him, and I hope that somehow he will find his way out of the dark."

"As do I," Maryann said. "But I do not know what to tell you. The only one who got through to him…well, at least a little, I suppose…was his friend Oliver."

"Oliver Cornell?" Ellie asked, remembering that hot summer day many years ago.

Maryann nodded. "He was at the wedding. Do you know him?"

"Not really."

"Well, shortly after Frederick had returned, he came for a visit. I don't really know what happened, but after his visit, Frederick seemed different. Less cold and detached, and yet, more hopeless. As though he had just realised that life held nothing for him anymore. At least, nothing good. Leopold was very concerned."

Ellie sighed. From Frederick's own behaviour as well as the bits and pieces his family had provided, Ellie knew that her hopes did not hold a bright future.

She was his wife, and yet, she hardly saw him. They even lived in the same house, but the only time he allowed her within his presence was when he visited her chamber at night. Although Ellie had hoped that he would warm to the idea of sharing her bed, the distance between them seemed even greater now than it had on their first night together. Sometimes Ellie thought that he might feel something for her. However, in the next moment, he would pull away with such desperate force as though he feared his feelings would destroy him should he allow them to surface.

What had he suffered that he felt the need to raise such an insurmountable shield around himself? And even keep his own wife out?

16

A GARDEN PARTY

fter years of hoping for a child, the Earl of Drenton and his wife had finally been blessed with a healthy baby boy. Overjoyed, they felt the need to celebrate their happiness with their friends and neighbours mere weeks after the child had been born. Since it was a pleasant summer, a garden party was arranged and invitations sent. One such invitation found its way to Elmridge.

Frederick groaned in agony as he received it. However, since he had weaselled his way out of the last three events, he knew that he could not escape this one. After all, the earl and his wife were long-standing friends.

And so before he could change his mind, Frederick found himself walking down the hall to the front drawing room. This time of day, the ladies of the house generally enjoyed a little refreshment in the west-facing parlour.

Upon entering, three sets of eyes turned to him, and he swallowed. While not completely at ease in anyone's company, Frederick at least felt more or less comfortable in his mother's as well as Maryann's presence. His wife, however, unsettled him every time he laid eyes on her.

Why? He did not know, but her deep blue eyes always looked at him as though they could see right through him, as though she could tell by a simple look what he was thinking. At night, when he visited her bedchamber, the dark wrapped him in a safe cocoon. She could not see him then, and neither could her eyes unsettle his resolve.

During the day, however, he felt as though he was at her mercy.

Frederick cleared his throat while keeping his eyes fixed on the card in his hand. "We have received another invitation." Quickly, he related the details, and as expected, his mother's face immediately took on a delighted glow.

"I am so happy for them," she said. "I know what a strain it has been on them to wish for a child so dearly and not be blessed with one."

Maryann nodded. "I am so glad I have Mathilda." Her voice caught slightly as she went on. "Without her, I probably wouldn't have survived Leopold's death."

Although she remained silent, Elsbeth rose from her seat by the window and sat down next to Maryann. Her hand brushed over Maryann's arm and then came to rest on her slightly clenched hands.

As though transfixed, Frederick stared at her, his eyes following her every movement.

Until his mother cleared her throat.

Instantly, his head snapped up. "Well, I thought to send a quick note with our congratulations," he said, suddenly terrified by the thought of spending a whole afternoon in his wife's company, "and explain that we are still in mourning."

His mother glanced at Elsbeth before returning her sharp eyes to him and shook her head. "Maryann and I are in mourning. However, you and Elsbeth should attend. Although we will surely miss her," she said, a doting smile playing on her lips as she looked at his wife, "a young wife needs to get out of the house every now and then." Her eyes narrowed as she turned back to him. "As do you, my son."

Hesitating only for a moment, Frederick nodded. "As you wish, Mother." Then he bowed to the ladies and departed quickly.

Knowing that Theresa meant well, Ellie tried to calm her rattled nerves. For days, she had tried to hint to her mother-in-law that she did not wish to go out; however, it had been to no avail. Theresa was determined to give her new daughter-in-law a little time away from the family, alone with her husband.

Alone with her husband? Ellie mused, meeting her own eyes in the vanity mirror. If only they would be alone. On the contrary, a large number of guests was expected. The Season in London was drawing to a close, and many friends and neighbours had decided to return to the country early in order to celebrate with the earl and his wife.

"Are you cold, my lady?" Betty asked, glancing down at Ellie's trembling hands. Her own hung in mid-air, a strand of her mistress' blond tresses dangling from them.

"No, I'm fine," Ellie assured her, desperately trying to shake the apprehension that settled in the pit of her stomach like a rock. Looking up, she met her maid's eyes and managed an encouraging smile. "Really, I am fine. It is just nerves."

Betty nodded knowingly and returned to fixing Ellie's hair. "Do not worry yourself, my lady. I am certain everyone will receive you kindly."

Ellie sighed. That was the problem. They were *always* kind. They were *always* concerned for her. They never gave her a tangible reason to be upset – which was all the more upsetting. Ellie had never enjoyed being the object of others' pity, and now, it was all she was.

Once again wishing that she could simply stay home, Ellie stopped when her thoughts were interrupted by a sweet melody drifting to her ears. Looking up, she saw Betty's face in the mirror, her eyes had a dream-like expression and a lovely smile played on her lips as she hummed under her breath. Her hands worked without conscious thought, once again pinning Ellie's hair up and leaving only a few tendrils to fall from her temples.

A smile came to Ellie's face as she watched her. "You seem happy."

Betty flinched, and her features tensed. She met Ellie's eyes in the mirror, and a hand clamped over her mouth. "I'm so sorry, my lady. I didn't mean to get distracted."

"Do not worry yourself," Ellie assured her. Rising to her feet, she took Betty's hands in hers and looked at her with a deep smile on her face. "I am glad you are happy. Cherish it, not all of us are this lucky."

A shy smile came to Betty's face, and she averted her eyes just as a slight blush came to her cheeks. "Thank you, my lady," she whispered and then took her leave.

Ellie took a deep breath. If only she could be this happy! Whoever had put that smile on Betty's face, Ellie hoped that he was worthy of her maid's tender heart. She sighed and left her chamber.

Twenty minutes later, Ellie was trapped in a moving carriage with only her husband for company. Sitting diagonally from the other, both sat at the far right end as close to the window as the bench would allow. With nothing to say, they both stared at the moving landscape passing by outside.

Inwardly, Ellie moaned.

In the beginning, she had asked a few noncommittal questions, to which her husband had found equally noncommittal answers, most of which had been monosyllabic. All the while, his gaze had been focused out the window, and a scowl had decorated his otherwise handsome features.

When Ellie finally remained quiet, he seemed to relax.

Disappointed, Ellie watched the earl's estate come into view. How she had wished for some time alone with her husband! However, without the company of others, who allowed them to converse only in a more distant fashion, he seemed unable to speak to her. What was he afraid of? She wondered. Were they doomed only to exchange unimportant pleasantries for the rest of their lives?

When the carriage came to a halt under the earl's roofed drive leading up a few steps to the front doors, a footman opened the door, and her husband stepped out. Then he stood aside and allowed the same footman to help her out of the carriage as well.

Ellie was severely disappointed. She had hoped to feel the touch of his hand against hers, even if just for a moment. Did she so repulse him that he could only touch her when the lights were out?

Following him inside, she contented herself with the fact that at least he had offered her his arm. However, she could feel the tension that tightened the muscles in his shoulder and arm.

Walking into the large ballroom, they found that the doors leading to the gardens had been opened, allowing a fresh breeze to dance among the many guests. Large tables held refreshing foods, and a vast array of flowers decorated the entire room. Outside on the terrace, tables and chairs stood in shaded corners, and delighted laughter echoed to their ears from everywhere.

Ellie tensed when heads began to turn and conversations broke off. It was not as though silence fell over the room at their entrance; however, Ellie could hear her heart beating in her chest as she once more found herself the focus of her neighbours' pitying stares.

Clinging to her husband's arm, she took a deep breath.

Although Frederick was far from enjoying these events, they did not turn his stomach upside down. On the contrary, anger regularly rose at the mindless comments that usually were directed at him at some point during the evening or in this case afternoon. However, if people insisted on asking rude questions, he would simply give rude answers.

He had no patience for their misguided need for gossip.

However, when they walked into the ballroom, Frederick felt a jolt go through his wife's arm as though she had been slapped, and his gaze involuntary turned to her.

Her eyes were wide and her skin pale as she swallowed and then raised her head. Despite the tremble that shook her frame, he saw determination shining in her eyes.

Shifting his gaze from his wife to the guests already gathered in the earl's summer home, Frederick finally understood that she, too, found herself facing people whose insensitive behaviour caused her pain. Although he saw smiles on most of the faces turned toward them, Frederick had no trouble detecting the underlying hint of pity that accompanied them all.

Instinctively, the arm that held hers tightened, pulling her closer. Then he guided her away from the throng of people and onto the terrace. The sun shone brightly, and a handful of children played in the gardens. "Would you like some refreshment?" he asked, wondering what had brought on this sudden desire to shield her from the world.

Was it simply because he could relate? Or because he felt it his duty to protect his wife?

"Yes, that would be lovely," she said, a delighted smile on her face. "Thank you." Her eyes looked into his as though searching for an answer to something she did not understand.

When he stepped back, Frederick felt her reluctance to let him go in the tense muscles of her arm. He nodded to her then, and she smiled back at him.

As he turned around, she whispered, "Hurry back."

This short, heart-felt plea touched a place deep down that Frederick couldn't quite name, and as he headed for the refreshment table, he felt a shiver run over him. However, he wasn't sure if it was a shiver of dread or anticipation. All he knew was that something had changed.

Nothing earth-shattering had happened, and yet, something was different now.

Don't overthink it! His heart cautioned, and after retrieving a glass of fruit punch for each of them, he returned to the terrace. Stepping through the doors, he found his wife surrounded by a group of gossip-hungry hyenas.

"My dear marchioness," Lady Betram beamed although her eyes had narrowed into slits, "I am so relieved to see you here. No one expected to see you out in society." Silence fell over the group, and suddenly aware of her blunder, Lady Betram coughed and added, "I mean so soon after your wedding. My heart-felt congratulations by the way. We were all quite delighted when we heard about your betrothal. So unexpected!"

Supportive murmurs echoed through the group, and Frederick lifted his eyes to his wife's face. The forced smile on her lips told him everything he needed to know, and he hurried to her side before another insensitive comment could be made or she would lose the control over her emotions and fuel their gossip even more.

"My dear, here is your punch," he said loud enough for all to hear. Handing her the glass, he heard the relieved sigh that escaped her lips upon seeing him returned. For a moment, their eyes locked, and he had to force himself to look away. "It is such a beautiful day. What do you say we take a stroll about the gardens, my dear?" Taking her by the elbow, he turned back to the hyenas listening closely to every word of their exchange. "Please excuse us, my ladies."

Frederick offered a quick bow and then guided his wife down the steps onto the meticulously cut lawn toward the laughing children. The echo of their delighted voices stood in stark contrast to the conniving remarks of their mothers.

"Thank you," his wife gasped, a deep red colouring her otherwise pale skin. "I never know what to do. Sometimes I wish they would simply say what they truly think."

Frederick nodded. "Then you would be justified to put them in their place."

Elsbeth turned to him then, her eyes searching his. "You know what it is like, do you not?"

Frederick shrugged his shoulders, gesturing toward the empty bench below a large oak tree. "To my great regret, I have recently become aware of it. Before, I never knew how insensitive people could be."

Sitting down, his wife sighed. "I do enjoy company," she said, lifting her eyes to his, "but I do not wish to be the object of their pity." Her gaze remained on his as she looked at him openly, and Frederick understood the question she was asking.

Taking a seat himself, Frederick said, "Only those who would see life as a burden deserve our pity, and I can see that you cannot be counted among them." A dazzling smile came to her lips, and Frederick felt his own tug up in response. "You enjoy life, do you not?"

"I try, but…"

"But they make it difficult for you," he finished for her, wondering about the woman across from him; the woman he did not know, but who was his wife nonetheless. "The sadness in your life comes from them, not your own heart."

Staring at him as though he had just shared a secret with her, she smiled, and her eyes lit up like stars in the night sky.

Transfixed, Frederick looked at her, and a sense of warmth washed over him. However, instantly dread settled in his stomach as her eyes swept his face, clearly seeking a deeper understanding of him.

Clearing his throat, he rose to his feet. "I should speak to…a few people and offer our congratulations. Then we can leave." Stepping back, he nodded to her. "Remain here. I doubt anyone will bother you, but I promise I will keep an eye out for the hyenas."

"The hyenas?" A quizzical expression came to her face before he saw understanding dawn on her. "Ah, yes, the hyenas. Perfectly named, indeed!"

With a last look, Frederick turned to go. His steps, however, were heavy, and his feet felt weighted-down as though they regretted the direction he had chosen and would have preferred to stay.

As expected, he did not quite escape the gossiping gentlemen among the earl's guests. Cornered in the back drawing room, he answered their questions with as much patience as he could muster.

"Is Napoleon truly as short as they say?" *I'm afraid I've never met the man.*

"Is it true that a cannon ball can cut through a stone wall?" *It cuts through a human being with even greater ease.*

"Why exactly does one attach a bayonet to the front of one's musket? Is it meant to support one's aim?" *No, it's another way of killing your enemy.*

Exasperated, Frederick tried to step past them. However, the gentlemen would not allow him to escape, their eager faces burning a hole in his soul. With drinks and cigars, they tried to keep him in place, and Frederick felt his control over his emotions slipping. Soon, he would answer them as rudely as their questions were to him and thus cause affront.

His mother would not be pleased.

"There you are, my dear," his wife's soft voice cut through the crowd. How they even heard her above the roar of their own voices, Frederick would never know. However, they did, and instantly, the throng of men parted, allowing her through.

With a soft smile on her face, she stepped toward him, and the moment she reached his side, he offered her his arm and led her away from his own group of hungry hyenas.

Finally offering their heart-felt congratulations to their hosts, they also bid them goodbye and made for the carriage immediately lest they be cornered again. Only when they had sunk into their seats and the carriage rumbled down the lane did they breathe a sigh of relief.

"Thank you for coming to my aid, my lady," Frederick said, knowing only too well the fears she had faced to save him from his own. "I truly am grateful."

A shy smile came to her face, and a touch of crimson coloured her cheeks as she averted her eyes. "It is no more or less than you yourself did for me."

17

ADMITTING DEFEAT

acing the length of his study, Frederick glanced out the window as the sun slowly lowered itself behind the horizon heralding the approaching night. Now and then, he would stop, stare at the glowing fireball in the darkening sky, then rake his hands through his hair and ultimately resume pacing.

Only too well did he remember his wife's glowing eyes as well as her charming smile. Even more did he remember his own reaction to it.

Closing his eyes, he shook his head.

There was no way for him to share her bed that night and still maintain the distance between them. Even in the dark, she would no longer be faceless. Too well did he remember those penetrating blue eyes as they had looked into his with such deep understanding that he had felt stripped to his core. How was it that she could look at him that way? They had only met a few weeks ago; how could she possibly know him?

And yet, when their eyes had met that sunny afternoon for a brief moment, Frederick had thought to see a kindred spirit. She knew agony and suffering just as he did. People looked at both of them and saw only what they wanted to see, and the pain their misjudgement brought tortured them even more. However, one aspect remained that opened up a bottomless ravine between them which nothing would ever be able to bridge.

Unlike his own, darkness did not rule her heart.

Despite the cruel hand fate had dealt her, her soul was pure, loving and innocent. The pain she suffered came from the people around her, not from within herself. Somehow she had walked through hell untouched, and a part of him desperately wanted to know how she had found the strength to do so.

However, it did not matter.

As much as he wanted her to find happiness after everything that had happened, Frederick knew that an intimate relationship between them was not possible. If he was forced to bare his soul to her or anyone for that matter, it would destroy him.

Not even he dared to look at the blackness that resided in his heart and mind. He surely would not survive another's judgement. Would she despise the man he was if she knew what he had done? He knew that he had no right to find happiness. Unlike her, he had been the cause of the misery he had suffered. It had been his own doing, and now, he had to live with the consequences.

His wife, however, was innocent and deserved whatever happiness life could bring her. If nothing else, it was his duty to see to that.

In addition, if he went to her now, he would lose that sense of detachedness that had always brought him peace of mind. Her touch would force him to explore the dark emotions that rested in his heart, and he knew he would not have the strength to survive such a confrontation.

He needed to see his family safe, and he could not do that if he did not keep everyone at an arm's length. He had to stay the course until everything was settled and he could leave.

If he was lucky, she was already with child.

My dear. He had called her, *my dear.*

Smiling at herself in the mirror, Ellie danced around her bed-chamber in her nightgown. Humming under her breath, she remembered the few moments they had shared that afternoon. Moments free of silence and distance. Moments that had reminded her of that one summer day long ago before adult burdens had started to weigh them down.

Was it truly possible? Could he come to care for her?

Feeling the butterflies flutter in her belly, Ellie smiled.

After extinguishing most of the candles, she retired to bed, her heart beating excitedly in her chest at the possibilities that night held. She snuggled into the covers and waited.

When the moon had risen and fully replaced the sun, its silver rays sparkling on the wall, Ellie was still waiting. By then, the butterflies in her belly had stilled and a sense of trepidation had settled in their place.

And still Ellie waited.

Finally, when the grand clock in the hall downstairs struck midnight, its loud strokes echoing through the silent house, tears streamed down Ellie's face.

She had to face the truth; he wouldn't come.

Disappointed beyond words, Ellie cried into her pillows as nagging thoughts of self-doubt invaded her mind. Did he truly not like her? Or was it her scars that he could not see past? Was she so hideous?

For a long time, Ellie wept, allowing the pain in her heart to grow and spread until her limbs felt heavy and her mind became numb. Images of the fire that had destroyed her life rose from the depth of her memories, and in that moment, Ellie fervently wished it had claimed all of her and ended her misery then and there.

Instead, it had doomed her to continue her life on the cusp of other people's happiness, just watching, never experiencing for herself. Was her life even a life still worth living?

As these thoughts echoed in her head, a small voice rose from the depth of her being. Whispering in her ear, it spoke with a resoluteness that forced Ellie to listen.

Rising from the bed, she brushed away her tears and walked over to her vanity. As she stood in the dim light, staring at her own face in the mirror, anger spread through her heart. It was not the scars that caught her attention as she looked upon her own face, but the utter defeat she saw in her swollen eyes.

Shocked, Ellie stared at the woman she had become.

Although she would never have referred to herself as brave, she had always been confident. With her head held high, she had walked her path, knowing her limits but not allowing them to confine her. Never had she turned away from a problem. Never had she averted her eyes so she wouldn't have to see what was before her. Never had she succumbed to her own, perceived insecurities.

What had happened to her? At what point had she allowed her scars to define her? Yes, she worried that Frederick might never find her desirable, and yes, that would surely pain her greatly, but was it reason enough to consider her own life worthless? To consider herself worthless?

Beyond the shadow of a doubt, she knew that Frederick had suffered greatly. She couldn't even imagine what he had lived through on the continent and how the loss of his father and brother had affected him. However, she, too, had suffered. She, too, had faced pain and horror. She, too, had faced the loss of someone she had loved.

And still she had triumphed.

Or at least at first. However, at some point, she had succumbed to the misjudgement of others, of all those people who believed that her life was over, that she had no reason to hope for the future.

Her hands balled into fists, stretching her scarred skin, and her jaw clenched as she stared at the woman she had become.

Disgust settled in her stomach at the very sight of her own face. Never had she thought it would come this far. And never would she allow for it to happen again.

Taking a deep breath, Ellie unclenched her hands. Then she turned and faced the closed door to her husband's bedchamber.

Frederick needed time. She knew she ought to be patient and not rush him. However, that did not mean she ought to allow him to wallow in his misery. Doing so would only bring him to the brink of surrender. Did he entertain the same thoughts that had only just now shocked her into realising that she had admitted defeat after all?

Ellie didn't know, but she knew with a certainty born out of personal experience that ignoring his pain would not destroy it. In fact, it would only return stronger and destroy him instead. Somehow, she had to find a way to break down his defences and make him feel.

Whether he wanted to or not.

She would be patient, and she would be gentle, but she would not allow him to dictate the terms of their relationship.

She was his wife, and whether he wanted to or not, she would not only save his life but also his soul as well.

Now more than ever, Ellie knew that she deserved her happily-ever-after, and by God, she would get it.

18

A WORD GIVEN

e can be rather mule-headed at times, can he not?" Maryann asked, twirling the parasol in her hands.

Ellie sighed. "In my opinion, that is quite an understatement."

Maryann chuckled.

As they walked along the shore line of the lake to the east of Elmridge, Ellie's eyes shifted to Mathilda lying on a blanket in the shade of a large juniper tree, fast asleep. After spending the whole morning swimming in the cool, clear blue water, the young girl was exhausted and had barely been able to keep her eyes open during the little picnic they had brought.

"Did he do something?" Maryann asked, her eyes serious. "The last few days, you seemed different. Rather annoyed with him, to tell you the truth."

Ellie shrugged. "I'm still trying to find my way, I suppose." Picking up a small pebble, she flung it into the water. "At the garden party, he seemed to warm to me, but now...," knowing how much his family cared for him, Ellie chose her words carefully, "he is even more distant than before. I only wish I knew what scared him that day."

"Scared him?" her friend asked. "What makes you say that? Leopold often said that Frederick was fearless, which is why he's always been so concerned about his brother especially when he went off to join the war against France."

A delicate smile tugged on Ellie's lips, then she turned to Maryann and met her eyes. "There are many areas in which someone can be fearless. However, being fearless in one does not make you fearless in all of them."

For a moment, Maryann's eyes rested on Ellie's face before she nodded and said, "I suppose you are right. I remember when Mathilda was born, Leopold was...terrified. It was a difficult birth, and I lost a lot of blood. Dr. Madison later said that I was lucky to be alive. When Leopold heard that, he went pale, and for a moment, I thought he would pass out."

Ellie nodded. "The thought of losing you scared him like nothing had ever before, didn't it?"

"It did," Maryann confirmed. "For a long time, he refused to share my bed," a hint of red came to her cheeks as she averted her eyes, "because he was afraid to get me with child again. He was afraid of losing me."

"And yet, he was a strong man, was he not?"

Maryann nodded. "What do you think Frederick is afraid of?"

Ellie shrugged. "I don't know...yet." She swallowed before a determined smile spread over her face. "But I will find out."

Maryann took her hand then and gave it a gentle squeeze. "I am so glad he married you," she said, and Ellie's eyes went wide. "Not only for Frederick's sake, but selfishly also for my own. I love Theresa dearly, but she is rather a mother than a sister." Again, she squeezed her hand, and Ellie felt her heart ache at her sister-in-law's honest words. "And I have so wished for someone to talk to, someone who can understand."

"I feel the same way," Ellie whispered as tears pooled in her eyes. "If it wasn't for you, I would surely go mad. Promise me that we will always talk to each other, that we will always share with each other what burdens our hearts."

As a tear ran down Maryann's cheek, she nodded her head vigorously. "I promise, dear Sister."

Embracing each other, they almost lost their footing and would have ended up in the lake had Ellie not stepped back to break their fall, her foot sinking into the chilled water.

Squealing, Maryann pulled her back up the shoreline. "Are you all right? I am so sorry."

"Don't be," Ellie said, laughing. "It felt wonderful actually. Refreshing." After glancing around, Ellie sat down in the soft grass. "Come on. Take off your shoes and stockings."

"What?" Maryann gaped. "What if someone sees?"

"There is no one around," Ellie assured her as a rush of excitement went through her. "Otherwise, you wouldn't have allowed Mathilda, would you?"

Maryann swallowed, then her eyes shifted to her sleeping daughter before returning to Ellie. "Are you sure this is a good idea?"

After setting down her shoes, Ellie pulled off her stockings and holding up her skirts stepped into the lake. A deep smile spread over her face as the cool water swirled around her legs, cooling her heated skin. "It is a wonderful idea!" she sighed.

Although a hint of reluctance remained in her eyes, Maryann sat down and quickly removed her shoes and stockings. Then she followed after Ellie, and as her feet sank into the cool wet, the delighted look on her face said more than a thousand words. "I've never done this before," she whispered as though betraying a secret. "Have you?"

At the memory, Ellie bit her lower lip, unable to suppress the wicked grin that came to her face.

Maryann stared at her. "What? Truly? When? I never knew you were this daring!"

Ellie laughed. "It was a while ago, but…it was well worth it."

"Did anyone see?" Maryann asked, honest shock on her face.

Again, Ellie grinned.

"Really? Who?" Maryann gaped, almost letting go of her skirts. Before they could end up in the water, she pulled them tighter around herself and took a step back up to the shore. "Tell me!"

Remembering that one fateful summer day, Ellie couldn't help but wonder. "It was Frederick actually." She laughed at her friend's shocked expression. "Maybe I should bring him here," she said, looking around the peaceful oasis somewhere far away from all the things that stood between them. "Maybe it would help him remember the man he used to be."

Returning to the stables, Ellie handed the reins of her mare to the stable boy. Another beautiful day had led her across the pastures surrounding Elmridge. Feeling the wind in her hair, she had chased the sky until a growling stomach had persuaded her to return home.

"You were gone a long time," observed a quiet voice from above.

Startled, Ellie caught her breath. "Mathilda?" she asked, then noticed the ladder leading up to the hay loft. "What are you doing up there?" After a moment of hesitation, Ellie approached the ladder. Glancing up, she quickly assured herself that no one was watching and swiftly found her way up to the hay loft. On unsteady feet, Ellie picked her way through the mounds of hay until a small head with rather dishevelled chestnut locks appeared as though out of nowhere.

"Shhh!" Mathilda cautioned, putting a finger to her lips. "Pearl and her kittens are sleeping."

"All right," Ellie whispered, and after taking a few more rather precarious steps, she sank down into the hay beside Mathilda. "If they are sleeping, then what are you doing here?"

"I'm watching over them," the girl stated as though it was the most natural thing in the world to watch over sleeping cats. "I'll make sure that nothing happens to them. I promised Pearl."

"I understand," Ellie said nodding her head as a suspicion formed in her heart. "You are true to your word. That is very honourable of you."

A delighted smile came to the girl's lips. "She trusts me."

"And rightly so," Ellie assured her, watching with delight as Mathilda's eyes began to shine with pride. "I can see that Pearl is sleeping soundly, knowing that you are watching over her and her babies."

"I wouldn't let anything happen to them!" Mathilda stated with vehemence.

Squeezing the girl's hand, Ellie smiled at her. "You are watching over them just as your mother watches over you."

A shadow fell over the girl's face at hearing her words, and her head sank.

"What makes you sad?" Ellie asked, trying to look into her face. "Is it about your mother?"

Mathilda shook her head.

"Can you not tell me?"

Shrugging her shoulders, the girl lifted her head, big, round eyes searching Ellie's face. "I am not sure you would understand. It is a question of honour."

"I see," Ellie mumbled. For a moment, she felt confused about the girl's stated reason, considering it rather odd. However, then something her father had once said to her little brother shot into her head, and she suddenly knew what Mathilda meant.

"I think we all know about honour," she said, watching the girl intently. "In our own way. Keeping a promise once given is very honourable."

Mathilda nodded.

Once Pearl and her kittens awakened, Ellie left her niece to care for them and returned to the house. She went upstairs to change out of her riding habit and then proceeded straight down to her husband's study.

Never before had she entered it, but today, his rather solemn mood of the past few days would not keep her out.

After a quick knock, Ellie opened the door and stepped across the threshold. Her husband's head snapped up from the stack of papers before him on the large desk. Closing the door behind her, Ellie approached him and found herself looking into widened eyes. Clearly, he had not expected her to seek him out.

However, Ellie was determined to pull him out of his self-inflicted isolation by force if necessary, and now, she even had a reason why she needed to speak to him. After all, it was a family matter.

"Is there anything I can do for you, my lady?" he asked, rising from his chair. Taking a step forward, he stopped as though uncomfortable with the dwindling distance between them. "May I offer you a drink?" he asked before a frown settled on his face. Apparently, he had just remembered that ladies did not drink brandy in the middle of the day. Or at all, at least as far as she was concerned.

"Thank you, no," she declined his offer and took another step toward him. Seeing his eyes narrow, she decided not to push him further. At least, not today. "I have come to speak to you about Mathilda."

"Mathilda?" he echoed, and his eyes opened wide with alarm. "Is something wrong? Has something happened to her?"

Ellie shook her head. "I apologise for alarming you. No, she is fine." He visibly relaxed, and Ellie smiled at the evidence that his heart was not as cold as he wanted her to believe.

"Then why are you here, my lady?"

With regret, Ellie noticed that he did not call her *my dear*, and in the spur of the moment, she decided to call him on it. "At the garden party, you called me 'my dear'," she reminded him, watching with delight as his eyes fell from hers and his hands began shuffling papers on his desk.

"You said you wished to speak about Mathilda," he reminded her.

Ellie smiled. "As you wish, my lord." His eyes met hers, and for a moment, she saw a hint of wonderment at her unexpectedly bold conduct. "I am concerned for her. She seems rather saddened, and I believe it would do her good if you spoke to her."

"Me?" His eyes widened, and he stared at her as though the mere thought was preposterous. "Why me? Why not her mother?"

"Maryann has spoken to her, and I believe their relationship is on the mend," she explained, taking a step toward him. His eyes followed her. "They have shared their grief over your brother's loss. However, I have reason to believe that Mathilda's current, rather strange behaviour is due to something your brother told her."

"And what would that be?" Frederick asked, his eyes now determined to ignore her.

Ellie shrugged. "I am not sure, which is why I need you to speak to her."

A frown came to his face before his eyes reluctantly focused on hers. "Then how do you know I am the one who can help her?"

Ellie smiled. "Are you so determined not to speak to her?"

Flustered at her open words, Frederick turned away, his feet carrying him over to the window. "I assure you I am not," he said, but his voice vibrated with emotions. "I merely ask because…my time is limited, and at the moment, there are quite a few issues that require my attention."

Ellie laughed, and he turned his head to stare at her before focusing his valuable attention out the window once more. "Have it as you wish, my lord," Ellie said, her steps carrying her closer to him.

At every soft *clunk* of her shoes on the parquet floor, Frederick's shoulders seemed to tense as though he thought himself the prey and her the predator. Ellie's heart softened toward him, but she refused to alter her behaviour simply because he currently disapproved.

"Well, then to answer your question, my lord," Ellie spoke to his turned back, "something she said reminded me of my father. I remember walking by his study one day, and since the door stood ajar, I heard him speaking to my brother." Slowly, Frederick turned around, honest interest in his eyes. "He spoke to him of duty and family honour." Shaking her head, Ellie laughed. "He was five at the time. However, my father never thought it too early to instil in his children a sense of duty to their family. All the same, when Mathilda told me how she had given her word to Pearl to watch over her..."

His eyes narrowed, and a confused frown appeared on his face.

"Pearl is the mother cat in the stable," Ellie explained.

A hint of a smile touched his lips before he nodded. "I see."

"Well, it felt to me as though she was acting out something her father had taught her or spoken to her about."

"But why?" Frederick asked. "Why to a cat?"

A soft smile on her face, Ellie lifted her hand and placed it on his upper arm, from where it slowly slid down before dropping to her side again.

Although she had wanted to touch him since the day they had met, now her hand had moved without conscious thought. The situation had inspired a physical sign of understanding and comfort, and she had given it without thinking about it twice.

Upon seeing Frederick's rather disconcerted face though, Ellie experienced a moment of unease. However, ignoring her own doubts, she smiled up at him. "Because she misses him, and as a child, she does not know how to handle grief any other way." Her eyes looked deep into his. "Even adults are often at a loss when something happens that changed everything they held dear, everything they believed in."

Frederick swallowed, his eyes, however, remained on hers.

"You knew your brother best," Ellie said. "Do not worry. You will know what to say." She smiled at him encouragingly, and he still did not look away. "She is a remarkable child, and sometimes children have a way of seeing the world at its simplest. They see the simple truth when adults are lost in its complicated details. Listen to her, and maybe you will find answers to your own questions."

Frederick's mouth opened then, but he only stared at her as though she was an apparition. No words left his lips, and yet, his feet

took a step forward as though her closeness was not as unbearable as it had been a moment before.

Then he smiled at her. "I will speak to her."

"Thank you," she whispered.

He nodded his head and turned to go.

"Frederick," she called after him, delighted at how his name felt on her tongue.

Again, he turned to look at her, and his eyes held a glimmer of joy as though he enjoyed hearing his name on her lips as much as she had enjoyed saying it.

A slight flush warmed her cheeks, and for a moment, her eyes dropped to the floor before meeting his once more. "Maybe one day, you will call me 'my dear' again."

His eyes narrowed, and yet, the expression on his face remained pleased. "Maybe," he whispered and left the room.

For a moment, Ellie thought she would faint as joy flooded her heart and her head began to spin.

19

SIMPLE WISDOM

aybe.

The word echoed in Frederick's head as he left the house and headed over to the stables. Before his inner eye, he saw his wife's glowing eyes and charming smile. The way she had looked up at him had taken his breath away, and he didn't even know why. In all honesty, she was not a beauty, and yet, he thought she was beautiful. The kindness and compassion, the determination and directness he always saw within everything she did amazed him. After everything that had happened to her, how could she remain so life-affirming?

Stepping into the stables, Frederick lifted his head. The scent of fresh hay tickled his nose, and he inhaled deeply. Since his return, he had spent too much time indoors, and he felt the smell of the world outside beckon him with each step he took.

A soft rustle above his head drew his attention, and reluctantly he directed his thoughts to the task at hand.

Climbing the steps to the hay loft, Frederick craned his neck, trying to spy his niece among the mounds upon mounds of golden hay.

Finally, when he was almost ready to give up, chestnut curls peeked out from a particularly large pile of the golden ears.

"Mathilda?" he called, and her head appeared, round eyes staring at him as though she was seeing a ghost.

"Uncle Frederick?" she gasped before her eyes narrowed, and she looked at him with a hint of suspicion. "What are you doing here?"

Thinking that his wife would probably advise him to be honest, Frederick said, "I came to speak to you." Her dirt-stained face remained unreadable, and he thought that she would probably make a talented spy. Shaking his head at such an absurd thought, Frederick sank into the hay beside her. "What are you doing up here?" The moment the words left his lips, his eyes caught the curled-up ball of fur beside her.

Lost in sleep, Pearl and her kittens looked completely at ease.

"I am watching over them," Mathilda answered, a sense of importance ringing in her voice.

Frederick nodded. "What makes you think they need someone to watch over them?" He glanced around. "They seem quite safe here."

Mathilda shrugged. "Everyone needs someone. Nowhere is truly safe. Bad things can always happen."

As her words echoed in his head, Frederick remembered what his wife had told him, and he realised that she had been right. As young as Mathilda was, these few simple words showed that deep down she understood the ways of the world. She knew that happiness was not a constant. It could be lost. And while her young eyes clearly saw the dangers the world held, she was still determined to do what she could to make it a safer place for those in her care.

Pride filled his heart. She was barely six years old, and yet, she already showed qualities that usually only came with age and experience.

Experience. Frederick mused.

Since the day her father had died, Mathilda had experienced many previously unknown emotions, and despite her young age, she had found a way to handle them. Deep down, Frederick envied her, knowing that he was far from such simple wisdom that his little niece possessed.

"What about you?" Frederick asked. "Who is watching over you?"

Eyes focused on her charges, Mathilda twirled a corn stalk between her fingers. "I'm not sure. Father used to."

"Would he sit by your bed and watch you sleep?"

To Frederick's surprise, Mathilda broke out laughing. However, when her charges began to stir, she reduced it to a slight chuckle.

Confused, but smiling at her nonetheless, Frederick said, "I haven't seen you laughing like this in a long time. I like it."

"Me, too," Mathilda agreed. "But you mustn't distract me like this. Pearl needs her sleep. Her kittens are quite rambunctious."

"Not unlike someone else I know," Frederick observed.

His niece viewed him through narrowed eyes. "I do what I have to in order to protect them," she defended herself. "They are young and don't yet know about the world."

Frederick nodded. "But you are young, too," he objected. "Who is watching over you?"

Mathilda shrugged.

"You miss your father, don't you?" Frederick asked, feeling a lump in his throat. "I know I was gone for a long time, but I remember how you used to play together."

Mathilda nodded. "Father never insisted I had to be a lady."

Again, Frederick laughed. "Yes, I remember finding the two of you up in a tree one day."

A deep smile came to the girl's face. "I dared him to climb up, and then he got stuck and couldn't get down. I had to go up and get him."

Frederick chuckled. "So, you were watching over each other?"

Mathilda nodded. "Wherever I went, he would always find me. He would come and make sure I was fine." Moist eyes rose to meet his. "Sometimes when I climb a tree and I almost fall, I feel like he is standing down there, ready to catch me." Absentmindedly, she twirled the corn stalk between her fingers. "I know that is silly. I know he is gone."

Covering her small hands with his, Frederick shook his head. "It is not silly." He took a deep breath. "You know, I do that, too, sometimes."

Mathilda's head snapped up. "Really? You climb trees?"

Frederick chuckled, then shook his head. "No, I don't climb trees, but sometimes I like to believe that someone is with me who I know is gone forever."

"Who?"

Frederick took a deep breath. A part of him wondered why he was telling her this—little niece of all people. Had Elsbeth known this would happen? Did she even know what the girl's secret was? If she had, why would she have asked him to speak to her? "I lost a friend of mine in the war, and he would always lecture me about being too careless. I remember riding into battle and hearing his voice in my head, screaming at me to be careful. I also remember that sometimes I tempted fate only to feel as though he was still there, watching over me." He shook his head. "I haven't heard his voice in a long time."

"You're not careless anymore?"

Frederick shook his head. "Not like that. Lately, life has changed."

"I know. Many things are different now," Mathilda agreed. "Mother cried a lot after Father died, and although she tried to smile whenever she saw me, I knew she didn't really want to." Again, her gaze met his, only this time a tentative smile played on her lips. "And then after your wedding, things changed again."

Frederick's eyebrows went up. "They have? After my wedding? How?"

"Because of Ellie."

"Ellie?" Frederick echoed, and although the name sounded unfamiliar, it stirred a strange sense of recognition. From the depth of his soul, it drew forth the soft sound of a babbling brook and the feel of the sun on a hot summer's day on his skin. And yet, the details of the memory eluded him.

"She spoke to Mama," Mathilda elaborated, one hand stroking Pearl's fur. "After your wedding, I found them sitting in the gardens. Mother cried, and at first, I was scared, but then she spoke to Ellie and," the girl sighed, and her little shoulders trembled, "and then Mother seemed better." She lifted her eyes to him. "She didn't look so sad anymore even though she was still crying. Do you know what I mean?"

Frederick nodded. He remembered the day Mathilda was talking about. He, too, had seen the two women sit in the shade and speak to each other. He had seen Maryann weep as his wife had held and comforted her.

Apparently, his mother had been right. Elsbeth had been exactly what they all needed. Not only did his mother look less exhausted with the strain of taking care of everyone, but also Maryann had finally found a way to deal with her husband's loss. She still grieved his passing, and yet, she now remembered that life still held wonders that she could not ignore. One such wonder now sat beside him, and Frederick marvelled at the change that had gone unnoticed by him. How had he not seen the improvement in their spirits? Right under his nose, his wife had worked her magic; now, he suddenly realised, she was trying to help him as well. She had sent him to speak to his niece, not only because she hoped he could help the girl but also because his niece's wise words held a deeper meaning for him as well.

Did it? He wondered. Could he actually benefit from what Mathilda had told him?

Everyone grieved in their own way, and for the first time, Frederick realised that he himself grieved by suppressing every emotion that might prove his undoing. In the beginning, it had merely been the pain, the sense of loss, of hopelessness that he had ignored, that he had pretended did not exist and could, therefore, not hurt him. However, after a while, even that had not been enough. Today, Frederick realised, he suppressed almost all emotions; be they good or bad, it did not matter. The only moments any sense of feeling had returned had been moments he had shared with his wife. How had she done it? How had she breached his walls and touch his heart? Even now, he only sat here, touched by his niece's honest words, because his wife had asked him to be there. Had she known what would happen?

Shaking his head, Frederick didn't know what to think. What was he to do now? After all, emotions were not part of his plan. Everything had gone so well up until now. Ought he to stay the course? Frederick didn't know, and yet, he knew that anything but denial would open old wounds.

And he knew he could not risk that.

20

THE HEART OF A LION

Standing at the front drawing room window, Ellie gazed out into the rain. Through the curtain of water, she watched as the sun slowly began its descent, giving the world a magical glow. For days now, the rain had confined them all to the house, and while Mathilda's spirits seemed suddenly lifted, Frederick walked the halls with his gaze fixed to the ground. Whenever they happened upon one another, he would speak to her in a polite, but rather detached tone, his eyes never meeting hers. Somehow, Ellie had hoped that helping Mathilda would help him as well. Could he not see that the world still held wonder? Had the strength of a little girl not also instilled in him the wish for better days?

Ellie sighed, wondering what else she could do to breach the wall he once again seemed determined to defend against any outside influence. Did he see her as a threat?

"Elsbeth."

Startled, Ellie spun around and found Theresa standing in the doorway.

"Forgive me, Child," her mother-in-law said, coming toward her. "I did not mean to alarm you. Do you have a minute for an old woman?"

"Certainly," Ellie said, taking Theresa's offered hand, and the two of them sat down on the settee. "Is something wrong? You do look rather heavy-hearted."

Theresa took a deep breath, then turned to Ellie. "Ever since your wedding day, I have been meaning to speak with you. I know that my son is less than forthcoming with regard to family affairs as well as his own thoughts on these issues so that I deem it my responsibility to explain to you the steps that led to your wedding."

Staring at Theresa, Ellie took a deep breath. "I always thought it was you who chose me for him."

A pleased smile lit up the old woman's features. "You are an intelligent woman, Elsbeth, and I beg your forgiveness for bringing you into this house without your consent."

Ellie smiled and squeezed Theresa's hand. "I cannot deny that the offer of marriage came as quite a shock to me, but I can honestly say that it was not unwelcome."

Theresa sighed with relief. "You have no idea how good it is to hear you say that, my dear girl. Especially now that I have come to love you like a daughter, I would not wish to see you unhappy."

Touched beyond words, Ellie met Theresa's honest eyes as her own filled with tears. "Thank you," she breathed. "I think of you as a mother as well."

A delighted smile on her face, Theresa patted her hand. "You have been a blessing on this house. Everyone under its roof has benefited from your presence here, and in time, my son will come to see this, too."

Averting her eyes, Ellie took a deep breath. Finally, she could ask the many questions that had plagued her since the day of the proposal, and yet, she feared to learn the answers. Raising her eyes to her mother-in-law's once again, she asked, "May I enquire why you chose me?"

Theresa smiled. "Why would I not?"

Shaking her head, Ellie closed her eyes. "I have tried very hard not to allow people's opinion affect who I am," she whispered as though to herself. "However, I have recently come to realise that I am not as strong as I like to think." Gazing at her scarred hands, Ellie shrugged. "I may have survived the fire, but many things have changed." She looked up and met Theresa's gaze. "When people learnt of the proposal made to me, they were surprised, shocked even. They can see that I am no equal to your son."

Once again, Theresa squeezed her hand, her eyes lingering on Ellie for a moment. "Let me tell you why I chose you."

Ellie nodded, feeling her hands tremble beyond her control.

"For the first time, I saw you one night at a ball. Like many others, I cannot deny that my eyes were drawn to you. I saw your scars and remembered the stories I had heard. And then I looked at you and saw something that I'd never thought possible."

When Theresa remained quiet, Ellie asked, "What? What was it?" Feeling her fingernails dig into her palm, she held her breath.

"I saw you smile," Theresa said, and although her eyes held tears, pride shone on her face. "It was a heart-felt smile, a smile that spoke neither of duty nor perseverance. It was not forced or half-hearted. You were enjoying yourself, and in that moment, I realised that a woman who cannot only endure such physical pain but also rise above the whispers and stares around her had to have the heart of a lion."

Tears streamed down Ellie's face. "But I don't. I am weak. I thought I was strong, but lately I feel like I cannot bear these scars any longer."

"We all feel alone sometimes and disheartened." Lifting Ellie's chin, Theresa made her look at her. "Sometimes we all want to give up and lie down and die because we believe that we do not have the strength to go on or because we do not believe the struggle worth it." A knowing smile crinkled her lips. "But the moment passes, and in the next, we are strong again."

"But I am not—"

"Yes, you are," Theresa insisted. "But you are not only strong. You are also kind and caring, and when I saw my son or rather the shadow he had become, I remembered you. I remembered your strength, and I knew that if there were one woman on this earth who would be able to save him from himself, it would be you." Theresa squeezed her hand, her eyes intent on Ellie's. "You know the meaning of pain, of loss, of struggle and of hopelessness. You have walked through hell, and yet, you are still an angel inside. If anyone can help him, it is you."

As Ellie broke down sobbing, Theresa held her, smoothing back her hair as a mother would. She rocked her, and she stroked her back, and slowly Ellie calmed down.

"Thank you," Ellie whispered, brushing the tears from her eyes. "It means so much to me to hear you say that, to know that you have such faith in me." Although Rosabel had voiced a similar thought about why Frederick's mother had chosen her, hearing the truth from Theresa now soothed the ache in Ellie's heart. To stand alone against doubts as well as those around her who expected her to fail was daunting, and to know that there was someone walking with her meant the world to Ellie.

Handing her a handkerchief, Theresa looked at her with sad eyes. "Although I know what it feels like to be at your wits' end, to have your heart broken and the world to look like hell itself, I now know that I cannot help my son. Maybe it is simply because I am his mother. As much as we love each other, I suppose some things you cannot speak about to your mother." She shrugged. "I suppose it is the same where the mother is concerned." Theresa took a deep breath, and a sad smile came to her face. "When my husband died, Frederick was on the continent, but I remember I could not talk to Leopold, either. He was my son, and he grieved, too, and I didn't want to burden him." Theresa's eyes became distant, and Ellie watched her quietly, knowing only too well the pain memories could cause. "The one I could speak to was Maryann. As much as she means to me, I never held her as a baby. I did not spend twenty-odd years worrying about her heart and soul, her well-being and health. I cannot explain it any better, but I know it is different when it is your child. Unfortunately, Maryann knows that now, too. I've seen how she desperately tried to shield Mathilda from her own pain because the need to protect her child, to keep it away from pain is stronger than the desire to confide in someone about your own feelings of loss." Blinking, Theresa shook her head, and her eyes focused on Ellie once more. "I apologise. I did not mean to speak of such gloomy matters."

Gently squeezing her mother-in-law's hand, Ellie asked, "How did your husband die?"

Theresa inhaled deeply, and Ellie saw how acutely she still grieved his passing. "He died of a cold."

"A cold?" Ellie asked, unable to suppress her surprise. "How do you mean?"

A sad smile on her face, Theresa shook her head. "He had a slight fever and a mild cough. It lasted a couple of days, and finally he agreed to send for Dr. Madison. The doctor said not to worry, and Archibald insisted I attend the function that night. I don't even remember what it was. Everything else is burned into my mind, but these details are gone. Whatever they were, they did not matter." She took a deep breath. "I kissed him goodbye, and he laughed at me for looking so distraught. Against my own better judgement, I left, and when I returned home, he was dead."

Shocked, Ellie stared at her mother-in-law, not knowing what to say.

"You see, my dear, life is unpredictable and fleeting. When I look at my son, I fear not only for his well-being, but also for his life. After losing his father and brother, I could not bear to lose him, too. To be honest, I brought you into this house for selfish reasons." She shook her head vehemently as tears stood in her eyes. "I cannot lose more of my family. I won't survive."

Nodding, Ellie drew the frail-looking woman into her arms and let her mourn the losses she had suffered. "I will do what I can," she whispered in her ear. "I promise."

21

TEMPTATION

"*B*etty, have you seen Lady Mathilda any-where?" Ellie asked as she saw the maid entering the second floor from the servant staircase. "She said she wanted to go outside into the gardens. How-ever, I cannot seem to find her."

Betty shook her head, and a heavy lump settled in Ellie's stom-ach. "I have not seen her, my lady. Would you like me to ask around?"

"Yes, please," Ellie replied. "But quietly. I do not wish to alarm her mother. She is probably just hiding somewhere. Would you mind going down to the stables? She loves to sit in the hay loft. I'll go speak to her mother and try to find out if she knows where Lady Mathilda went."

Betty nodded eagerly and immediately set off, the hint of a smile on her lips.

Taking a deep breath, Ellie headed downstairs as well. This time of day, Maryann usually sat in the back parlour over some em-broidery.

Every step felt heavy, though, and she could not shake the dread that settled in her heart. Had something happened to the little girl? It was not unusual for her to hide out somewhere; however, in the past week, she had been particularly cheerful. Ellie suspected that Frederick had something to do with that. Whenever Mathilda saw him, a deep smile lit up her features, and she waved to him, a cheerful word on her tongue. Ever since he had gone to speak to her, they had seemed closer somehow, like confidantes sharing a secret.

Although she did not know what they had spoken about, Ellie loved him for the change he had brought about in the little girl. Seeing them smile at each other—even though Frederick's smile seemed a bit reluctant—truly warmed her heart and made her hope for the future.

Gathering her composure, Ellie entered the drawing room, hoping that Betty would find Mathilda before circumstances would force her to alarm Maryann.

However, as she turned to the settee under the tall windows opening to the gardens, she found mother and daughter sitting side by side, heads bent over a cushion. Slowly, Maryann guided the needle through the fabric as her daughter watched in silent awe. Maryann's lips moved, and a quiet word was exchanged between them, one that brought a sparkle to Mathilda's eyes and drew a soft chuckle from her lips.

Touched by the peaceful sight before her, Ellie retreated quietly. Walking back to the foyer, she realised that she had never seen mother and daughter in such intimate togetherness. A surge of hope, of blissful lightness lifted her heart, and a single tear escaped, running down her cheek. Closing her eyes, Ellie stood in the large hall, savouring the moment before she heard footsteps echo on the marble floor.

"Are you all right, my lady?" Frederick asked as she opened her eyes. His own were narrowed as they followed the wet trail the tear had left on her cheek. "Did something happen?"

A deep smile came to her face, and she stepped toward him. Although he did not retreat, she saw him tense. "I just found Maryann and Mathilda sitting in the drawing room, embroidering a cushion." A confused frown came to his face. "Thank you for that."

The frown deepened. "I'm afraid, I do not understand."

Again, she took a step toward him and placed a hand on his chest, right above his heart. He drew in a sharp breath, and even through the layers of fabric, Ellie could feel it quicken its pace. "Whatever you said to Mathilda, it helped her with her grief. I think her little heart is beginning to heal."

Absentmindedly, he nodded, his eyes looking down into hers. "I am glad," he whispered. "She deserves to be happy."

Ellie shivered as his breath tickled her skin, and for a short moment, she forgot everything around her. Nothing mattered. Not her scars. Not his grief. Not the distance between them. In that moment, Ellie felt like her old self, and an old instinct took over, an instinct fuelled by desire.

Without conscious thought, Ellie found her hand moving upward until it curled around his neck. All the while, his eyes remained on hers, and although he did not draw her into his arms, neither did he withdraw from her.

His lips were so close that Ellie could smell the hint of mint tea on his breath. More than anything, she wanted to know what it would feel like to kiss him.

Before she could make up her mind, he suddenly blinked, and the spell was broken.

Eyes flitting around the room, lingering anywhere but on hers, Frederick cleared his throat. As he stepped back, her hand fell to her side. "I apologise, my lady," he croaked, then bowed to her and quickly departed.

Staring after him, Ellie tried to maintain her composure. She knew he needed time, and still, that knowledge did not keep away the pain that invaded her heart. The only comfort she could draw around herself like a thick blanket on a cold winter's day was that for a moment he, too, had seemed tempted.

What had ultimately made him withdraw? She wondered. Had it been her scars? Or rather a scar of his own?

If she only knew.

Shaking her head, Ellie forced her thoughts back to the present. Even though he had not kissed her, the distance between them did not seem as insurmountable as it had before. Step by step, she was bridging the gap, and eventually, he would come to realise that there was no need to protect himself from her.

She only had to be patient.

Feeling the sudden need to move in her limbs, Ellie returned upstairs and changed into her riding habit. The careful control she had to exhibit around her husband proved a greater strain on her nerves than she had anticipated, and a chase across the green pastures around Elmridge would surely allow her to release some of that strain.

Striding across the front court with long strides, Ellie wondered where Betty was. She had not responded to her ringing. Was she still in the stables looking for Mathilda? Ellie hoped she would find her there and put her mind at ease. The child was safe, after all.

Entering the stables, Ellie welcomed the smell of fresh hay. She inhaled deeply, and a smile spread over her face. Compared to the blinding sunshine outside, the dim light in the stable proved soothing to Ellie's nerves, and she welcomed the peaceful silence around her.

Until a soft giggle echoed to her ears.

Instantly, her head snapped around, eyes staring down the aisle between the two rows of boxes. *Betty?*

For a moment, Ellie remained rooted to the spot as her ears listened intently, and she tried to understand the sounds she was hearing.

Betty was not alone. From the quiet whispers she heard, Ellie suspected it to be Peter, the stable master.

Intrigued, Ellie quietly proceeded down the aisle. A part of her knew she should simply return to the house and pretend none of this had happened. However, another part of her wondered what exactly *was* happening.

Feeling the almost desperate need to confirm her suspicions and satisfy her curiosity, Ellie placed one foot before the other, always careful not to make a sound and alarm the two people so lost in each other. Every time she approached on open door to an empty horsebox, her breath caught in her throat and her heart hammered as though it wanted to burst from her chest. Only upon seeing that the box was indeed empty—not only of horses but also people—did it resume at a more normal rhythm.

By the time Ellie reached the far wall of the stable with only one more box on either side of the aisle, her skin was crawling with anticipation held in check. Almost swaying on her feet, she balled her hands into fists and forced her nerves back under control. Oh, how humiliating it would be to be discovered by them now!

Taking a deep breath, she leaned forward, her ears humming with the sounds of pleasure rising from the box to her left. Back pressed against the wall, Ellie peeked around the corner, and once again, her breath caught in her throat.

Arms wrapped around each other, Betty and Peter stood leaning against the far wall. Holding her close, Peter trailed kisses down her neck while his hands eagerly explored her body. To Ellie's relief, Betty's eyes remained closed as she arched her neck and bit her lip.

A rush of heat flooded Ellie's cheeks at the sight; however, she couldn't seem to avert her eyes. When Peter lifted his head and captured Betty's lips, Ellie felt like she would faint any second. Her heart hammered in her chest, and a wave of desire washed over her. Why was it that Frederick's touch didn't make her feel like this?

Because he barely touches you, her voice of reason whispered.

Stepping back, Ellie leaned back against the wall and closed her eyes. Her ears, though, still listened to the cacophony of sounds the two lovers made, and a sudden anger came to Ellie's heart. How dare Frederick keep that from her? As her husband, was it not his responsibility to teach her the pleasures of the marriage bed? Then, why hadn't he?

Looking down at her burned hands, Ellie swallowed as tears came to her eyes. Did he not desire her? She had to know. Somehow she had to find out if they could ever have what she had witnessed today.

THE ONE QUESTION

ll night, the images of Betty and Peter danced before her eyes, and more than ever, Ellie wished that Frederick would come to her.

But he didn't. He hadn't, not since the garden party.

The next morning, when she joined the rest of the family in the breakfast parlour, Ellie felt a deep flush come to her cheeks as she met her husband's eyes.

Without thinking, she quickly averted her own.

"Are you all right, my lady?" he asked, his voice tinged by concern and a hint of curiosity. "You seem rather flustered."

A slight gasp escaped her lips before she once more raised her eyes to his. "I am fine. Thank you."

For a moment, his gaze remained on hers as though trying to decipher what she would not tell him, and as though he could read her thoughts, he suddenly blinked and returned his gaze to the plate before him, clearing his throat. "I am glad," he mumbled into his muffin.

Intrigued, Ellie watched him. Had he somehow known the line of her thoughts? Had there been something in her eyes that had told him about her desires? Could he somehow tell that she wanted nothing more but to feel his lips on hers, his hands on her body?

Blushing at her own thoughts, Ellie smiled into her napkin.

Walking the gardens after breakfast, lost in her own thoughts, Ellie started when Maryann suddenly came upon her. Hand clutched to her chest, she closed her eyes and took a deep breath.

"I apologise," her sister-in-law said. "I did not mean to startle you. Are you all right?"

"Do not worry," Ellie assured her. "I was just…thinking."

"And smiling," Maryann added, a big grin on her face.

"I was?"

Nodding her head, Maryann drew Ellie toward the bench under the oak tree by the water fountain. "Tell me what is going on. I have never seen you smile like that or, at least, not until breakfast this morning."

Ellie's eyes grew round, and she stared at her friend.

"Don't worry. No one else saw," she chuckled, "except for Frederick, I suppose."

Burying her heated cheeks in her hands, Ellie sighed. "I don't know what to do."

"About what?" Maryann asked. "Tell me what is on your mind. I can see that something has changed between the two of you."

Licking her lips, Ellie didn't know where to begin. She did not want to compromise Betty and Peter, and yet, she needed to tell someone or she would burst. "Well, yesterday I saw something or rather someone and they…" Seeing the frown on Maryann's face, Ellie knew she needed to be a lot more explicit in order for her friend to understand what she was talking about. "All right, but you have to promise me not to breath a word to anyone about what I am about to tell you."

Taking Ellie's hands in hers, Maryann nodded. "I promise."

Relieved, Ellie took a deep breath. "Yesterday, I wanted to go for a ride. However, when I came to the stables, I…I heard something." Again, she saw a puzzled look on Maryann's face. "So, I walked past the row of boxes to the far wall, and there in the last box, I found…Betty and Peter." Biting her lower lip, Ellie looked at her friend.

For a moment, Maryann just looked back at her before her eyes opened wide and an astonished "Oh!" escaped her lips. Shifting in her seat, she swallowed. "You mean, they were…?"

As more heat rose to her cheeks, Ellie nodded.

"All right," Maryann mumbled as though to herself before her eyes once more rose to meet Ellie's. "May I ask? How does seeing them make you smile? I don't understand. I thought something had happened between you and Frederick."

"Well, I…eh…" Wringing her hands, Ellie sighed. "To be honest, I am a little uncomfortable talking about this." She shook her head, trying to decide what to do. "And yet, I feel like I need to because I really don't know what to do."

An understanding smile on her face, Maryann looked at her with gentle eyes. "Again, I promise not to breathe a word of this to anyone. Please, do not feel as though you cannot talk to me. After all, it was you who reminded me how important it is to be able to express your feelings and have someone listen." She took Ellie's hands in hers. "You did that for me. Please, allow me to do the same for you."

Touched, Ellie smiled at her friend. "You're right. And believe me it is not that I do not trust you to keep this to yourself. It is just a little embarrassing. To tell you the truth, I am not sure how I feel about it myself."

"All right," Maryann said. "I think I understand. From what you have said so far, I assume…it has something to do with the marriage bed." As a slight flush rose to Maryann's own cheeks, she glanced into Ellie's eyes. "Am I right?"

Ellie nodded, a sense of relief washing over her. "You are." Taking a deep breath, Ellie tried to put all her contradicting emotions into words that Maryann could understand. "From what I saw at the stables, I think that…eh…Betty enjoyed Peter's touch." Saying out loud what she had thought about all night felt oddly liberating, and yet, a hint of humiliation came to her heart at revealing her innermost thoughts to someone else.

"And you don't enjoy Frederick's?" Maryann asked. Although Ellie could clearly see that her friend felt rather uncomfortable discussing this topic as well, Maryann would not be deterred, determined to return the gesture of friendship Ellie had given her.

"He barely touches me," Ellie admitted, her head bowed as though revealing a character flaw of her own. "And he hasn't come to my bed in weeks. Quite obviously, he did not enjoy it, either." Taking a deep breath, Ellie looked at Maryann. "Can I ask you? What was it like for you and Leopold?"

Maryann swallowed. However, the hint of sadness that still lingered in her eyes at the mention of her husband's name was quickly replaced by a delighted twinkle. She met Ellie's eyes then, and a smile spread over her face. "It was always very…enjoyable. For both of us."

"From the way you speak about him, I thought it had been," Ellie said. "Just as it is for Betty and Peter. Is it only if two people are in love? I cannot help but wonder. Betty clearly loves Peter. She's been humming and singing for weeks now, and a constant smile decorates her features. Now, I know why." Ellie squeezed Maryann's hand. "And I know that you and Leopold loved each other very much."

Maryann drew a deep breath and nodded, tears collecting in the corners of her eyes. "We did," she mumbled and dabbed at her eyes. Then she shook off the sadness that had claimed her so suddenly and turned to Ellie. "But you do care for Frederick, do you not?"

"I do," Ellie admitted. "I just don't know if he cares for me." When Maryann opened her mouth to object, Ellie stopped her. "Listen, I know that he is a kind man and that the past holds its sway over him. I also know that…well, I think that he likes me, the person I am inside. And every now and then, when our eyes meet, I think that there could be more, but he always turns away and leaves." Ellie swallowed, trying to keep her wits about her as dark emotions encroached on her heart. "I suppose what I am wondering is if he could ever feel about me the way that Leopold felt about you. I know I am not beautiful anymore, but am I truly so hideous that he could never enjoy touching me? I think it is mostly this question that is holding me back. Yesterday, I almost kissed him, but then…I wasn't brave enough. I don't know if I could live with his rejection. Maybe I'd rather not know." Again, Ellie took a deep breath, finally realising the one question she needed to have answered. "So, I suppose what I want to know, what I need to know is, is it *my* scars keeping us apart or his?"

"Why don't you ask him?" Maryann suggested. "I'd think not knowing, always wondering is worse than anything else. It will torment you for the rest of your life."

Ellie nodded. "I know it will, but even if I could find the courage to ask him, would he tell me the truth? Or would he simply lie to spare my feelings?"

Maryann remained silent.

"No, asking him will not give me an honest answer," Ellie determined. "The problem is I don't know what will. And until I find out what is standing between us, nothing will ever change."

23

A MESSAGE

Spending his days locked up in his study, Frederick noticed the veil of detachment once again fall over his heart. By now, he knew that the good always came with the bad. He could not experience joy without pain, and the pain that lived in his heart would overwhelm him should he ever dare release it. And so he kept himself isolated from the people around him. He had noticed smiles and laughter returning to the manor, and a small part of him was glad for his family. However, another, larger part of him did not care, at all.

A knock on the door shifted his attention from the papers before him.

Wilton entered, giving a slight bow. "You have a visitor, my lord. Lady Charlotte."

The blood drained from his face as Frederick stared at his butler. His muscles grew tense, and the pain in his heart strained against its shackles.

Swallowing, Frederick rose to his feet. "See her in."

Wilton bowed and left, returning moments later with Charlotte in his wake.

Her usually glowing eyes seemed dim as they met his. Hair tucked back under her hat, she did not look like the young woman she was. Incredible sadness tainted her beautiful features, and the weight of her stare almost brought Frederick to his knees. Looking at her, he couldn't help but wonder where she found the strength to rise in the morning.

"Hello Frederick," she greeted him, and her voice sounded as weak as her body looked. In fact, she seemed almost terminally ill, and Frederick had to keep himself from taking her by the elbow and escorting her to the seats under the window front.

"Charlotte," he whispered instead, glancing past her at the closed door. "Did you not bring your mother?"

An almost soundless chuckle rose from her throat. "I do not care about my reputation. Any hopes for a future died with Kenneth."

Frederick took a deep breath as her eyes remained fixed on his. He felt as though he was being weighed. At a loss, he offered her a refreshment, but she declined.

Instead, she walked over to the armchair facing his desk and sat down. Opening her reticule, she drew out a letter. "I came to give you this."

Reaching out, Frederick took the letter from her hand. As his eyes slid over the front, he recognised Kenneth's handwriting, *To Sir Frederick Lancaster.*

As the world began to spin before his eyes, Frederick sank into his chair. Staring at Charlotte across the desk, he noticed that her eyes were still focused on him. She didn't even blink.

"It's all right," she said. "Open it."

Running his fingers over the smooth paper, Frederick hesitated. "How did you get this?"

"Before you left for the war, Kenneth gave me a small box." She swallowed, then drew in a deep breath. "He made me promise only to open it should he not return home. It sat on my vanity all this time. I looked at it every day. At first, I hoped I would never know what was inside, that he would come home safe and sound. But then, when…" For a moment, she closed her eyes. "I couldn't bring myself to open it. Opening it would mean he was truly gone." Her eyes once again dug a hole into his soul. "I only opened it this morning."

"I see," Frederick mumbled, not knowing what to say. The pain he saw etched in her eyes echoed through his heart, and his own strained against its shackles with greater force.

Once more, his eyes returned to the letter in his hand, and for a second, he could almost believe that Kenneth was still alive. His finger skimmed the words written there, and Frederick wasn't sure if he wanted to know what message lay beneath.

"He left me a letter as well," Charlotte said, her eyes resting on his. "I haven't opened it yet. I need you to open yours first."

"Why?"

She shrugged. "I just do." She swallowed. "Do you mind?"

Breaking the seal, Frederick drew out the single sheet of paper. Gently, he unfolded it, then turned his eyes to his friend's writing.

Dear Rick,

I feel compelled to write this letter because in my heart I know I shall not return. I cannot say what makes me certain of this, but the need to protect those I love still remains.

All my life, you've been the brother I never had. I love you dearly, and I know that we were always meant to walk through life side by side. From where I am now, I will continue to watch over you, be assured of that, for I know that guilt now resides in your heart.

As often as I have lectured you, I also know that you've turned a deaf ear most of the time. But listen to me now. We all make our own choices, and we all need to make our peace with them. I have made mine for better or for worse, the way I saw fit, and even if you think you could or should have swayed me from my path, know that you could not have. Just as I have never been able to sway you from yours.

Do not blame yourself as I know you do. You are a good man, a good friend, and I wish you well. Remember me, but do not forget the people who need you and love you. One day, we shall meet again, I am certain. But until then, do not waste your days in darkness.

I ask only one thing: look out for Charlotte. She will have need of your strong arm as well as your kind heart. Protect her as you would your own.

Your brother-in-arms and in life,

Kenneth

153

As his eyes shifted from the words before him, Frederick felt tears stream down his cheeks. Why was it that Kenneth's death plagued him so when his father's and brother's barely touched his heart?

"He has a way of knowing exactly what to say, does he not?" Charlotte whispered, her own eyes bathed in tears as well.

Frederick nodded, brushing the wetness off his cheeks. "More than once, I thought he knew me better than I know myself. I do not know how to go on without his counsel."

Charlotte nodded. "Neither do I."

"I do not know what to say, Charlotte." Frederick put down the letter and met her eyes. "But my offer stands. Should you ever need anything, all you need to do is ask."

"Thank you," Charlotte whispered, rising from her chair. "I will remember that."

Stepping around his desk, Frederick opened the door. "Allow me to escort you to your carriage."

"I came on horseback."

Frederick stopped in his tracks and stared at her.

"All my life, I have lived by the rules," Charlotte said, her voice sounding defeated. "And it has brought me nothing but misery. If I hadn't…" She gritted her teeth and for a moment closed her eyes as though forcing the words back down. "Now, I will do as I please, and I ask you to respect that."

Frederick nodded, understanding only too well the sense of hopelessness that shone in her eyes. All of a sudden, nothing mattered anymore as though her own life had ended the day Kenneth had died. And yet, everyone around her expected her to care about the pettiness of life. Frederick knew it had to drive her mad.

Standing on the front stoop, he bid his friend's fiancée good-bye. "Be well, Charlotte."

Not saying a word, she mounted her mare. Then her eyes turned to him once more, and the pain he saw there almost choked the life from him. What suffering had he brought on her? If he had only insisted Kenneth stay home. If he had only…

Watching her ride down the drive, Frederick raked his hands through his hair. His muscles clenched, and he felt the desperate need to move, to run, to fight. If only he could return to the continent and throw his pain and misery into battling the enemy. The hatred he felt surge to the surface could be released no other way without hurting the few remaining people he still cared about…deep down.

Storming across the yard, he stripped off his overcoat and flung it on the ground. As he rushed into the stables, Peter jumped up. "Good afternoon, my lord. Is there—?"

Ignoring his stable master, Frederick strode down the aisle to his gelding's box. He grabbed his saddle resting on a hook on the wall and threw the bridle over the bay's head. Gritting his teeth so hard he thought they would crack, Frederick swung himself into the saddle that had carried him around the world and urged on his horse.

Without regard for anything, they shot out of the stable and up the hill leading to the expansive pastures surrounding the manor. As they flew across a sea of grass, Frederick closed his eyes, then opened them again.

The world remained the same.

The wind whipped in his face and burned in his eyes. Tears streamed down his cheeks, and pain burned in his heart. Would it ever end? Would he be forced to continue his life on the brink between dull detachedness and crippling pain? Was there no safe way to feel?

Spurring his gelding on, Frederick screamed with frustration. Remembering the moment that had torn Kenneth out of life, he wished for a sudden attack. Some unseen force that would unhorse him. That would throw him onto the ground, breaking his bones. That would finally end this agony.

In that moment, the saddle girth snapped.

24

BLINDING PAIN

As her husband stormed across the courtyard, Ellie retreated back into the manor. Who was that woman that had brought such a pained expression to Frederick's eyes? She had looked familiar, but only when Ellie saw Frederick's expression, did she remember the night Leopold had died.

That night, the woman had come to the Midnight ball and spoken to Frederick on the terrace. Then, too, his face had taken on a tortured expression. What news had she brought? What past did they share?

Feeling a sense of dread settle in her stomach, Ellie walked through the house without a sense of direction. In her heart, she knew that the woman's effect on her husband bothered her more than she liked to admit. Could it be that Frederick did not warm to her because he loved another? Did they share a doomed love? Why had he not married her instead? His mother surely would not have refused his wishes.

Ellie's head spun, and she sank onto the settee in the front parlour.

How long she sat there, Ellie could not say. However, her inner reflections were suddenly interrupted when a soft hand came to rest on her shoulder.

Instantly, her head snapped up, and she looked into Theresa's gentle eyes.

"She was his friend's fiancée," her mother-in-law said, and a relieved sigh escaped Ellie's lips as she clasped her hands to her face.

Feeling Theresa sit down beside her, Ellie did her utmost to stop the tears that threatened. Never before had she realised just how deep her feelings for Frederick ran.

"His name was Kenneth Moreton, Viscount Hutchins," Theresa said. "He was killed in battle six months before Frederick returned home."

As her hands sank into her lap, Ellie turned to her mother-in-law. "I have heard his name before," she whispered, once again remembering the day she had waded into the brook. "They were friends since childhood; were they not?"

Theresa nodded. "Despite their differences in character, they were like brothers. Kenneth always followed wherever Frederick would lead, and Frederick always watched over Kenneth no matter what the circumstances. There was a special bond between them."

Remembering the agony in Frederick's eyes upon seeing his dead friend's fiancée, Ellie realised that most of her husband's pain stemmed from the unresolved issues caused by his friend's death. It was the incident that had torn apart his soul, keeping him from opening his heart to all that had followed, be it his father's and brother's death or the love of his family.

"He never speaks about him, does he?"

Theresa shook her head. "No, he refuses to. Only Oliver sometimes dares to open these wounds Frederick so carefully shields. However, to this day, I suppose it has done little good." Turning sad eyes to Ellie, Theresa patted her knee. "Oliver does not understand the meaning of pain, physical or emotional. As much as he tries, only personal experience can make us truly understand such agony."

Ellie nodded, seeing clearly in her mother-in-law's eyes the hope that she as his wife would find a way to ease her son's suffering.

Ellie only hoped she would not disappoint her.

For all their sakes.

The remainder of the day, Ellie spent pacing the front parlour. After everything her mother-in-law had said, her mind reinterpreted every situation she could remember. Trying to look at her husband's behaviour in a different light, Ellie came to understand the fear that lived in his heart. Despite his strong exterior, he was terrified of the weakness he knew could swallow him whole.

When the blazing sun slowly dimmed and evening approached, Ellie's head snapped up and she finally realised how late it was. Hours had passed since Frederick had stormed off, and yet, he had not returned. Or had he? Had she been so occupied and not noticed?

Walking back to the front hall, Ellie stopped Wilton in his tracks. "Have you seen his lordship?"

"I believe he went for a ride, my lady."

Fear settled in her heart. "He has not returned yet?"

"No, my lady."

"Thank you," she mumbled and hastened to find her mother-in-law but then stopped before she had taken more than a few steps. Ought she to alert Theresa? After all, she wouldn't know where Frederick was, either. If Wilton said her husband had not returned yet, then he simply hadn't. Wilton always knew where everybody was, maybe with the exception of Mathilda. The young girl often disappeared without out a trace, hiding in every nook and cranny all over the manor and its side buildings, only to reappear suddenly out of thin air.

Stepping outside, Ellie gazed across the gardens and then proceeded around the manor toward the stables. Frederick had stormed off in anger. Could he be so blinded by his emotions that something had happened to him? Her insides twisted at the thought.

Determined, Ellie entered the stables. "Peter, saddle my horse," she instructed, ignoring his rather stunned expression. After all, her dress was suitable for having tea, not chasing her husband across his estate. However, there was no time to change, and so Ellie led her mare out of the stables and swung herself into the saddle.

Following in the direction Frederick had taken, Ellie urged her horse onward and circled the stables toward the pastures that lay beyond. Her eyes scanned the horizon, finding nothing but endless sky, nothing to give her a clue as to where he had gone.

When she was about to spur her horse onward and up the slight hill, she stopped as her eyes finally settled on something.

Or rather someone.

A small distance from her, Ellie spotted a man walking up the hill toward her, his horse trotting by his side. Although he was tall, he held himself hunched-over, his right arm clutched to his left shoulder. As she stared, his face came into view.

Ellie drew in a sharp breath at the pain she saw there. "Peter!" she called, then urged her horse onward.

Her mare shot forward and within a few long strides, she was by his side. Sliding out of the saddle, Ellie rushed to her husband. "What happened?" she asked, seeing blood run from a cut on his forehead.

Panting under his breath, Frederick looked like he would faint any second.

In that moment, Peter and a few stable hands reached their side, taking the horses and helping her husband down the slope and into the manor.

Wilton's eyes grew wide at the sight of his master's distorted face.

"Call for Dr. Madison," Ellie instructed, and the butler hurried off. Then she turned back to the stable hands and pointed up the large staircase. "Take him upstairs to his chambers. I'll be up immediately."

Gritting his teeth, Frederick eased himself onto the bed. Instantly, a blinding pain shot through his shoulder, and for a moment, he thought he would crumble to the ground. Only Peter's steady hands held him upright. "It's dislocated, my lord."

"I know," Frederick snarled taking a deep breath and waited for the pain to subside. He closed his eyes and tried to breathe evenly.

Footsteps approached, and then his mother's voice drifted to his ears, "Frederick?"

Opening his eyes, he forced a reassuring smile on his face and met her worried gaze. "Hello, Mother."

Shaking her head, she inspected his shoulder. "It's dislocated."

"So I've heard," he forced out through clenched teeth. If they would only leave him alone!

"If you would please leave us now," his wife spoke, and Frederick glanced around his mother. Elsbeth stood by the doorway, ushering everyone outside. "Send Dr. Madison up as soon as he arrives." Then she closed the door.

After setting a wicker basket on the bedside table, she came to stand beside his mother, her eyes gliding over his injuries. Never before had Frederick felt so vulnerable as when her gaze slid over him in such a perusing way, and he averted his eyes.

"I will clean the cut on his forehead," she said, then returned to the bedside table and retrieved a bottle of cooking port and a clean cloth. "Do you have any other injuries beside this cut and the dislocated shoulder?"

"I don't think so," Frederick answered, starting to feel more and more uncomfortable with the level of contact this situation forced on him.

After pouring some of the port on the linen cloth, his wife came to stand beside him, and his heart nearly stopped when she placed a gentle hand under his chin and carefully tilted up his head. Never had she touched him like this before!

As she began cleaning his wound, he barely felt the sting of the alcohol. Instead, he felt her warm breath on his cheek, and a shiver went down his back. He swallowed, and his eyes were once again drawn to her. Her brows slightly furrowed in concentration, she bit her lower lip as she worked, and despite the pain in his shoulder, Frederick wondered what her lips would feel like on his own.

"There," she finally said, straightening up. "The cut should heal fine." When her fingers left his chin, Frederick regretted the loss of their touch immediately. Clearing his throat, he swallowed, forcing his thoughts back under control.

After a short knock, the door opened, and Dr. Madison strode into the room. "I heard you took a little tumble," he joked, and Frederick rolled his eyes at the haggard-looking doctor. Thin like a broomstick, Dr. Madison, with his few remaining hairs and child-like smile, approached the bed, eyeing him carefully. "I never thought I'd live to see the day you fall off a horse."

Frederick grunted. "I didn't fall. The saddle girth snapped."

Dr. Madison shrugged, probing a gentle finger at his injured shoulder.

A growl rose from Frederick's throat. "Was that necessary, Doctor?"

Grinning, Dr. Madison shrugged, and Frederick wondered if the doctor had any undisclosed issues with him. "We need to remove the shirt."

His mother stepped forward and tried to slide it off his shoulder.

Instantly, a searing pain brought Frederick to his knees.

Soft hands kept him from falling flat on his face, and as he looked up, he found his wife's eyes only a breath's length away from his own. Pulling on his uninjured shoulder, she eased him back onto the bed. "Look in the basket. There should be a pair of scissors," she said to his mother and held out her hand to receive them. Then, she carefully cut away his shirt.

As her fingertips brushed over his heated skin, another shiver went down his back, and the dull pain in his shoulder was almost forgotten. It had been a long time since gentle hands had touched him!

"Very well then," Dr. Madison said, rubbing his hands. "Shall we?"

Staring at the thin, old man, Frederick wondered if he even possessed the strength it took to relocate a shoulder. "Are you certain you can do this?" he asked, sounding doubtful.

A grin on his face, Dr. Madison ignored him and dragged the heavy wooden chair from the desk in the corner into the centre of the room. "Please, be seated."

As Frederick tried to rise to his feet, a crippling pain returned to his shoulder, and he would probably have fallen had it not been for his wife's steady hands. Gently, she guided him to the chair, her hands supporting his uninjured shoulder.

Dr. Madison approached then. He set one leg on the chair's seat right behind Frederick's injured shoulder before carefully lifting up the arm and placing it over his knee.

Gritting his teeth, Frederick waited, hoping Dr. Madison knew what he was doing.

The doctor then placed one hand on his patient's shoulder and the other on his upper arm. From one second to the next, he then leaned forward, simultaneously pushing down on shoulder and arm.

A sharp pain shot through Frederick, and the breath caught in his throat.

Then a soft *pop* echoed through the room, and the shoulder was back in its socket.

"There, all done," Dr. Madison announced cheerfully, patting him on the shoulder.

Frederick winced, but the sharp pain had indeed vanished. Only a dull echo remained. "Thank you," he grumbled.

"Yes, thank you," his mother said, enormous relief showing on her face. "I'll escort you out."

With a last wink for his patient, Dr. Madison followed his mother out the door.

"He is a rather strange man, is he not?" his wife observed, a hint of humour in her eyes. "To tell you the truth, I didn't think he had the strength to do this."

Frederick snorted, carefully rising to his feet. "Neither did I."

"Let me help you," she said, rushing to his side.

Frederick was about to protest when her soft hands touched his skin. His heart began to hammer in his chest, and once more the breath caught in his throat. He swallowed but did not object. Gently, she led him to the bed, fluffed up his pillow and then drew the blanket up to his chin.

"You should rest," she said, closing the curtains. "I will have some food sent up later."

"Thank you," Frederick mumbled, unable to keep his eyes off her.

She smiled at him then and as though on impulse reached out her hand and brushed a lock off his forehead. "Sweet dreams," she whispered and left.

For a long time, Frederick lay in his bed wondering. Although his eyelids were heavy, his mind could not abandon the memory of her touch. With sure, yet gentle hands, she had taken care of him, her quick mind knowing exactly what he needed.

No one had taken care of him in a long time. Not like that. Especially now that he was the head of his family, he was the one to look after others. But even long before becoming the marquess, he had always taken care of those around him.

His mind—always cautious—ushered a warning about the vulnerable position he suddenly found himself in. His heart, however, objected, again and again conjuring the soft brush of her fingertips against his skin.

Closing his eyes, Frederick fell asleep.

25

TO LIVE OR DIE

*U*nable to stay away, Ellie slipped into her husband's bedchamber. The sun had long since disappeared behind the horizon, and the house lay silent. She knew she ought to get some rest. She knew he would ring if he needed anything. And yet, she could not stay away.

Closing the door behind her, Ellie tiptoed her way across the dark floor until her bare feet touched the soft Persian rug leading up to his bed. In the dim light of a single candle burning on the desk in the corner, his features looked almost haggard and pale as though a life-threatening disease was about to claim him. For a short moment, the breath caught in Ellie's throat, and unable to move, she stared at his chest, willing it to rise and fall.

When it did, she almost fainted with relief.

What are you doing here? An obnoxious voice whispered. *There is nothing you can do for him.*

Ellie knew that, and yet, she couldn't leave.

Despite the slight chill in the air that drifted through her nightgown, she stayed. Silently, she lifted up the chair Dr. Madison had used to relocate Frederick's shoulder and carefully carried it to his bedside. Fortunately, the slight exertion served to warm her chilled muscles.

Sitting down beside him, Ellie's heart rejoiced.

For the first time, she had the opportunity to look at him openly without the need to avert her eyes as soon as he felt her gaze on him.

In the dim light, his dark hair looked almost black on the white linen pillow while the tone of his skin appeared to have a touch of silver. His eyes were closed, and his breath came in even intervals. He was a handsome man. Ellie had always thought so; however, these days, his rugged features were often contorted by the pain that had claimed his heart.

As he continued to sleep peacefully, Ellie inched forward.

The cut on his forehead had closed, and she reached out a tentative hand, brushing the back of it over his cheek and forehead. Relieved to see that no infection had set in—at least not yet—, she watched him sleep.

For once, the tortured expression his face bore on most days had vanished. The muscles along his forehead and around his mouth seemed relaxed, and the corners of his mouth even curled up into a soft smile every now and then.

Seeing it, Ellie smiled in answer. What was he dreaming about? She wondered. What had made him smile?

Leaning onto the bed, Ellie soon rested her head on her folded arms. As her eyes continued to gaze at her husband, she noticed that her eyelids began to grow heavy. At first, Ellie fought the warming blanket of approaching sleep with all her might. Too much did she enjoy this moment of peaceful silence with her husband. However, before the clock in the hall downstairs struck twelve, Ellie was fast asleep.

Inspired by the rare smile that had played on her husband's lips, Ellie slept peacefully, her own dreams continuing in the direction her heart desired until tortured moans drifted to her ears and found their way into her dreams.

Coming awake, Ellie squinted her eyes, trying to shake off the last remnants of sleep. The room was still dark, and the candle in the corner had almost burned down, its dying light casting eerie shadows across the bed.

Still asleep, Frederick began to stir. His head jerked from side to side. However, his eyes were squeezed shut. Occasionally, a pained moan would rise from his throat, and his hands were balled into fists, tearing at the bed sheet.

"Frederick?" Ellie whispered, carefully touching his arm. "Everything is all right. You are safe." Staring at her husband, Ellie was at a loss. She could see the dark memories that tortured his dreams plainly on his face, and yet, it was evident that he did not hear her.

She shook him a little, but to no effect. How could she wake him? Should she wake him?

Touching his bare skin was strangely exhilarating, and yet, Ellie felt her own inhibitions stir below the surface. Would he object to her touch? Would he rather she call someone else?

To hell with what he wanted! Ellie thought as another agonised moan rose from his lips. There was no time. He needed her now. She had to wake him.

Climbing onto the bed next to him, Ellie leaned forward and gave his uninjured shoulder a rough shake.

Frederick didn't even flinch. Instead, his body tensed, and the muscles in his arm felt as though they were about to snap. Then his mouth opened. "Kenneth! NO!"

Recognising his friend's name, Ellie knew what memories held him trapped. Determined to loosen their hold, she grabbed her husband's face with both hands. "Frederick, wake up!" Again and again, she called his name, her fingers almost digging into his scalp.

Seconds ticked by. Seconds that felt like a small eternity as Ellie desperately tried to make him hear her.

Frederick, however, was lost in his own past, once again battling the demons that haunted him day in and day out. His head still jerked from side to side when his hands suddenly flew up and tightened around Ellie's arms.

Before she knew what was happening, he rolled over, taking her with him. Pinned into the mattress, she stared up at his unseeing face.

His eyes snapped open then, and a growl rose from his throat.

"Frederick!" Ellie called, feeling her skin crawl as his weight pushed down on her. "Wake up!" When he still didn't react, she lifted her hand and slapped him across the face as hard as she could with her arms still held tight in his iron grip. "Frederick! Wake up!"

He blinked then, and Ellie felt relief flood her heart. Again, she spoke his name. Softer this time and with less force, but this time he heard her.

As his eyes focused on her, she smiled up at him, suddenly acutely aware of his naked chest resting on hers, his face only a breath's length away from her own. Even in the dim light, she could see a golden glimmer in his dark eyes.

His gaze narrowed then, and a hint of shock came to his eyes as he realised that she lay pinned under him. Rising, he almost fell off the bed as he stumbled backwards.

Sitting up, Ellie grabbed his hand and pulled him back. "Are you all right?"

Still staring at her, he glanced about the room, and she could see the memory of the past day resurface. He cleared his throat then and slid off the bed, his eyes not meeting hers. "I apologise, my lady, I–" He winced, and his right hand went to his injured shoulder.

In the dim light, touches of blue and purple decorated his skin.

"There is no need to apologise," Ellie assured him. Sliding off the bed herself, she stepped toward him.

He drew in a sharp breath that Ellie doubted was due to the pain in his shoulder. For some reason, he was terrified of her touch, and despite her own doubts, Ellie thought that her scars were not the reason. "You should return to bed. Your shoulder will need time to heal." When he didn't move, she placed a hand on his arm.

He flinched and drew in a deep breath. Eyes looking at everything but her, he stepped around her. "I suppose you are right. I am sorry I woke you, my lady. Please, return to your own bed. You, too, need rest."

"I am fine."

As he carefully eased himself back under the blanket, his eyes fell on the chair by his bed before they looked up at her, a question resting in them.

"I was watching over you," Ellie admitted, sitting back down in the chair she had only abandoned a few minutes ago. To her, it seemed like hours had passed since then.

"There is no need…"

She smiled at him, and his voice trailed off. "Did I not promise to look after you?" she asked, her tone lightly, hoping to banish the darkness in his eyes back to where it had come from. "Be it in sickness or in health?"

The ghost of a smile flitted across his features, and for a moment, he averted his eyes. "I am most grateful for your kindness, my lady."

"You are welcome," Ellie whispered, willing this moment to last forever. Never before had he looked at her the way he did now. His eyes held hers openly, and a gleam of honest appreciation and maybe even affection shone in them as a tentative smile curled up his lips.

"You must be cold, though," he said, his eyes shifting to her bare feet. "I assure you I am fine. Please, return to your own bed. I do not wish for you to catch a cold."

Unwilling to leave, Ellie grasped at the one straw he had offered her. "Who is Kenneth?"

Instantly, his smile vanished, and he stared at her in shock. "How...?"

"You said his name in your sleep."

Closing his eyes, he nodded. "I see." Then he looked at her, and for a moment, Ellie thought he would demand that she leave. Instead, his eyes softened, and a resigned expression came to his face. "You will not go, will you?"

An apologetic smile on her lips, Ellie shook her head.

"All right." Gritting his teeth, he carefully moved backward to the other side of the bed, then gestured to the spot he had just vacated. "If you don't mind, my lady."

Touched by his thoughtfulness, Ellie slid into the bed, welcoming the warmth his body had left behind. Her cold feet began to tingle, and her heart hammered in her chest. "Thank you."

Frederick lay back, his eyes focused on the ceiling. "What did I say?"

Resting on her side, Ellie watched him. "Not much. All you did was call his name in a way that..."

"I see." He cleared his throat. "Kenneth was my friend," he finally said. "He died in the war."

"You saw it happen?"

His eyes closed, and for a moment, Ellie thought he would send her from his bed. "I did." His voice sounded hoarse when he finally spoke. "He broke his neck as a cannon ball cut down his horse."

Lying in the almost dark, Frederick waited for his wife to express her sympathy. People generally did. They would say that he was lucky to be alive. That at least his friend hadn't suffered. That they were both heroes now. That he should take comfort in knowing his friend died for a greater cause.

However, when his wife finally spoke, the words that left her lips were evidence of a perception few people possessed. "There is no glory in dying young, is there?"

For a moment, Frederick remained silent, unprepared for the understanding that rang in her voice. "Dying is always ugly and always a tragedy." He knew that he sounded bitter, but how could he not?

"Few people think of dying when they speak of war," his wife pointed out. "They speak of causes and victories, of enemies and defeat. They think of banners blowing in the wind. Of glory and parades."

Frederick turned his head to look at her and winced at the slight pain the movement brought to his shoulder. Ignoring his discomfort, his eyes searched hers in the semi-dark, wondering how she knew the thoughts that echoed within his own heart as well. "You sound like a war-weary soldier," he observed and was touched by the soft curl that came to her lips.

For a long time, she simply lay beside him, her eyes distant as though she was collecting her thoughts. "I have never been on a field of battle like the one that your friend died on," she stated the simple truth, "but I know the meaning of pain and fear. I know what it is like to feel death reaching out its hands for you." She shook her head, and a single tear rolled down her cheek. "I remember how scared I was, how terrified. And yet, a part of me welcomed the nearing end."

Frederick's breath caught in his throat, and he closed his eyes, remembering the feeling she spoke of.

"I wanted it to end," she admitted, a slight catch in her voice as she spoke. "I didn't want to bear the pain any longer. I didn't think I could. If death means an end to your suffering, then there is no shame in welcoming it." For a moment, Frederick's heart stopped before a sigh of relief left his lips. Ever since Kenneth had died, he had wished for death, and he had always felt guilty to be so willing to throw away something that others valued so highly. "Who would choose pain if there was another way?"

Again, he looked at her, and again, he saw the honesty of her words in her eyes. "Most people would disagree."

A sad smile on her face, she met his eyes. "I suppose it is always difficult to judge something that you have never experienced yourself. People simply assume what something feels like, how they would feel, but they don't know." She took a deep breath. "When they look at me, they think they know how I feel. They think I ought to sit at home in the dark and mourn my fate because they cannot imagine that life could ever look beautiful again. I do not deny that what happened that day was horrible and that I mind the scars that I now bear. But does that mean my life is over?"

Inhaling deeply, she closed her eyes, and Frederick realised that he did not know beyond the common gossip what had happened to her. "I have thought about this a lot. For wherever I turn, people make me feel as though I have no right to be enjoying my life." She raised her head a little. "It is the same with you, is it not? Your scars are not visible, and, therefore, people assume you have none."

"Unfortunately, the visible scars I have are generally hidden under layers of clothing," Frederick observed, suddenly feeling the need to lighten the mood. Seeing the pain that crossed her face at the memories she shared with him, Frederick felt the almost desperate need to shield her from them. After everything she had suffered, she deserved happiness, peace of mind.

At his words, her eyes travelled to his left shoulder, and even in the dark, he could see a slight flush come to her cheeks.

As he felt the heavy weight of her gaze on him, a new surge of guilt flooded his heart, and he swallowed.

Somewhere under the blue and purple bruises, an ugly scar rested; a scar that would always remind him of Kenneth. A scar that would always remind him that he had failed his friend. All his life, Frederick had looked out for Kenneth, and when his friend had needed him most, Frederick had simply watched him die. It had been Kenneth who had come to his aid, not allowing the bayonet to take his life but merely to mark him for the betrayer he was.

"You blame yourself for what happened to your friend," his wife observed, her eyes resting on his face.

Lost in contemplation, Frederick's eyes snapped up, staring at her across the short distance separating them. By now, he knew her eyes so well. Even in the dark, the soft blue shone like sapphires, delicate and gentle, and yet, their depth spoke of an unyielding character, one that had been tested time and time again but could not be broken. What did she see when she looked at him? What did his own eyes reveal about him?

Her simple statement spoke to his heart in a way nothing before ever had. She had not asked; yet, somehow she had known. Gently her eyes moved across his face as though she could read the truth where others had failed.

The truth was that he did not know what to say. His heart ached in his chest, and yet, he knew not how to put the pain he felt into words. His mind knew that he blamed himself for Kenneth's death, and yet, the pain in his heart went much deeper. How could he even begin to explain something he did not understand himself?

Searching for the words that eluded him, Frederick saw a slight curl come to her lips as her gentle eyes looked into his and her words took the burden to answer from his shoulders. "The day of the fire started like any other," she began, and a shiver went down Frederick's back. Somehow he knew that what she was about to tell him she had never before shared with another. "In retrospect, I often thought that there should have been something to mark this day as different, as life-altering, as dangerous. Maybe there had been. Maybe I simply didn't notice."

Taking a deep breath, she licked her lips. "The first thing I heard were the servants' screams. I will always remember that sound. It chilled me to my bones, and from one second to the next, a perfectly pleasant day turned into a nightmare. I rushed upstairs as my heart hammered in my chest and the pain radiated through my whole body. I never thought the beating of my own heart could ever hurt."

For a moment, she closed her eyes, and Frederick knew the strength it took for her to go on. "When I hurried down the corridor, smoke hung in the air, growing thicker with each step. When the coughing started, I held a handkerchief before my face to keep the smoke from my lungs. Servants rushed by me, pointing down the way they had come, their faces contorted in horror. Fire had broken out in my little brother's room, and he was trapped inside." A single tear spilled over and was instantly absorbed by the pillow underneath. "Fear gripped my heart at their words, and I rushed on. As I turned the corner, I found his nursemaid, Agnes, standing just outside his door. Tears streamed down her face as a coughing fit shook her body, her pale face illuminated by the dancing flames inside the room."

She took a deep breath, and for a second, Frederick thought she would not go on. "I remember that I wanted to turn and run. I didn't want this to be happening. I knew what it meant, and I wasn't ready to handle something so horrible." Her eyes met his, and Frederick understood that the only reason she was reliving the moment of her greatest pain was to help him with his own. "But I stayed. As much as I wanted to, I couldn't run. Instead, I stepped up to the door and looked inside. The bed was aflame as were the curtains and the rugs and everything else that can be consumed by fire. My brother lay on the floor in the corner. His eyes were closed, and through the flames, I could not tell if he was still breathing. My heart stopped, and the absence of the pain was even worse than the pain itself."

Was she right? Frederick wondered. Could there be anything worse than pain? Ever since he had returned from the continent, Frederick had done his utmost to gather his pain and guilt and hopelessness in one place and lock it away. He had schooled himself not to feel, and the absence of his emotions had brought him peace. Hadn't it?

"For a long time, I just stood there," she whispered, and her own guilt shone in her eyes openly. "I could not bring myself to save him. I just stood there, hoping someone would come and help. But time passed, and nothing happened. Only the fire continued to dance, and the smoke grew denser. Then the flames touched him." She swallowed and took a deep breath. "His pant leg caught fire, and yet, he didn't move. His failure to react scared me more than anything else in my life. Something snapped then. It was as though something else took over. I heard myself scream his name, and then I rushed through the flames into the room. I remember the heat on my skin as it grew from warm to hot and then became painful and ultimately unbearable. But my body still moved. I put out the small flame on his leg, picked him up and cradled him close to my body, trying my best to shield him from the fire. My hands and arms wrapped around him, I stared at the wall of fire that stood between us and the door. I closed my eyes then...and ran."

Tears streamed down her face, wetting the pillow and shining in her eyes. "I don't remember much else. I dropped to the ground in the corridor. I heard Agnes scream his name, then mine. My hair must have caught fire because the skin on my face and neck began to burn with a heat so intense that blackness soon engulfed me, and I welcomed it." Again, she met his eyes, willing him to hear her words and understand them for what they were, the naked truth. The ugly truth was that life could be painful, and that sometimes one simply didn't have the strength to handle it.

Frederick swallowed as her words coursed through his veins. "Did your brother live?" he asked, remembering the little boy that had accompanied his family to his sister's wedding.

A deep smile illuminated her face. "He did."

"What is his name?"

"Stephen," his wife whispered. "His name is Stephen."

"Does he bear any scars?" he asked, his eyes travelling over her beautiful face. For the first time, he saw her scars as a part of who she was. He understood them to be a part of her. Without them, she would not be the woman she was today. The fire had scarred her soul as well as her body, and in that moment, Frederick wished that he, too, had been marked more visibly.

"No," his wife said. "He has no scars. The skin on his leg was irritated for a few days, but it healed nicely."

"You saved his life," Frederick said as his gaze met hers. Despite an underlying fear that threatened to consume him, he withdrew the veil that usually clouded his eyes and let her see the guilt that still lived in his heart. Although he admired the strength she had conjured in reliving her own painful past, he wanted her to understand that her story was different from his own, that her scars were not the same as his, that his guilt was justified. After all, Kenneth was dead. She had saved her brother, but he had failed his friend.

Her eyes searched his for a long time, and Frederick could see the understanding of his message on her face. Like no one else, she understood him despite the few words he spoke.

"Yes, I saved his life," she agreed, and her gaze held his as though by a magnetic pull. "I saved his life...because I could." The soft blue of her sapphire eyes hardened. "I was there when it happened. I could reach him in time, and the danger that threatened him was within my power to ward off."

Transfixed, Frederick stared at her as the simple truth washed over him.

"Could you have stopped the canon ball?" she asked, her tone filled with challenge. "Could you have caught him as he fell?"

Frederick swallowed. "I should have."

Her eyes narrowed. "Could you have?"

Drawing a deep breath, Frederick shook his head. "It is not as simple as that. I should—"

"Could you have?" she repeated. Lifting her head off the pillow, she stared at him, her gaze holding him immobile. "Could you have?"

Again, Frederick swallowed. "No," he forced out through gritted teeth as a new sense of failure came over him. All his life, he had protected those he loved. His ability to watch over them had made him feel strong, powerful, in control. Now, it lay shattered at his feet. If he could not protect the people he loved, what value did he have?

A soft curl came to her lips as she lay her head back down. "We all feel guilty when a tragedy happens." The sharp tone vanished from her voice as she spoke. "We all think we should have been able to prevent it. It is not wrong to think that way. It simply means that we care, that we wish we could have done something to prevent it. But the truth is often another. As much as we wish for it to be different, few things are within our reach."

Resting his head on the pillow, Frederick stared into the dark. Everything that he had been, everything that he had believed came crashing down around him. First, Kenneth, then his father, and now his brother. They had all died under his watch. It had been his responsibility to protect them, and he had failed miserably. Who would be next? He wondered, and his eyes shifted to the woman beside him.

Once again, her eyes shone soft and clear in the dim light, searching his face. In them, he could see the deep desire for him to understand, for his heart to understand that he was not at fault, that he ought not to blame himself. And although he wished for nothing more but to set her mind at ease, Frederick knew deep down that the guilt that had followed him home from the continent still lived. Maybe it had retreated into the shadows, lurking and waiting, but it was not gone. One day, it would return and claim his soul for good.

"Sometimes we have to let go of the things that hold us back, that prevent us from finding happiness," she whispered, and for a short moment, he could feel the soft warmth of her breath brush over his cheek. "I know that heart and mind are often at war. Only because the mind comes to understand, the heart might still be far from *feeling* the truth the mind has come to accept. It takes time. Allow yourself that time. Feel the guilt. Do not ignore it for then it only grows stronger. It is your choice. No one else can make it for you." Her eyes looked deep into his, and Frederick could feel their touch as though her hand had reached across the pillows. "Do you want to live? Not just exist, but live?"

A small spark of hope, of desire soared into life, warming his heart and melting the ice that had settled upon it long ago. And yet, a shadow lurked in the depth of his being, and it spoke only of the betrayal he had committed. "I don't think I have the right to—"

Elsbeth shook her head. "You have every right," she said, and the conviction that rang in her voice warmed his heart even more. Slowly, he felt the shadow retreat. "Do not doubt yourself. If you want to live, live! If not, the pain will never go away. You will become a shadow of yourself, and the life you have will be wasted." She swallowed then, and a hint of fear shone in her eyes. "Do you want to live...or die?"

Staring at her, Frederick knew that she was right. He had to make a choice. Only before tonight, he had always thought that he had made that choice long ago. That he was only here to take care of his family and fulfil his duty.

Now, all of a sudden, a new desire rose in his chest. A desire to live, to feel...to love. His eyes swept over her, seeing the soft curve of her lips and the honest way her eyes looked into his. She bit her lip as though nervous, as though his answer held sway over her heart as well.

And all of a sudden, Frederick knew what he wanted.

But could he trust his own desires?

Would the darkness in his heart allow him to live?

Did he truly have a choice?

Or was he just fooling himself?

26

A WALK IN THE GARDENS

alking the gardens, Ellie hummed under her breath. The sun shone brilliantly, and the few snow-white clouds drifted lazily across the clear blue sky. Birds chirped in the trees and crickets in the high grass, their echoing sounds in harmony with Ellie's cheerful tune.

Despite the seriousness of their conversation, Ellie's mind rejoiced each and every time it drifted to their shared time a few nights ago. Again and again, she relived moment for moment, seeing a new light come to Frederick's eyes and hearing true emotions ring in his voice. Never had she imagined that her husband would talk to her the way he had: openly, honestly, without holding anything back. He had confided in her about his greatest fears and darkest thoughts.

And he had listened.

From the stillness of his body as he had lain beside her, Ellie knew that he had listened intently, absorbing each word that had left her lips. Although she could not be certain that her advice would help him out of the abyss his friend's death had plunged him into, Ellie thought that the honesty with which he had answered her questions—despite the mortification plainly visible on his face—spoke of a great desire to find what he had lost. She knew he felt guilty about his friend's death. She knew that he thought he had no right to live, to be happy for his friend would never have the chance to be. Kenneth's life had ended, and nothing could bring him back. Even if Frederick lived his life in sorrow or ended it for good, it would not change the fact that his friend was dead. Nothing he did would change that.

Ellie only hoped that deep down Frederick had finally come to understand that, and that it would help him accept that he could not spend his life mourning the dead. Remember, yes. But not mourn, not the way Frederick did.

"There you are," trilled a voice from behind her, and Ellie spun around.

Beholding her friend's face, Ellie rushed toward her, a deep smile curling up her lips. "Madeline," she called, embracing her friend. "I am so glad to see you!"

"As am I, dear Elsbeth." As she stepped back, Madeline's sharp eyes slid over Ellie's face in a way that brought a blush to her cheeks. "I see that married life agrees with you," her friend commented. Then she took Ellie's hand and pulled her over to a shady spot under a tall oak tree. "You look radiant. Am I right to assume that your husband has finally come to understand how fortunate he is to call you his wife?"

Sitting down on the stone bench by the water fountain, Ellie could not help the smile that lifted up the corners of her mouth. "I am not certain," she admitted. "However, I am hoping that he will one day."

Madeline's eyes narrowed. "I have to say that you do not look hopeful at all. You, my dear Elsbeth, look like a cat who is not hoping to catch a mouse but has done so already."

Ellie laughed. "Do you think of me that way? That I trapped him into this marriage?" If anyone else had said what Madeline had just admitted to, Ellie would have been hurt.

Shaking her head, Madeline chuckled. "Well, if anyone trapped him, then I suppose it was your mother. At least, she keeps telling everyone who comes within earshot of the wonderful match she so selflessly procured for her daughter. According to her, she was the one who inspired him to ask for your hand despite your tainted beauty." Shaking her head, Ellie stared at her friend. What was her mother thinking? "I assure you I simply meant to point out that the smile on your face and the glow in your eyes speak of a woman very much in love."

As inexplicable joy coursed through her veins, Ellie met her friend's eyes. "Oh, I am, Madeline. I really am. I just don't know how he feels about me."

Madeline's eyes narrowed in thought, and she put a finger to her lips. "I wish I could stay for supper. Quite frankly, no one reads people better than me. I suppose I could find out if he truly loved you."

"Thank you," Ellie said, knowing that her friend tended to overestimate her own abilities in this regard. While Madeline definitely had a way with people, more specifically with men, she often misread their true intentions or maybe she simply saw what she wanted to see. "But there is no need. He will come to it in his own time."

"As you wish," Madeline relented before she lifted her head and almost craned her neck, looking past Ellie's shoulder.

"What is it?"

"I thought I saw something?"

"Something?"

A wicked grin came to Madeline's lips. "Well, someone."

As Ellie turned around, she was surprised to see her husband walking around the long hedge that shielded the small oasis by the water fountain from the rest of the gardens. By his side, she found Oliver Cornell.

For a moment, Frederick looked uncomfortable as he beheld them. Then, however, he exchanged a few quick words with his friend, and they came walking toward them.

Rising to their feet, the two women glanced at each other, each brushing down their dresses.

"Who is *he*?" Madeline asked, her gaze resting on Frederick's friend, and Ellie detected a curious twinkle in her friend's eyes.

Ellie smiled. "That is Oliver Cornell, a friend of Frederick's."

Madeline's eyebrows rose into arches. "You mean the Earl of Cullingwood?"

"I suppose so."

A satisfied grin spread over Madeline's face.

Ellie laughed, "You cannot be serious?"

"He is an earl, is he not?" Clearing her throat, Madeline put on her most dazzling smile as the two men approached.

Offering a quick bow, Frederick greeted her and Madeline and then introduced his friend. All the while, his eyes rested on her as though she were the only one there. Ellie felt her heart thudding in her chest, its echo pulsing through her veins.

"It seems I was not the only one who deemed this day a good day to call on a friend," Oliver chuckled, a friendly smile on his face.

Glancing at Ellie, Madeline quickly turned her attention back to the earl within her reach. "You are certainly right, my lord. It is a beautiful day, and I did not mind the time in the carriage at all. I had the windows open the whole journey here. The air is wonderful, is it not? So fresh and invigorating."

Ellie had to suppress a chuckle at Madeline's efforts to beguile her husband's friend. She quickly averted her eyes lest she laugh out loud.

"It is beautiful indeed," Frederick agreed. His gaze, however, rested on Ellie, and an excited tingle went over her as his eyes held hers. Was he talking about her? Did he think she was beautiful? Oh, if she only knew!

All too soon, the two men excused themselves. Clearly disappointed, Madeline did her utmost to continue their conversation; however, Oliver was adamant. Maybe he had something important to discuss with her husband, Ellie thought, and with a sad eye, she watched Frederick walk away. Before he was lost from sight though, his eyes returned to her, and instantly, Ellie's heart jumped into her throat. For a second, she thought she would faint.

"What could they possibly have to discuss that we shouldn't hear?" Madeline complained. Sinking back onto the bench, she crossed her arms. "I think they were very rude to leave us here."

Catching her breath, Ellie sat down by her friend. "Do not pout, Madeline. There are more earls in the world than just this one."

A wicked smile lit up Madeline's face as she turned to Ellie. "You see right through me, do you not?"

"Like a piece of glass."

Looking at each other, they both broke out laughing.

"I've missed you," Madeline admitted. "I've missed us."

"Me, too."

"To tell you the truth, I might not ever forgive your husband for taking you away from me." Feigning outrage, Madeline lifted her chin. "It was in very poor taste. Very poor taste, indeed."

"I am surprised you even noticed my absence," Ellie stated, still feeling the excitement of her chance meeting with her husband pulsing through her veins, "with all the husband-hunting to keep you busy."

Madeline's mouth dropped open. "I resent that, my dear Elsbeth. I do not hunt. I am not the moth, but the flame. I cannot help that they feel drawn to me."

Ellie laughed, and Madeline's features softened. "Will you be back in Town next season?"

"I don't know," Ellie admitted. "At the moment, I am not sure of anything."

Giving Ellie's hand a gentle squeeze, Madeline met her eyes, a warm smile on her face. "But I am," she all but whispered. "He cares for you deeply."

At her friend's words, Ellie's heart stopped, and yet, she didn't dare hope.

"He does," Madeline insisted. "Whether he knows it or not, he does. Do not allow him to persuade you of the opposite. Seize the day, and win his heart." A hint of wickedness returned to her curved lips. "Men are often lost when it comes to matters of the heart, and, therefore, I wholeheartedly believe that it ought to be women who make the proposal, not men." She chuckled. "They still have so much to learn."

"Thank you for coming," Ellie whispered, pulling her friend into her arms. For a moment, she closed her eyes, enjoying the soft breeze on her skin and the warmth that engulfed her heart.

Today was indeed a beautiful day.

27

A DAY FOR VISITING

eturning to his study in the late afternoon, Frederick offered Oliver a drink. All day long, his friend had seemed determined to speak to him, and yet, he had not said a word that would have justified his keen observation of Frederick's person. "May I be frank?" he asked, handing Oliver the glass.

"Certainly." Sinking into the large armchair, Oliver took a sip, his eyes watching Frederick with open curiosity.

"Why have you come?"

Oliver snorted, "Do you want me to go?"

"I did not say that," Frederick corrected his friend. "I merely asked why you came. I sense that there is something on your mind. However, so far we have talked of mere trifles. All I ask is that you say what you came here to say."

Nodding, Oliver set down his glass. "Your eyes did not deceive you. However, the reason I came here was not only because I wished to speak with you about something, but also to see how you were."

Frederick shrugged, and a small stab of pain coursed through his shoulder.

"There!" Oliver exclaimed, finger pointing at Frederick. "That is exactly why I came!"

Confused, Frederick stared at his friend. "Because I injured my shoulder? Because I was thrown off a horse?" He shook his head. "I'm afraid I do not understand."

"Do you truly not see what is going on here?" Oliver asked, rising from the chair. His features tensed as he searched for the right words to explain himself. "First, your father, then your brother, and now *you* almost died, too. Does that not worry you? It's almost as though a curse was put on your family."

Frederick laughed. It had been a long time since he had heard anything so ludicrous. "My dear friend, you appear to have lost your mind," he jested. "I merely fell off a horse. I did not even come close to dying, believe me."

"You could have broken your neck," Oliver objected. "And besides, do you even remember the last time you fell off a horse? Do you not wonder why your saddle girth snapped to begin with? Has your saddle not always served you well? It has carried you around the world and back, and now it simply snaps?"

Frederick shrugged, wondering what had caused Oliver's worry. "Sometimes leather becomes brittle and snaps. These things happen."

"Have you spoken to your stable master?" Oliver insisted. "Did you ask him why he did not replace the girth if it was indeed brittle?"

Frowning, Frederick stared at his friend. He could honestly say that that thought had never occurred to him. "What do you want, Oliver? Did you only come here today to warn me about some ominous curse? I never knew you believed in such superstitions."

Rubbing his hands over his face, Oliver sighed. "I don't know. I suppose…I came here because I was worried. After losing Kenneth, I cannot imagine losing you, too."

"I understand," Frederick said. "But I am fine. I assure you, I am." Seeing the slight shadows under Oliver's eyes, Frederick wondered what demons haunted his friend. Did he feel the same guilt for staying home and not accompanying them that Frederick did for not having been able to save Kenneth? Was everyone's life ruled by guilt in one form or another?

"Will you, at least, promise me to be careful?" Oliver asked, his eyes clouded with concern he could not seem to shake.

"I promise," Frederick said although he had no idea how to fulfil that promise. In what way ought he to be careful? And when? All the time. Lying in bed? Sitting down for supper? He could not be more careful than he already was. His friend's worry simply stemmed from an overly creative imagination.

"Good." Oliver nodded, and reaching for his glass, he took another sip. "Thank you." He cleared his throat and put on a happier face. "Well then, tell me about your wife?"

Frederick cringed.

Oliver stepped toward him. "My concern for your life is not the only reason I came," he said. "I am also still concerned for your well-being, your state of mind." He shook his head, and a slight chuckle escaped his lips. "Considering all the concerns that plague me, I am surprised that my hair hasn't gone white yet."

Anxious laughter slipped from Frederick's lips. "As I told you, your concerns are unfounded. I assure you that everything is fine. There," he said, forcing a smile on his face, "you should be able to sleep well tonight. How long are you planning on staying?"

A wicked grin spread over Oliver's face as his eyes calmly rested on Frederick. Gone was his agitation and the slight shadows under his eyes seemed to have retreated. "Are you so determined to rid yourself of me?" he asked, his keen eyes watching Frederick closely. "Are you displeased with what I have to say or with the questions I ask?"

Frowning, Frederick shook his head. Stalking to the other side of the room, he took his time refilling his own glass. "Do not be absurd. I merely asked to have the guest room prepared should you decide to stay." Willing his features to relax, he turned and met his friend's scrutinising eyes. "You know you are always welcome here."

"Why can you not talk about her?" Oliver asked. Like a predator stalking its prey, he began to move forward, slowly approaching his friend before stopping in his tracks, only to move closer a moment later. "Even if your mother chose her for you, you have been married to her for a couple of months now."

Frederick swallowed, knowing only too well how persistent Oliver could be. "What is your point?"

Shaking his head, Oliver sighed in exasperation. "Rick, she is your wife. Your wife! I simply want to understand why you never speak about her. You never even mention her. It's as though she does not exist. At least, not to you. Is being married to her so awful?"

"What?" Frederick's eyes snapped up as his heart thudded in his chest. Oliver's words were like a stab to the heart, and Frederick stared at him in surprise.

After bidding her friend goodbye, Ellie walked back through the front hall and toward the back parlour where she knew Theresa and Maryann would be sitting with their embroidery. As she walked down the corridor, distant voices drifted to her ears, and she stopped, straining to listen.

Her husband's voice she recognised instantly and, therefore, presumed the other one to belong to his friend Oliver Cornell. Unable to make out their words, Ellie proceeded down the hall until the door to Frederick's study came into sight.

It stood slightly ajar, the voices drifting out into the hallway beckoning her closer.

Ellie hesitated, knowing that it was wrong to listen to their private conversation. Her heart, however, longed to know what was spoken between the two men.

Frederick was a guarded man, who rarely shared his innermost thoughts and desires with anyone else. A few nights ago, he had finally allowed her a glimpse of the man he was underneath duty and responsibility, and Ellie's heart had instantly recognised him as a kindred soul.

The guilt that plagued him, the doubts he could not shake echoed within herself as well. Never before had she spoken to another the way she had bared her soul to him, revealing her own fears, her own weaknesses and failings. Speaking to him in the dark had been liberating indeed. She had felt her heart beat with a strength and joy she had not known before. Her limbs had felt lighter as though relieved of a heavy burden, and her soul had soared into the night sky, dancing among the stars and welcoming the new freedom she had finally found.

What scared her most was the thought of losing that connection to him again. In quiet moments, she wondered what she would do if he went back to the indifferent politeness that had been between them since the day of their wedding. Deep down, she knew she could not live with such loss. She'd prefer he scream and yell at her. At least then, he would communicate his feelings, allow her to be a part of his life, instead of live side by side with him without them sharing anything about themselves.

But how was she to keep him from withdrawing from her again? Although she knew more about his inner self today than she had a week ago, many questions still remained unanswered.

Ellie glanced at the door up ahead, and as though of their own accord, her feet proceeded down the hall. With each step the voices grew louder, and her ears were able to discern individual words. But Ellie wanted more.

She swallowed, then stepped up to the door standing slightly ajar. Peeking through the gap, she could not see either one of the two men. However, every sound now travelled to her ear unhindered, and a shiver went down her back at her husband's voice. "What is your point?" he asked, a hint of apprehension clouding his words. Where they arguing? Ellie wondered.

Footsteps echoed on the parquet floor. Then Oliver spoke, his voice filled with agitation barely held in check. "Rick, she is your wife. Your wife!" Ellie froze, all breath knocked from her lungs. "I simply want to understand why you never speak about her. You never even mention her. It's as though she does not exist. At least, not to you." Ellie's heart grew heavy, and she felt the cool touch of tears as they clung to her eyelashes. Her head sank, and she turned to walk away. "Is being married to her so awful?"

"What?" Frederick's voice sliced the heavy silence like a whip, and Ellie's head spun back around.

After Oliver's words had clawed at her heart, the honest ring of consternation in the single syllable that left her husband's lips was like a healing balm, gently easing the pain.

Returning to the door, she stood quietly, her ears begging him for more.

A slight chuckle echoed through the room before Oliver spoke again. "What are you afraid of, Rick? That you actually might have come to care for her?" Ellie's heart sped up as excitement began to bubble in her veins. "I've seen the way you looked at her today. You do care for her, do you not?"

Ellie held her breath.

Frederick cleared his throat. Oh, how she wished she could see his face! "She is a wonderful woman, yes," he said, and his voice sounded strained. "However, I do not understand what concern she is to you."

184

"You are of concern to me," Oliver snapped, sounding exhausted with his friend's inability to answer his questions satisfactorily. "I can see that you care about her, so do not deny it. However, I don't understand why you look so glum if you have actually come to love the woman you're married to."

The word *love* echoed in Ellie's ears, and a myriad of butterflies took flight in her belly. Dancing on her toes, she fought to keep quiet lest she draw their attention and lose every opportunity of learning her husband's true feelings.

Frederick sighed. "Oliver, this is a personal matter. I—"

"I am your friend, Rick." The sound of footsteps reached Ellie's ears, and when Oliver spoke again, his voice echoed over from Frederick's corner of the room. "Look at me. Do you even hear what I'm saying? I am your friend. I have always been your friend. All the things we have been through together, and now, you cannot talk to me about this?" Oliver drew in a laboured breath, which spoke volumes of the exhaustion and disappointment he felt at his friend's stubborn insistence. "Please, Rick. Talk to me."

"It is not that I do not wish to answer your questions," Frederick said, exhaustion ringing in his voice as well. "I simply do not know what to tell you."

"All right. Then just answer my questions. I don't need elaborate explanations, just the simple truth." A moment of silence hung about the room, and Ellie was afraid that Frederick would deny his friend's request. Then heaving a sigh of relief, Oliver whispered, "Thank you."

Ellie frowned. Had her husband indicated his acquiescence?

"Do you care about her?" her husband's friend asked yet again.

Frederick drew in a deep breath as though in need of courage. "I do, yes." Ellie's heart soared into the sky, and the corners of her mouth curled up in a way they had not in a long time. Breathing heavily, she tried to calm herself.

"Do you love her?"

Instantly, she froze.

"I don't know if I can," her husband admitted, and a pang of disappointment washed over Ellie's heart. Listening to him was like walking a tightrope. Any second she could lose her balance and plummet to her death.

"Why?" Oliver asked. "Is it her scars? Do you not find her attractive?"

This was it, Ellie thought, and for a moment, time stood still. If she would ever get an honest answer to this all-consuming question, then it was now. Frederick had no reason to lie to his friend or to want to cushion the blow. He did not need to protect Oliver's feelings. He could be brutally honest.

Ellie only hoped that her own fragile heart would survive the truth she had longed to learn for months. Taking a deep breath, she closed her eyes and her hands curled into fists at her sides.

"No," Frederick said, and Ellie held her breath.

No to what? Did he not mind her scars? Or did he not find her attractive? Straining to listen, her fingernails dug into her palms.

"I do not mind her scars." Ellie almost sagged to the floor as relief washed over her. "Her scars are a part of who she is. Without her own, she would not be…she would not be the only one who seems to understand mine."

A smile vibrated in Oliver's voice. "You sound like you admire her."

"I do." Frederick sighed. "Life made her walk through hell, and yet," he hesitated, and Ellie's nerves almost snapped, "and yet, she seems untouched. After everything that she went through, she managed to find her way back into life. A part of me wishes I knew how she did it while another believes I have no right to it."

"Did you speak to her about Kenneth?"

A short laugh touched Frederick's lips. "She made me. She wouldn't leave. I…" He paused, and once again, Ellie wished she could see his face. "She knows that war is about dying, about loss and pain. She knows it to be a tragedy, and she never once spoke of heroes or glory. Everyone else does, but not her."

"Then speak to her," Oliver went on. "If she is the one who understands you, talk to her."

"I don't know if I can."

"Why not? You sound like you care for her deeply. Sharing your past with her will only help you grow closer. Or are you afraid she will think badly of you?"

"I don't think she would," Frederick replied, and Ellie rejoiced at the trust he had in her. "But I am not sure I should involve her in this. She has been through so much. I do not want to see her hurt again."

"What hurts her is the distance you force between the two of you," Oliver snapped, his patience slowly running out.

"How would you know that?"

"Because she looks at you the same way you look at her," Oliver stated, and for a long time, Frederick remained silent. "She cares about you, and I think she would want you to share your thoughts with her. Have you ever talked to her about this?"

"I wouldn't know what to say. Ever since returning from the continent, I feel incapable of speaking to others about anything beyond the importance of daily trifles."

"Except for her," Oliver objected. "You said you've spoken to her about Kenneth. Don't you think she would like to learn a bit more about you? What are you afraid of?"

"Afraid?"

"Yes, afraid," Oliver insisted. "I cannot shake the feeling that you're running away from something. As much as you care about her, there is something you're not telling me. You said you don't mind her scars, but do you find her attractive? I know I might be overstepping here, but have you shared her bed?"

Ellie swallowed, feeling the heat rise to her cheeks.

"That is none of your business," Frederick growled, his footsteps echoing through the room as he walked toward the window.

Oliver followed him. "Is she with child yet?"

Frederick whirled around. "Maybe you should leave!"

"Throw me out of your house if you want, but I will not allow you to return to that war," Oliver said, his voice heavy with determination. "I remember well our conversation from the night of the Midnight Ball. I know that you feel once you've done your duty and provided for your family, you are free to get yourself killed." Ellie's blood froze in her veins. "I have already lost one friend to that ridiculous cause, I will be damned if I lose another. I swear, I will do everything within my power to stop you. Do you hear!"

Frederick remained silent as unspoken words hung heavy about the room. Frozen to the spot, Ellie saw her husband before her mind's eye as he stood silent like a column, his eyes narrowed, staring at his friend as though he were the enemy.

"If you do not answer me, then I will simply have to speak to your wife!" Oliver threatened, his voice as cold as ice.

Ellie clearly understood what his friend's threat would mean for Frederick, a betrayal of the worst kind. Oliver had to be quite desperate to go to such length. Merely thinking about it made Ellie's skin crawl.

"You will do no such thing," Frederick growled, measured steps taking him closer to the door. "I think it best if you left now. I do not wish to detain you any longer. Return to your own family and meddle in their affairs."

Oliver scoffed. "You are my family, you mule-headed idiot! I only hope that your wife can find a way through that thick skull of yours. If not, I swear I will knock you out and lock you up before I let you do anything stupid. I'd rather you are furious with me than dead."

Closing her eyes, Ellie stepped back from the door. More had been revealed than she had hoped for. Holding her breath, she turned away and walked back the way she had come. Crossing the front hall, she slipped out the side door and hurried into the gardens.

The green oasis welcomed her: its sweet scents easing her heavy heart and confused mind, and she breathed a sigh of relief.

Long strides carried her across the lawn and toward the water fountain. Its soft babbling sounds as it rose into the air and cascaded down into itself soothed her nerves. Exhausted, she sank onto the bench under the large oak tree. The sun had long since begun its descent and merely shone as a red disk in the darkening sky.

Oliver's voice echoed in her mind. Was Frederick truly planning to return to the war and allow himself to be killed? Was his pain that great? His guilt? Did he truly have nothing worth living for?

A painful stab in the heart drew a sob from her throat, and Ellie buried her face in her hands.

Despite everything that had happened, despite the many losses, Frederick still had a family who loved him. Only his own heart had closed to the meaning of that love. Even if his mind knew it to be true, his heart told him that such love was of no consequence. And even if he doubted his heart, ultimately, it would be his guilt that would convince him that he did not deserve it no matter what he did. He could not win.

Considering everything she had heard, Ellie understood Oliver's fears and knew them to be justified. If Frederick was allowed to follow his own course, it would lead to his destruction.

Her hands began to tremble, and a cold chill ran down her body making her shiver as Oliver's words echoed in her mind once more. *I only hope that your wife can find a way through that thick skull of yours.*

Oliver put all his hopes in her. If she couldn't convince Frederick that life was worth living after all, then no one could. Just like

Theresa, he put his faith in her, hoping that she could save Frederick's life.

The burden of their trust weighed heavily on Ellie's heart. What if she couldn't? Not only would she lose Frederick herself, but he would be lost to others as well.

What was she to do?

28

A CLOAK OF DARKNESS

Staring out the window of his study, Frederick forced his anger back under control. Taking slow breaths, one after the other, he tried to calm his racing heart as it thudded in his chest. His hands linked behind his back, his shoulders tensed with each breath that left his body and again when his lungs once more filled with air.

All the while, the darkening sky spoke to his soul in a strange way.

Although the day had started out promising, everything had come crashing down around him. Despite the anger still boiling in his veins, Frederick tried to remind himself that it had not been Oliver's fault. His friend had merely pointed out his own shortcomings, dragged his inability to function in normal society into the light of day, his inability to love and trust.

Frederick knew that he was not the man he used to be. He also knew that he never would be again. The war and everything around it had changed him, and deep down, he had come to accept that.

Only those around him—his family, his friend and his wife—could not see the truth. They clung to the hope that with time he would return to them, that someday he would wake up and realise that everything had only been a bad dream.

However, that would never happen.

Taking a deep breath, Frederick knew what he had to do. Despite Oliver's threats, he could not abandon his chosen course for he knew it to be the right one. If he stayed, the darkness within his heart would ultimately poison all those around him, and eventually, they would come to resent him for it. If he left, however, they would mourn him for a little while—the way they mourned his father and brother—but then they would dry their tears, and a smile would return to their faces.

And so he would leave.

The only thing left to do was to father an heir to ensure his family's future.

Frederick swallowed, knowing that his wife's touch proved the greatest danger to his mind's determination. Only if he could suppress all sense of affection and intimacy, only when the veil of detachment hung closely around him, distancing him from her, could he touch her and not have her affect him, not have her sway him from his path.

For his family's sake, he had to try.

Sitting at her vanity, brushing out her hair, Ellie stared at her own reflection. Her eyes, however, remained distant, the rhythmic movement of her hand, brush stroke for brush stroke, soothing her heart.

Again, her mind conjured the moment her hand had brushed against Frederick's, and the scene unfolded before her eyes.

A few days ago after supper, they had risen from their chairs to return to the drawing room for some entertainment. Maryann and Mathilda had been practising a duet on the pianoforte for days, which they wished to share with their family that evening.

When they had filed through the doorway to the drawing room, Theresa had stopped in her tracks, turning back to Wilton, asking to have her shawl brought down. As she had stepped aside, Ellie had come to a halt as well, wondering if something was wrong. She had meant to lift her hand and place it on Theresa's arm to enquire after her well-being when Frederick had approached.

The moment her hand had come up, his had been right beside her, and the instant, her skin had touched his, a jolt had gone through them both.

Meeting his eyes, Ellie had felt his stare to the very core of her being. Her hand had tingled with anticipation, and her heart had thudded in her chest, making her catch her breath. Frederick had looked equally affected before a hint of displeasure, of disappointment had come to his eyes. Not with her, but rather with himself.

Without a word, he had walked away, not even excusing his absence.

Since then, he had kept to his study. When they happened to meet, he was always polite, always cordially enquiring after her sensitivities, but the connection she had felt before had been gone as though it had never been.

Disheartened, Ellie had spent the last few days walking the halls of Elmridge alone. More than once, Theresa and Maryann had enquired after her, but Ellie did not know what to say. Only too well did she understand what Frederick was doing. He was shutting himself off from her, from everyone. What she didn't know was what she could do to prevent it.

When the sun had finally disappeared behind the horizon, Ellie still sat at her vanity. Shrouded in darkness, she stared at her own reflection, barely able to see the line of her nose or the curve of her lips. No echo of recognition registered in her mind, and her heart remained untouched by what her eyes could not see.

Not a single candle burned in her room, and the summer's warm nights made a fire in the hearth unnecessary. Seeing the shadows dance across the walls behind her, Ellie's eyes shifted to the silvery crescent in the night sky.

Truly, it was a night for ghosts to roam the earth, to haunt the living.

That thought struck a spark, and Ellie's mind took her back to the first night Frederick had come to her bed as well as all the ones following. Upon entering, he had kept his gaze fixed on the floor and immediately extinguished each and every candle. More than once, Ellie had wondered why.

Now, she knew.

Haunted by his own ghosts, Frederick tried to hide in the shadows. As much as his heart might long for human companionship, it also feared the closeness that grew from it and, therefore, fought to protect itself. Only with the dark between them, keeping him safe like a shield, he would use to defend himself against an enemy, had he come to her bed.

A wicked smile curled up Ellie's lips as understanding dawned, and she realised that the dark could be her ally. Obviously, Frederick considered himself safe from her touch as long as the night wrapped its cloak about him.

Only the safety he sought was no safety at all, and she would make him understand. Deep down, his heart longed for more, but since he was not willing to see that in the light of day, then she would convince him in the dark of night.

Remembering the passion she had witnessed between Betty and Peter, Ellie smiled. Other senses might be more persuasive than the sense of sight.

A soft chuckle escaped her lips at the wickedness of her plan.

However, if Oliver was right, then Frederick would not leave unless she was with child, and, therefore, he would need to visit her bed.

And when he did, she would give him a reason to stay.

29

ONLY TO FEEL

A week passed, and every night, Ellie waited for her husband. After extinguishing all the lights, she would crawl into bed and lie in the dark, her body trembling with hope as well as the fear of disappointment. As the hours ticked by, her optimism would abandon her, and ugly doubt would creep into her heart. Some nights, she was determined to suffer this torture no longer and simply solve the problem by visiting him in his chambers. However, her courage always failed her. She never got further than her hand on the door handle.

This night was no different. The clock had already struck eleven, and the house lay in utter silence, a deafening silence that drummed in her ears and taunted her resolve. Rolling onto her side, Ellie hugged her arms around a pillow and closed her eyes to the pain of her husband's repeated rejection.

Feeling a soft draft caress her cheek, Ellie frowned. Had the door come ajar?

Turning onto her back, she lifted her head off the pillow and stared into the semi-darkness around her bed. Faint shadows hung on

the walls; however, one of them seemed to move, quiet footsteps carrying it closer.

Ellie's breath caught in her throat.

Although she could barely make out his silhouette in the dark, Ellie knew that he was there. Her skin tingled as it always did when he was near, and once again, her heart quickened its pace as though expecting her to run a marathon.

Quiet footfalls brought him closer, and his white nightshirt shimmered in the dark as he moved into the single beam of silvery light filtered in through a gap in the curtains. Ellie held her breath as though faced with a strange apparition and not her husband, a man of flesh and blood.

In the dark, however, he seemed otherworldly somehow. No sound came from his lips, and his eyes were hidden in the shadows. For a terrifying moment, Ellie's mind whispered, *What if it isn't him?*

Swallowing, Ellie pushed her fears aside, breathing in his familiar scent as it slowly bridged the small distance between them. As though completely torn, he smelled of fresh air and sunshine mingled with a sense of oppressive despair that settled on her nerves.

Again, Ellie swallowed as she realised how very conflicted he was. Had he indulged in spirits yet again in order to find the courage to come to her bed? Was he so terrified of allowing someone to come close?

As he sat down on the bed, it was as though a shock wave rolled across the mattress, washing over her before receding. Breathing in deeply, her head sank back onto the pillow while her eyes remained focused on his shadowy form, trying to find their counterparts in the darkness that hid his face.

In a slow, fluid motion, he slid under the blanket, and the warmth from his body reached out to her with tantalising fingers. Goosebumps rose on her arms and legs before he had even touched her, and Ellie wondered if her tingling nerves would allow her to proceed with her plan.

Inch by inch, the warmth radiating from his body came closer until it engulfed her whole. For a moment, Ellie closed her eyes and took a deep breath, willing her wits not to abandon her.

When she opened them again and looked up into the dark, she could barely make out his form as it hovered above her, his hands fisted into the mattress on either side of her head. His warm breath touched her skin, and more goose bumps broke out all over her body.

Staring into the eyes she could not see, Ellie marvelled at the sense of peace that came over her, and a loving smile touched her face.

This was where she ought to be.

When she felt his hand through the fabric of her nightgown as it moved up, pulling her nightgown along, the breath caught in her throat, and for a second, Ellie thought she would lose her nerve.

Caught in the memory of their previous encounters, Ellie felt her body grow rigid. Never had he touched her, not her bare skin, and clearly he had no intention of doing so tonight. A lump formed in Ellie's throat, and she allowed herself a moment of self-pity. *Why could he not feel the slightest bit of passion for her?*

However, as quickly as the emotion had seized her, it vanish, and her breathing continued in a slightly elevated rhythm, which her heartbeat matched, sending shivers throughout her body. If he wouldn't touch her, then it was up to her to take the first step.

Drawing in a deep, yet shaky breath, Ellie slowly lifted up her hand and reached out. In the dark, she could not see his face and was, therefore, forced to merely rely on her tactile sense. It did not lead her astray.

The moment, her fingertips touched his cheek, he froze, his hand resting on her thigh.

Hearing him draw in a slow and deep breath, Ellie moved her fingers down his cheek, skimming her thumb across his cheekbone. Her fingertips leisurely grazed his jawline, detecting a slight stubble, before she cupped her open palm to his cheek.

He exhaled slowly, almost painfully, and Ellie bit her lip as excitement coursed through her body.

For a moment, she remained still, her hand to his cheek, and waited.

When he made no move to stop her, Ellie lifted up her other hand and touched it to his face the same way. Her thumbs moved in small circles over his cheekbones before she drew her hands down, her fingers tracing the line to his mouth, over his lips and down the small dip along his chin.

All the while, he remained frozen in place as though untouched by her actions. Ellie, however, could feel his blood pulsing under her fingers matching the slow beat that echoed within her own.

Encouraged by his silent reaction, she skimmed her thumbs over his lips and was delighted when they parted slightly, his warm breath rushing over her fingertips.

Growing bolder, Ellie moved her hands back over his cheeks, around his neck and buried them in his thick hair. Her fingers traced the hard contours of his head as well as the soft skin in the back of his neck. Feeling the comparatively coarse texture of his nightshirt's collar touch her skin, Ellie pulled her hands back momentarily before reaching out once more and sliding them down his neck and under his shirt onto his shoulders.

A slow moan escaped his lips, and he sank down onto his lower arms, burying his face in the curve of her neck.

Shocked at his sudden reaction, Ellie lay still, her hands resting on his shoulders. The muscles in his back trembled ever so slightly, and tears came to her eyes as she realised the effort it took him not to run from her, from himself.

Gently, she trailed her fingers over his tense muscles, moving her hands down his back and then up to his shoulders. Smooth skin met her, interspersed with small scars from nicks and cuts. When her fingertips moved sideways to the soft skin below his shoulder blades, Ellie gasped.

Under his left shoulder, a larger scar rested, circular in nature as though an arrow had pierced his flesh. She drew her hand upward then over the ridge of his shoulder and down the front, finding an identical scar just below his collarbone.

A bayonet—she thought, closing her eyes to the horrible image conjured by the scars marking his body. *How had he survived such an attack?* She wondered, unwilling to picture the moment he had almost lost his life.

Kenneth.

The name shot into her mind like a lightning bolt. He had saved Frederick's life. She knew it to be true as though he had just confessed it to her. Kenneth had saved him while Frederick had been unable to return the favour.

Ellie closed her eyes, wrapping her arms around his strong shoulders. No wonder guilt had been able to sink its talons into his heart.

Holding him tight, Ellie took a deep breath, willing the images away. They had no place here in this bed.

Determined to return to the sensual pleasures her body had only just begun to explore, Ellie flattened her hands to his skin, then drew them up his back and over his shoulders to his neck, gently touching his skin as though her touch could heal the wounds that remained unseen.

All the while, his head remained buried in the curve of her neck, his warm breath tickling her skin, and surprised, Ellie noticed that his body no longer hovered above hers. At some point during her explorations, the distance between them had slowly grown smaller until his body had come to rest upon hers.

His weight pressed her into the mattress while his warm body covered her like a blanket, safe and secure. Turning her head, she felt her cheek touch his, and the sensation sent new shivers through her body. Her hands moved to his face, her fingers once more tracing his jawline and brushing over his lips.

He lifted his head then, and a part of Ellie mourned the closeness they had shared.

Looking up into his face, she wished she could see his eyes. What would they tell her? Were they peaceful, gentle, loving even? Or would she find a tortured expression resting in them? A hint of guilt? Of regret?

Swallowing, Ellie pushed all thoughts from her. For once, she would not think, not wonder, not doubt. The time for words would come, for her to ask and for him to explain. Now, however, she would only feel.

Gently cupping his face in her hands, she pulled him down to her, softly brushing her lips against his, revelling in the sweet sensation that spread from the small nerve endings in her lips to the rest of her body.

A jolt went through him at the first touch, and she brought his face close to hers again and again, her lips caressing his like the soft brush of a rose petal or a feather. Fleeting. There one moment, gone the next.

All her senses narrowed into this one sensation, focused only on the small place where their lips touched.

Time stopped until a strangled moan escaped his lips. As his arms moved up, his hands slid into her hair, and his body pressed deeper into hers. His mouth opened and covered hers in a desperate attempt to get closer.

For a tiny second, Ellie was stunned into silence as his hungry lips devoured hers and his hands caressed the slim line of her neck. She marvelled at the feelings that shot through her as though her body was under attack from an outside force. An attack she revelled in. An attack she never wanted to stop.

When his lips freed hers and moved down the line of her jaw, trailing kisses in their wake, Ellie closed her eyes, her teeth sinking into her lip. Holding on to him, she relinquished the control that had been hers and allowed him to take charge, enjoying the new sensations his lips and hands stirred within her body.

Never before had she felt like this. Never before had anyone touched her like this.

When his thumb skimmed over her cheek and his hand slid down the side of her neck, his fingertips gently brushing along her scarred skin, tears came to Ellie's eyes.

He did not retreat, did not pull back at the reminder of her tainted beauty. Instead, his hand retraced his path, exploring her scars as she had explored his, before it once again cupped her cheek, his lips finding hers once more.

In that moment, Ellie's heart soared to the heavens. In that moment, everything was perfect, and all thought left her body. For once, she wanted only to feel.

Doubts would return soon enough.

Returning his kiss, she wrapped her arms around his strong shoulders, curious about the pleasures that awaited her, and abandoned all thought.

30

THE MEMORY OF A TOUCH

inking into his bed, Frederick rolled onto his back, staring at the dark ceiling. His breath came in small gasps, and his heart drummed in his chest. Closing his eyes, he moaned and rolled over, his hands curling into fists. He buried his face in the pillow and growled in...

Was it frustration? Despair? Agony?

Settling back onto his back, Frederick focused on drawing one long breath after another into his body. After a small eternity, his heart calmed down, and his mind began to clear.

A mere hour ago, he had finally worked up the nerve to seek out his wife in her bedchamber. The decision had not been easy. However, he had always known that he could not leave his existence here at Elmridge behind without providing an heir to continue his family's line first. He knew his duty, and he had acted upon it. After all, he had shared his wife's bed before without it leading to further complications.

Only tonight, things had been different. *She* had been different.

Closing his eyes, Frederick once more felt her soft body beneath his, her gentle hands caressing his face, sliding up and under his shirt. He remembered the shock that had gone through him when her fingers had first touched his skin. Disbelief had clouded his mind then, and for a moment, he had thought himself lost in a dream. Then her soft lips had startled him awake, and although he had known that it was more than just foolish to allow her to continue, he had not been able to stop himself, let alone her. Instead, a deep desire, buried under layers of pain and guilt, had fought to the surface and claimed him whole.

His body had taken over then, devouring her with a hunger he had long since thought lost, and with each kiss, with each caress, the veil of detachment he had draped upon his shoulders had slid off, falling to the ground in a crumpled heap, all but useless. Unguarded, his heart had opened to her, to the soft whispers of her soul as her gentle fingers found the marks on his body. The story she had read there had echoed between them, guiding his own hands to the pain of her past in return. Feeling the scarred tissue of her neck beneath his fingers, he had sensed the pain that had been hers that fateful day long ago, and just as her touch had healed his pain, his own hands had moved over her skin with the same compassion and understanding that she had shown him.

He remembered her lips curling against his in a gentle smile as his fingers had touched the place of her shattered life. He remembered her heart beating against his chest, his own abandoning its own rhythm and joining hers. He remembered thinking that he loved her.

That thought had jolted him awake, terrified him to his very core, and he had fled her room like the coward he knew himself to be.

Cringing at the memory, Frederick rubbed his hands over his face. What kind of a man shared his wife's bed, took her body and then rushed from the room like a common criminal?

When his demons had risen to the surface, he had not even looked back at her before closing the door separating their rooms. Now lying in the cold dark, he wondered if her face had held the same disappointment and hurt he still felt in his own heart. And yet, the warmth from her body still clung to his skin, sending shivers up and down his back, and his lips tingled with the need to feel hers once again. His body ached with the need to feel her, and his soul felt all but hollow at the absence of her touch.

How was it that she could tear down his defences so easily? What was her secret?

Deep down, his soul recognised hers, and yet, his mind could not remember the hot summer's day years ago when his defences had been non-existent, and her curious eyes had seen into his heart with no difficulty.

A deep smile on her face, Ellie lay in bed amidst her crumpled sheets, remembering Maryann's words. To describe her recent experience as *enjoyable* would be an enormous understatement, and a giggle rose from her lips as she remembered the blush that had come to her friend's cheeks upon her rather inquisitive questions.

If she had known the sensations her body was capable of experiencing, Ellie would have demanded her marital rights a long time ago. Still, it was easy to speak in retrospect. After all, before tonight she had not known how Frederick would react to her touch. She had not known that he would respond so eagerly, and neither had she known that he would not in the least be appalled by her scars.

Snuggling into her blanket, Ellie remembered how his fingers had traced the marks the fire had left on her skin. Goosebumps had risen all over her body, and she had held her breath, only exhaling when his own explorations of her body had continued without any sign of delay or hesitation after what his nimble fingers had discovered.

Her scars were a part of her as his were a part of him, and although she wished she could take the pain and guilt off his shoulders, she knew he would not be the man he was without the experiences that had formed him.

Grinning, Ellie bit her lip, wondering if Frederick lay awake in his own bed as well. Was he also staring into the dark, remembering her touch on his skin? Did shivers run down his body at the thought of her lips on his?

Even at the memory, Ellie's heart thudded in her chest, quickening its pace as her thoughts travelled to the regions of his body that had brought her such pleasure. Her fingers ached to touch him again, and she had to fight herself to remain where she was and not tiptoe across the room, open the door and seek him out.

Ellie giggled at the shocked expression that would undoubtedly come to his face should she dare to do so.

Without warning, a hint of disappointment sneaked into her heart as she remembered how he had fled the room immediately after their love-making. And yet, she should have expected his reaction, she reminded herself. After all, her own surprise at what had happened could be nowhere near as great as his had to have been.

He needed time, and she would be patient; however, she would not wait forever.

Whether he liked it or not, she knew now what he could give her as well as what she could give him. And if fear should keep him away once more, then, by God, next time, she would be brave enough to seek him out instead.

Snuggling into the blanket, Ellie closed her eyes, a smile on her lips, and was soon fast asleep. In her dreams, she pictured the moment they would first lay eyes upon each other after what had happened between them.

31

VULNERABLE

As she descended the large staircase on her way to the breakfast parlour, Ellie felt her heart hammer against her ribcage, her hands trembled, and her breathing was far too rapid for someone who had only just risen from her bed. Even Betty had noticed her rather odd behaviour. Like a fool, Ellie had twirled a strand of her hair around her index finger, a wide smile on her face that seemed somewhat inscrutable. Although she had seen the slightly amused grin on her maid's face in the mirror, Ellie had not been able to persuade the corners of her mouth to return from the peeks they had risen to. Only now, when she was but a few steps away from meeting her husband in the light of day did the smile slide off her face, replaced by a rather strained expression that Ellie knew spoke of her nerves stretched to the limit.

On shaky feet, she proceeded down the corridor. Then before stepping into the breakfast parlour, she took a deep breath, trying to steady her nerves and willing her body to stop trembling. Was Frederick equally nervous about meeting her? About looking into her eyes after what had happened in the dark of her bedchamber?

Ellie only hoped that he would not treat her with indifference or worse polite detachment.

Arriving somewhat late, Ellie found the rest of the family already seated around the large table. The brilliant sun shone in through the tall windows, sending shimmering lights all over the room and sparkling in the polished silverware neatly laid down on each place setting. Smiling faces turned to her, a friendly greeting on their lips. Ellie, however, could scarcely pay them any attention as her eyes were drawn to the dark man at the head of the table.

As he beheld her, the teacup in his hand froze halfway to his lips, and his eyes met hers with an intensity that sent a shiver down her back and made her heart jump in her chest. Taking a deep breath, Ellie rounded the table, only vaguely aware of her lips mumbling a greeting to the rest of her new family. Her eyes, however, could not be forced to leave his, and as she sank down onto her chair, the butterflies in her belly fluttered about like never before.

Frederick cleared his throat, his gaze returning to the plate before him, a hint of unease tugging at the corners of his mouth.

Instantly, Ellie felt as though cast into the shadows, missing the light that shone in his eyes like the flowers missed the sun in the dark of night. Fortunately, she did not have to suffer for long as his gaze quickly returned to hers as though of its own accord. Although she could see the reluctance on his face, he could not keep his gaze from meeting hers, gliding from her eyes to her lips and further down, lingering in all the places that he had explored the night before.

Feeling her heart quicken, Ellie bit her lower lip as a tingling heat rose to her cheeks.

The ghost of a smile flashed over Frederick's face at seeing her reaction before he averted his eyes once more, distress clouding the joy that had played on his features only a moment before.

Ellie took a deep breath, glancing at the others seated nearby, too close for her liking as the atmosphere between her and her husband seemed suddenly charged with desire barely hidden underneath their polite exterior.

If at all.

Turning her head to look at Maryann and Theresa, Ellie tried to determine whether or not they had noticed the silent exchange between them. Both, however, were absorbed in conversation with each other and at least at the moment paid her little attention.

Relieved, Ellie returned her eyes to her husband.

Although he did his utmost to appear disinterested, as though her presence did not affect him in the least, his eyes would venture to hers again and again betraying the lie that he wanted her to believe.

Delighted with his inability to hide his feelings, Ellie smiled at him, her heart beating in her chest with such joy that she felt it would burst. She openly met his eyes then, sharing the depth of her own feelings without restraint, letting him see the place he held in her heart.

Drawing in a deep breath, Frederick swallowed, and she could see his understanding of what she had just revealed to him in his eyes.

Stunned, he stared at her, and Ellie could not help but wonder what thoughts went through his head at that moment. Was it so difficult for him to believe that she cared for him? Deeply? Could he not imagine that the scars and tears they had shared would bring them closer?

"Frederick?" Theresa called, and he blinked, clearing his throat. "Frederick, are you listening to me?"

Taking a deep breath, he turned to his mother, his eyelids blinking rapidly as though trying to clear the images still lingering in his mind. "Yes, Mother, what…? I apologise. I was…lost in thought."

The slightly tense expression on Theresa's face vanished, and she smiled at him before her eyes darted to Ellie for a split second. "I merely wondered," she asked, her voice strained, "whether or not you intended to attend this year's Midnight Ball?"

Ellie froze as the mention of Lord Branston's annual event brought back the memories of Leopold's death. Eyes darting to Maryann, Ellie found her gaze fixed on her plate, hands hidden in her lap. Instantly, her heart went out to her new sister-in-law, and she felt the almost desperate need to comfort her. Glancing at Frederick, Ellie could not imagine how his death would affect her. It was the worst fate possible.

"I am not certain," Frederick answered his mother's question, his own voice tinged with regret. "Do you wish to attend?" His eyes shifted from his mother's to Maryann's face.

Leopold's widow sighed before lifting her tear-heavy eyes off the remnants on her plate. Her gaze went around the table, lingering on all of them as though asking for advice, as though seeking an answer to a question she had not wanted asked in the first place. She took a deep breath then and licked her lips, but no sound could be heard.

Theresa reached out then, her hand closing around Maryann's. "It is all right, Dear." Her voice betrayed the same grief visible on her daughter-in-law's face. "There is no rush. The ball is still a few weeks away. I am certain Lord Branston will not hold it against us if we delay our answer."

Maryann nodded, a hint of relief playing on her beautiful features.

After breakfast, Frederick retreated to his study, and Ellie's eyes followed his tall form all the way down the corridor until he disappeared from sight. Tempted to go after him, she took a hesitant step forward.

"Elsbeth, do you have a moment?" Theresa asked, coming up behind her.

For a second, Ellie closed her eyes, reluctantly letting go of the delightful tingle that had settled over her at the thought of spending time alone with her husband. Compelling her features into a friendly smile, she turned to her mother-in-law. "Certainly. Is something wrong?"

"Come, walk with me," Theresa said, slipping her arm through hers. They went out the side door and into the gardens where the early sun glistened in the morning dew droplets still clinging to the hedges. "I meant to ask your advice. It is about Maryann."

"Is it about the Midnight Ball?" Ellie asked, feeling a sense of unease crawl up her back. Although she had not known him, the night of Leopold's death was etched into her mind. How hard was it for his mother and wife to return to a place where they had lost someone so dear to their hearts? A place that would not mourn his passing but celebrate life instead? Would they be able to bear that?

Theresa nodded. "It has almost been a year since Leopold was taken from us, and," she took a deep breath, her voice heavy with tears held in check, "a part of me believes that it is time for Maryann to move on."

Ellie stopped, her eyes searching her mother-in-law's face. "Do you truly believe that she ought to find a new husband so soon?"

Theresa shook her head. "I am not talking about a husband. I simply think that after a year of mourning Maryann needs to be reminded that life still holds beauty and joy." She took a deep breath and sank onto the bench, and Ellie sat down beside her.

"I am an old woman, and I have lived a wonderful life. Of course, I wish I hadn't seen the death of my son, but I take comfort from knowing that I will see him again soon." A delicate smile curled up the corners of her mouth, and Ellie took Theresa's hand in hers.

"But Maryann is young. Who knows what life still has in store for her? And I am so glad that she has found her smile again, her laughter and the joy of being with her family."

Theresa gently squeezed Ellie's hand. "I am so grateful that you have come to us," she whispered, and Ellie felt the heat of embarrassment touch her cheeks. "You have healed this family in a way I never thought possible. I see it every day when I look at Mathilda and Maryann. I feel it in my own heart, and lately, I've seen it in my son as well." Ellie's heart stopped, and a hopeful smile touched her lips. "Do not give up, dear child," Theresa whispered, giving her hand a gentle squeeze. "He is as mule-headed as his father, but his heart is in the right place. He wants to love you. I saw it in his eyes this morning."

An excited shiver went over Ellie as she remembered the veiled desire she had seen in his gaze. The struggle she had seen there proved Theresa's words to be true.

"He is afraid though," her mother-in-law continued. "More afraid than he ever was in his life. Allowing yourself to love, to be vulnerable is a great risk, and after everything he has lost within the last two years, he is hesitant. Do not give up on him."

Smiling at Theresa, Ellie tightened her hold on her hands. "I won't."

"Good," her mother-in-law said. "Now, about Maryann: do you think it would be too early to persuade her to go out into society again? I do not wish to push her too soon, but I know that she will need some convincing, or she will spend the rest of her life locked away on this estate."

Ellie shrugged. "I am not sure. Maybe it is not too early in general, but maybe the Midnight Ball is the wrong occasion. It is bound to bring back memories of Leopold's death. How could anyone expect her to be in good spirits when faced with the memory of her husband's death?"

"You're right," Theresa nodded. "But you do agree that she ought to go out among people again, do you not?"

"I do, yes."

"Good. Then we'll just have to find an occasion that will allow her to forget her sadness for a night and be the young woman that she is."

A smile on her face, Ellie nodded.

32

DESIRE

Standing before the window, Frederick stared past the water fountain at the two women seated on the bench while the stack of paperwork on his desk remained as it was. What were they talking about? He wondered.

Again and again, he dragged his eyes from the window and forced his feet to carry him across the room, and yet, before long he would always find himself back in this very spot, staring at his wife. It was as though she had cast a spell on him, drawing his thoughts to her despite his efforts to focus on something else.

Rubbing his hands over his face, he began to pace the length of the room.

In his mind's eye, he once more saw her radiant smile as her gaze had met his over breakfast, the memory of the previous night edged into them. Heat had flared up in his veins, and the breath had caught in his throat. As she had bitten her lower lip, he had almost lost control, the desperate need to touch her coursing through his veins.

What had he done? How could he have been so careless? Not only had he gone to her bed, but he had also allowed her touch to tear down the walls he had so painstakingly erected around himself. And now, he was not only risking his own heart, but hers as well.

Despite his daftness when it came to matters of the heart, Frederick could not have overlooked the love and desire that had shone in her eyes that morning. He knew that she cared for him, that she might even love him, and that thought terrified him more than anything else.

Once he left, she would be the one to suffer. Instead of protecting her, he had placed her in harm's way. How could he have been so careless?

His jaw firmly set, he glanced outside at the by now empty bench, determined to protect her, even if it meant from himself. Never again would he share her bed; it was too great a risk.

As an almost painful sense of regret flooded his heart at the mere thought of never feeling her soft skin under his hands again, a rather obnoxious voice whispered in his head, reminding him of the yet unresolved issue of an heir.

Cursing under his breath, Frederick raked his hands through his hair, welcoming the dull pain as he tried to pull it out by the roots.

A knock sounded on his door, and Frederick spun around. For a moment, he closed his eyes and tried to regain his composure before calling for the person on the other side of the door to enter.

Grabbing a handful of papers from his desk, Frederick looked up as dainty footsteps echoed on the parquet floor, and his heart nearly stopped when he found himself looking at his wife, who just then closed the door behind her.

They were alone.

Frederick swallowed, retreating until he felt the desk in his back. "My lady?" he whispered, his mind unable to form a coherent sentence as it was currently occupied with the way her lips curled up into a soft smile that lit up her beautiful eyes. Those eyes that had seen into his soul more than once and that always seemed to know just how to render his defences useless.

"Frederick, I need to speak with you."

"Frederick?" he repeated, gawking at her.

She stopped a few steps in front of him, and her eyes met his as a rather mischievous curl came to her lips. "Do you not consider it appropriate?" she asked, a kind challenge in her voice, and took a step closer.

Stiffening, Frederick drew in a sharp breath.

"Is something wrong?" she enquired, eyeing him curiously. "You seem stressed." Again, she took a step closer and then another until she stood before him, the sweet scent of her soft skin muddling his mind.

Taking shallow breaths, Frederick tried to ignore the siren's call that echoed in his blood. How was it that he could suddenly not be in the same room with her without feeling the desperate need to wrap her in his arms?

Striding over to the window front, Frederick cleared his throat and took a deep breath. Yes, a little distance helped clear his mind. Turning to face her once more, he linked his hands behind his back, thus, hopefully avoiding any unwise initiation of physical contact from his side. "What can I do for you, my lady?"

A knowing smile played on her lips as she met his eyes. "It is about Maryann. I just spoke to your mother, and we agree that the Midnight Ball might not be the best occasion for Maryann to return to society."

Transfixed by the way her lips moved as she spoke, Frederick barely heard what she said as his mind recalled the softness of her lips and his own began to tingle in pleasure.

"However, we also agree that it will be time soon to persuade Maryann to accompany us to an appropriate event," his wife continued, and Frederick tried to force his attention to the soft words spoken with her beautiful voice. "It is not good for her to spend all her time alone with only us for company. She needs to see other people and come to realise that it is all right for her to be happy again. Do you not agree?"

Frederick froze. From the sound of her voice, he knew that she had just asked him a question; however, his mind was unable to provide him with any content to which he could reply. Still transfixed by her lips, he watched them turn into a beautiful smile, a smile that slowly moved toward him.

Clearing his throat, Frederick blinked. His eyes finally settled on hers as she crossed the last few steps between them, and he drew in a sharp breath.

Standing before him, her deep blue eyes looked up into his, and again, a somewhat mischievous smile curled up her lips before she spoke. "Do you wish to kiss me?"

Heat shot up Frederick's face, and he mumbled unintelligible sounds like an idiot. At a loss, he took a step backward as all rational thought abandoned him.

A delighted chuckle rose from her throat, and once again, she bit her lower lip, the hint of a blush colouring her own cheeks. However, unlike him, she did not appear witless, but instead a spark of determination came to her eyes, and she closed the distance between them once again. Holding his gaze, she lifted her hands and gently placed them on his chest.

Frederick drew in a sharp breath, feeling his resolve melt away.

"May I ask a question?" she whispered as her warm breath brushed over his skin.

Gritting his teeth, he swallowed and just barely managed to nod his head.

The smile still on her face, she asked, "How come you have never kissed me? Do you not want to?"

Jolted awake, Frederick stared at her, his gaze once more drawn to her soft lips. "Yes, I do…I mean, I…I have." Embarrassed by his own inability to voice his thoughts in a coherent fashion, Frederick turned away, but her hands still resting on his chest stopped him.

"I meant outside of the bedchamber," she clarified as her own cheeks turned a deeper shade of red; and yet, despite her own embarrassment, her eyes never left his. "And was it not I who initiated that kiss as well?"

"I do believe so," he said, watching his words fall against her lips. Releasing the tight grip he had on his hands, his arms came forward, slowly reaching for her.

Her hands pressed tighter against his chest as she moved into him, her head tilted upward, welcoming his lips.

Surprised, Frederick noticed that his head was beginning to lean down toward her, her lips closer now than they had been a mere moment before. His heart thudded against her hands, and he cursed under his breath as his voice of reason issued a warning.

An agonising growl rose from his throat then, scaring away all objections his mind could possibly bring before him. Desire took him, and his hands came around her, pulling her closer.

Her breathing had quickened as well, and her fingers dug into his shirt.

Unable to resist any longer, Frederick lowered his head, his mouth hungry for hers, when voices suddenly echoed through the door, quickly followed by a short, but determined knock.

As his head snapped up, his eyes burned a hole into the door. "May the devil take them all," he growled, frustration ringing in his voice.

"I will see you tonight," his wife whispered as she stepped out of his embrace, a delighted smile playing on her lips. Her eyes held his a moment longer before she turned away and opened the door.

Damn them all to hell, Frederick thought, watching her leave.

33

IN HIS HANDS

Never before had Frederick noticed the intricate wavy grain of the door that connected his bedchamber to his wife's. As the moon slowly climbed the horizon, its crescent hanging high in the sky watching over the sleeping world, Frederick remained frozen to the spot. Staring at the heavy wooden door, he lifted a hand, reaching for the doorknob, only to pull it back as though slapped a moment later.

Raking his hands through his hair, he groaned, then spun around and started pacing the room. The skin covering his skull ached, and he thought that should this continue he would surely be bald soon—and mad.

As his blood boiled in his veins, making it increasingly difficult to maintain a clear head, Frederick felt his muscles tense, trying to hold on to the control he felt slipping away.

Her siren call was as strong now as it had been this afternoon. Only too well did he remember his own surrender and the desperate need to hold her in his arms and feel her soft lips on his own. Had his mother and Maryann not knocked on the door to his study at precisely that moment, he would have been lost, his resolve melted away by her radiant blue eyes. And even after she had left the room, his mind had been solely focused on her; he barely remembered what his mother and Maryann had meant to tell him. He sincerely hoped it had not been important.

Approaching the window, he stared at the night sky, the moon's soft, silver light touching the earth with gentle fingers. Frederick didn't know why, but the dark had something soothing, calming as though the brightness of day hurt his eyes and the night provided the necessary relief to regain his strength and face another day.

Resting his forehead against the cool window pane, he closed his eyes. Even though every fibre of his body argued against it, Frederick knew that he had to take a stand. There could be no further intimacies with his wife for his resolve, weak as it was, would not survive it. Somehow, he would need to make her understand that it was for the better.

A soft knock echoed through the door, and Frederick's eyes snapped open.

Unable to move, he listened, knowing that the knock had not come from the door leading out to the corridor, but instead from his wife's bedchamber; and the struggle within him began anew.

How could he take a stand when his own resolve was non-existent?

Lifting his head off the glass, he turned around, staring at the door, willing it to open while at the same time fearing that it would. How could anyone be so conflicted and not go mad?

His eyes fixed on the door handle, he watched it move downward, slowly, quietly before the door began to slide open. Holding his breath, Frederick took a step backwards and collided with the wall, feeling the cool glass of the window against his fingertips.

The moment his gaze met hers, Frederick knew he was lost.

The soft light of the moon touched her deep blue eyes, lending them a sparkle that made him catch his breath. A shy smile curled up her lips as she tiptoed into his room in nothing but her nightgown, her bare feet making no sound on the wooden floor. In her right hand, she held a candle, its warm, orange glow the only colour in an otherwise dark world.

"Are you avoiding me?" Her melodious voice asked, dancing across the room and touching his heart so effortlessly. "I've been waiting." Even in the dim light, he could see the soft glow that came to her rosy cheeks as she once again fought down her own nerves and pursued her heart's desire.

How could such strength live within her when his own legs had turned to pudding at the mere sight of her? He wondered. However, maybe the difference lay within the fact that while she followed her heart's desire, he, on the other hand, was fighting his.

"I assure you, my lady, I am not avoiding you," he croaked, then cleared his throat. "I merely...I...You ought not to be here." Taking a step forward, he met her eyes, willing his face to remain unaffected by her sweet scent that drifted to his nose. Once again, he linked his hands behind his back and straightened his shoulders, hoping to portray the determination he did not feel.

"I am your wife," she whispered, slowly approaching him. A delighted smile played on her lips, and her eyes shone with a devotion that almost choked the air from his lungs. "Why ought I not be here?"

Realising that he could not fool her, Frederick swallowed. Despite his best efforts, she could still see through his mask to the core of his being, his own desires reflected back to him in her open eyes. "My lady, the hour is late. You ought to be in bed."

"I was." Grinning, she bit her lip, taking another step toward him. "However, this afternoon, you led me to believe that you would join me. Have you changed your mind?"

Watching her approach, Frederick drew in a deep breath, and his arms returned to his sides.

When she came to stand an arm's length before him, her eyes melted into his as though trying to help him see the futility of his efforts to keep himself locked away from the world. "At some point," she whispered across the small dancing flame, "we all need to face our fears."

Lifting her other hand, she licked her thumb and index finger. Then she took a deep breath, and Frederick noticed that her hands were trembling. Holding his gaze, she extinguished the flame, and a small shiver went over her as she exhaled.

Then the smile returned to her lips, and she set down the candlestick on the desk beside them. "Fear must be felt and faced," she said, once more placing her hands on his chest, "before we lose ourselves to it."

Frederick swallowed, feeling her soft skin through the thin fabric of his shirt. The warmth of her body so close to his engulfed him whole and melted away the ice that clung to his heart. "Does fire not frighten you anymore?" he whispered, brushing a stray curl from her forehead, his eyes gliding over her scars before returning to look into hers.

"It does," she admitted, and a soft tremble shook her lips. "But I do my best not to let that fear control me. It is a struggle. Every day." Her lips relaxed before a smile reclaimed them once more. "But it is worth it."

Nodding, he looked down at her, his hand cupping the side of her face.

"I know that you feel more at ease in the dark," she whispered, her eyes never leaving his. "I know that at least for now you need it to let down your guard." She swallowed, then inhaled deeply before speaking again. "What I'm asking is are you willing to share it with me? Or do you rather want me to go?" The hands that rested on his chest began to tremble.

Looking down at her, Frederick realised that her fear of fire was not the only thing that still haunted her. Despite the courage she so often portrayed, she, too, risked her heart by so openly offering it to him, and the fear of having it broken was clearly edged into her eyes.

For so long his sense of self-preservation had dominated his actions. Fear of the sufferings human interaction would bring had made him shy away from everyone in his life, had made him determined to keep himself at a distance because deep down he knew that he was only one step away from losing his mind and giving up his life for good.

However, in that moment, when she stood before him and opened her heart to him, allowing herself to be vulnerable, everything changed.

Gazing into her eyes, Frederick smiled, and a sense of peace washed over him that he had not felt in a long time. "I don't ever want you to go," he whispered, and a smile spread over her face that could have lit up the night.

Pulling her into his arms, his eyes caressed her face, gliding from her own to her lips and over the scars that had brought them together. He could look at her for hours, feeling her warm body moulded against his.

His arms tightened around her then, pressing her closer to him, and the moment changed. In her open eyes, he could see tenderness slowly be replaced by desire as it pushed to the front. She raised her chin, her eyes dipping to his lips.

Frederick took a deep breath, knowing that there was no turning back, not that he wanted to. Slowly, he lowered his head and captured her mouth with his. A soft moan escaped her, and she melted against him as his strong arms held her.

Just as she had done the night before, she handed over the reins and allowed him to guide her through the sensual pleasures of the marriage bed, her trust in him unwavering.

And for the first time since he had returned home, Frederick did not flinch at the thought of someone else's happiness resting in his hands.

34

A SEVERE CASE OF INATTENTION

hen Ellie awoke the next morning, the memory of the previous night still played on her lips, and she stretched lazily before even opening her eyes. It had been a long time since she had slept this well.

Reaching out her hand, she found the other side of the bed empty, and a stab of disappointment penetrated the love pulsing in her heart.

Despite everything they had shared the night before, Frederick had left. He had even risen from his own bed in order to avoid waking up next to her.

Ellie sighed.

Sitting up, her eyes shifted to the window where brilliant sunlight filtered in through the half-closed curtains, casting a beam across the floor, which touched her nightgown that still lay in a crumpled heap on the Persian rug.

A smile tugged at Ellie's lips at the memory of how it had gotten there, and an excited shiver shot up and down her body as the warmth returned to her heart.

He loved her; she was sure of it. However, his demons still plagued him, and as she had so observantly noted the night before, he felt safest in the shadows. The light of day scared him; it was too revealing, too painful.

Ellie reminded herself that she would have to be patient, and yet, she knew that treading too lightly would only make things worse. Frederick's way of dealing with the pain in his past was avoidance, which would only lead to more heartache. At some point, he would need to turn around and face his fears, and if he was not willing to do so on his own, then she would have to see to it herself.

Slipping back into her nightgown, Ellie returned to her chamber and rang for Betty. After putting on a new gown and having her hair styled in the casual fashion she had come to like, Ellie went downstairs for breakfast.

Upon approaching the back parlour, chatty voices drifted to her ears, and Ellie realised that she was late yet again. Apparently, spending the night in her husband's arms caused her to oversleep.

"Good morning," she greeted the rest of her family, who welcomed her with equal delight. Taking her seat, she met her husband's eyes and found a warm glow on his face as he gazed at her. Although clearly still suffering from a touch of self-consciousness, his eyes did not have the slightly shocked expression that she had seen there the day before.

Breakfast was a delight as Ellie's doubts with regard to her husband's feelings seemed to have evaporated. Instead, she revelled in the shy smiles they exchanged under their family's scrutinising eyes, and whenever her gaze met his, her heart danced in her chest.

It was truly a wonderful day.

Or at least, a wonderful morning.

After spending an hour in the drawing room with Theresa and Maryann as they discussed their upcoming tea party, Ellie began to feel the separation from her husband acutely. Fidgeting in her seat, she glanced at the door again and again, hoping that he would join them; what rational reason there was for him to do so, she could not say.

"Why don't you go see him?" Theresa suggested, and Ellie's head snapped around. Her mother-in-law smiled at her, then reached out and patted her knee. "Go talk to him, and ask if he has any objections to the date we've chosen."

Staring at Theresa, Ellie raked her brain but could not recall the conversation her mother-in-law was referring to. "The date," she mumbled, glancing at Maryann, whose lips were stretched into a knowing smirk. "Yes, the date. Well…"

"We thought September the 28th would be fine," Theresa reminded her, an amused smile playing on her lips. "Two weeks after the Midnight Ball."

"Yes," Ellie said, rising to her feet. "I'll ask him." Excusing herself, she turned to the door, hoping that neither woman would notice the slight skip in her step. At the mere prospect of seeing her husband, her limbs seemed to be unable to remain calm and allow for a graceful exit.

"Take your time," Theresa called after her before the door closed.

Drawing in a deep breath, Ellie hastened down the corridor, crossed the grand foyer and approached her husband's study in record time, her heart racing in her chest. Before knocking on the door, though, she took a few calming breaths, feeling suddenly shy at the thought of him seeing her excitement.

Hearing his voice bidding her to enter, Ellie clenched and unclenched her hands, willing them to stop trembling. Then she opened the door, and the moment her eyes met his, all air was knocked from her lungs.

To her great pleasure, Frederick stared at her with the same childish delight she felt in her own heart, the paper in his hand long forgotten. Before long he swallowed and cleared his throat. "Is there anything I can do for you…Elsbeth?" he asked, returning the paper to his desk and coming toward her.

A glorious tingle surged through her body at hearing her name on his lips, and a deep smile came to her own. Unable to bear the distance between them any longer, Ellie closed the door behind her and approached him. "I came to speak to you about the tea party?" she said, hoping her voice did not sound as unsteady as it felt. "We agreed that the 28th would be perfect."

A frown drew down his eyebrows, and for a moment, Ellie feared that something was wrong. "Tea party?" he asked. "What tea party?"

Eyeing him curiously, Ellie took another step forward. "The tea party for Maryann." When the confused expression on his face did not clear, Ellie laughed. "They came to speak to you about it yesterday. Do you not remember?"

For a moment, his eyes widened as though the suitable memory had come to him at last. However, a second later, he averted his eyes and cleared his throat as though embarrassed.

"Is something wrong?" Ellie asked. "Is there a problem? Have you changed your mind?"

"No, no." He shook his head, hands suddenly linked behind his back. "The 28th is fine."

Narrowing her eyes, Ellie looked at the slightly flustered expression on his face. "You really do not remember that they came to talk to you about that?"

"Well, I…" He swallowed, his hands gesturing futilely. "I was distracted," he finally admitted. Returning to his desk, he shuffled through the papers before him, moving them from one side to the other and back again.

"Distracted?" Rounding the desk, she came to stand before him. "What distracted you?"

Straightening, he closed his eyes and took a deep breath. Then he turned to her and met her enquiring gaze. A soft smile curled up his lips as he spoke, "You."

Ellie's eyes opened wide. "Me?" A delicious warmth spread through her body, and she swallowed as his eyes burned into hers. "But I…I wasn't even in the room. How could I have…?" Her voice trailed off when realisation dawned and she finally understood just how she could have posed as a distraction even in her absence.

"You were still on my mind, though," he admitted somewhat sheepishly, confirming the line of her thinking. "I admit I did not hear a word they said."

Once again, butterflies took flight in her belly, and Ellie would have loved nothing more than to dance around the room in his arms. However, the hint of apprehension, almost hidden in the corners of his eyes, told her that he was not ready for such displays of affection. So instead, Ellie smiled at him, her hands once more coming to rest on his chest as though they belonged there. "I myself experienced a similar inattention only this morning," she confessed, feeling his heart jump against her palms at her open words. "Your mother had to remind me of the date we had agreed on for I honestly could not recall it."

A soft laugh left his lips and fell onto her own. "I have never experienced anything like it."

Ellie smiled, holding his gaze. "Nor I."

35

A TRUTH FELT

A few days later, her hand gently brushed down his arm as she stepped by him and followed his mother into the front parlour. Despite the layers of fabric, his whole body froze at the soft touch, its echo pulsing into every region of his being. Staring after her until the door closed and erased her from sight, Frederick forgot the world around him.

Moments passed, and still he remained rooted to the spot, hypnotised by sensations he had thought himself incapable of.

Over the past few weeks, his life had changed considerably, and yet, he did not know how to feel about it. On the one hand, he delighted in the love he shared with his wife. Yes, after days of denial, he had finally admitted to himself—although not yet to her—that he was in love. How she had breached his defences; he still didn't know. However, her gentle, yet insistent love had awakened his cold soul. Long forgotten desires soared to the surface of his being, demanding to be heard, and despite his own insistence, he was unable to stay away from her.

The nights they spent in each other's arms, shrouded in darkness. In these moments, Frederick could pretend that his past did not matter, that he was free to love and be loved in return for she knew who he was. With her, he held nothing back, sharing not only the scars on his body but also those edged into his soul.

And despite the doubts he initially had, she understood. She did not judge or pity him. She simply listened, and she cared.

Her gentle touch was like a balm for his soul, soothing the many cuts it had suffered. Not since before he had left for the war had Frederick felt this alive.

However, despite everything he felt during the night, the sun rose every morning, bringing with it the guilt and pain that the dark had so effectively hidden. A part of him wondered if it was the loss of her touch that brought back his doubts, for whenever they would come upon each other during the day, the magic of the night would return. A mesmerising smile on her lips, she would come to him, her hands brushing over his arm or taking his hand in hers. Her fingers would skim over his cheek before her arms would come around him, and he would feel whole again, all doubt banished by the love that shone in her eyes.

The most rational part of his mind that remained undisturbed by the guilt he felt in his heart reminded him day in and day out that Kenneth's death was not his fault; there had been nothing he could have done to save him, the same was true for his father and brother. His heart, however, could not be swayed. Deep down, he felt guilty, and no matter what he did or what he told himself, the feeling would not leave. It was there when he woke, and it was there when he went to bed. Sometimes, he could make himself forget or ignore it, but it never ceased to be.

One afternoon, Frederick sat in his study, his face buried in his hands. His head throbbed, and his heart ached. All day he had spent wading knee-deep through the issues that arose from a large estate such as Elmridge. Tenant quarrels had taken up most of his time, delaying the paperwork that needed to be completed. Minute by minute, the lightness that had carried him through the early morning had vanished, making room for the dark thoughts that always lingered nearby.

More than anything, he felt deficient. Unlike him, his father and brother had single-handedly run the estate with a smile on their faces. The anger that sometimes rose in his heart had never overtaken them. They had been strong while he was weak.

Not his brother, but he, Frederick, should have died that night of the Midnight Ball.

Stomping around the room and tearing at his hair, Frederick felt tempted to punch the wall or to throw the decanter through the window and hear the glass shatter. Dark thoughts, destructive thoughts entered his mind, and his limbs trembled with the effort to hold himself in check.

A knock sounded on the door, and an agonising growl rose from deep in his throat for Frederick knew that his nerves were close to snapping, and he feared for anyone in his presence when that happened.

When his wife entered, it was like a punch in the gut, and Frederick nearly toppled over. He stumbled backward to put as much distance between them as possible until his back hit the wall.

The second her gaze came to rest upon his face, the smile died on her lips and she froze. Her eyes narrowed, searching his own as though hoping to find an explanation for his erratic behaviour.

"Leave!" he hissed wringing his hands, not knowing what else to do with them. It had been only a matter of time before he would lose his mind. Although the last few weeks had lulled him into a false sense of security, Frederick had always known that.

"What happened?" she asked, coming toward him.

Frederick shook his head, backing away. "Don't!" Stepping behind his desk, he pointed to the door. "Leave!"

For a long moment, she looked at him, the blue in her eyes deepening, before she slowly shook her head.

"Please!" he pleaded, his fingers curling around the backrest of his chair, their sinews standing out white. "I do not wish to hurt you."

A soft smile came to her lips then, and she approached him, coming to stand on the other side of his desk. "You won't."

The certainty he heard in her voice he did not feel in his heart, and so he raked his mind for some way to make her leave. "Get out!" he snarled. "I don't want you here!"

Instead of the shock he had hoped to see on her face, her eyes merely narrowed. Squaring her shoulders, she stood up tall and met his gaze, her own as unwavering as his. "What is your problem?" she asked, and her voice sounded cold.

Stunned, Frederick stared at her.

She scoffed then and shook her head at him. "I am tired of this. You are the marquess now, and you need to find a way to handle your issues without succumbing to your guilt." She exhaled loudly, sounding impatient. "What bothers you today? Is it your friend? Or your brother?"

Still staring at her, Frederick couldn't believe his ears.

"Speak!" she snapped, annoyance hardening her voice even more.

"How dare you?" he snarled, leaning forward and bracing his hands on the desk. "You know nothing of the burdens I carry!"

His wife laughed. "Forgive me, my lord," she mocked, "but the scars you bear do not even begin to compare to mine." Her lips pressed into a tight line, she glared at him. "All your life, you've had it easy. The second son, freed from all responsibility, and yet, you only saw yourself as deprived of the honour bestowed upon your brother. And then you had to play soldier!" She shook her head, a hint of disgust in her eyes.

His blood rushing in his ears, Frederick rounded the desk, a snarl contorting his face. "What would you know of being a soldier?" he growled. "You have never experienced such hell!"

"Hell?" she asked. "What hell? Nothing happened to you! A few cuts and bruises and you demand the pity of everyone around you?" A snarl on her lips, she shook her head. "No, that right is not yours to claim. Instead, it was your friend who died a hero. He gave his life to save yours, and you let him!"

Feeling her words like blows to his body, Frederick groaned in agony. Panting for breath, he stared at her. "Why would you speak to me like this?" he barked. "I did not let him!"

"From what your mother told me," his wife continued, her voice as cold as ice, "your relationship has never been one of equals. He followed you wherever you led. You knew that! You knew he would give his life for you, and yet, you insisted he accompany you."

"I didn't!" Frederick growled. "I merely informed him of my decision. He was the one who offered. It was his decision!"

His wife sneered at him. "It was not, and you know it! You know as well as I do that nothing could have kept him from your side. He even abandoned his own fiancée, the woman he loved, to follow you on this childish quest! And now, he is dead, and she is alone, heartbroken; the man she loved is gone forever." His wife shrugged, and the derision he saw in her eyes knocked the breath from his lungs. "But you're alive. Better him than you, isn't that what you think? You're glad that he is dead, that you could return home to safety, to your family and the title that now is yours. You have finally gotten everything you've ever wanted!"

His jaw clenched painfully, and his hands balled into fists. Panting under his breath, he stared at his wife as rage surged through his heart. All the dark thoughts and emotions he had suppressed for so long poured out of him and rose to the surface of his being. His muscles tensed, strained to the point of breaking. "You will not speak of him!" he roared, feeling his pulse thudding in his neck, and without conscious thought, his hands shot forward and grabbed his wife by the arms, holding her in an iron grip. Lowering his face to hers, he snarled, "You know nothing of Kenneth! Don't you dare speak of him again!"

Oblivious to everything around him, Frederick's head snapped up when the door suddenly opened. Their eyes wide and faces pale, his mother and Maryann rushed into the room, staring at him in open shock. "What is going on?" his mother gasped, her eyes shifting to his wife. "What are you doing? Release her! Now!"

"Out!" Frederick bellowed. "This does not concern you!"

"But—" his mother began to object before his wife silenced her. "Leave us," she whispered, her eyes, however, remained on his, their depth fixing him with an icy stare.

After a moment of hesitation, his mother and Maryann retreated. The door closed, and he was alone with his wife once more.

"Like a shadow, he followed you wherever you went," she hissed and raised her chin, her arms straining against the tight grip of his hands. "You took him for granted and repaid his kindness and devotion with indifference. You did not care whether he lived or died so long as you were safe, so long as he kept you safe."

The tip of his nose touched hers as he snarled at her through clenched teeth. "I would have given my life for him!"

"Then why didn't you?" she demanded. "Why didn't you save him?"

"Because I couldn't!" Before he had formed a conscious thought, the words flew out of his mouth and echoed in his heart, releasing the pain he had hidden from since the day Kenneth had died. "I couldn't," he repeated as though to himself. "He was gone before I even knew what was happening." Swallowing, he closed his eyes as grief slowly swept through his body.

"It was not your fault." Like a soft melody, his wife's voice touched his broken heart, and he opened his eyes, finding her own full of love and compassion. "You loved him," she whispered, "and I know you would have given your life for him." A sad smile curled up her lips, and she lifted her hands, placing them on his chest where they belonged. "It's what you do for a brother."

As his eyes swept her face and he finally felt the truth of her words in his heart, his hands loosened their hold on her arms. His muscles hurt from the unbearable burden that he had carried with him for so long, the burden that was slowly growing lighter. Gently, he drew her against him, resting his forehead against hers and closed his eyes.

"It is always easier to give your own life," his wife whispered, her soft breath brushing over his lips, "than to lose someone you love and go on without them." She inhaled deeply, and a faint shiver went through her. "I know my brother would have felt guilty had I died saving his life, and yet, I never would have wanted him to," she lifted her head and placed a hand under his chin to make him look at her, "because what happened to me that day was not as bad as losing him would have been." Tears stood in her eyes. "I know that I got the easier end of the bargain. My brother is alive and well while Kenneth is not." She swallowed and took a deep breath. "But I need you to believe right now that it was not your fault. We all make our own decisions, and even if Kenneth's motivation to join the army stemmed from his deep desire to protect you, it was still his decision. He knew that he could not live with himself if he didn't do everything within his power to assure that you would return home safely." Gently, her hand cupped his face. "Your pain would have been his, and he didn't want that. Just as you would never have blamed him for staying home, you must not blame yourself for him going with you. You are not responsible for the fate of the world, not even for that of your own small world."

Frederick nodded, and for the first time, it was not his mind he felt agree with her words. Yes, her reasoning was rational and made absolute sense, and yet, the words she spoke did not matter because in that moment Frederick was listening with his heart.

A lightness spread through him that he remembered from innocent days of his childhood, and although grief flooded his heart, still as fresh and painful as it had been the day of his greatest loss, he did not mind it. Kenneth was gone, and so were his father and brother; however, the love he had for them remained. He felt it in the grief that echoed in his heart and brought tears to his eyes, and despite the agony that shook his body, he welcomed it because without grief it was as though love had never been. Only love led to grief, and so the pain that brought him to his knees was a testament to the love he felt for them.

Clinging to his wife, he wept, not ashamed of his tears because he knew that they were the means to a new beginning. He had spent the past two years locked away in misery, his inability to cope with the loss he had suffered casting dark shadows over his entire family. They, too, had suffered, but no more.

He would cry for the ones he had lost, and he would remember them, but he would not join them. He would walk through life with a smile on his face and the woman he loved by his side.

Feeling her arms wrapped tightly around his shoulders, he smiled as tears continued to roll down his cheeks and onto her already soaked sleeve. "I love you," he whispered, grateful beyond words that she had come into his life.

"I love you, too," was the last thing he remembered her saying before the world around him lost all meaning, and all there was was her.

36

A DIP IN THE LAKE

Taking off her shoes and stockings, Ellie brushed her bare feet across the smooth grass, feeling its blades tickle her soles. As the autumn sun continued to burn down on her head, she pushed herself off the ground, lifted up her skirts and took a tentative step toward the shallow bank of the lake.

"Is it not cold?" Frederick asked from behind her as she dipped the tip of her left foot into the clear water. "You are not seriously planning to swim, are you?"

Laughing, Ellie turned to look at him, a smile on her face. "Not at the moment," she said, biting her lower lip, and he smiled at her. "Please, it is truly wonderful. You should join me, my lord."

"My lord?" he repeated, and his eyes narrowed before the corners of his lips drew up into a knowing smile. "Are you trying to bait me, *my lady*?"

Delighted with their friendly banter, Ellie took another step backwards, feeling the cool water swirl around her ankles, her heated skin welcoming the rare sensation. "I have to admit I am rather surprised to find you such a stick in the mud, my lord," Ellie mocked, enjoying the amused curl that came to his lips. "I would have thought you more daring."

Grinning from ear to ear, Frederick kicked off his boots and then proceeded to pull off his stockings, all the while keeping his eyes fixed on hers. Then he strode toward the water, and Ellie took a few steps backward as he came toward her, not slowing down as his feet slipped into the water. Within a moment, he was before her, his arms coming around her waist, pulling her closer, his lips seeking hers. "Is this daring enough for you, Elsbeth?" he asked and immediately captured her mouth, not letting her answer.

Losing herself to the moment, Ellie dropped her skirts—which were instantly claimed by the lake's cool water as it slowly travelled upward, moulding the thin fabric to her legs. Her attention, however, was currently directed elsewhere as her heart thudded in her chest at the feeling of her husband's hungry lips on hers. His arms pulled her tighter against him, and she buried her hands in his thick hair.

When he finally released her, she was panting for breath, her cheeks flushed.

Gazing down at her, Frederick smirked. "You seem flustered, my lady. Is something amiss?" Then his eyes shifted down, and he noticed her soaked skirts. His eyes instantly became serious. "I'm sorry, Elsbeth." Taking her hand, he pulled her toward the shoreline. "I shouldn't have done that. You'll catch a cold wearing a wet dress."

"It is just the hem," Ellie objected, determined to hold on to the lightness that had carried them through the day. Stepping onto the dry land, she lifted up her skirts and twisted the fabric in her hands to remove as much water as possible.

"Here, let me help." Kneeling down, Frederick took the hem of her dress from her hands. Pulling it tighter around her legs, he began to twist and squeeze the fabric, and a small puddle formed by her feet. As he looked up at her, a mischievous smile curled up his lips. "Maybe this wasn't such a bad idea at all—"

"Who said it was a bad idea?" Ellie interrupted, but he ignored her.

"—after all, the view is rather spectacular."

Lifting her head, Ellie gazed into the distance, her eyes sweeping over the clear, blue water, almost entirely encircled by a dense tree line. Late bloomers poked their head through the tall grass here and there, their brilliant colours sparkling in the warm sun. "Yes, it is beautiful here, is it not?"

Frederick coughed, a devilish grin still on his face. "That is not the view I was referring to." He raised his eyebrows at her, and she followed his gaze to her wet legs.

A flush shot up her cheeks, and in mock outrage, she slapped his shoulder. "You are truly a scoundrel, my lord. No gentleman ought to behave like this."

As she lifted her hand for another slap at the back of his head, he ducked out of the way…and froze.

Seeing the shock on his face, Ellie felt her stomach twist into knots. "What's wrong?" she asked as cold fingers settled around her heart, squeezing it with an iron grip.

He did not answer her, though, but instead lifted his hand and skimmed a finger over her wet skin.

Looking down, Ellie found him staring at the small birthmark just below her left knee, the little bird spreading its wings, free of all restraints, and the breath she had been holding flew from her lungs in a burst of relief.

Dropping the hem of her skirt, Frederick rose to his feet, his dark eyes searching hers. A hint of recognition sparkled in them as he narrowed his eyes, almost squinting at her as though trying to look even closer.

He swallowed then, slowly, ever so slowly, and shook his head in disbelief. "Ellie?" he whispered, his eyes holding hers as though afraid she would disappear into thin air. "Ellie?"

A deep smile spread over her face as tears filled her eyes and a lump settled in her throat. Unable to speak, Ellie simply nodded as her tears spilled over and streamed down her face.

At her affirmation, a slow smile lifted the corners of his mouth before he crushed her to his chest. Rubbing his hands over her back, he mumbled her name into her hair again and again.

Holding on to him, Ellie revelled in the love that flowed through her; they had finally come full circle.

Deep down, she had hoped, wished, prayed that maybe one day he would recognise her, that maybe he would remember that day long ago. Still, she had never truly believed it would happen, always knowing that that day had meant more to her than it had meant to him.

Suddenly standing back, Frederick held her at an arm's distance, his eyes gliding over her face. "I cannot believe it is you," he whispered, awe ringing in his voice. "I can't believe I…" Speechless, he shook his head. "I can't believe I didn't see it before."

Resting her hands on his chest, Ellie looked up at him. "It has been a long time, and…," she swallowed, "I have changed."

He shook his head vehemently. "No, you have not. The light I saw in your eyes that day," a devoted smile curled his lips, "it is still there. Maybe even brighter now than it was then." Cupping her face in his hands, he drank in the very sight of her. "I cannot believe it is you, Ellie. My Ellie." Pulling her closer, he brushed her lips with his own. "Thank you," he whispered. "Without you, I would have been lost." Then his mouth closed over hers, and words became obsolete.

37

GENTLEMEN UNWELCOME

"What do you mean 'I cannot come'?" Frederick asked, his look of hurt disbelief threatening to melt her resolve. "This is my house, and you are telling me I cannot go where I please?"

"I am." Meeting his eyes, Ellie stepped closer, her fingers skimming over his cheeks and trailing down the side of his neck until they came to rest on his shoulders.

At her touch, his eyelids had lowered, and she could tell from the relaxed expression on his face that the tea party had slipped from his mind.

As she brushed her lips over his, his arms came up and around her waist, drawing her closer. His mouth devoured hers with a passion Ellie had only just come to cherish, and a hazy fog settled over her mind, threatening to make her forget the tea party as well.

"I have to go," she mumbled against his lips, forcing herself to draw in a deep breath and focus her thoughts on the guests due to arrive any moment and not the sensual tingles her husband's skilled lips stirred within her own.

"No, you don't," he disagreed and pulled her back into his embrace.

Feeling her resolve weaken once more, Ellie squeezed her eyes shut, then pushed away his hands and took a few hasty steps back. "Yes, I do," she insisted, hoping her voice sounded more convincing than she felt. Brushing down her dress, she pinned a few loose curls back up, fixing her husband with a determined stare, hoping he would keep his distance and allow her to regain her composure.

"Why can't I come?" he asked, his eyes roaming her body in a rather scandalous way that sent excited chills down Ellie's back.

Swallowing, she did her best to ignore him; however, the amused crinkle of his lips told her that he knew very well what effect he had on her.

Walking over to the window, Ellie feigned indifference as her eyes swept over the many tables set up across the upper lawn. Large umbrellas offered shade while allowing the slightly cooling breeze to sweep gently through the gardens while refreshments waited on the terrace in the cooling shade of Elmridge's walls.

When her nerves had calmed down, Ellie turned around to face him. "Today is for Maryann," she reminded him. "Despite her earlier doubts, she is looking forward to this afternoon. Do not ruin it for her."

"Are you saying my mere presence would ruin the day?" Frederick asked dumbfounded, and Ellie had to suppress a chuckle.

"In this case, yes." Stepping closer, she placed her hands on his chest and looked up into his eyes. "No gentlemen are allowed today. Maryann needs to be at ease in order to realise that social events are not simply about finding a new husband. She is not ready for that, yet, and we think an event only for women and children will allow her to relax and enjoy herself."

Looking slightly disgruntled, Frederick nodded. "Fine."

"You will stay away?"

"I'll do my best."

Ellie pinched him through his shirt, and he flinched, staring down at her. "That was uncalled for!" he complained, rubbing a hand over his chest.

"Then be serious!"

"I am serious!"

"No, you're not," Ellie objected, fixing him through narrowed eyes. "You're trying to make me feel sorry for you, so that I'll let you attend."

At her words, the miserable expression slid from his face, instantly replaced by a mischievous smirk. "You can't blame a man for trying!"

Fighting down an answering smile, Ellie glared at him. "Yes, I can, and I assure you I will find an appropriate punishment if you do not behave yourself."

"You cannot be serious?" he said, a hint of doubt in his voice as his eyes tried to see behind her calm mask.

A satisfied smile came to her lips, and she batted her eyelashes at him. "Believe me, you won't like it!"

He drew in a sharp breath. However, before he could say another word to dissuade her, Ellie turned around and left, her teeth digging into her lower lip as she fought the grin that threatened to steal her composure.

As expected, she found Maryann and Theresa in the foyer. While her mother-in-law looked rather pleased, Maryann was fidgeting nervously from one foot to the other, her cheeks a little pale. However, when their guests began to arrive, her nerves slowly relaxed, and before long, Ellie saw an honest smile light up her face.

Coming to stand beside Ellie, Theresa reached for her hand and gave it a gentle squeeze. "We did well," she whispered into her ear.

Ellie nodded. "She does look happy."

As per their request, no gentlemen were in attendance; however, most women who were already mothers had brought their children, and although Mathilda had been nowhere to be found only that morning, she soon abandoned her secret hiding spot and came forward to curiously inspect potential playmates.

Not only had most of Elmridge's direct neighbours answered their call for a social gathering among women, but also Ellie's friend Madeline and her cousin Rosabel had arrived. While Madeline seemed somewhat disappointed that no men were in attendance, Rosabel was delighted to be able to bring her two children.

"Your belly is growing rounder," Ellie observed, hugging her cousin. "Are you certain it is not too exhausting for you to come today?"

"I feel perfectly fine," Rosabel assured her, patting her son's dark curls as he clung to her skirts. At age two, Christopher John Astor peeked at the world with curious eyes, but did not yet dare venture far from his mother. "Graham was a bit concerned as well, but you know how men are. They always worry about things they do not understand. It was the same when I was expecting Christopher." Again, she stroked his unruly curls. "But I really wanted to come, and he trusts my judgement."

"I am glad you are here," Ellie beamed, enjoying the radiant smile on her cousin's face. Hers had been a marriage of convenience as well; however, the love that Rosabel and Graham shared today was truly without compare. Well, almost. Ellie thought as Frederick's adoring gaze appeared before her eyes.

"You seem happy," Rosabel observed, jarring Ellie awake, and with a twinkle in her eye asked, "Has he come to appreciate you after all?"

A deep blush surged up Ellie's cheeks, and she bit her lower lip to keep the face-splitting smile that immediately announced itself under control.

Rosabel laughed. "That is all the answer I need." She took Ellie's hand and gave it a gentle squeeze. "I am truly happy for you, dear Cousin."

Before long, the mothers were seated at the many tables dotting the lawn while their children chased each other through the green maze of the garden, playing hide-and-go-seek until their growling bellies sent them to the buffet tables.

Cheerful voices filled the air, and children's laughter echoed across the lawn while toddlers crawled around their mothers' chairs. Maryann's eyes glowed as she watched Mathilda walk hand in hand with Rosabel's daughter Georgiana to the buffet, where they retrieved a piece of lemon cake for each of them and then retreated into the shade by the water fountain. "I haven't seen her this happy in a long time," Maryann observed with a sigh.

"She is a truly beautiful child," Rosabel said, a winning smile on her face as she looked at Maryann, and before long, the two women were conversing easily about the one thing that brought irresistible smiles to their faces: their children.

Glimpsing Madeline, Ellie walked over to her, offering her a piece of lemon cake. "There are no gentlemen here. You might as well eat a slice without fearing for your reputation."

Madeline rolled her eyes. "Do not remind me," she pouted, a hint of distaste in her eyes as she watched a group of little boys tumble

238

around on the lawn. "Who in God's name allowed them to bring their children?"

"I did."

As her eyes flew open, Madeline turned to her, disbelief drawing down her brows. "Why would you do such a thing? They're so…unsanitary." Her nose crinkled in disgust as a little boy wiped his runny nose on his sleeve before his nanny had any chance of retrieving a handkerchief.

Ellie laughed. "Feel free to leave if you're truly appalled by the guest list," she whispered in jest before the smirk left her face. "I for one am truly glad to see you."

Madeline's eyes softened, and she smiled at Ellie. "As am I. Even if I had known about the extended guest list," her eyes darted to another rowdy band of boys and girls, "I would have come in order to see you."

"I feel truly honoured," Ellie said, not even the slightest hint of sarcasm in her voice. "So? Any news on the marriage front?"

Looking displeased, Madeline shrugged. "I have come to realise that men are idiots no matter what their title."

Ellie chuckled. "Does that mean you are not set on marrying a high-ranked gentleman any longer?"

"Oh, please, dear Elsbeth," Madeline scoffed. "If I am to put up with the vices and follies of a husband, I, at least, expect him to be of the highest possible rank. If not, what on earth is the purpose of ever binding yourself to one of their kind." She shook her head as though the notion of love had never crossed her mind; Ellie supposed it really hadn't. "After all, following a year of marriage, you generally find yourself stuck with one of…those as well." Again, her nose crinkled in disgust as she pointed at young Christopher, who in that moment plucked a bogey from his nose and plopped it into his mouth, chewing happily.

A shiver went through Madeline, and determinedly, she turned her head away. "Gross!"

Suppressing yet another laugh, Ellie batted her eyelids to keep the tears from coming. "Am I to understand," she cleared her throat, "that you are no closer to choosing a husband than you were in the spring? Your parents must be growing impatient."

Madeline shrugged. "While they are not pleased with this delay, I assure you they would never deny me the right to choose a husband freely."

"I am glad to hear it." As her eyes swept over her friend's raised chin and she noticed the determined look resting in her eyes, Ellie couldn't help but ask, "Has it ever occurred to you that you might be happier without ever choosing a husband?"

Looking at her sideways, Madeline shrugged, and Ellie noted that her question had not taken her friend by surprise. "If it weren't for social pressure, I most certainly would."

Ellie sighed, hoping that one day, Madeline would meet a man who would sweep her off her feet and that her friend would not be too stubborn to admit that her heart had been stolen.

"Who is that?" Madeline asked, her voice drawing Ellie back from her inner contemplations.

"Who?" Turning her head, she glanced at the group of mothers standing in a circle by the terrace doors.

"Not them," Madeline objected, her hand unobtrusively gesturing to the young woman, standing alone in the shade of the large oak tree. "Her."

For a moment, Ellie was at a loss as her eyes swept over the woman's chestnut hair and hazel eyes, a handkerchief clutched in her hands. Although she was not crying, her gaze spoke of unbearable sadness as though the scene before her eyes only served as a reminder of what she herself had lost.

Instantly, Ellie's eyes opened wide. "Charlotte," she whispered, and her heart went out to the young woman.

"Who?"

"Lady Charlotte Frampton," Ellie elaborated. "Her fiancé died in battle. We invited her in the hopes that such an event would help her move on."

"I don't think it is working," Madeline observed casually. "I sincerely hope this wasn't your only idea."

38

A TEA PARTY

alf-hidden behind the curtains of the small back drawing room, Frederick stood with his nose almost pressed to the windowpane. His ego chided him for his behaviour, calling him childish and immature. His heart, however, rejoiced at the sight of his wife as she chatted with friends and neighbours, always the gracious hostess, a kind word for everyone on her lips. The sunlight touched her golden hair, half piled atop her head and half cascading down her back and flowing freely over her slender shoulders. Her deep blue eyes shone like sapphires, and her rosy lips beckoned him forward, their siren call echoing in his bones.

When exactly he had lost his heart to her, Frederick didn't know. All he knew was that she possessed it; and yet, he did not feel threatened or vulnerable in the least. On the contrary, he had never felt so safe in his entire life!

A deep smile curled up the corners of his mouth as he contemplated the future before them. Since the day she had saved his soul from perpetual torment, the shadows had receded, allowing him to enjoy the love she so openly bestowed upon him. Joy tingled in every fibre of his being, and he wanted nothing more than to run out there and wrap her in his arms.

Instead, he stood hidden, stealing a glance at his own wife like a common thief!

Frederick sighed, glancing at the clock on the mantle. *How much longer till the guests would leave?*

When he turned back around, his wife had just abandoned her post beside her friend—*Madeline, was it?*—and was walking down the small slope of lawn toward the old oak tree by the water fountain. Following her with his gaze, Frederick's eyes grew wide when he beheld the small woman standing in its shade. "Charlotte," he gasped, and his heart constricted painfully.

Although he had called her 'friend' once, the loss of Kenneth had changed everything. He could not set eyes upon her without being reminded of what they both had lost. Frederick supposed she felt the same way for she had only come to see him twice since his return home. Why was she here today? He wondered. However, when his eyes swept over his wife's gentle features as she sat down beside Charlotte, Frederick knew why.

As she had done for the rest of his family and him as well, Ellie was intent on helping those who had no strength left to fight for themselves. Her eyes held the same determination as they had when she had told him that Maryann needed to see that life was still beautiful, that she could still find happiness. Obviously, his wife was on a mission; and although Frederick could have done without the stab of guilt he felt at Charlotte's presence, he could not help but love his wife all the more for her diligence in bringing peace to the people he cared about.

For a long while, he simply stood there, gazing longingly at Ellie as she spoke to his friend's former fiancée. Gently, she touched the woman's hands, her head lowered in confidence while Charlotte's gaze was fixed on something in the distance. After a while, though, she nodded, her eyes shifting to his wife, and smiled.

Frederick was amazed. How did she do it? How did she know exactly what to say? He shook his head. Words often eluded him.

Walking around the room, he tried to shake off the touch of stiffness that had come to his legs and back from his rather unfortunate position behind the curtains. From outside, happy laughter and chatty voices reached his ears, and despite his misgivings about not being invited, Frederick realised that it had been a long time since such innocent joy had echoed through the halls of Elmridge. Not since before he had left for the continent had he felt this content, and the corners of his lips curled upward in happiness.

"May I ask what you are smiling about?"

At his wife's voice, Frederick spun around.

Ellie laughed. "Do not worry! I will not breathe a word of this to anyone," she assured him, a mischievous twinkle in her eyes as she approached.

"I assure you, my lady, I have not the slightest inkling as to what you are referring," he said, trying to look innocent. "Maybe you are not aware of the fact that this is my favourite room in the entire house. I spent hours here, reading and…thinking." A grin spread over his face, and again, she laughed. "How did you know I was here?"

Her gaze shifted to the window before returning to his. "I saw you, my lord."

His eyes grew wide.

"Do not worry. I doubt anyone else saw. However, I would advise against spying on your guests in the future."

A frown on his face, Frederick grumbled, "I was not spying on my guests. Why would I? I have no interest in their affairs."

"I see," Ellie nodded, coming to stand before him. Her eyes gazed into his in a way that made the breath catch in his throat. "Then who were you spying on?"

Wrapping his arms around her, Frederick pulled her closer. "You," he whispered against her lips before his mouth claimed hers.

As she melted against him, Frederick lost all sense of his surroundings. The only thing that mattered was her and the way she made him feel. The way she felt lying in his arms. The way her lips moved against his. The way her hands ran up his chest and wrapped around his neck, pulling him even closer. Before Frederick knew what was happening, he pulled her down onto the settee.

Unfortunately, that was when she stopped herself and by extension him.

"This is unwise," Ellie gasped. Rising to her feet and brushing down her dress, she glanced at the window. When none of their guests seemed to be gawking back at them, her features relaxed and she turned back to him, an amused curl to her lips. "My lord, you made me forget my manners," she chided him before turning to leave.

Jumping to his feet, Frederick reached for her, pulling her back into his arms.

"I do need to go," she protested, snuggling against him.

"But you don't want to."

"That is of no importance." Drawing in a deep breath, she straightened, extracting herself from his embrace.

As she did so, Frederick could see the reluctance to leave in her eyes, and his heart beat faster.

"I will see you tonight," she whispered, a wordless promise dancing in her eyes. Then she took another step backward, and a deep smile curled up her lips before she tore herself away and finally turned to leave.

His wife took another few steps before her arms came up for balance and she started to sway on her feet.

As his heart stopped, Frederick lunged forward. He barely managed to grab a hold of her before she sagged against him, her body going limp as though every strength had suddenly left her.

"Ellie!" he called, his voice sounding hysterical to his own ears. Turning her over in his arms, he breathed a sigh of relief when he found her eyes open.

A bit disoriented, she blinked, then focused her gaze on his face, slow breathes moving her chest.

Carrying her to the settee, Frederick gently settled her into the cushions. "Are you all right?" he asked as a new fear gripped his heart. "I'll send for Dr. Madison immediately."

Before he could jump up though, her hand curled into the fabric of his sleeve, holding him back. "There is no need," she whispered, her voice not as weak as he had feared. "It is just a spell of dizziness. I suppose I should have eaten something."

"You haven't eaten anything?" Frederick snapped, glancing at the many tables laden with food. "It is late afternoon. When was the last time you did eat?"

Her eyes narrowed, and for a moment, she said nothing. "I suppose it was at breakfast."

"Breakfast?"

Her eyes shifted to him and narrowed in a completely different way. "Don't speak to me as though I am a silly child," she objected, pushing herself up into a sitting position. "It was a very busy day, and I was distracted. It could have happened to anyone."

"I'm sorry," Frederick mumbled. "I didn't mean to insinuate that you cannot take care of yourself. I was merely worried."

Her features softened. "I know, and I'm sorry, too. I did not mean to snap at you."

"Thank you." Reluctantly, Frederick held out his hand to her as she tried to stand up. "Are you certain this is a good idea? I could get you something to eat."

Grinning at him, she shook her head. "Do not use this as an excuse to join the party. I am perfectly capable of walking out there by myself."

"All right," Frederick mumbled, watching her go. Although she did not sway anymore, neither did she look too steady on her feet. Frederick swallowed as every fibre of his body told him to follow her, to see her safe, to protect her.

However, hoping that he could trust her judgement, he stayed behind, quietly watching through the window as she reappeared on the terrace. To his relief, she took a seat in the shade and had a footman bring her something from the buffet.

Seeing the colour return to her cheeks, Frederick sighed before his heart froze as an unexpected flashback seized him.

For a reason he could not name, he found himself reliving the moment he had returned from the terrace at the Midnight Ball and had found his brother on the floor, writhing in pain, his face as pale as death itself.

To this day, they did not know what had taken Leopold's life. The doctor had suspected poison, and yet, there had been no way to know for sure.

Wallowing in his guilt, Frederick had not given it much thought at the time. After all, dead was dead. Nothing he could have done would have brought his brother back.

Now, however, his thoughts had cleared and the turmoil of his heart had ceased. Again, Oliver's voice echoed in his head, *It's almost as though a curse was put on your family.*

First his father, then his brother and now…? Had he almost died when the saddle girth had snapped? Frederick wondered. Were Oliver's concerns justified? Had it been cut deliberately? Did someone want them dead?

But who? And why?

His father had been an only child. The few relatives they had were quite distant. Was someone after Elmridge and the title? Who would inherit if he died?

Frederick didn't know since he had never before contemplated such a scenario. Even when he had been determined to seek out death on the battlefield, he had hoped that his son would be the one to carry on the title.

His son. He marvelled. Never before had he thought of himself as a father. He had only ever seen his son as the means to his deliverance. The means that would set him free.

However, everything was different now.

Watching his wife eat her lemon cake, Frederick smiled. Nothing and no one could ever make him leave her. He loved her beyond hope, and he would spend the rest of his life by her side, raising their children together.

Was there a threat out there, though? A threat not only to their happiness, but also to their lives?

Not hers, he reminded himself with some relief. Her death would not affect the line of succession. His, however, would. What ought he to do? Maybe he ought to speak to Oliver. After all, he had been the only one to ever voice any concern in this regard.

Again, his eyes travelled to his wife as she sat amongst her friends. Her eyes sparkled with delight, and the smile on her face spoke to the happiness within her heart. She looked like life itself. At the very least, she was his life, and all of a sudden, the thought of ending his own seemed as preposterous as snow in July.

39

SONS & DAUGHTERS

alking through the gardens with her mother-in-law, Ellie drew her shawl tighter around her shoulders. At least, the weather had stayed fine long enough for their tea party to be held outdoors; it had been well worth it. Ever since that day, a smile had been more firmly fixed on Maryann's face and the thought of re-joining society, even at a mixed event, did not bring frown lines to her forehead anymore. Ellie was pleased.

"The leaves are starting to change," Theresa observed as the wind tugged a strand of her greying hair from her bun. "It's been a year of great change."

Ellie nodded as her gaze slid over Theresa's face, noticing the sad curl to her lips and the hint of tears forming in her eyes. "It has seen a lot of sadness," she whispered, pulling her mother-in-law's arm through hers.

"It has," Theresa nodded before she stopped and turned to Ellie, her own wrinkled hands grasping Ellie's scarred ones. "But it has also brought a lot of joy," she said, and despite the tear that rolled down her cheek, a smile came to her face, "and you are the reason."

Ellie opened her mouth to protest, but Theresa shook her head to silence her. "I know praise makes you uncomfortable, and you do not see anything special in the kindness you bestow on others, which makes it even more precious because it is heart-felt and not due to a duty you believe to be yours." Squeezing Ellie's hands, she looked deep into her eyes. "I don't know what happened that day Maryann and myself came upon you and Frederick in his study." As though chilled, a tremble went through her. "I thought for sure all hope was lost. But then the next day, everything seemed to fall into place."

Remembering the intimacies she had shared with her husband that day—physical as well as emotional—Ellie averted her eyes, feeling uncomfortable. "It is difficult to explain."

"I don't need you to explain," Theresa assured her. "I knew you would find a way, a way neither one of us could have walked." A warm glow came to her eyes. "I haven't seen him this happy, this…carefree in a long time. It is as though a heavy burden was lifted off his chest, and he can finally breathe again." A delighted smile lit up her features. "I can see that he loves you."

A warm blush rose in Ellie's cheeks, and she bit her lower lip self-consciously.

"Don't be ashamed," her mother-in-law chided lovingly. "Love is nothing to be ashamed of. From the very beginning, I had hoped that this day would come. That you two would come to love each other. I just wanted you to know that."

"Thank you, Theresa. You have no idea how much your words mean to me." Ellie took a deep breath as the cool wind rushed over her cheeks. "I feel at home here," she said, a hint of awe in her voice as her eyes swept over the gardens that had heard so many of their secrets before returning to the woman before her. "And it is not just because of Frederick, but because of all of you. You've welcomed me with open arms and open hearts, and I will be eternally grateful for that."

More tears rolled down Theresa's cheeks before she wrapped her daughter-in-law in a tight embrace, her thin arms holding a strength that her frail-looking body rarely exuded.

Despite a sense of familial loyalty, which urged her to refrain from speaking her mind, Ellie felt the almost desperate need to have Theresa understand just how much she meant to her. "I am very close to my sisters and my brother," she began, "and my cousin Rosabel is like another sister to me. However, my parents have always been rather distant. They were never unkind, but less emotional. I cannot recall the last time I hugged either one of them." A sympathetic smile on her face, Theresa squeezed Ellie's hand. "I do love them, but it's a different kind of love. I don't know if you can understand considering how close you've always been to your sons."

Theresa sighed. "Well, it's not always easy to love someone unconditionally, the way parents tend to love their children. Especially when they get older, it is sometimes difficult to show the love you feel in your heart. Circumstances put a distance between you and them that neither one of you can bridge easily." Her eyes sank, overshadowed with past difficulties, and Ellie wondered about the depth of pain and fear Theresa had felt when Leopold had died and Frederick had seemed determined to walk in his brother's footsteps. "I would not judge your parents for appearing distant for I do not know the reason they felt the need to guard their hearts." Lifting her gaze to Ellie's face, Theresa smiled. "However, I am overjoyed that you see us as your family. I gave birth to two sons, but I consider myself the mother of two sons and two daughters."

Touched beyond words, Ellie closed her eyes, savouring the moment. Then she looked at her mother-in-law and said, "Thank you for bringing me here. I cannot imagine being anywhere else."

"Neither can I," Theresa whispered. "You belong here with us, and we will never let you go."

Ellie laughed as tears ran down her cheeks. "You wouldn't ever be able to get rid of me."

Chuckling, Theresa smiled. "I wish you only happiness, Elsbeth. You and my son. After everything you've been through, you deserve it." A wistful twinkle came to her eyes. "In many ways, seeing Frederick with you reminds me of my own husband. He was just as helpless without me as Frederick is without you. Always remember, men are no good without women by their side."

40

SUPICIONS

"I have to admit I was surprised to receive your note," Oliver said as he sat down across from Frederick. "I thought after last time you wouldn't want to see me for a while. If I recall correctly, you were quite upset."

Frederick chuckled. "And with good reason, I might add. However, that is of the past."

"Obviously," Oliver remarked, staring at his friend in a somewhat incredulous manner, his eyes searching the other's face as though looking for an explanation. "Have you finally spoken to your wife?" he asked, a devilish grin on his face. "Is she the reason for that dreamy look in your eyes?"

Clearing his throat, Frederick straightened in his chair as the smile slid off his face. He hadn't been aware his feelings were so obvious. Could everyone tell how much he loved his wife simply by looking at him?

Oliver laughed, slapping his knee. "She truly must be an extraordinary woman to accomplish what I feared to be a hopeless task. How did she do it?"

"That is none of your concern," Frederick snapped, feeling somewhat disconcerted that his friend could read him so well.

Oliver chuckled, and Frederick noticed that the smile on his face was not overshadowed by lines of worry as it had been during his friend's last visit.

Instantly, Frederick felt sorry for causing his friend such distress. He was still coming to realise how deeply he had hurt the people around him, not to mention frightened them nearly witless by his intentions of leaving for the continent again. Had they all known why he had intended to return?

"So?" Oliver's voice brought him back to the here and now. "Why did you ask me to come? I assume it is not because you wished to share the good news of your improved spirits with me."

Remembering why he had asked Oliver to come, Frederick drew a deep breath and his lips thinned as he collected his thoughts. Apparently, Oliver could read him quite well after all because he instantly grew serious, almost nervously fidgeting in his chair as he waited for Frederick to speak.

"I know I have not been myself lately," Frederick began. "Many things escaped my notice, and I've only now come to realise that there are still things that I have left unresolved."

"Such as?"

Leaning forward, Frederick rested his elbows on his knees, his eyes fixed on Oliver's. "Do you remember, during your last visit you suggested that…someone might have manipulated the saddle girth?"

Oliver's eyes went wide, and he leaned forward as well. "What are you saying?"

"I don't know," Frederick admitted, and some of the tension left Oliver's shoulders. "The strangest thing happened when we had a tea party here the other day."

"So I've heard." The hint of a smile came to Oliver's face. "Women only? That must have been a sight."

A strained chuckle escaped Frederick. "It was. However, what annoyed me most was my wife's insistence that I stay away."

"Well, you're a man," Oliver pointed out flatly.

"But it's my house!"

"So?"

"So I should be able to go wherever I please!"

Oliver chuckled before he swallowed and his face grew serious again. "I heard Charlotte was here."

Frederick nodded. "I believe Ellie invited her. After all, the whole point of having that tea party was to give Maryann the opportunity to mingle without the pressure of looking for a husband. I suppose Ellie thought Charlotte would benefit as well. However, from the way she sat by herself, I don't believe she appreciated the invitation. I couldn't help but wonder why she accepted it."

"She has not been out in society since Kenneth died," Oliver stated. "It is a shame they did not get married before he left. After all, she is a most diligent widow."

"Well, it is her right to mourn him, do you not agree?"

"I certainly do," Oliver said. "However, her parents seem to be of a different mind."

"What do you mean?" Frederick asked, feeling a chill run down his back. If only they had been married, Charlotte would have been afforded all the respect due a grieving widow. Maybe she would have even been with child, thereby securing her own future as well.

"From what I heard, her parents are strongly *encouraging* her to accept Lord Northfield's proposal," he explained, and Frederick's eyes went wide. "I know! That man has no honour! It baffles me why her parents would even consider him."

Clearing his throat, Frederick swallowed, his pulse still thudding in his neck. "Didn't Charlotte always have a handful of suitors? Especially since she and Kenneth did not marry, I would assume that still to be the case."

"It is," Oliver nodded. "It makes you wonder, does it not?"

"Indeed." Drawing in a deep breath, Frederick met Oliver's eyes. "We should keep an eye on her…and Lord Northfield."

Again, Oliver nodded. "Agreed."

"I suppose I could ask Ellie to invite her for tea and…speak to her," Frederick suggested. "Maybe she can find out what is going on."

"That's a good idea," Oliver said before a smirk drew up the corners of his mouth. "Ellie, is it?"

Suppressing a smile, Frederick leaned back. "It is, yes." A part of him wanted to remind Oliver how they had met Ellie years ago, but he stopped himself in the last moment. That memory was his alone. He would not share it with anyone but his wife.

And so instead of reminding his friend, he reminded himself why he had asked Oliver to come. Clearing his throat, Frederick took a deep breath. "Let's not stray off topic. The reason I mentioned the tea party in the first place was to tell you that being the hostess kept my wife so busy that she forgot to eat, and the result was that she almost fainted."

"Is she all right?" Honest concern creased Oliver's forehead.

"She is. However, the image of her pale cheeks as she lay in my arms, and then later as she sat on the terrace finally eating something, for some reason it brought back another memory." Frederick exhaled, feeling a slight tremble in his hands. "Of the night my brother died."

Oliver frowned, his eyes moving over Frederick's face as he tried to work out what his friend was trying to tell him. "You are wondering who murdered your brother."

Frederick's head snapped up, and his jaw fell open. "I do, yes," he mumbled after a while. "I cannot believe it never occurred to me to ask these questions before. I guess—"

"You had other things on your mind," Oliver interrupted. "I am sure your brother would understand."

"Thank you." Relief washed over Frederick at his friend's words. Upon realising that he had all but ignored his brother's murder, new guilt had settled in his heart. Why was it that guilt continually threatened to undermine the good that happened to him?

Shaking his head, Frederick took a deep breath. "Well, it made me think about my father's death, then Leopold's and then…"

"Your accident," Oliver finished for him. "Do you believe your father was murdered as well? I thought Dr. Madison had ruled it a severe case of pneumonia."

Frederick shrugged. "I don't know." Rising to his feet, he began to pace the length of his study. "I keep thinking about what my mother told me. That he seemed fine, even insisted she go out that night." He spun around, fixing Oliver across the backrest of the chair before him. "When she came home, he was dead. Does that sound natural to you?"

Oliver shrugged. "I don't know. I admit it sounds…unusual." He rose to his feet then and came to stand before Frederick, his eyes intent on his friend's. "Are you saying you believe that someone is killing off the male members of your family in order to…what? Inherit the title?"

"I've been wondering that, yes," Frederick admitted, feeling a hint of relief at having shared the oppressive thoughts that had kept him awake the past few nights. He had not confided in his wife because he did not wish to alarm her. He had put her through enough these past few months. "Now that my father and brother are dead, I am the marquess." He met Oliver's eyes. "I am the last of our line. What if it was not an accident? What if you were right and someone deliberately caused the saddle girth to snap?"

Oliver took a deep breath, then raked his hands through his hair. "Just for the record, I didn't want to be right."

"I know. But what if you are?"

Looking around the room as though hoping for the answer to reveal itself, Oliver shrugged. "We need to find out what happened." Although seemingly at a loss, his head began bobbing up and down. "And we need to make sure nothing happens to you."

For a moment, Frederick closed his eyes. "I have to admit a part of me hoped that you would be able to refute my suspicions."

"Believe me, there's nothing I'd rather do," Oliver said, clasping a hand over Frederick's shoulder. "Well then, tell me, who would inherit should you pass?"

"I am not sure," Frederick admitted. "After the thought first occurred to me, I went to the library and looked at the family tree. However, since my father was an only child and the title can only be passed on through the male line, whoever inherits is someone I have never met before." Walking over to his desk, he picked up a rolled up parchment. "Here, let me show you."

As they leaned over the family tree, Frederick pointed to various generations of his family. "As far as I can tell from this, my father's father, my grandfather, had a younger brother, who in turn had a son as well. However, at that point, the family tree ends on that side. Does that mean the son died childless? Or were his children simply not added? To tell you the truth, my father rarely spoke of his family. I suppose there must have been some kind of falling-out."

Stepping back, Oliver started pacing the floor, his brows drawn down in a concentrated frown. Before long though, he spun around. "Here is what we'll do. I'll write to my father. If anyone knows anything about that generation of your family, it's him. He is so obsessed with genealogy and enriching our 'noble' line," Oliver said, his voice sounding exasperated, "that he sinks his talons into every bit of information he can obtain."

Frederick nodded. "Good. Thank you."

Taking a step closer, Oliver glanced at the door before continuing. "Have you noticed anything out of the ordinary around here? Especially around the time of the accident?"

"No, nothing. However, I suppose I was not the most reliable witness at the time."

"Have you recently hired anyone new? Did someone come to visit?"

Frederick shrugged. "I'll speak to my steward, but I don't think he'll be able to help us." A long sigh escaped him, and he shook his head. "I cannot believe that someone would truly seek to kill us in order to inherit the title. Wouldn't that be rather obvious? Wouldn't whoever inherits the title be subjecting himself to such suspicions?"

Oliver shrugged. "In my experience, people who are willing to kill for profit have left reason behind a while ago. Whoever he is, he may not even think that far ahead." Coming to stand before his friend, Oliver met Frederick's eyes. "In case I have not yet made this clear, I am not leaving your side until this is resolved. Do you understand? And I'd appreciate it if you didn't fight me on this."

Frederick nodded, a grateful smile curling up his lips. "I won't. Thank you, Oliver."

Slapping him on the shoulder, Oliver grinned. "This is the most excitement I've had in years."

"I am pleased to be able to provide adequate entertainment during your visit," Frederick replied with a chuckle. Deep down, however, he knew how concerned his friend was for him as lines of tension were clearly visible on Oliver's face. "But promise me not to breathe a word of this to anyone. I do not wish to alarm my wife or my mother."

Oliver nodded. "Agreed."

41

DREAMS & NIGHTMARES

Rolling onto her side, Ellie closed her eyes and inhaled deeply through her nose, fighting down the rising nausea. For a moment, she feared she would be sick, but then the feeling passed, and she opened her eyes, her left hand coming to rest on her belly.

A knock sounded on the door, and in a weak voice, Ellie called, "Enter."

Instantly, the door swung open and her husband burst into the room. "Are you all right? Betty said you were indisposed." With eyes full of worry, he hastened to her side. Gentle hands brushed stray hairs from her forehead and caressed her cheek until they ran down her arm and held on to hers. "Should I call for Dr. Madison?"

"No," Ellie objected, trying to smile at him reassuringly. "I am fine. This is nothing to worry about."

"Nothing to worry about?" he echoed, the expression on his face clearly stating that he disagreed. "You're as white as a sheet." He swallowed, and she could see the effort with which he held himself in check as panic rose to the surface.

"All right," Ellie said, determined to put him out of his misery. Lifting her head off the pillow, she sat up as Frederick grabbed a hold of the pillow and propped it up so that she could rest comfortably against the headboard of the bed. "Listen, I am not entirely certain yet, which is why I haven't spoken to you about this."

His eyes fixed intently on her face, he swallowed, and she could see that he was expecting awful news as the muscles in his jaw clenched and unclenched repeatedly. "This?"

Pulling his hand into hers, she smiled at him, momentarily forgetting the hint of nausea that still remained, and gently laid his hand on her belly. A deep smile spread over her face as she met his eyes.

For a moment, he remained very still as his eyes slid over her face before understanding dawned, and they went as round as plates. As though jolted awake, he almost jumped to his feet, still holding on to her hand. "Are you saying...? You...?" His voice trailed off as his gaze shifted back and forth between her belly and her face. Then he swallowed and sank onto the mattress beside her. "Why didn't you tell me?"

Seeing the stunned expression on his face, Ellie couldn't help but laugh. "I am sorry," she whispered, wringing her hands, suddenly nervous about his reaction. "I didn't mean to keep this from you. However, I wasn't certain I was expecting before...well, a part of me still has doubts. I didn't mean to say anything before I could be absolutely certain. I didn't mean to raise false hopes. I didn't..."

Gently, Frederick placed a hand on her belly and the other on her own, trembling hands. A deep smile shone on his face as he looked into her eyes. "I understand. But I have to say from the looks of it, I do not have any doubts."

Ellie took a deep breath as joy flooded her heart and tears sprang from her eyes. "After the accident, I was so sad about never having children. I hadn't thought about it as much before, but once I knew it would never be, it really hurt."

Pulling her into his arms, Frederick held her tight as her tears ran down her cheeks and she quietly sobbed against his shoulder. "You will be a wonderful mother," he whispered in her ear. "I don't have any doubts about that either."

"Thank you," Ellie sniffled, then sat back and looked into his eyes. "Please do not tell anyone yet."

Smiling at her, he shook his head. "I wouldn't dream of it, but I doubt that my mother and Maryann will take long figuring this out."

Ellie laughed. "I suppose you're right about that. But not to-night. Tonight, I want them to enjoy themselves."

"They will," Frederick assured her. "I will tell them that we need a little time alone, and they will go without—"

"No," Ellie objected. "Go with them. They'll need you."

Disappointment edged into his features, he stared at her.

"I know that Maryann puts on a brave face, but I think she can use all the support her family can give her tonight." Gently, Ellie brushed her fingers over his cheeks and kissed his forehead. "It has been a long time since she has been to a ball, and I don't want her to feel pressured." Running her hands down his arms, she snuggled against him. "So, if any gentleman becomes too insistent," she instructed, then brushed her lips against his, "you will interfere. Promise me!"

Frederick swallowed, and as Ellie sat back, she could see that he had his eyes closed. "Were you even listening to me?"

As his arms came around her again, he murmured into her ear, "I didn't hear a damn word you said, and you've got only yourself to blame for that."

As her family's voices slowly faded away and the sounds of the carriage receded down the drive, Ellie snuggled into her coverlet. Although she would have loved to watch Maryann take her first tentative steps back into society, Ellie was relieved that at least Frederick would be there. His watchful presence would assure that Maryann could enjoy the evening. Would she dance? Ellie wondered. If a gentleman asked, would she agree? Oh, how Ellie wished she could have gone!

However, although the nausea had retreated after Ellie had nibbled a piece of stable bread, she felt far from able to dance the night away. She would probably faint in the middle of the dance floor. A slight giggle escaped her at the thought. What would her mother think? No doubt she would consider Ellie's behaviour highly inappropriate and look down at her with righteous condemnation!

Sighing, Ellie pulled the blanket tighter around her shoulders and closed her eyes, a soft smile playing on her lips.

Despite the heartache of the past, the present had turned into a wonderful place, and the future looked even more promising. Frederick had successfully battled his demons, Maryann had found her smile again and Mathilda spent more and more time with her family instead of hiding from them.

Gently brushing a hand over her flat belly, Ellie mused that in the future their home would be filled with even more laughter and joy. Remembering the delight in Frederick's eyes, Ellie smiled. He would be a wonderful father—she was certain of it—and after all her doubts, she would be a mother after all.

"Life could not be any sweeter," she mumbled before sleep finally claimed her, and her dreams allowed her a glimpse at the future that awaited her.

By the time Ellie's consciousness returned from the beautiful corners of her sleeping mind, all light had disappeared; not even the smallest ray reached through her closed eyelids and touched her optic nerve. With eyes still closed, she rolled over, determined to hold on to her wonderful dreams, and reached out with her hand, sliding it over the mattress, wondering if Frederick had returned yet.

When she found the other side of the bed empty, Ellie sighed with regret as she would have loved nothing better but to snuggle into his arms and rest her head on his shoulder.

Once again, she drew the blanket tightly around her shoulders, enjoying the warmth of her cocoon, when her nostrils picked up a familiar scent.

A scent that made the little hairs in the back of her neck stand on end.

A scent that had tortured her in her nightmares time and time again.

A scent that chilled her to her bones.

Fire! Ellie's mind screamed, and she shot upright, eyes wide with terror, her body frozen in shock.

The room lay in darkness, and although the curtains were still open, no moonlight reached inside. As her eyes turned to the door leading to her husband's bedchamber, an orange glow peeked out from under it, shining brightly in the darkness surrounding her.

Frederick! Ellie's mind screamed, and her heart constricted painfully.

Instantly, her earlier paralysis fell from her, and she jumped out of bed, urged onward by her worst fears. "Frederick!" she called in a panic. "Frederick, are you in there?" As she reached the closed door, a sudden warmth jumped out at her as though she had run into a wall.

With trembling hands, Ellie reached for the door handle but stopped when the heat radiating off it singed her already scarred skin. Tears sprang from her eyes as her mind conjured imagines of the inferno that had to be raging inside.

As panic crawled up her spine, threatening to engulf her, Ellie remembered Frederick's loving eyes, and a new strength surged through her.

Swallowing, she brushed away her tears, then returned to the bed and reached for the thick coverlet. Before she could even begin to think about doing anything else and alert the house to the fire, she had to know if Frederick was in his room.

Wrapping a corner of the coverlet around her hand, she approached the door once more, feeling the heat emanating from it painfully on her skin. Pressing herself to the wall beside the door handle, she reached out, knowing that she would have to be fast.

For a quick moment, Ellie closed her eyes, then took a deep breath and before panic could take her once more, her padded hand snapped out like a whip and pushed down the door handle.

Instantly, the door flew open, and Ellie jumped backwards as a wall of fire surged forward, reaching out its hands for her. Large flames licked at the wooden floor, touched the cabinet by the side wall and within minutes the small bouquet of dried flowers Mathilda had given her was ablaze.

Staring into the flames, Ellie felt herself moved backwards through time.

Again, she saw her little brother's body lying on the floor as the fire closed in on him. Again, she heard his nursemaid's screams of terror. Again, she felt her heart hammering in her chest and panic flooding every fibre of her being.

As though paralysed, Ellie stood in the corner of the room as the wall of fire slowly moved forward, threatening to cut off her only escape: the door leading out into the corridor.

Out of nowhere, a wave of nausea washed over her, and Ellie blinked.

Shaking her head, she forced the sense of numb detachment from her mind, and her hand went instinctively to her belly, shielding the precious life within. This time she would not be able to sacrifice her own life in order to save someone she loved. This time her child would die with her…if she failed to save herself.

Fresh tears came to her eyes, and for a moment, despair settled on her aching limbs as the smoke grew denser around her, drawing racking coughs from her body.

Again, nausea returned, and Ellie groaned, one hand braced against the wall to keep from sinking to her knees. One hand clutched to her belly, she staggered forward as a slight chill went over her. Stopping in her tracks, Ellie felt a presence within herself that she hadn't noticed before as though her child was urging her not to give up, reminding her of what she had to lose.

Holding the fabric of her sleeve before her face, Ellie drew in a shallow breath as her eyes surveyed the situation before her.

From what she could see, Frederick's chamber was completely engulfed in flames. If he was in there, …

Ellie swallowed and determinedly pushed that thought aside. It served no purpose. She had to think of her child.

The only way out that remained was the door to the corridor. However, she would have to move fast since the flames entering her bedchamber through the open door were already blocking her way, reaching out their orange tongues for her bed. Should the bedding catch fire, she would be trapped by a wall of flames on all sides.

Gathering up her nightgown, Ellie shot forward and flung herself across the mattress, rolling off the other side with such force that she hit the floor painfully. A sharp pain shot through her shoulder, reminding her of the day Frederick had fallen off his horse. As she tried to move her arm though, only a mild pain pulsed in her shoulder, which suggested that the joint had not been dislocated.

Scrambling to her feet, Ellie stumbled forward, eyes fixed on the door. The short distance suddenly seemed insurmountable, and her heart sank.

Nonetheless, she pushed onward as a wave of dizziness washed over her, and she staggered forward like someone too deep in the cups. The world blurred before her eyes, and she reached out a hand to keep from running into the door head-first.

As her hand made contact with the door, it felt as though her wrist was snapped in half. A blinding pain shot through her body, and heaving sobs rose from her throat. Gritting her teeth, Ellie swallowed, slowly drawing in a breath through her nose.

When the pain subsided, she reached out her other hand for the door handle, feeling its relatively cool surface against her heated skin, and pulled.

The door wouldn't open.

As panic rose once more, Ellie frantically moved the handle up and down, pulling on the door with all her might.

However, it remained closed, and her foggy mind finally realised that it was locked.

As the bedding behind her went up in flames, Ellie stood staring at the keyhole in dumbfounded incomprehension. She could not recall a single day that this door had been locked. Why would it be locked now?

42

A LIGHT IN THE DARK

"IT was a wonderful evening," Maryann enthused, her eyes glowing like the stars themselves in the dim interior of the carriage. "I truly enjoyed it." Her gaze shifted from him to Oliver and on to his mother sitting beside her.

Theresa smiled and gently squeezed her hand. "You are welcome, child. My heart soared seeing you so happy tonight."

"I have to admit you are still the superb dancer that you've always been," Oliver said, a hint of regret in his voice.

Frederick laughed. "I'm afraid you will always be the worst dancer at any event no matter who is or is not on the guest list. Not even lack of practise could bring Maryann down to your level."

Shooting him a disgusted look, Oliver crossed his arms, the hint of a pout on his face as Maryann tried her best to suppress a giggle. His mother shook her head at him; however, she refrained from commenting on his lack of manners.

As the carriage rumbled along, silence filled the small space as each one of them turned to their own thoughts. Finally freed from his promise to watch over Maryann's happiness, Frederick felt his mind instinctively return to his wife and the secret she had shared with him that day.

He would be a father! The thought echoed in his ears, and yet, Frederick had trouble believing it to be true.

A few weeks ago, such news would have sent him packing; only now, everything was different. The thought of leaving his wife and child was so ludicrous that he could hardly believe it had sprung from his own mind.

A loud rapping echoed through the carriage roof, and their heads snapped up. "My Lord, you might want to take a look at that."

Instantly, the carriage stopped, and the door swung open.

Stepping outside, Frederick turned to his coachman. "What is it, Thompson?"

"Over there, my lord." Jumping from his seat on the box, the coachman pointed into the distance.

Turning his head, Frederick stared into the night.

At first, he could hardly make out his surroundings as the sky seemed to be a black abyss, swallowing up all light. However, as his eyes slowly adjusted, the faint light of the stars allowed him to glimpse the outline of Elmridge in the distance. "What is it?" he mumbled just as a heavy cloud moved onward, revealing the small sliver of moon that hung in the sky.

The added light instantly froze Frederick's features.

Despite the late hour, the front yard bustled with activity as people ran in a disorderly fashion from here to there, their movements and occasional shouts not merely betraying haste but panic as well. However, what froze the blood in Frederick's veins was the soft orange glow emanating from the back of the house.

"Oh, God, there's a fire!" Oliver called next to him.

"What?" his mother's and Maryann's voices echoed over from the carriage before they, too, joined them, staring out into the distance at the only colour on an otherwise black canvas.

"Ellie," Frederick gasped in horror.

Only a moment later, Maryann's shriek pierced the night, "Mathilda!"

Gritting his teeth, Frederick took a deep breath, then spun around. "Oliver and I will take the horses! The rest of you stay here."

As the coachman began to unhitch the horses, Frederick shrugged off his overcoat.

"This is taking too long," Oliver observed, pointing at the many buckles that needed to be opened to free the horses.

"You're right." Drawing a small dagger from his boot, Frederick began to cut through the leather, oddly reminded of his own accident. He still didn't know if his saddle girth had been cut.

"You carry a dagger in your boot?" Oliver asked, staring at him.

Not looking up, Frederick nodded, then handed the reins of the first horse to his friend and bent to work on the next. Before long, they mounted the animals, who pranced around nervously, feeling the agitation that hung in the air like smoke.

Racing through the night, his eyes focused on the orange glow as it slowly grew bigger, Frederick prayed that they wouldn't be too late.

Moments seemed to stretch into hours as the cool night air brushed over his face, and his fingers began to ache as he held them curled around the reins in an iron grip.

When they finally descended the small hill leading down toward the drive, Frederick saw a line of servants leading from the small well in the back to the house, handing buckets of water from one to the next and passing the empty ones back.

Stopping by the front stoop, he slid off his horse, Oliver close behind him. "Where is my wife?" Frederick called, his eyes searching the yard, hoping to catch a glimpse of her golden hair.

As though out of nowhere, Wilton appeared, bowing stiffly. "My lord, I am so relieved to see—"

"My wife!" Frederick snapped, grabbing the butler by his shirt front. "Where is my wife?"

"We believe she is upstairs," Wilton answered hastily.

Almost tossing him aside, Frederick bounded up the stairs to the front door.

"Uncle Frederick!"

Stopping in his tracks, he turned to the voice, and his heart skipped a beat as Mathilda came racing toward him in her nightgown. He caught her in his arms, hugging her close. "Are you all right?"

The girl nodded, tears running down her cheeks.

"Stay here," he said, setting her back down. "Do not come into the house."

Then he turned around and, followed by Oliver, crossed the front hall and sprinted up the stairs, taking two at a time.

Rushing down the corridor toward his wife's bedchamber, he found a throng of people outside her door. No fire was visible, but dark smoke hung in the air, sneaking into his lungs. "What is going on?" he coughed. "Where is my wife?"

Peter, his stable master, stepped toward him, his face and hands darkened by the small particles drifting through the air. "The door is locked, my lord," he gasped, breathing heavily, "and the key is missing."

"What?"

"We've been trying to break it down, but it won't budge." Wiping his sleeve over his forehead, he pointed at the men still at work behind him. "Your bedchamber is completely ablaze, my lord. We are not sure about the condition of your wife's room. From the window, it does—"

"The window," Frederick mumbled and spun around, racing back the way they had come.

Stepping outside, he breathed in the fresh night air, and his body instantly felt rejuvenated. In large strides, they rounded the house, passing by the stables as two men emerged, carrying a long ladder.

"My lord!" they called, gesturing toward the gardens.

Unable to keep still, Frederick sprinted ahead until he came to stand below his wife's window.

A wave of relief washed over him as he saw her standing by the open window, coughing vigorously, her face streaked with soot.

When her eyes beheld him, her face lit up and a relieved smile spread over her face. "Frederick!" she called as sobs tore from her throat.

Unable to tear his eyes away from her as the men set the ladder below her window, Frederick froze as the dark behind her suddenly shone more brightly and flames moved into his field of vision. The breath caught in his throat, and his heart constricted so painfully that he thought he would faint.

Rushing forward, he pushed the men aside just as his wife climbed onto the windowsill. In a matter of seconds, he climbed the ladder and the most wonderful feeling swept through his heart as she sank into his arms. Holding her tight, he glanced over her shoulder at the raging inferno.

Truly, they had no time to lose. If they had only been a few moments later, she would have been lost to them—to him—forever.

Closing his eyes, Frederick pushed that thought aside and carefully carried her down the ladder.

43

MATHILDA'S MOMENT

uddled under the tall oak tree by the water fountain, Ellie pulled one deep breath after the other into her lungs. The fresh air tickled her insides as though her body was slowly waking up. Suddenly away from the unbearable heat, a cold chill went up and down her back, and she pulled the blanket tighter around her shoulders.

Glancing up, she found Frederick nervously pacing the lawn, Oliver by his side, before he once again strode over and sat down beside her, his arms coming around her as though he was still afraid to lose her.

"I am fine," she whispered, snuggling into his shoulder. Only a mild pain in her wrist and shoulder remained.

"Are you certain?" His gaze burned into hers, then dipped lower to where her hand still rested protectively on her belly.

Smiling, Ellie nodded, and the relief that washed over his face brought tears to her eyes. She reached up then and cupped her hand to his cheek. "We are both fine."

He crushed her to his chest then, burying his face in her hair, and for a long time, they sat locked in each other's embrace, oblivious to their surroundings.

Since everyone had finally been accounted for, the underlying panic had finally died down and only the desire to save as much of the manor as possible hastened people's movements. The line of servants still supplied water although even a full bucket was little more than a drop in the ocean. At least, for the moment, the fire didn't seem to spread, the massive oak doors charred but unyielding under the raging inferno.

"Where is Mama?" Mathilda's tear-heavy voice reached their ears, and reluctantly, they pulled back.

Letting go of Betty's hand, the little girl came running toward them. "Where is Mama?"

"She will be here soon," Oliver said before Frederick had even opened his mouth. "They are still with the carriage, but I've sent men to retrieve them." He brushed a hand over her unruly curls. "Do not worry. She will be here soon."

Opening the blanket, Ellie drew the little girl onto her lap and wrapped them both in it as though huddled inside a cocoon. Then she leaned back into Frederick's arms, her limbs suddenly heavy. "I'm afraid I will fall asleep any moment," she whispered, unable to suppress a yawn.

Frederick cleared his throat and moved her in his arms so that he could see her face. "Can you tell me what happened? How did the fire break out? And why was the door locked?"

Through the haze that threatened to cloud her weary mind, Ellie felt a familiar suspicion rise to the forefront of her thoughts. "I don't know," she whispered, trying to recall what had happened. "I fell asleep, and when I woke up, I...I smelled fire." A shiver went over her, and Frederick's arms tightened around her shoulders. "I saw its glow coming from under the door to your bedchamber." She met his gaze and knew that he understood the fear she could not put into words, the fear to lose someone she loved. "I needed to be certain you were not in there, and so I opened the door." Frederick's eyes widened, but he didn't interrupt her. "Instantly, the flames lashed out at me, and...I suppose for a moment, I...I couldn't move. I remembered the fire that..."

"It's all right," Frederick mumbled into her ear, his hands brushing up and down her arms. "You don't need to speak about it."

Ellie drew in a deep breath, then swallowed and closed her eyes. "I made it to the door, but it was locked." She shook her head, still unable to believe what had happened. "Why was it locked? I've never..." Again, she took a deep breath, trying to calm her rattled nerves.

"You didn't lock it?" Oliver asked, standing before them, his forehead furrowed in concentration.

Ellie shook her head. "Why would I?"

"Maybe it was the woman," Mathilda's sleep-deprived voice peeped up from under the covers.

"Who?" they all asked in unison.

"The woman," Mathilda said as though their question was ludicrous; she couldn't possibly be any more specific. "I couldn't sleep," she mumbled, and her eyelids closed.

"Mathilda?" Frederick called, giving her a soft shake.

Again, her eyelids opened. "Mama?"

"She will be here soon," Oliver said, kneeling down before her. He took her little hands into his, rubbing them gently. "Can you tell us about the woman you saw? It is important."

Slowly, Mathilda's head bobbed up and down. "Well, I couldn't sleep," she began her tale, her round eyes shifting back and forth between them, "so I thought I'd get one of the kittens from the stables. Their fur is so soft." A little smile drew up her lips before her eyelids closed once more.

"Mathilda?"

Again, her eyes snapped open.

"So, you went to the stables," Oliver said, trying to keep her focused. "What then?"

Mathilda shook her head. "No, I wanted to, but then I heard a noise."

"A noise? What noise?" Frederick growled, and the tone of his voice sent a shiver down Ellie's back.

"Footsteps," Mathilda said. "So I hid. I thought it might be Wilton, and I didn't want to get in trouble." She looked at them with open eyes, seeking approval of her reasoning; so Ellie nodded her head in encouragement. "That's when I saw her."

"Who?" Impatience rang clear in Frederick's voice, and Ellie could feel the muscles in his arms tremble. "Who did you see?"

"The sad woman from the tea party," Mathilda mumbled, her eyelids closing. "I've seen her before. At the stables. The day…" Her voice grew quieter before it finally trailed off.

While Frederick and Oliver bore similarly puzzled expressions, Ellie felt the blood freeze in her veins, and she closed her eyes, hoping against hope that Mathilda had been wrong.

"Who?" Frederick asked before his gaze turned to her, and she could read on his face that he understood. "You know who she is talking about."

Ellie nodded. "I think I do," she whispered, her eyes shifting back and forth between Frederick and Oliver. "She is talking about Charlotte."

"Charlotte?" Oliver exclaimed in confusion while Frederick closed his eyes, his lips pressing into a tight line. "Why would she lock your door?" Oliver asked, starting to pace the lawn. "What would she even be doing here to begin with? This doesn't make any sense." He spun around. "What did you see next?" he asked Mathilda, only to realise that sleep had finally claimed her. "Mathilda!" he called, coming toward her.

"No, don't," Ellie whispered, wrapping her arms tighter around the little girl. "Let her sleep. She is exhausted."

"But we need to know what happened," Oliver snapped. For a moment, he stared at her, then swallowed and took a step back. "I apologise. I did not mean to speak so harshly. I just…"

"I know," Ellie said, offering him a weak smile. "There is no need to apologise." Then she shifted her attention to her husband, who sat staring into the distance. "Are you all right?"

He looked at her, offering a weak smile of his own. "I don't know. I don't understand any of it. Why would she do this? Lock your door in the middle of the night?" His face paled. "Did she set the fire as well?" His eyes shifted back and forth between her and Oliver. "Did she set the fire and lock you in? Did she want you to…?"

Ellie felt the muscles in his body tense with the need to move, and yet, he sat perfectly still, holding her in his arms.

"Why would she do that?" Oliver asked, raking his hands through his hair. "She barely even knows you. What reason could she possibly have to want to hurt you? Or Frederick?"

Frederick swallowed and closed his eyes, his head sinking to his chest. "Maybe that is the answer. Maybe she meant to hurt me the way I hurt her."

"What?" Oliver asked, his eyes so wide they looked like they would pop out of their sockets any moment.

From across the courtyard, Ellie saw the carriage pull around the house and stop by the entrance to the gardens. Theresa and Mary-ann climbed out, their faces pale with fear as they glanced up at the smoke billowing out of Frederick's as well as her bedroom windows as the fire slowly died down.

"Go," Ellie whispered, and Frederick looked at her through narrowed eyes. "I am all right. You need to go and find her. You need to find out what happened."

"Are you certain?" he asked as his muscles flexed with the urgent need to be off.

Cupping her hand to his cheek, she smiled at him reassuringly. "I am. Now, go."

Gently, he set her down onto the bench, Mathilda still sleeping in her arms, and gestured for Oliver to follow.

Watching them stride across the lawn toward the stables, Ellie prayed that they would find her and that Frederick would be able to handle the answers he would receive. If his old demons found a way to reclaim his heart, he would be lost to her for good.

As Theresa and Maryann hastened toward them, a single tear rolled down Ellie's cheek, and for a moment, she buried her face in Mathilda's hair.

Please!

44

POETIC JUSTICE

As they chased the moon across the fields, Frederick's heart alternately burned with rage and ached with guilt. Had Charlotte truly tried to murder his wife in her sleep? His Ellie. His wife. His sweet, innocent wife, who only ever had a caring word for Charlotte.

Why had she done that? He growled under his breath, only to feel the flame of anger doused by the guilt-ridden realisation that he knew the answer to that question only too well. Not Ellie, but he had been Charlotte's target. Frederick was as certain of it as he was of the sun rising in the east, and deep down, he could even understand why.

After Kenneth's death, his own guilt had almost consumed him, and he had no trouble understanding why Charlotte had placed blame on him as well.

"Do you truly believe she will be there?" Oliver called, his voice almost drowned out by the deafening howl of the wind.

Instead of answering his friend's question, Frederick urged on his gelding, guiding him down the small slope and into the thicket of the forest. Only slightly slowing down, the horse found its way along the familiar path, jumping fallen trunks and dodging tree stumps. Before long, the lake of his childhood came into view, the thin crescent reflected in its calm surface, gleaming in the night sky. It had been such a peaceful place when Ellie had taken him there not too long ago.

This night, however, it promised to be the scene of a tragedy.

Scanning their surroundings, their eyes glimpsed little more than vague shadows whenever a dark cloud moved in front of the faint light of the moon and all that remained were minuscule stars shining above their heads as they always did.

As they approached the shoreline, the sky cleared, and Frederick drew in a sharp breath as his eyes fell on a lonely figure, standing knee-deep in the ice-cold water.

"Charlotte!" Oliver called, sliding off his horse, and raced toward the water.

Instantly, she spun around, fixing them with a stare that had Oliver stop in his tracks and froze the blood in Frederick's veins.

The woman before him might have resembled the Charlotte he had known since childhood. However, the deranged look in her eyes told him that she barely remembered those times.

"What are you doing?" Oliver panted, shaking his head before holding out his hand to her. "Get out of the water!"

Charlotte, however, barely looked at him, her accusing eyes burning a hole into Frederick's soul. How could he not have seen it before?

"It was you," she growled low in her throat, and Frederick felt himself reminded of a cornered animal. "You killed him."

His gaze shifting back and forth between them, Oliver stood at the shoreline, clearly at a loss.

Sliding off his horse, Frederick approached the water, torn about what to do.

Charlotte had been a friend, and on top of that, Kenneth had entrusted her into his care. How could Frederick deny him this last request? He shook his head. Seeing the crazed look in Charlotte's eyes, he realised that he had already failed him by allowing this to happen.

At the same time, however, Frederick could not banish the image of his wife trapped in her burning bedchamber from his mind, and all feelings of sympathy vanished into thin air.

"Did you set the fire?" Frederick growled, needing confirmation before proceeding any further down this path.

A disturbing grin contorted her soft features before she threw her head back and laughed.

"Did you set the fire?" Frederick snarled, striding forward into the lake. "Answer me!"

Instantly, her laughter stopped, and she stared at him. "Yes!" she hissed, her gaze unflinching.

Frederick gritted his teeth, desperately trying to control the anger that surged through his body as he strode toward her. "Did you lock her in?"

"Yes!"

"Why?" he bellowed, standing merely an arm's length away from her. "Why? Damn you! Why?" As his pulse hammered in his neck, Frederick felt his hands ball into fists, and he desperately wished for something to pummel.

Her face contorted in a snarl, Charlotte took a step toward him, her eyes crazed as they slid over him. "Do you truly need an explanation?" Her lips thinned, and she looked at him with disgust in her eyes. "I wanted you to know what it means to lose the one person you truly need." She swallowed, then drew in a deep breath. "A life for a life."

"Then why didn't you take mine?" Frederick snarled as his muscles began to ache from the exertion of keeping them under control. "Why did you have to go after hers?"

"I tried," Charlotte said, a hint of disappointment coming to her face. "I tried."

The realisation hit Frederick like a punch to the gut. It had been Charlotte. She had manipulated the girth on his saddle. She had known which saddle was his. She had known that he would never use another nor allow anyone else to use his. She had known that it had been a gift from his father and that it had a special meaning for him.

I've seen her before. At the stables. The day... Mathilda's small voice rang in his ears.

"It should have been so simple," Charlotte spat, her words echoing through the night. "You were gulping down one drink after another, so lost were you in your own perceived misery to notice anyone else around you." Her nostrils flared as she stepped toward him. "Why did you let him take it from you? Why didn't you hold on to it?"

Staring at her, Frederick swallowed as his mind once more conjured up the night of the Midnight Ball. "Leopold," he gasped before his gaze found hers, and his eyes narrowed into slits. "You poisoned him! You poisoned my brother!" Like a serpent ready to strike, he shot forward, his hands curling around her throat in an iron grip, squeezing the air from her lungs.

With wide eyes, she stared up at him, her arms hanging limp at her side.

"Frederick, stop!" Oliver's voice cut through the silence that had suddenly descended upon the lake. "Frederick!" Moments after the sound of churning water reached his ears, strong hands grasped his own, trying to break his hold on Charlotte's neck.

Endless seconds passed before Oliver managed to loosen Frederick's hold and pull him back, sending them both stumbling backwards.

Charlotte sank to her knees, rasping breaths tearing from her throat. "Why did you stop him?" she snarled. "Why couldn't you let him do it?"

Shaking off his friend's restraining hands, Frederick stared at her. "Is that why you came here? Because you knew I would look for you here?" Stepping closer, he searched her face, unable to believe that the girl he knew had tried to manipulate him into taking her life.

Laughing, she glared at him. "It would have been poetic justice, do you not agree?" Brushing wet strands of hair out of her face, she staggered to her feet. "You killed my fiancé, and now, I killed your wife. I knew you would seek revenge, so here I am. Take it. It's yours. Kill me, and then you will be ready to kill yourself."

Staring at her, Frederick shook his head, only now understanding how broken she was, and despite the rage burning in his heart, he could not help but pity her. Could he have ended up like her if Ellie had not saved him? The thought brought an icy chill to his bones.

Swallowing, he met her eyes. "Ellie is not dead."

The heinous smile slowly slid off her face and was instantly replaced by a look of sheer rage. "You're lying," she snarled.

Frederick shook his head. "I am not. She is fine." Lowering his head a fraction, he looked deep into her eyes. "She and our baby are fine."

"Baby?" Charlotte whispered, and her eyes grew wide as she stared at him, all anger suddenly gone.

For a moment, before her eyes rolled back and she slumped down into the water, Frederick thought he had seen a glimpse of the old Charlotte, the sweet girl who had always teased him.

As her head disappeared below the water, Frederick and Oliver reached for her, pulling her back to shore.

"What will you do now?" Oliver asked. "Shall we turn her over to the authorities?"

Sighing, Frederick sank down into the grass. "I do not know. But whatever it is, it'll either be a betrayal of my friend or my brother." He looked up and met Oliver's eyes. "What would you do?"

Shaking his head, Oliver sat down beside him. "That I cannot say."

45

A SAD STORY

Almost a week had passed since Frederick and Oliver had returned by the early light of the next day, an apathetic Charlotte with them. Staring into the distance, she had not uttered a single word, and Ellie doubted that she had any idea what was going on around her.

While Oliver kept an eye on their charge, Frederick drew Ellie aside, sharing with her the news he had acquired that night.

Shocked beyond words, Ellie was relieved nonetheless to see boiling emotions under his seemingly calm exterior, and when she looked deep into his eyes, she saw the man she knew him to be. Wrapping her arms around him, she wept with relief that his demons had not gotten a hold of him again. Although the guilt that plagued him was clearly edged in his face, it had not succeeded in squeezing the will to live from his chest as his heart beat steadily beneath her fingers as they rested gently on his chest.

After a quick explanation, they had departed again, taking the carriage to make Charlotte comfortable. Despite his anger, Ellie knew that Frederick still cared for her well-being. Better than anyone, his heart understood how she had lost her way, how her actions had not come from the kind-hearted girl he had known all his life, but from the pain of loss that had overwhelmed her and made her its slave.

Each morning, Ellie glanced out the window of her temporary bedchamber, hoping that Frederick would come home that day. Although she had done her best not to reveal her pregnancy to the rest of her family until Frederick would return, her mother-in-law's keen eyes had soon noticed the subtle differences that were unique to a woman carrying a child under her heart.

Overjoyed, Theresa and Maryann had congratulated her, expressing their heartfelt joy that after all their heartache finally everything was falling into place. Although touched by their words, Ellie could only force a smile on her face as she knew that both women did not yet comprehend the full truth of Charlotte's desperate deed.

Before his departure, Frederick had merely told them that she had set the fire in order to avenge her dead fiancé since she blamed him, Frederick, for his death. Too shocked to ask any more questions, Maryann and Theresa had accepted his words and were soon distracted by the comings and goings of everyday life.

Elmridge needed to be restored to its former charm. Fortunately, only Frederick's and Ellie's bedchambers had suffered under the fire while the rest of the manor seemed more or less untouched. Only a thick layer of dust and ashes had been carried from room to room. However, after a thorough airing-out—thankfully, temperatures were still pleasant—and an equally thorough cleaning, the majority of the house was just as impressive as it had been before.

"A penny for your thoughts."

Ellie spun around and a smile spread over her face at the sight of her travel-weary husband. "Rick!" she exclaimed flying into his arms. "You've returned."

Wrapping his arms around her, he held her tightly, breathing in the scent of her. "I hurried back as soon as I could." He stepped back, gazing into her eyes before they dipped lower to her belly. "Believe me, nothing but a dire emergency could have made me leave you in a time like this. Are you all right?"

Nodding, Ellie smiled. "I feel just as nauseous as I did before." His brows furrowed in concern. "I actually take that to mean that the baby is fine," she assured him, and he laughed, guiding her to the settee under the large windows.

As he sat beside her, her eyes travelled over his face, trying to determine the harm the last few days had done. "Tell me," she whispered.

Clearing his throat, Frederick nodded. "They never suspected anything."

"Did they not notice her absence?"

Frederick nodded. "They did. However, I do not know where they believed her to be." Rising to his feet, he started pacing. "I don't know what happened. From what I remember, Charlotte's parents have always been quite considerate of her wishes, and despite the freedom granted her, Charlotte never took advantage of it. She was always the dutiful daughter." Turning to look at her, he shrugged his shoulders. "Ellie, I honestly do not understand how they could not have seen her misery." He shook his head. "I know I did not fully understand the demons that plagued her myself until the night at the lake; however, it still was obvious to me that she was suffering. I simply never thought it my place to offer her comfort." Sighing, he sat back down beside her and took her hand in his. "I would have, though, had I known that she was so alone."

Squeezing his hand, Ellie rested her head on his shoulder. "What will happen now? Will they turn her over to the authorities?"

Frederick took a deep breath, and Ellie could feel his muscles flex as contrasting emotions tore at his heart. "No," he finally said. "They will not." Sitting back, he turned to look at her. "I could not bring myself to demand it, and I hope Leopold can forgive me."

Cupping her hand to his face, Ellie looked deep into his eyes. "It is not wrong to show mercy."

Frederick swallowed. "They will find a place for her in an institution. After all, she needs medical help. Judging from the depth of her pain, she might never fully recover."

"So, they will lock her away?"

Closing his eyes, Frederick exhaled slowly. "I'm afraid they have to. After what she did to Leopold and what she tried to do to us, she cannot be allowed to live freely. There is no telling what she might do next."

As the pain tore at his heart, Ellie snuggled closer, slipping her arm through his and resting her head on his shoulder once more. "Theirs is a sad story," she whispered. "Kenneth's and Charlotte's. If only he hadn't died, they could have had everything."

"If only," Frederick whispered back, planting a soft kiss on her temple.

Looking up, Ellie smiled at him. "I am glad you are back."

"As am I." A soft smile touched his lips as he leaned down and kissed her softly, pulling her into his arms where she belonged. "My Ellie, what would I do without you?"

EPILOGUE

Ten Months Later

*S*itting in the rocking chair in the nursery, Ellie smiled down at her little son. At three months old, Leopold Kenneth Lancaster cooed up at his mother, his bright blue eyes following her every movement. Gently, she placed the tip of her finger on his forehead and slowly ran it down to the tip of his nose.

Watching her with rapt attention, Leopold blinked as her finger reached his nose, then giggled and waved his little fists about as his mother's delighted laughter filled the sun-bathed room. Ellie could not remember ever having been happier than at this very moment.

"You look beautiful together." Smiling, Frederick came walking in through the door that connected the nursery to their bedchamber.

After sharing a temporary bedroom in another part of the house for the time it took to have their old rooms fixed up—for in the first few weeks after the fire, nightmares had haunted Ellie's sleep—they saw no need to change what had turned into a comfortable routine. Falling asleep with Frederick's arms wrapped around her, Ellie could not imagine ever giving that up. At the same time, she felt an almost desperate need to be near her child after almost losing him so early in her pregnancy.

Today, the three of them were inseparable, and it filled Ellie's heart with joy to see Frederick so devoted to his son.

"Rick." Rising from the chair, she came toward him, and he instantly held out his arms to receive his son. "Are they here?"

"They are," was all he said before his son claimed his undivided attention. Grinning stupidly, sticking out his tongue or wiggling his eyebrows, Frederick did his utmost to make him laugh again and again until even his wife joined in, unable to keep a straight face at the silliness that seemed to have overtaken her otherwise serious husband.

Sinking into the rocking chair once again, Ellie brushed the tears from her cheek. "Are they in the front drawing room?"

Finally looking at her, Frederick nodded, bouncing in his step.

Ellie took a deep breath. "They will love him, don't you think?"

"Of course," Frederick agreed, frowning at her in feigned outrage. "He is their nephew. We are family."

"I know. I think Stephen will be taken with him the most." Feeling excitement bubble up, Ellie rose to her feet, almost dancing as she took a turn about the room. "After having only sisters, he probably welcomes a male relative a little closer to his age."

"Closer to his age?" Frederick gawked at her. "Isn't Stephen already nine years old? He seemed quite grown up as he bowed his head to me just a few minutes ago."

Ellie sighed. "That's my father's influence. Maybe we should invite him to spend the summer here with us."

"I have no objections," Frederick said, an amused curl to his lips. "However, I doubt that he'll be wanting to spend his time with an infant."

"I didn't mean it like that. However, in a few years—"

"In a few years, Stephen will still be nine years older than Leo. I doubt a twenty-year-old will want to spend much of his leisure time with a ten-year-old."

"Oh, forget what I said," Ellie sighed, waving his comments away. "I just thought…"

"I know," Frederick interrupted. Walking over with a sleeping baby in his arms, he gazed down into her eyes. "It was a lovely thought, and I do agree that Stephen might benefit from a little distance to his father. That man certainly is a stick in the mud."

Ellie giggled. "You have no idea."

As his gaze returned to their sleeping son, Ellie thought to detect a hint of sadness in his eyes. "Is something wrong?" she asked, placing a tender hand on his arm. "You seem to have a dark cloud hanging over your head."

The ghost of a smile travelled over Frederick's face. "You know me too well."

"What is it then?"

He took a deep breath, and an apologetic smile drew up the corners of his mouth. "I'm sorry. I didn't mean to spoil your day."

Ellie swallowed, bracing herself. Had something happened to her family? "Then it is bad news?"

"Yes, I suppose it is." Walking over to the crib, he gently laid Leopold down before he returned to her side. "There was a fire at the Winham Institute." Ellie drew in a sharp breath, and Frederick squeezed her hands. "From what I heard, there are few survivors, especially among the patients, which is not surprising considering that most of them were locked up when it happened and, thus, could not save themselves."

A cold shiver went down Ellie's back as memories of the night of the fire returned in startling clarity. "Charlotte?" she asked as heat suddenly surged through her body.

Holding her gaze, Frederick drew in a deep breath. "As far as I know, she was not among those recovered alive."

Ellie closed her eyes, and instantly, her husband's arms came around her. Silent tears rolled down her cheeks and onto his coat as she whispered a quiet goodbye to a woman who had lost everything: the man she loved, her sanity and now, her life. Despite everything that had happened, Ellie had never wished her ill.

Lifting her head from Frederick's shoulder, she searched his face. "How are you?"

"I'm not sure," he admitted as a slight tremble shook his broad frame. "To tell you the truth, a part of me is relieved. Would you want to spend your life in an asylum after losing everything you loved?" He shrugged. "I know I wouldn't. At least now, she is at peace."

"Maybe you're right."

Again, his arms came around her, and his eyes held hers as though with an invisible force. "I don't know what I would have done had I lost you that night," he choked out. "I owe you my heart, my life and my soul for without you I would have been lost. You brought me back from a place that I never want to see again, and now, every day,

you are the reason that life is precious to me again." His arms tightened around her possessively, and the breath caught in Ellie's throat as she read his love for her in his eyes. "Promise me that we will walk through life together."

A smile on her lips, Ellie nodded as tears ran down her face. "I promise. We belong to each other—now and forever."

ABOUT BREE

USA Today bestselling author, Bree Wolf has always been a language enthusiast (though not a grammarian!) and is rarely found without a book in her hand or her fingers glued to a keyboard. Trying to find her way, she has taught English as a second language, traveled abroad and worked at a translation agency as well as a law firm in Ireland. She also spent loooong years obtaining a BA in English and Education and an MA in Specialized Translation while wishing she could simply be a writer. Although there is nothing simple about being a writer, her dreams have finally come true.

"A big thanks to my fairy godmother!"

Currently, Bree has found her new home in the historical romance genre, writing Regency novels and novellas. Enjoying the mix of fact and fiction, she occasionally feels like a puppet master (or mistress? Although that sounds weird!), forcing her characters into ever-new situations that will put their strength, their beliefs, their love to the test, hoping that in the end they will triumph and get the happily-ever-after we are all looking for.

If you're an avid reader, sign up for Bree's newsletter at www.breewolf.com as she has the tendency to simply give books away. Find out about freebies, giveaways as well as occasional advance reader copies and read before the book is even on the shelves!

Thanks you very much for reading!

Bree

Abandoned & Protected – The Marquis' Tenacious Wife

#4 in the Love's Second Chance Series

A bear of a man. A twig of a girl.
And a love that was destined to be.

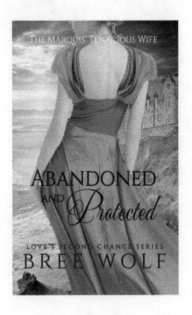

After what her father did to her mother, HENRIETTA TURNER's worst fears are to be realised when her uncle decides to marry her off to a Scot. Gentleman or not, Henrietta knows that at his core he is still a barbarian. What will she suffer at the hands of this savage?

CONNOR BRUNWOOD, Marquis of Rodridge, can't believe he fell head over heels in love with this thin, pale twig of a girl. However, the moment he saw her, he knew he had to make her his wife. If only she didn't hate his guts!

However, when his life is suddenly in danger, an assassin lying in wait, everything they thought they knew is put to the test.

Will Henrietta betray her husband or stand by his side? Will she take the opportunity to rid herself of him forever? Or will she risk everything to save his life...as well as her heart?

LOVE'S SECOND CHANCE SERIES

For more information, visit

www.breewolf.com

Printed in the USA
CPSIA information can be obtained
at www.ICGtesting.com
CBHW031945220724
11977CB00010B/67